It was a lovely warm July day in Munich, so he decided to walk to his lunchtime appointment rather than have the company driver take him. The previous day, he had received a strange request for an appointment from one of the bank's original shareholders. The request was for a meeting at the Hofbrauhaus, rather than at the Head Office of the AH Bank which was situated on Widenmayer Strasse overlooking the river Isar.

Reinhard Heinrich loved the city of his birth. It was the perfect size, he always said -big enough to have all the conveniences of a substantial city yet small enough to feel personal. He walked alongside the river before turning into Maximilian Strasse. The trees were full and bursting with the energy the summer sun had provided. The sun felt warm on his back as he walked with his usual purposeful stride. He kept wondering why Adolf Eicke had chosen such a strange venue for a meeting. If it wasn't for his connection with the bank, and that he was a personal friend of his father, he would have refused the request. He didn't particularly like the Hofbrauhaus, which was always filled with foreign tourists and seemed like a caricature of a German beer hall. Reinhard Heinrich, CEO of one of Germany's lesser known private banks, was not known for his flexibility.

As he got closer to the beer hall, he couldn't help noticing the increased number of tourists. The demographics had changed over the years, he reflected. At first it was the waves of Americans- loud clothing and loud mouths. They came with the then all-powerful dollar and were generous tippers. After that, cheap flights brought in the British – less generous than the Americans but a lot more adventurous. Quiet groups of Japanese then filtered in. Fearful, they stayed close to their umbrella-wielding guides, and seemed intent on taking home hundreds of often meaningless photographs of dustbins and street signs, all snapped with the latest Nikon or Panasonic cameras.

2

The Crooked Star

Today it was the turn of the nouveau riche – Russians, Chinese and Indians were now arriving in increasing numbers. Heinrich walked into the entrance of the Hofbrauhaus.

The Hofbrauhaus was originally built in 1897. It was destroyed in a bombing raid on the 25th of April in 1944 and then faithfully rebuilt after the war. It has always been popular with the locals but only achieved international fame in the 60s and 70s when tens of thousands of tourists started coming to the annual Oktober Fest. Today it is the symbol of the festival and indeed Munich.

Reinhard looked around the crowded hall, hoping that Eicke had managed to get a table in the garden but was disappointed when he spotted him at a small table in a corner close to the bandstand.

As he approached the table, Eicke extended a hand in greeting.

The Crooked Star

'My dear Mr. Eicke, what a pleasure to see you,' smiled Reinhard, as he shook the elderly man's hand and sat down opposite him. He knew from the bank records that Eicke was seventy-seven years of age, although he could easily pass for someone ten years younger. His tanned face was lined in an attractive way and with his swept-back grey hair, he resembled the actor, Curt Jurgens.

'A beer is okay, ja?' enquired Eicke.

Reinhard nodded. Eicke beckoned to a waitress, who was dressed in a traditional Bavarian skirt and blouse and ordered two steins. He had a good look at her ample cleavage, which is a definite asset for any aspirant beer hall waitress.

'I had some private business to attend to in Munich so it seemed convenient that I combine it with some bank business as well. I have to admit that I still love summer in this city. Not that Vienna is unpleasant, but Munich comes alive with the warm sun. I am sure you are wondering why

I have chosen such a venue for a meeting. I am going to come straight to the point and tell you, that I think that there has been a security breach at the bank. I did not feel comfortable discussing my problem at your offices, in case they have been bugged.'

Reinhard raised his eyebrows in a display of disbelief.

'Mr. Eicke, of course I am willing to hear what you have to say. I must tell you that we employ a security firm to conduct debugging procedures at the bank regularly. We have also installed the latest firewall technology on our computer system. We all know nothing is totally secure, as we have seen with Wikileaks, but I am confident that we have the most sophisticated security systems of any bank.'

Eicke waited while the beers were placed on the table before he spoke again.

'Reinhard, I accept what you are saying, but after what I am going to reveal to you, perhaps you will understand why I have taken these precautions today.'

'Please go ahead,' Reinhard said, as he raised his glass in salute.

Eicke removed a small notebook from the inside pocket of his jacket and opened it at the first page.

'Three weeks ago, on the 9th of June, I received an email accusing me of having stolen Jewish money. I ignored it. Then earlier this week a second message arrived. This was more detailed and gave the number of my account held at the Vienna branch. It included the exact balance in the account and also your father's name, which is why I am here. I was shocked that someone had access to secure information, so I immediately contacted Mr. Schmidt at the bank in Vienna and told him about the messages. Like you, he said the bank had all kinds of defences and that the weak link must lie with my computer.

He arranged for someone from a private IT company to visit me. The very next day a young man arrived at the house and spent the better part of two hours working on my computer. He went away without telling me anything. Yesterday Schmidt contacted me and said that he was getting a complete forensic audit done at the bank.'

'Schmidt has yet to contact me in this regard, but I have the utmost confidence in him,' said Reinhard. Although he did not reveal it, he was inwardly fuming that he had been made to look ill-informed about such a potentially important security breach in the bank.

'I almost forgot, here are copies of the emails,' Eicke said, reaching into his inside jacket pocket again. He handed the e-mails to Reinhard with a shaking hand.

Reinhard opened the folded sheets. The second e-mail did indeed mention his father – *tell your friend and co-conspirator, Hermann Heinrich, that we know where he lives and we know his real name.*

Reinhard let out a loud sigh and looked up at Eicke.

'I agree this is serious and I thank you for arranging this confidential meeting. Under the circumstances, I think I should leave right away. I want you to know that I will take personal control of this investigation.'

Eicke held up his hand, 'First finish your beer. Although you may not know it, it was here at the Hofbrauhaus that I first met your father all those years ago. At the time, we were completely unaware that our fathers had actually known one another. People say there is no such thing as fate. Tell me, how is Hermann? Why doesn't he have an e-mail address like everyone else? We have not had any contact in years.'

Reinhard smiled. 'He is fine physically, but psychologically he never got over the death of my mother.

8

He has become a recluse. He paints and he now has a small dog. He has no E-mail and no television. Do you remember a security guard at the bank called Helmut? Well, when father retired, he and his wife came to Garmisch to look after him. I suppose one would call Helmut a manservant. They stay in a cottage on the property and so effectively, my father lives alone in that big house - alone that is except for his dog, Blondi.'

'So his dog is called Blondi,' Eicke grinned. 'Hermann still hankers after the old days, but I suppose having a dog with the same name as the Fuhrer's dog, is innocent enough.'

Reinhard shrugged his shoulders, 'He doesn't talk much about that period and I have never pried, although I would like to know something about my ancestors, even if they were not angels.'

Eicke looked down at the table.

The Crooked Star

'People who survived the war, all have silent nightmares and secret thoughts which we are obliged not to say anything about. It was one thing to lose the war but we also lost our memories. The conquerors shoved our guilt down our throats. Do you know the resentment I felt when it was announced that Sputnik was put into space by the Russians or that the Americans landed the first men on the moon? We were restricted from shouting out- *these are German achievements*- and there was Werner von Braun waving a little stars and stripes flag like some bloody Yankee. They say it takes a century for history to be written objectively.'

Reinhard made a show of draining the last dregs of his beer, hoping that the exaggerated gesture would enable him to leave without appearing too rude or impatient. In Germany, there is still a strong sense of formality and someone from an older generation is always granted due deference. In this case, Reinhard would wait for the old man to terminate the meeting.

'I can see you are anxious to leave, and I fully understand your concern. I will rely on you to sort out this problem. Thank you for meeting with me today and remember to give my regards to your father and your charming wife.'

Reinhard stood up and shook Eicke's hand.

'I will get to the bottom of this nonsense and I will keep you informed of our progress. Good day, Mr. Eicke.' He turned and walked out of the hall just as the Oompah band resumed playing, after having taken a short break.

Once outside, he was pleased to be able to breathe in some clean air again. As he made his way back to the office, he had a terrible feeling in his stomach that something dreadful was unfolding. Reinhard's generation was the first in Germany for whom war and deprivation were historical. From the age of ten, he in fact only knew an easy, almost luxurious life as the son of one of the founders of the Bank. He was sent to an exclusive private

11

school and later attended University, followed by a year at the Harvard Business School where he obtained an MBA degree. On his eighteenth birthday, he was given a Mercedes Benz sports saloon. Despite his familial connections, he proved to be a very able bank employee and received deserved promotions to management level. Everyone agreed, when he took over as CEO after both his father and Eicke retired in the same year, that he was 'the man for the job'. In 2008 he had managed to keep the bank solvent, despite the loss incurred by the branch in America. As he walked back to the office, he kept thinking to himself that he didn't like the sound of this problem that had now been thrust upon him by Eicke.

On returning to the bank, Reinhard immediately called a meeting with the bank manager Rudi Muller and the IT manager Karl Kreie. He arranged for Alfred Schmidt, the branch manager in Vienna, to participate via a conference call.

The discussion started off very acrimoniously, with Reinhard demanding to know 'why the hell he had been kept in the dark.' He calmed down somewhat when he was told that a report was sitting on his desk, although it had only been put there some thirty minutes earlier. He glanced at the report which stated that the initial investigation indicated, that the bank's firewall may have been penetrated. Alfred Schmidt explained, that at this stage, they had employed the services of a small IT company in Vienna which was contracted to their branch. They had examined Adolf Eicke's computer, which appeared to have been hacked into, but were unable at this point to trace the origins of the break-in. Karl Kreie indicated that he knew of very sophisticated IT companies, some with offices in Munich, who may have to be called upon in order to assist in the tracking operation.

Reinhard asked everyone to co-ordinate their efforts and said that he wanted a strategic document to be presented at a follow-up meeting the next day. Although no one commented, they clearly realised that a lot of midnight oil would be burnt that evening. A bank like AH pays generous bonuses and expects pounds of flesh in return. Reinhard ended the meeting abruptly, as he wanted to drive to Garmisch-Partenkirchen to confront his father.

CHAPTER 2

The trip from Munich to his home usually took just over one hour but today Reinhard was keeping the BMW 7 Series between 160 and 180 kilometres per hour and so the

14

journey would be considerably shortened. The E533 Autobahn between Munich and Garmisch-Partenkirchen, is arguably one of the most scenic in all of Germany, but Reinhard was too preoccupied to enjoy the green, undulating, pine-covered hills or even the splendid first glimpses of the Alps that appear after Penzberg. He arrived at the gates of the family estate just forty minutes after leaving the office. He drove straight past his own house, around the line of birch trees and up to where his father lived.

In the 1980s, the Algemeine Handels Bank or AH as it was known, grew exponentially and started making huge annual profits. Hermann Heinrich decided to use some of his profit share to develop the farm, previously owned by his mother's sister, into a luxurious estate. He commissioned a leading firm of architects to design an immense house with ten bedrooms, in the typical traditional Bavarian style of architecture, complete with colourful murals on the exterior walls. The huge basement which ran under the total footprint of the house, contained an extensive wine cellar, filled with premium wines from Germany and France, as well as South Africa, where Hermann had a share in a wine estate in Stellenbosch. The house was named "der Adlerhorst"- Eagle's Eyrie- undoubtedly influenced by Hitler's obsession with eagles and the Alps. The views of the Zugpitze, Germany's highest mountain, and the surrounding Alps, were breath taking and the bank's most important clients vied for a weekend invitation to Adlerhorst. In the summer, these usually consisted of rambles through the delightful countryside, followed by superb meals prepared by hired, professional chefs. They were always accompanied by a selection of wines chosen personally by Hermann, who invariably gave an informed lecture on their provenance. The guest list was carefully chosen so that there would be an eclectic mix of leading industrialists and businessmen, together with politicians, as well as the odd socialite thrown in for some glamour. After the death of his wife, these weekend gatherings came to an abrupt halt as Hermann retracted into his hermitage. When Reinhard announced his intention to marry Sabine Kreisler in 1998, Hermann had the old farmhouse demolished and in its place he had a modest, if six bedrooms can be considered modest, copy of Adlerhorst built, insisting on the same exacting standards to which the original house had been built. He also arranged for a row of birch trees to be planted halfway between the homes, so that there was a distinct division between the two properties, thus ensuring the privacy he craved, even from his own family.

Alerted by Blondi, his two-year old Jack Russell, Hermann opened the door of the house just as his son was about to ring the doorbell.

'I don't recall that we had an arrangement to meet today,' Hermann said, with a puzzled expression. Even between father and son, there existed this formal arrangement whereby appointments were made prior to visits. The only exception was Eva, Reinhard's four year old daughter, who was allowed to appear unannounced for her daily playtime with Blondi.

'My apologies, but an emergency has occurred at the bank and I need to speak to you urgently,' said Reinhard, as he stepped inside the entrance hall.

'It is very warm, so I suggest we sit in the north-facing lounge. Blondi come!' Reinhard and the Jack Russell followed the old man obediently.

Hermann Heinrich was dressed in dark grey trousers with military-like creases ironed into them. He wore a white shirt with a maroon tie, and his jacket was buttoned up. His attire would have been quite acceptable at any office in the city. He dressed this way every day, including for meals, where he sat alone at the table. When walking on the estate, he changed into a typical Bavarian outdoor set of clothes and allowed himself the freedom of not wearing a tie.

18

The Crooked Star

The lounge was a large, wood-panelled room with windows on one side. On the opposite walls, four heads of antlered deer, whose glass eyes stared unblinkingly with a blank and forlorn look, were mounted. Unlike his father, Reinhard preferred to shoot animals with his camera and whenever he looked at the stuffed heads, he couldn't help but wonder how much happier they would have been, grazing in some field rather than being affixed to a wall.

'Father, today at his request, I met with Adolf Eicke. He is very concerned because he has received two disturbing e-mails that seem to indicate that someone has hacked into his computer and maybe even into the confidential records of our bank. Your name is mentioned in the second one.' Reinhard handed his father the two e-mails.

Hermann read them twice before lifting his head and looking at his son, saying nothing for the moment.

'Sounds like some Jewish organisation, perhaps Wiesenthal, looking for more compensation. Once blackmail starts, it never ends. Even so, how can I help you?'

'I don't need direct help because we have access to top security people who can deal with hackers and the like. I want you to lift the veil of secrecy which hangs over our family's history, going back to your father, my grandfather, the infamous Reinhard Heydrich.'

'How dare you call your grandfather infamous? Don't you have any respect for him or me?'

The old man's face reddened and his breathing became more rapid. Reinhard realised he had touched a sensitive nerve, as his grandfather's name was never mentioned - initially from fear of reprisal, then later to protect the bank from any past political association.

'Father, I apologise. I chose the wrong word. I did not get to meet my grandfather and everything I do know about him, I have learnt by reading articles in newspapers and books. None of those have been flattering. When have you ever discussed him with me? If we have skeletons in our cupboards, I would rather know about them. That is why I am here - to ask you to open the cupboard doors. I need to know for the sake of the bank, as well. Can there possibly be any connection between our family history and these e-mails?'

Hermann's colour had returned to his face, and his breathing started to normalise.

'Why did I never discuss the war or my father? Because it was a terrible period in my life, that's why. I idolised my father who in turn idolised that man with the magnetic blue eyes.' He paused and then continued, 'You will never understand what it was like to be alive then. It was Germany's greatest hour, followed by Germany's most tragic hour. The Fuhrer was God incarnate. I remember my father taking us to a rally in 1940. He was on the podium along with Himmler, Goering and other dignitaries, and we were seated right in the front. Then the Fuhrer appeared and a mighty roar went up. He raised his hand several times in a half salute.' Hermann mimicked the well-known style of a half salute that only Hitler used. 'The crowd went silent. Then as he spoke, they interspersed his sentences with co-ordinated shouts of Sieg heil! Sieg heil! Sieg heil! Even now I can hear it in my head. This was the man who had saved our country, who gave us back our dignity. We did not know it then, in the euphoria of victory, that dark days lay ahead - that the dark would one day turn to pitch black. I... I never got over the murder of my father. Then the end came and in the East, we were overrun by barbarians who committed the greatest mass rape in the history of mankind. Fortunately, we came under the Americans here and so we were spared some of the atrocities that occurred in Berlin. Nevertheless, we were treated like dogs.' He banged his fist on the arm of the chair, causing Blondi to look at him quizzically.

Hermann paused for a moment before continuing. 'We scrounged for food in the garbage bins of the occupiers. We begged for sweets and cigarettes. There was no pride, only humiliation. Yes, we did terrible things in the war, I acknowledge that, but so did the other side. The rule is, that the loser is always guilty and the victor blameless. Ask yourself, did the Americans really have to drop two atom bombs on civilian cities and what did destroying Dresden prove, at such a late stage in the war? Was the killing by the British, of nearly 30 000 Boer woman and children, more than ten percent of the population, also not an act of genocide? Not if you are the victor. What about the illegal invasion of Iraq, this century?' Hermann's chest was heaving again, and he was clearly in an emotional state.

The Crooked Star

'So you want to know about your grandfather, about the war and about the formation of the bank. You want to know all my secret memories. I will tell you, but first I am going to order some coffee for us and a biscuit for Blondi.' He picked up a telephone that was on a small table beside his chair and mumbled into it. Then he turned once again to his son.

'The war ended sixty-five years ago - that is two generations. Why do we Germans, living in the 21st century, have to continue to bear the burden of guilt for something our forefathers did? Sure, I was in the Hitler Youth here in Garmisch, but I was only nine years of age when the war began. You were born twenty-three years after the war was over. When will all this shit come to an end?' Hermann looked directly into Reinhard's eyes.

'I agree,' replied Reinhard, 'I don't feel at all personally guilty or responsible for anything that happened in the war. People of my generation and younger, are aware of what happened and that is why we vigorously support the democratic system and why, for example, there is so much opposition to having our troops in Afghanistan. In the bank's business dealings with the rest of the world, it is important that we adopt a completely neutral stance with regard to the Nazi period in our history, however, I am concerned that if we were to discover some Nazi skeletons, that the public exposure could damage the bank. As you know, we count some high-ranking political figures among our client base.

There was a tentative knock at the door, which was open. Hermann's aide, Helmut, came in with a tray, on which were placed two mugs of coffee and a small bowl with a bone-shaped biscuit for Blondi. Helmut acknowledged Reinhard with a nod of his head. After placing the tray on a small table, he turned and walked out of the room, closing the door behind him. Hermann held up the biscuit and within a flash, Blondi had jumped onto his lap and grabbed it. Reinhard shook his head when he saw

25

the dog jump down and proceed to eat the biscuit on a rare Persian rug. As a child he would never have been indulged in this way.

'I am sorry that you never got to meet your grandfather. Despite what you may have read about him, the father that I knew was a strict but gentle man, a very talented man I may add.'

CHAPTER 3

The Crooked Star

Two men, from very different backgrounds, had both advanced rapidly into the upper echelons of the Nazi Party. One, Theodor Eicke, the son of a minor station master, was born in the then German province of Elsass-Lothringen in 1892. At the Treaty of Versailles, this province was ceded to France and became known as Alsace-Lorraine. In 1914 Eicke enlisted in the Kaiser's army. Young Theodor proved to be an able soldier and like Adolf Hitler, was awarded an Iron Cross Second Class for bravery. After the war, along with millions of others, he scoured the streets vainly looking for work, but there was mass unemployment and rampant inflation, caused by the horrendous reparations placed on Germany by the victors. He realised that his provincial background and poor education, equipped him poorly in those terrible times for obtaining any meaningful employment. He developed an intense hatred of the Government of the Weimar Republic, which he blamed for all the ills that had befallen Germany. Soon he drifted into one of the many radical factions which had formed across the country, finally choosing the Nazi Party, as more than any other, it met all of his political and social inclinations, including anti-Semitism. It was not long before his fanatical extremism and loyalty to the party were noted, and he rapidly moved up the ranks, eventually becoming an SS-Brigadefuhrer in 1934. Later that year, he became Commandant of Dachau concentration camp.

The other man was Reinhard Heydrich. He was the son of Richard Bruno Heydrich, opera singer and founder of the Halle Conservatory of Music. It was his talented father who taught him how to play the violin. He also instilled in him, through many whippings, an understanding of what blind discipline to orders involved. No deviation or any questioning of even a minor instruction was allowed. It was this credo that was to rule Heydrich's behaviour for the rest of his life. It also made him the ideal candidate for a leadership position in the Nazi Party, which he joined in 1927. By 1934, he was the head of the SS intelligence division, the SD.

The Crooked Star

There were never ending power struggles in the pre-war Germany, many of them orchestrated by Adolf Hitler, who successfully used a divide and rule policy to maintain his supreme position in both the party and country. One such struggle took place in 1934, when the ambitious Heydrich tried to wrest control of Dachau Concentration Camp from Eicke. Eventually, Himmler intervened and Heydrich backed off.

Theodor Eicke decided that it was not a good idea to have the powerful Heydrich as his enemy, so it was with this in mind that he requested a private meeting. It took place at the Hofbrauhaus in Munich. After some small talk, Eicke came straight out with a proposal that he and Heydrich could make some money, as he said, for the time when they would no longer be in uniform. Heydrich was not someone who was concerned about money, except as a means to providing for the necessities of life. He decided to go along with Eicke's scheme from a strategic alliance point of view, rather than from the greed which was

29

driving Eicke. The plan was very simple and involved persuading mainly Jewish inmates, to hand over family gold and jewellery in return for favours, including not having other family members arrested. Over the next year, they amassed a substantial amount of loot which Heydrich kept hidden in a box at his father's house in Halle. They drew up a private agreement, stating that at a convenient time in the future, the proceeds would be split equally. They each had a copy of this agreement.

As the war progressed the two men's careers took them in different directions. Eicke was put in command of a Totenkopf division, which became known for its unmatched brutality and war crimes involving the murder of captured soldiers and POWs. In January 1943, he was appointed S.S. Obergruppenfuhrer and a few weeks later on the 26th of February, he was killed when his Fiesler-Storch reconnaissance plane was shot down over the battlefield near Kharkov in the Soviet Union.

The Crooked Star

The urbane and scholarly Heydrich, on the other hand, was spotted by Hitler and earmarked for high political office. In 1941 he was appointed Deputy Reich Protector of Bohemia and Moravia in the former Czechoslovakia, with his headquarters in Prague. This supremely arrogant young man, liked to drive through the streets of the city in an open-top, green Mercedes Benz, without an armed escort. He was a cruel and unyielding governor and became a universally hated symbol of Nazi oppression throughout the country. In January 1942, he was asked to chair the infamous Wannsee conference – The Final Solution to the Jewish Question, which would produce the blueprint for the elimination of all the Jewish people in Europe and the Soviet Union, some seven million people. The minutes, which were taken by Adolph Eichmann, quoted Heydrich in his opening address: 'Europe will be combed of Jews from east to west' - the reference to hair lice being obvious. While most documentation related to the Holocaust was deliberately couched in euphemisms and vague generalities, it was rumoured that Heydrich had very revealing private correspondence with both Hitler and Himmler, copies of which disappeared after the war. Extensive searches for this material proved fruitless. Heydrich returned to Prague and on a fateful day in May of the same year, a bomb was thrown into his car and shots were fired at him. He managed to chase after his attackers, shooting and killing one, before collapsing on the pavement. He was rushed to hospital and despite the efforts of top surgeons flown in by Himmler, he succumbed to his injuries and died a few days later. He received an enormous state funeral. Later hundreds of Czechs were rounded up and shot in reprisal.

* * * *

Hermann looked at his son, his lips tightly clenched together.

The Crooked Star

'Most of what I have told you, with the exception of the story about the box, you could have read in history books. First, I think we should have something stronger to drink, than coffee.'

He got up and went over to a display cabinet. He poured two whiskeys into lead-cut crystal glasses. He returned to his chair, and handed one glass to Reinhard. He raised his glass.

'Right. The whisky has come out of the cupboard and now it is time for the skeletons to follow. When we heard about the death of my father, we cried for days. At the grand funeral, Hitler came and shook my hand, referring to my father as a hero of the Fatherland. It was a terrible time and then one-day Uncle Heinz rushed in and said that the Eastern front was collapsing. Soon hordes of Russians would be invading our country, raping and looting. My mother packed up everything and we moved to the farm her sister had, right here in Garmisch. Nine months later the war ended. You cannot imagine the absolute hell that Germany was plunged into. In many ways we were lucky, as we had a roof over our heads as well as vegetables and chickens. We sold eggs to the American garrison and we subsisted on a variety of vegetable soups. I can tell you, my mother was a very creative cook. She worked her fingers to the bone, especially after her sister died. She would get up at sunrise to work in the fields, where we also helped, and then the chickens needed to be fed and the eggs and produce sold. I would sometimes see her at night, patching our clothes and darning our socks. She was like a saint.'

Hermann stopped to wipe tears from his eyes.

'Father, I understand if you do not wish to carry on.'

'No, no. I will continue. After leaving school I had a number of odd jobs. I struggled for almost a year and then I applied for a job as a clerk in the bank in Munich,

34

which I got. I rented a room in an old house and lived very frugally. Then in my second year, I was called into the bank manager's office and told that the bank would pay for my studies for an accounting qualification. I was overjoyed and I can tell you that I had a few beers to drink that night.'

He hesitated for a few moments to catch his breath. 'I am going to jump in time to a day, a warm day like today, when on my way home I decided to go to the Hofbrauhaus for a beer. It was crowded. I looked around and saw a table at which a young man was seated. I asked if I could join him. He agreed, and we got talking. It was apparent from some of his remarks, that he was involved in the black market which had developed after the war, and that he had recently moved to Munich. I found him to be an agreeable sort of person, even if I frowned on his morals. We arranged to meet on the Saturday, so that I could show him around the city. Well, we became good friends - we both liked cycling and the outdoors.'

Hermann took a sip of his whisky. He was apprehensive at what he was about to reveal to his son. 'Then one day I took him to meet my mother,' he said smiling. 'As we walked into the house, I said, 'Mother, I would like to introduce my friend, Adolf Eicke.' Well, it was if she had seen a ghost. She called me aside into the kitchen and asked if I knew who his parents were. I said I didn't, but I would ask him. I was a bit embarrassed but eventually I got up the courage to ask him outright. He told me his father had been a general in the army and had been killed on the Eastern front. He said he avoided talking about it because of the connection with Dachau and because the country was in denial about the Nazi period. I then explained to him that our real name was Heydrich and when he heard that he just laughed, from relief I suppose. The knowledge of who our fathers were, proved to be a lasting bond.'

Hermann swirled the whisky in his glass before taking a sizeable mouthful.

'The following day my mother took me up to her bedroom. She opened a velvet- lined box that contained old photos of my father, taken with us at different times, as well as some with Himmler and Hitler. She pulled out a note with two signatures at the bottom, written in my father's handwriting. It was headed, Hofbrauhaus Agreement. It said in simple, non-legal terms, that the articles in my father's possession, were to be shared jointly by my father and Theodor Eicke, or their immediate heirs. I asked my mother what the articles referred to. She said they were in a trunk, that to this day she had never opened, for fear she would be arrested by the Allied occupiers. All she had been told, was that the contents once belonged to Jews who were now dead.'

'Oh no!' Reinhard cried, 'don't tell me that the seed money you and Adolf used to form AH Bank, came from the proceeds of the Jewish articles?'

Hermann nodded. For a while neither man said anything. Then Reinhard broke the silence.

'How many people knew about the trunk? Why, after all this time, is someone raking up the past? Maybe it has nothing to do with the box at all. If they have found out about our true background, perhaps they are taking a chance. Let's face it, there was a lot of looting during that period, especially of Jewish property.'

'According to my mother,' continued Hermann, 'until that day, only four people knew about it and three were dead. I do not believe any record was kept as to whom the gold and jewels belonged and tracing them would be nigh impossible. I arranged for Adolf to visit the farm once more and after a discussion, it was agreed that the split would be in thirds, with my mother and I getting a third each and one third to Adolf. This was also the initial shareholding in the bank. I think in later years, when I inherited my mother's share and therefore was clearly the majority shareholder, that recriminations came from Adolf, who claimed he had been cheated and deserved fifty percent. Anyway that is another story.' He paused and took a sip of whisky.

'We opened the trunk, which was filled to about halfway with gold coins and all sorts of jewellery, as well as a book with coded messages and a few miscellaneous papers. Adolf and I sold the gold anonymously on the black market. The diamonds and some miscellaneous pearls and rubies, we sold in Antwerp. I know it sounds ironic, but the man to whom we sold the jewels in Antwerp was a Jew – a survivor from the camps, no less. Can there be a connection between those events so long ago and these e-mails?'

'Right now we have little evidence of anything,' said Reinhard, looking decidedly grim. 'We need to trace the origin of the e-mails and establish if this is a real threat to any of us, and of course, the bank and deal with it. I am concerned that we could come under severe pressure if it emerged that we had assisted possible war criminals - someone such as Josef Mengele, for example.'

'We never knowingly assisted people like that. What we did, was not to query if the name given to us was true or false. Sure, we knew they were ex-Nazis but then that applied to millions of Germans. Only a small percentage of the population were actual war criminals, even by the definition of the victors.'

'I am not saying that you are in any direct danger but do you want me to arrange for a security guard to be posted here?' asked Reinhard.

'Are you crazy? Blondi here, alerts me to the faintest sound and I have my rifles for protection. I am not afraid.'

'I have been amazed,' said Reinhard,' at how clearly you have recalled events from such a long time ago. They are obviously strong memories.'

'Something that I have learnt as I got older, is that the human mind doesn't move in the same time continuum as ones' age. My mind is still around the forty-year mark, about half of my time age.'

'Father, that is very interesting and I have to say that this has been a very enlightening day, in a dreadful sort of way. Something that has just struck me, is how the Hofbrauhaus has featured in our family. Perhaps Adolf chose it deliberately today. Nevertheless, it is rather uncanny. Tell me, was there anything else in that trunk?'

His father shrugged his shoulders, 'As I said, just a notebook filled with meaningless numbers and some notes in my father's handwriting. I kept the trunk hidden for a few years and then one day I decided to get rid of it. I dumped it where it will never be found.' He abruptly changed the subject, 'Well, it was the Beer Hall Putsch in Munich that brought Hitler into prominence. Let's hope we have a better conclusion. I want to make it clear, that I do not want to be part of any investigation process you get underway, but I do wish to be kept fully informed. Do you understand?'

'Of course, I do. I must go and don't worry, I will let myself out.' Reinhard bent down and gave Blondi a pat.

Hermann looked up at Reinhard with sad, wrinkled eyes, 'One last thing before you go. Eva came across today and after playing with Blondi, she asked me to read to her from a book about Heidi. She says I am the grandfather, and she is Heidi. Reinhard, that little girl has given my life a new meaning. After your mother passed away, I lost all interest in life but with Blondi and Eva, life is once again beautiful.'

For the second time that afternoon, the old man had tears in his eyes.

The Crooked Star

Reinhard left without saying anything further. He looked back and saw his father standing thoughtfully at the window, watching him.

CHAPTER 4

Reinhard drove slowly around to his house. He was having difficulty coming to terms with the shocking information his father had just revealed about their past. The empty hole in his stomach seemed to be eating away at him. He parked the car outside the front door.

The sound of the car must have alerted his wife, Sabine. She opened the door and a surprised look crossed her face.

'My God, Reinhard! I didn't expect you home so early.'

The Crooked Star

He kissed her on the cheek and bent down to pick up his daughter Eva, who had rushed up to him.

'Papa have you got a present for me?' she asked, kissing him and throwing her arms around him.

'Not this time little one, I am sorry.'

He put her down and looked at his wife. He shook his head, which only made her more apprehensive.

'Don't worry. We have a problem at the bank and I needed to speak to my father. Let me relax for a few minutes and I will explain it to you.'

Reinhard had already decided that he would not mention the episode concerning the box, partly because he was concerned that she would let it slip during one of her many daily calls to her mother and friends.

Sabine was a fine-featured woman, six years younger than her husband. She usually wore her blonde hair swept back in a bun, so that she looked like everyone's

45

idea of the perfect Teutonic beauty. She was constantly worried about her figure and needed assurances as to the size of her derriere every time they went out. Not that there was anything wrong with her figure, as she had been a leading figure-skater as a young girl. Right up to the present time, she cycled or walked every day in the summer and skied in the winter.

Her father was the Managing Director of a large paper company in Hannover and they certainly encouraged her romance with the son of the founder of AH Bank, even paying for their honeymoon on the island of Mauritius. Reinhard got on well with his in-laws, in no small measure because they had an extremely busy social life and he only saw them two or three times a year when they would spend extended weekends at the Kleine Adlerhorst. Reinhard knew at the beginning of their relationship that Sabine had been very spoilt and would demand nothing but the best of everything - from the Porsche 911 Carrera 4S she drove to the spa treatments she went to religiously every month and of course, the de rigueur week at Cannes, during the film festival, where they had a fixed annual booking at the Carlton Hotel.

They went inside, with Reinhard going into the lounge, while Sabine took Eva to her playroom. A few minutes later she returned and sat opposite her husband.

'Well, what is the problem? Why not pour some drinks for us?' she demanded, in her usual abrupt manner.

'Not right now. Father poured me a stiff whisky a short while ago.'

'What about me? I want a drink. What has happened at the bank?'

'Well, someone may have hacked into the bank's database - we think just two accounts, those of father and Adolf Eicke. We will be conducting a highly confidential investigation and I have to insist that you do not mention a word of this to anyone, not even to your mother. Can you imagine the potential damage if this knowledge becomes public?'

'Can the bank really be damaged?' asked Sabine, inwardly worried about the personal consequences, should anything untoward happen that could impact on her lifestyle. 'Shall I get my father to give you some advice? He is far more experienced than you are.'

Reinhard went over to the far side of the room. He opened a cabinet which revealed several shelves filled with bottles of all shapes and colours. With a tot measurer he poured a gin and tonic, adding ice cubes from the concealed fridge.

'I don't think that is a good idea,' he said, handing Sabine her drink. 'If we keep it under wraps, then most likely nothing will happen. If it gets out, then it is anyone's guess. Following all the bailouts which many of the major banking giants received recently, clients are wary of anything even hinting that their funds may be at risk.

Banking has become a very sensitive financial sector. Please don't worry, as I am confident that we will have a smooth ride over this problem.'

'You look after the bank's affairs. I have enough on my plate running this house. I just hope that you will be able to get away for a few days in ten days' time.'

'I am not sure with this crisis. What is happening in ten days' time?'

'My mother has managed to secure tickets to a concert in London. Placido Domingo will be performing and of course, your favourite, sexy soprano, Anna Nebtrechko. You won't want to miss her, will you?'

'I would love to go, but I don't know how this problem with the bank will pan out. I cannot make a final decision until I know how this dilemma is going to be resolved.'

'Well I have already accepted, so you will have to delegate the responsibility for this silly investigation to someone else. Besides, everyone of any importance will be there, including royalty.'

Reinhard sighed, 'In that case, how can I refuse,' he said sarcastically. 'Now if you will forgive me, I need to spend some time alone, gathering my thoughts for tomorrow's meeting.'

Reinhard went outside and walked a short way from the house to an old bench that his grandmother had placed there many years before. It had a wonderful view of the Zugspitze, with its pointed peak. It was a place he often went to in times of sadness and stress - like the day his grandmother had passed away or when his mother lay dying from cancer, and he had sat there and pleaded with the Gods of the mountain to save her. All he had wanted was one more day to hold her hand and tell her how much he loved her - his wish had been granted. He looked across green-covered hills where cattle grazed, and he heard the faint tinkling of their bells as they moved around the pastures. Then his eyes followed the steep sweep up the side of the mountain. It was a truly majestic sight. Would the Gods be kind to him once more? Somewhere in his inner being, he knew that something of great import was starting to unravel - something that could bring down the house of Heinrich. Perhaps the Gods were seeking retribution for crimes committed by his Nazi grandfather, however, he could not afford to be tentative at a time like this. The family and the bank had substantial resources, enough to fight off or buy off any threat. He continued to watch the mountain, as the fading sun caused the colour to change from stone grey to shades of mauve, blue and purple. The trees became black shadows and the air a little crisper, as the night sky finally pushed away the light of the day. A few stars appeared and he looked up at the brightest one, wondering if it was perhaps a crooked star, like a swastika, that was there to shine down on Germany's guilt and never go away. Only when the mountain faded from view did he return to the house.

Reinhard had a restless night, as the revelations by his father brought their Nazi past rushing into the present. The bank was clawing its way out of the recession and the last thing it needed right now, was some Nazi connection. Just after midnight he went to the bathroom and swallowed a mild sleeping tablet. Two hours later he fell into a deep but fitful sleep.

CHAPTER 5

At 11 o'clock the following day, Reinhard reconvened the meeting in his office. Alfred Schmidt had flown in on the early flight from Vienna and went over and shook Reinhard's hand, before taking a seat at the table. For added privacy, Reinhard decided to hold the meeting in his office rather than the boardroom.

'Good morning and thank you for the long hours you no doubt put in last night. The problem is purely that of our security. We all know how sophisticated computer criminals have become, especially those from the former Soviet Union. It is important that we are always one step ahead of them. From the notes you have compiled, we will draw up an action plan. Before we continue, I want to tell you about certain conditions I would like applied to this investigation. Firstly, I want every one of you to sign a confidentiality agreement regarding anything that may emerge from this enquiry. All documents may only be circulated to the people around this table and even then, on a need to know basis. I am sure that I don't need to stress to you that the high-profile clients we have, could be scared away if they perceive there to be any breach of security at the bank. Secondly, I don't want any involvement by the police, government authorities or even well-known private investigators. If everyone is in agreement with these conditions, then we can proceed.'

Everyone nodded in agreement.

The Crooked Star

Alfred Schmidt raised his index finger, coughed and said, 'Mr. Heinrich, if I may make a suggestion. I think we are all agreed that we will need some third party help from professional IT experts, in order to trace the source of the invasion. In view of the low profile you want to maintain, I would like to suggest that we consider the firm we use in Vienna. They are a group of five young people, all very clever at the work they do and I am sure we can get them to agree to a secrecy clause.'

Reinhard looked at his IT manager.

'I met them once about six months ago. They seem very professional and I would have no problem using them.'

'If Karl is happy, I think we should stay with this company as I don't want too much third-party involvement,' said Reinhard, making a note on his pad. 'Alfred, see if you can set up a meeting tomorrow. I will fly to Vienna in the morning.'

The Crooked Star

Rudi Muller and Karl Kreie were given an initial budget of one hundred thousand Euros and tasked with increasing the firewall capability of the bank immediately. Reinhard would take personal control of the IT forensic investigation, to track the source of the hacking and e-mails. Although no one questioned his decision at the time, when they later discussed the meeting on their own, they were surprised that the CEO was personally involving himself in the investigation. No one was able to offer any valid reason for his action.

Reinhard was alone in his office when a text message came through on his mobile phone. It was just two words – "last night"? He could see it was from Inge Bauer, his secret mistress. At least, he thought it was a secret.

'Shit!' he said aloud. In the heat of the previous day's events, he had forgotten entirely that he had agreed to attend a concert with her at the Ludwig-Maximilian

University, or LMU as it is generally known. Inge was an Associate Professor in the Communications faculty.

Inge couldn't have been further removed from his wife Sabine. Whereas Sabine's entire life revolved around all the glamorous trappings that a never-ending supply of money made possible, Inge preferred being absorbed into the world of literature and the arts. Although not unattractive, she preferred make-up that was understated. Inge felt more comfortable if she blended in at a gathering, unlike Sabine, who encouraged eyes to follow her every movement. Reinhard sometimes questioned why he had Inge as his mistress, when he had a very attractive blonde bimbo as his wife. He had come to the conclusion that perhaps they should have switched places. He definitely preferred the intellectual conversations he had with Inge and the sexual side was pretty good as well, but he also liked having someone on his arm who made him the envy of all his fellow business colleagues. That's where it ended with Sabine, because not unlike his mother, she controlled him and ruled him. There was this very thin veneer of false charm, beneath which a fiery temper existed. She was totally self-centred, even about such minor things as having the best table at a restaurant or deciding which wine they should drink.

Reinhard was convinced that Sabine was unaware of just how she humiliated him with her attitude and hen pecking. She never used the words "please" or "thank you". It was always - Reinhard bring me a glass of water; Reinhard fetch the newspaper; Reinhard open the door. He obeyed like an eager puppy because he hated confrontations with her, that always ended with him having to apologise. The liaison with Inge was his way of getting revenge. He inwardly smiled when Sabine told guests about their perfect marriage.

He replied to Inge's message - "Major problem at the bank yesterday. I have to go to Vienna tomorrow. Will explain xxx R."

* * * *

Lufthansa flight, LH2324, taxied to the main runway some eight minutes behind schedule. Reinhard checked his watch for the second time in less than two minutes. Without realising it, this was a procedure that he performed scores of times during the day. Psychologists would no doubt put this down to an Obsessive-Compulsive Disorder, much like repetitive hand washing. He looked out of the window as the plane took off in a southerly direction, before gradually banking eastwards. Below him, the city sprawl of Munich gave way to orderly farm fields and then the Alps appeared, snow-capped even in summer. Soon the plains of Austria would come into view as the pilot set a direct course to Vienna.

Alfred Schmidt waited impatiently at the arrivals' hall in Vienna's main airport. He was dressed in a conservative, dark grey suit and clutched a folded newspaper in his left hand which he raised slightly in order to catch Reinhard's eye. The two men greeted one another and exchanged the usual pleasantries regarding the flight and the weather, as they made their way to the car park.

When they got into Schmidt's silver Audi 6, he turned to Reinhard and said, 'I have arranged for us to go directly to the offices of IT Wache, so that you can see their operation first-hand and meet the people running it. I must warn you that they are quite Bohemian, but very good at computer work.'

Reinhard had always thought that Vienna was a splendid city and was pleased when Strauss chose to drive along the Ring Boulevard to the offices of IT Wache on Berggasse. Today's route would take them past the Hofberg, Vienna's beautiful palace and home to the Spanish Riding School. The original building dated back to medieval times, and subsequent additions gave it an eclectic architectural style that ranged from Gothic to Art Nouveau. The Ring Boulevard, which was developed over a period of two hundred years through to the turn of the 20th century, contains some of Austria's finest public and private buildings, monuments and parks. These buildings include the Rathaus, the Burgtheater, the University, the Parliament and the twin museums of Natural History and Fine Arts. Vienna is also the city of music, and in the 18th and 19th centuries it was like a magnet for composers and musicians from all over Europe. Brahms, Haydn, Schubert, Mozart and even Beethoven spent long periods working in Vienna. Johann Strauss, of course, is commemorated in street names, statues and never-ending concerts, throughout the city. Imperial Vienna was the envy of Europe and even today, it is ranked as the number-one city for quality of life, in the world.

The offices of the IT company were situated in a non-descript, two-storey building and the company occupied three offices on the second floor. Reinhard and Alfred Schmidt were greeted by Dirk Siller, the de facto manager. They were ushered into a somewhat bare, small office which had a table surrounded by six chairs. A look of disdain appeared on Reinhard's face as he saw the pop band posters that adorned the walls.

'May I introduce my colleagues,' said Dirk, waving his hand towards three young people who had stood up when Heinrich and Alfred entered the office.

'This is Silke Kotter.'

Reinhard studied her youthful face and tried to guess her age. Perhaps eighteen he thought. She had beautifully formed lips that spread easily into a wide smile and her blond hair was pulled back into a pony tail that dangled over her right shoulder. He noticed that she had prominent cheek bones, which contrasted with the rest of her Nordic looks, but her striking looks belied a brilliant brain. She was reputed to be a brilliant computer expert, having designed several innovative programmes for clients.

'Novak Dokic and Heinz Villendorf.' Both of them were casually dressed in denim jeans and what appeared to be un-ironed shirts. They shook hands and resumed their seats.

Novak Dokic was something of a mystery, even to his colleagues. He had arrived in Vienna from Serbia on a tourist visa and simply stayed on, just another illegal immigrant adding to the millions living in the EU. He was highly computer literate but all he would ever reveal was that he had worked in the cyber- intelligence section of the Serbian army. Being a very private person, he mainly kept to himself after work, unlike Heinz Villendorf and Dirk Siller who were in the same class in high school and together had formed IT Wache some five years before. At every opportunity, they would find some reason to party well into the night, often arriving at work bleary-eyed and sporting terrible hangovers.

'Thank you Dirk,' said Alfred, starting the conversation. 'Mr. Heinrich, as you know, is the CEO of AH Bank and because you have already done some investigations into the hacking at the Vienna branch, you will know why we are here today. Firstly, I want you to tell Mr. Heinrich what your findings are to date.'

Reinhard opened his briefcase and took out a notebook. From the inside of his coat, he extracted a very expensive looking pen. He smiled and gave a slight nod of his head to indicate that the proceedings could begin.

Dirk Siller explained how he and Silke had gone to the Bank's office in central Vienna, and Novak had gone to Adolf Eicke's house in the Grinzing district. They had been able to determine that the firewall at the bank's computer had not been compromised. Novak then described how he had found that the unsophisticated protection on Eickes's computer had indeed been breached, but no damage to files had taken place. He had put in a trace but it ended at a server somewhere in Belgium. The danger, as Dirk explained, is that when such a breach is made, 'back-dooring' often occurs. This is where the hacker installs an opening deep in the system, that allows him to return unnoticed at a later stage. He went on to give a description of the various hacking techniques used by modern cyber criminals.

'Thank you for the explanation,' said Reinhard with a smile on his face. 'You have now added to my vocabulary with words like key-loggers, crackers, sniffers and super user-privileges. Now this is what I want to propose. AH Bank will involve itself with cleaning our computer system and installing new firewalls, etc. I want your company to concentrate on tracing the origin of the break-in. We will pay you well for this, including all expenses and a bonus on the successful conclusion of the search. You will be required to sign binding confidentiality agreements. Would you be interested in this proposal?'

Three faces turned to Dirk. They realised that this could be a real boost for a struggling outfit like theirs. They gave their thoughts away with the joyful looks on their faces.

'This is our game,' replied Dirk. He was trying to appear casual, so as not to leave too much money on the table. 'Novak here, is a hacking expert. He was involved with cyber-intelligence in the Serbian army, so he is well trained. Silke, and I hope she doesn't mind my telling you, has an IQ of one hundred and forty-five. She is bloody amazing. I would propose that they should both be directly involved in the search. Of course, we would back them up when required. You must understand that if this hacker is at all sophisticated, he will have all sorts of blind alleys put into the pathway and tracing it to its origin will be time consuming. However, before we say agree to this, we need to know exactly what you are offering us.'

Reinhard looked at Alfred, knowing that they had already discussed this aspect in the car.

'We will draw up a proper legal document with the full details and the responsibilities of both parties. We will offer you double your usual hourly fee – this includes when you are away from Vienna overnight. As I mentioned before, all expenses will be covered. We will agree on the level of hotel and car hire. If you are successful and we will define successful, you will be paid a bonus of fifty thousand Euros. Part of the confidentiality agreement is that not a single word about this may be discussed outside of this circle. All reporting will be directly to me, personally.' Reinhard looked at the four seated opposite him and the excitement was palpable.

'In principle, we say yes,' said Dirk, who was trying not to appear too eager. 'We will, however, wait for the agreement. If we are happy with it, we would like to commence as soon as possible, in case any links have been shut down by the hacker.'

'You will have the documents by this evening,' said Alfred, as both he and Reinhard stood up.

As soon as they had said good-bye and the door was closed, the four associates hugged one another.

'Fifty thousand Euro. This is exactly what we need to get our business to the next stage,' shouted Heinz. 'Come on, let's celebrate!'

'Wait, wait,' cautioned Dirk. 'First we must sit down quietly and work out our strategy. Silke and Novak will be excluded from the normal workload, so we may have to hire someone on a temporary basis. Silke, what about your friend...I think her name was Anna?'

'She is studying at the university but she has plenty of spare time. I will try to see her tonight, to find out if she would be interested.'

'Right. Now Silke, I want you and Novak to take over office number one and you can start planning right away.'

+++

On the journey to the AH Bank offices in Beatrixgasse, Reinhard made a call to Adolf Eicke, who suggested that they have lunch at his favourite restaurant in the Grinzing District where he lived. At the same time, Alfred Schmidt was arranging for a lawyer from their legal company, to be at their offices so that the urgent agreement with IT Wache could be drawn up.

Within thirty minutes of their arrival at the bank, a lawyer was ushered into Alfred's office. He made hurried notes as both Reinhard and Alfred bounced points off him. At Reinhard's insistence, he agreed to sit in a private office allocated to him, so that he could draw up the draft agreement. He was clearly not impressed with the instruction, as lawyers like to have time, not only to ensure that they have covered all legal loopholes but also to justify the large fees they charge, which would be difficult if an agreement could be produced in forty minutes.

At precisely midday, a taxi arrived at the bank to take Reinhard to his appointment with Adolf Eicke. He instructed the cab driver to drop him a short distance from the restaurant as he was early and wanted to have a walk around the lovely suburb of Grinzing.

It is situated on the outskirts of the city and is surrounded by the Wienerwald, Vienna's huge woodland area, which is also home to some fine vineyards whose wines are sold almost exclusively through the Heuriger restaurants in the district. It is an old part of town, with attractive architecture and a plethora of drinking and eating establishments. At night, it takes on a different look, as the hundreds of lamps that line the streets give it a soft, romantic feel. It has inspired a number of songs, including the well-known waltz, 'In Grinzing Back with You'.

The restaurant chosen by Eicke had a long name - Zur Schonen Aussicht Restaurant - which indicated the lovely views it has over the Wienerwald and central Vienna. At eight hundred years, it is the oldest house in Vienna and is one of the original Heurigen restaurants. In 1784 Kaiser Joseph II allowed wine-growers in the area the privilege of selling their wines for 300 days a year without a trading licence and this relaxation continues to this day. When Reinhard finally arrived at the restaurant, he found that Eicke was already seated at a table next to a window. He walked over and shook the old man's hand.

'So, we meet again Mr. Eicke, dare I say, in much more salubrious surroundings.'

Eicke smiled and gestured for Reinhard to take the seat opposite him.

'Come and sit down. You are now in my favourite eating and drinking place. I welcome you.'

Eicke beckoned to a waiter who immediately came across and stood next to him.

'May I do the honours and order the first bottle of wine?'

'Of course,' replied Reinhard, admiring the view as he looked over the vineyards spread across the valley.

Eicke pointed to a wine on the wine list. The waiter nodded and walked away.

'I have chosen a wine from a local variety called Grűner Veltliner. It is a young, off- dry, white wine with just a hint of fruit. You see, your father is not the only wine aficionado.' Eicke laughed out loud. 'I do, however, bow to Hermann's superior knowledge of viticulture. He seems to have an incredible knowledge of the background of every wine he offers. I once went with him on a tour of major wine-growing countries. It was three weeks of non-stop flying, including South Africa, to see his vineyard in Stellenbosch. It almost turned me against wine but thank goodness I recovered and I now drink at least half a bottle every day. They say it is good for the heart.'

'While I don't claim any expertise in wine,' said Reinhard, 'I do know what I enjoy and together with the odd beer, it is my main tipple. Tell me Mr. Eicke, if I may ask you, what brought you to Vienna after you retired from the bank?'

'As you know, I have lived for a large part of my life in Munich. I suppose I could have continued there or even gone down to Garmisch like you and your father. That is a very beautiful part of the world, but for me, Germany has changed far too much. I don't want to smell Turkish food on every street corner - you know, the meat turning around and around. Call me the old school if you like, but I can no longer see the Germany I grew up in. So I looked around and while I acknowledge that Austria too has an immigrant problem, it is not to the same extent as Germany. Then one day I found this house in the Grinzing district. It had views across the vineyards right down to the Danube. So I purchased it the very same day that I saw it, and my wife and I have been superbly happy here.'

Reinhard nodded in agreement, 'Yes, I can see that one could live a very good life here. I will definitely have to consider it in twenty, or so, years' time. Ah, here comes the waiter with the menus. What do you suggest to go with the delightful wine?'

'Today I am going to suggest the rösti topped with Norwegian smoked salmon and a side plate of garden salad. Shall I order two?'

Reinhard smiled and nodded his agreement.

'Now, Mr. Eicke, I promised to keep you informed of our progress and so here I am today. The company is going to do a complete overhaul of its computer security system and increase the level of our defences. We have also engaged the services of a local IT company. I believe one of their staff members, Novak Dokic, did some investigations on your computer.'

'Dokic?' questioned Eicke. 'So that explains his strange accent.'

'Apparently he is Serbian and well trained in hacking and cracking as they call it. Anyway, because of the confidential nature of the problem you raised with me the other day, we feel it is best if we conduct a small, surreptitious search for the person or persons responsible for the break-in and the e-mails. I am convinced that the bank will not suffer any negative impact from this. Of course, we are very grateful to you for raising the alarm so quickly.'

Reinhard paused, as he was concerned that the next point he was about to raise could be controversial.

He continued, 'My father has always been reticent about discussing the war or my grandfather. After reading the e-mails, I had this feeling that perhaps there was something in our family background which may have some bearing on, or connection to our problem. I have to tell you, that during the conversation I had with my father this week, he revealed for the first time, the secret of the trunk.'

Eicke looked surprised and licked his lips. Reinhard braced himself for a harsh response, as the old man was known for his bad temper and unexpected irrational outbursts.

'We had a solemn pact that we would never discuss the trunk with anyone else but I can see it is obvious that under the circumstances, you need to know. Reinhard, you are after all, the head of our bank now. I would like to suggest...no insist, that you restrict this information regarding the trunk to just the three of us. Yes, you are right. Hermann hated speaking about that time and I think I was one of the few people to whom he ever truly opened up his soul. You have to understand, that your grandfather had a very powerful influence on the impressionable young Hermann. Your family was at the top of the Nazi ranks and so they fell a long way when the end came. Hermann couldn't come to terms with it and to this day, he harbours deep-seated feelings of regret and revenge. We must never again mention the trunk.'

'Of course, that is exactly my feeling as well,' replied Reinhard. 'I need to ask you what you remember about the man in Antwerp to whom you sold the jewels.'

'Not an awful lot. As I remember, it was a small shop in the diamond section of Antwerp. Perhaps Hermann told you how surprised he was to see us, almost as if he knew one of us. He told us he was a Jew and a survivor from the camp system. We made some sympathetic remarks. I can't recall the address but I am sure if I went back to Antwerp, I would be able to find it. Wait. I have just remembered something. I took my wife there about twenty years ago and I bought her a diamond ring at the self-same shop. The Jew, who was present at our first visit, wasn't there that day. We were attended to by a middle-aged woman. Somewhere in my filing system at home, I could still have the receipt which I used for insurance purposes. I will look it up and send it to you. Do you think there could be a connection to these e-mails?'

'I am just clutching at straws. I will personally check it out once you send me the information. It may very well lead nowhere.' Reinhard checked his watch.

The waiter returned and placed the lunch plates before them. Two small round röstis were topped with twisted sheets of smoked salmon, forming a rose petal design. Sprigs of parsley were placed on either side of the food. A side plate of salad, consisting of lettuce, onion, tomato, celery and a light lemon-based vinaigrette dressing, was placed alongside the main plate.

The Crooked Star

The conversation over lunch consisted of polite, informal talk. Eicke reminisced about the early days at the bank and how for the first year he and Hermann shared a car, to keep expenses to a minimum. Reinhard studied the old man's eyes. They were dark blue and menacing, almost making the smile on his lips seem false.

'Why have you and my father not maintained any contact these last few years?' enquired Reinhard, changing the subject of the conversation.

Eicke looked a bit taken aback by the question and took a sip of his wine before answering.

'We had a major fallout when your father outvoted me on a question regarding the expansion of the bank into the American market. I was extremely annoyed that he had chosen to dismiss my objection and to belittle me in front of the management. I suppose it goes right back to the day when we looked at the agreement that our fathers' had made. It clearly stated that the proceeds would be split equally, but in my naiveté, I agreed to a three-way split that involved his mother. I was young and without much money and even a third seemed like a vast fortune. Hermann said at the time, that he would never use the two thirds majority to disadvantage me or to bully me.' Eicke could see that Reinhard was getting embarrassed by what he was hearing. 'After that meeting we had very harsh words and your father told me that if I didn't like the situation, I could always leave the bank. As you know, we both retired a year later. I left a few months before Hermann and he didn't even come to my farewell presentation. In a way it was like history repeating itself because our fathers too, had some bad blood between them. I have subsequently discovered other, how shall I put it -irregularities, which I will not discuss with you. I suppose I never forgave him. I was severely disadvantaged by the way he had manipulated his majority share.'

Reinhard, feeling uncomfortable, looked down at his plate and clenched his teeth. 'These last few days have been such a revelation to me. I am not in a position to discuss the disagreements that exist between you and my father. I am sure you will understand that I am going to have to devote much of my time to damage limitation and I may have to seek your help in this regard.' As was his habit, he looked at his watch.

'I am surprised that you do not appear to know about the differences between Hermann and myself. You were at the meeting when my objections were ignored.' Eicke seemed determined to force Reinhard to respond.

'I certainly do remember the occasion. At the time, I didn't think you were being humiliated in any way. Almost everyone else was in favour of opening up in America.'

'Perhaps you are choosing not to either remember or to be conscious of the situation. I was openly angry and my objections were correct. How much did the bank lose in

2008? Well over one hundred million Euros.' His smile had changed to a thin-lipped sneer.

'Mr. Eicke, where will this conversation get us? Yes, we did lose a lot of money, along with just about every bank in Europe and America. The present situation we find ourselves in, is potentially worse. Rather than dwell on the past, I would ask you to help us get over this present hurdle.'

'As a result of the losses and the way Hermann played around with the assets, I left the bank with a fraction of what I should have received. What do you say to that?' Eicke stared directly into Reinhard's eyes, in much the same way his father before him had stared at an adversary before ordering him to be shot.

'I would rather not comment on something I am not directly involved in. All I ask, is that you assist the bank in this matter,' responded Reinhard, somewhat meekly

'I am at your service, Mr. Heinrich, or should I say, Heydrich.'

The snide remark was not lost on Reinhard, but he chose to ignore it and not rise to the bait.

'I thank you for that,' Reinhard said, turning to summon a waiter.

'Please arrange for a taxi to take me to the airport,' he instructed the waiter. Turning back to Eicke he said, 'I have had a lot revealed to me in the past few days. The people of this country, it seems, still harbour dark secrets. I thank you for the frank conversation and the excellent lunch.'

'It is good that you should know the past, the white parts and the black parts. An eye for an eye and a tooth for a tooth, still applies even in the 21st century.'

Reinhard was puzzled by the biblical reference but decided not to pursue that line of conversation.

'Perhaps,' said Reinhard, standing up. 'I am the new face of Germany and the bank. One that does not have to keep looking back into the past with fear or shame.'

Reinhard bent forward and shook Eicke's hand.

The old man gave him a wry smile and watched as hurried out of the restaurant.

CHAPTER 6

The Crooked Star

Silke stood in front of the door of her bedsitter and fumbled in her coat pockets for the key. She was aware that the champagne that Heinz had produced after they had signed the agreement, coupled with the wine at the wine bar afterwards, had reduced her co-ordination severely. Once inside, she had already decided that a shower and a good sleep would enable her to be fresh for the start of their internet search the next day. She took a look at herself in the mirror. Despite the effects of a long night of drinking, she still looked very attractive. She had high cheek bones like her mother, no doubt the result of some Slavic genes in her bloodline. Silke swallowed two headache tablets before going to bed, as she believed there was nothing worse than staring into a computer screen with a hangover.

Silke Kotter was not her real name. Three years earlier she had assumed the identity of a young, baby girl who had died in a car accident along with both her parents. Silke and the baby girl were born in the same year.

The Crooked Star

Silke was in fact, the daughter of Pastor Rudolf Nuss and his wife Maria. Helga Nuss came into the world twenty-one years ago. Her father, the Pastor, was fifty-two years of age and had married late, after he had heard whispers in the community that being married was the correct thing to do. The Reform Church with the suffix HB, indicating that it was part of the Swiss Protestant movement, was a small church in a sea of Catholicism in Graz. Word had spread that there was something different about this small, unassuming building and the minister who ran it. People came from miles around to the Sunday service, including many Catholics, who secretly slipped into the back pews to hear Pastor Nuss' sermons, to be enthralled by the fire and brimstone rhetoric and the hidden warnings against Islam and immigration.

The smile with which he greeted parishioners didn't extend to his private life. He regretted having to get married and regretted even more the child that resulted from this unhappy union. He was a strict disciplinarian and kept a tight rein on the household budget. Beyond basic requirements for food and clothing, he had a long list of so-called 'luxury' goods which were connected to the devil. In fact, anything that was vaguely pleasurable was included.

'Please Papa, may I have an ice-cream?' the little girl would plead, as they strolled through the Stadtpark on a Sunday afternoon. There was always the same reply - that it was not healthy. While Helga was always neatly dressed, she never had the party dresses that other girls had or the latest toys, except for those which a few parishioners had given her. A small teddy bear, about six inches tall, was her favourite. It went everywhere with her, including to bed. Once, when she was five years old, her father caught her whispering to it and he took it from her, saying that she was now old enough not to have childish crutches. She didn't cry, but she spent days searching for it. She eventually found it hidden behind some books in her father's office and from that day on, she kept it well out of sight. It was also on that day, that her feelings for her father changed forever. He had taken away something she loved.

Helga was always at the top of her class at school and in Mathematics, she was considered to be a year or two ahead of her peers. In part, this was because of all the studying she did in the cold home in which she lived. While other children were playing, she was reading or working out complicated mathematical equations. Very few friends were allowed to visit and those who did, soon detected the lack of warmth and welcome that blew like the arctic wind through the house. Immersing herself in books, transported her to another world. Sometimes on a cold and miserable day, she would study the map of the world. She especially loved looking at the islands in the blue ink of the oceans. She knew the names of all the Mediterranean islands, including most of the ones in the Aegean Sea and she loved creating fantasy stories around them. In her mind she flew like Peter Pan from Crete to Naxos, across to Sicily and back to Skiathos. She made the bright

Mediterranean sun filter into the dark rooms of the Pastor's manse, where she studied and spent much of her free time. She longed to be there, among the olive groves looking at the blue sea, with a warm sun making her skin glow.

It was a few weeks after her eighteenth birthday, on a bright Sunday morning, as the congregation were inching their way out of the church that she first spoke to a young, good-looking boy not much older than herself. He spoke about a youth meeting he was going to that evening and asked if she wanted to join him. Later that day she finally plucked up enough courage to ask her father for permission to attend the meeting. She couldn't believe her ears when almost without hesitation he agreed. This would be her first outing on her own.

Three months later she realised that something was amiss with her body and despite all attempts at denial, she finally accepted the dreadful truth that she was pregnant. She considered the various options open to her - she could confide in her mother, which she knew would eventually result in a terrible confrontation with her father; she could commit suicide, but all the ways she considered, frightened her more than her father; she could run away but how would she cope with a baby and no work.

One day, while weighing up the options in her mind for the umpteenth time, Helga looked out of the window and saw her mother working in the garden. She knew she had to do it that day. She said a quick prayer as she took a few slow steps out of the room but then she lost her nerve and went back to the window. She practised a few opening lines, while looking at the figure of her mother bent over a small bed, where she was planting seedlings. Helga realised the futility of delaying the dreadful task any longer and once again walked out of her room and into the garden.

'Mother, I am pregnant,' she said in almost a whisper and then she burst out crying.

Her mother let out a howl of dismay and started crying as well.

'How are we going to tell your father?' were her first words. 'Please tell me it's not true,' she pleaded. She put her arms around her daughter and for the first time in many years Helga felt comforted by the contact she had so desperately desired as a young child.

The two women waited and secretly deliberated for three days, before they went into the Pastor's office where they both burst into tears before they revealed the news about the unborn baby.

Pastor Nuss folded his hands under his chin and sat in silence. Then he closed his eyes and prayed.

'Oh Lord, why have you let me father a daughter of Satan? Why has Satan been allowed to spill filth upon this house, to damn this House of God and all who reside in it? Why? Why, I implore You?'

Then he opened his eyes and pointed an accusing finger directly at his daughter, 'Romans: 8: 17.'

'Please father, what does that mean?' Helga's knuckles were now white as she clenched her hands together. Her mother sat with her head bowed. They were like two fearful women, waiting for a heavenly hand to strike them.

'The mind that is set on the flesh is hostile to God, it does not submit to God's law, indeed it cannot.'

He stared at her with eyes that were cold and unloving.

'You have forsaken the Lord your God. Eternal damnation awaits you and your offspring. Jeremiah: 2: 19. Your wickedness will punish you, your backsliding will rebuke you.' He waved his hand at her dismissively. 'I no longer see you as my daughter and I will have nothing to do with a child born out of sin.'

Helga looked at the man she called father and realised then that all connections between them were being severed. She had turned to him for help and all she got was eternal damnation. She desperately needed words of consolation but all she got was vicious rebuke. For the first time in her life she was determined to stand up to him. 'Luke: 6: 37,' she said through clenched teeth and trembling lips, 'Do not judge and you will not be judged. Do not condemn and you will not be condemned. Forgive, and you will be forgiven. You see I too can quote verses from the Bible.'

As she stood up and walked out of the office, he shouted after her.

'How dare you preach to me, you little whore?'

As the months dragged on, Helga was forbidden any freedom. Pastor Nuss refused to speak to her. Her mother, fearful as always, made clandestine visits to her bedroom, where Helga had all her meals. She stayed within the confines of the house and was only permitted to go into a small concealed section of the garden, situated at the back of the manse. Parishioners, who asked after her, were told that she was studying. It was here, in the little garden that she often looked up into the sky and prayed for herself and the baby growing bigger every day inside her. There were times when she prayed that the Angel of Death would release her from her purgatory. She came up with many plans as to how she would escape once the baby was a few months old. They would run away, perhaps to Vienna. At least she had a pen pal to turn to there. She would get a job and look after her child. She would give it something she had never had - love. Every day she would sit in this small patch of garden surrounded by a tall hedge, with a lone tree in one corner. It was here she would watch as the seasons changed, slowly at first with the temperature dropping a little every week. Then a sudden drop of five degrees occurred in one day and overnight the leaves changed colour and started falling on the ground. Winter was coming.

One day in early December, she felt painful spasms inside her. As had been prearranged, her mother summoned a mid-wife and her father made a call to Vienna. The mid-wife turned Helga's bedroom into a miniature delivery room with all the paraphernalia associated with basic obstetrics. It was only on the following day, the 8th of December, after hours of agony, that the baby entered the world. The scream from the baby would be the last and only memory she would have of her child. Unbeknown to her, the couple waiting in the next room were there to take the baby away. It would be registered as being born to them.

When Helga realised what had happened, she cried incessantly for two days. Sometimes her mother cried with her but her father retained his silence. Slowly her strength returned and on a Sunday, some two weeks later, while the church service was in progress, Helga packed a small suitcase with some of her clothing and the small teddy bear she had as a child. She knew where her father kept the church funds hidden and so she helped herself to enough money to see her through a month on her own in Vienna. As she walked past the church, she could hear the opening notes of the organ, followed by the congregation singing Silent Night, Holy Night. The cold, biting wind tore into her. She was walking into her own silent night.

Chapter 7

The building was grey and drab and looked very uninviting. Helga paused at the doorway and looked at the list of names. She spotted her friend's name, Anna Schmidt. She pushed the buzzer and waited. It seemed like an eternity and she started to panic. She had contacted her friend, so Anna was expecting Helga to arrive that day. Please answer, she cried silently. Helga waited. Then suddenly a voice came out of the speaker.

'It's me,' Helga shouted. She heard a click as the latch was released. When she arrived at the apartment which was situated on the ground floor, her friend Anna was standing in the open doorway, smiling.

'Oh my God, you look terrible,' Anna said, as she wrapped her arms around Helga and hugged her. 'Your eyes are so sunken and you must be dreadfully cold. Come in right away and I will make some coffee.'

The tears ran down Helga's cheeks as she battled to control herself. She sat down on a chair putting her suitcase next to her on the floor.

'Thank you, Anna. There is so much I have to tell you but you must please be patient, as I am still not sure I fully understand what has happened and is happening to me.'

'Now listen to me Helga. You do not have to worry about anything. I have cleared out a small room for you, I think it is called a box room, but it will be big enough. Do you not need to see a doctor?'

The two sat close together, holding their coffee cups in their hands for extra warmth. They reminisced about growing up in Graz and how so far apart their upbringing had been. Anna's father was an artist and her mother was an interior decorator. They had very liberal ideas when it came to giving their children almost complete freedom of choice and movement.

The next morning, over a cup of coffee, Anna announced that she would not be going home for Christmas as she had originally planned but would instead stay in Vienna with Helga. Anna was determined that she would try and get her friend's mind off the ordeal she had just been through, by taking her to Christmas markets, coffee houses and wine bars. On Christmas Eve Anna and Helga spent hours in the small kitchen preparing a feast for two, although they both admitted that their culinary skills were decidedly lacking.

It was just after Christmas when Helga decided that she should change her name. She researched the death notices on either side of her birth date and found that a week-old baby, named Silke Kotter, had died in the Innsbruck area. She checked the local newspapers and found an article describing a terrible car crash in which a father and mother and their new born baby had been killed. Four hours later, Helga was transformed into Silke. Her past ceased to exist except in the deep recesses of her mind. No one but she and Anna knew of the change in her identity.

It was at a wine bar in the old district of Vienna on New Year's Eve, that Silke was introduced to a friend of

Anna's, Dirk Siller, who together with two other friends had opened an IT consulting firm. He suggested that Silke should come around to their offices as soon as the festive season was over, as they had recently acquired two new accounts and could do with some additional help.

The months went by and Silke was now firmly entrenched as the fourth member of the firm. They were amazed at her knowledge of computer systems and she was often called in when they encountered really difficult problems. No one knew about her secret or how she often cried internally or how she added each day to the tally, starting with the birth of the baby, so that she knew its precise age every day. Was it a boy or a girl, she would ponder? What name had it been given? Oh, if only she could hold it close to her. She knew that one day she would find her baby. She wanted that more than anything in the world. A tortured soul is worse than torture of the flesh. She would often walk past shops selling baby clothes and on the odd occasion she would go in and pick up the tiny clothes and fondle them.

A year had passed and it was the 8th of December again – it was her baby's first birthday. She was now renting her own apartment and on her way home, she went to the baby clothes section at a nearby department store and purchased a pair of white crocheted booties, a small present for the baby. When she got home, she put the booties on the table, opened a bottle of champagne and toasted the baby's first birthday. Then she did something she had promised herself that she wouldn't do. She decided to give the baby a name. She decided that it was a girl and after thinking about the possible names she would have chosen, she narrowed the list down to five names. She pondered the list for a while, initially scratching out three names. She was left with Heidi and Odett. She recalled once reading about a very brave woman in the French Résistance during the war and her name was Odette and so

Odett became the chosen name. A toast confirmed the 'Christening'.

Another two years would pass before Silke finally came to the conclusion that the only way for her to overcome the constant despair she felt, would be to try and trace her baby. By now her computer skills had been honed to a fine degree and she knew how to infiltrate the most secure systems, not that she had ever attempted anything illegal.

She found that there are approximately two hundred births every day in Austria and if a birth has to be registered within fourteen days that would make a total of two thousand eight hundred births to investigate. A further complication was that she had no idea where the registration would have taken place. From the comments made by her mother, she believed that the birth was not registered in her name and that the people who had taken her child would have registered the baby as having been born to them.

It became such an obsession, that she spent most of her spare time, both at the office and at home, sifting through hundreds of births registered around the 8th of December. She made surreptitious calls to potential people on her list, often causing consternation. As she was concerned that someone could report her to the police, she decided against that avenue of investigation. Then one day she happened to pick up a newspaper left on a table by one of her colleagues and on page three, in a short article, she read that the annual meeting of the Synod of the Reform Church HB was to take place in Berne, Switzerland, later that month. She recalled that her father regularly attended the meeting, which took place on the last Friday of September every year. What if she could break into the manse, she thought? Silke was convinced that somewhere in her father's office she would find some clue to the identity of the people who had her baby. How would she get past her mother, she asked herself? She couldn't take the chance that her mother would assist her. She was at once very excited and very afraid. Silke kept asking herself what she would do with the information once she had it. She could go to the police or even the media. Austria had experienced some very bad cases of kidnapping and the media would no doubt love to get their hands on something like this. Did she want a big custody battle, with her baby torn between the mother and father she knew and loved or a strange woman she had never seen? Silke prayed and cried a lot but the burning desire to see her baby, perhaps just to touch it, compelled her to make the decision to go ahead with her plan.

First Silke needed to establish that her father was actually going to the meeting, so she approached Novak and asked him if he would do something for her and not ask a single question about it. Novak agreed and he was told that he had to phone the number she had given him. He was to ask for the pastor and tell him he was from

Google Earth and that they would be in the vicinity of the church on Friday 29th September and wanted to take 360 degree photographs of the church.

Novak phoned the number Silke had given him. The woman who answered the phone informed him that the pastor was not there and that she was his wife. She asked if she could be of assistance. After listening to Novak's story, she told him that there would be no one at the church for three days over that period, as they were all attending a conference. Silke gave Novak a hug when she realised that she would be able to break in with ease, as no one would be there. She already knew how she was going to achieve this. At the back of the house there was a small leaded window in the scullery. She would cut out the small pane carefully and enter through the window. On leaving she would glue the pane back in place. The scullery was dark and it was unlikely that anyone would notice what had taken place, possibly for years, if ever.

The Crooked Star

Early on the morning of the 25th September Silke took the early train from Vienna to Graz. In her handbag she had medical gloves, a glasscutter, a rubber suction device and a Leatherman multiple tool kit. As she alighted from the train, she started to panic and could feel that her rate of breathing and her pulse were way above normal. She hailed a cab and directed him to take her to a place two streets from the church. She was grateful that it was an unpleasant, windy day so she would not look out of place wearing a hood.

She tried to walk as nonchalantly as possible when she approached the church. The street was empty except for a man walking on the opposite side. Silke entered the church parking area and gave a start as she saw a car parked there. Then she noticed that the church door was open. As she got closer, the sound of a vacuum cleaner could be heard and Silke remembered that a cleaner came every Monday and Friday. With an audible sigh of relief, she quickly made her way to the back of the church and through the gate that led to the manse. When Silke saw the building that had been her home for eighteen years and latterly her prison, she started crying.

'Mother, do you love me?' she whispered. 'Please Lord help me in what I am about to do.'

Silke approached the leaded window and took out her tools and gloves. She applied the rubber sucker to the window and started cutting around the edges of the pane. As she neared the end, she held onto the sucker and made her final cut. She tugged at the rubber but the pane refused to budge. Although it was cold Silke could feel herself sweating. She tapped at the glass with the cutter and suddenly she felt it move. Silke pulled again and to her relief it came out of the frame. She inserted her hand into the opening and found the latch and managed to pull it upwards. Then she opened the window and climbed in as quietly as possible, just in case her mother had changed her mind and was in the house.

The Crooked Star

Walking through the house affected Silke emotionally, with all the smells and memories it imparted. Absolutely nothing seemed to have changed. Every item was still in its original place. She entered her father's office, the room of their final fight and parting. She did not know where to start. She pulled at a drawer on the filing cabinet, but it was locked. She was concerned that her father had taken the key with him. His desk was also locked. She was starting to panic. Had the trip been in vain? Along one wall there was bookcase filled with various bibles and reference books. On the bottom shelf she noticed piles of books, each six books high and when she bent down for a closer look, she recognised that they were her father's diaries. Silke pulled out four from the bottom of the pile and found one which was from three years previously. She sat down on the floor and opened it at the 8th of December. There was only one entry - a letter M next to the 10:00 slot. She paged back but each page only revealed the names of parishioners, who had asked to see the pastor. There were also some notes about purchases that had to be made, including light bulbs and paint. She was forced to read each page to see if any clue appeared. Silke began to despair. It didn't seem logical that her father would write about something on which he wanted absolute secrecy, in a diary. There were three entries on the 20th July. She recognised the names of two of the parishioners and the third entry was a letter M and a seven-digit number. Just in case there was a connection between the two entries with M, she wrote this number on a piece of paper and put it in her bag. She continued searching back a further three months without finding anything that offered any hope.

As Silke stood up, she heard a key turning in the lock of the front door. She grabbed her bag and raced for the kitchen. She now realised that the cleaning lady must have access to the manse as well. She would have to be both quick and quiet. She could hear something being dragged along the floor and the front door being closed.

She pulled herself onto the scullery counter and squeezed through the window, jumping to the ground. She found the pane of glass where she had left it. Taking some putty out of her bag she held the pane in place with her sucker and pressed lumps of putty around the edges. The pane seemed to be held in place. Silke looked back at her shoddy work and realised that anyone walking close by, would immediately notice what had been done but she couldn't wait any longer, as she now heard a tap being turned on in the kitchen next door. She pulled her hood over her head and walked briskly out of the church grounds.

Silke spent the weekend investigating if the number was a telephone number and who the owner was. She realised it had to be a Vienna number and it didn't take her too long to establish that it was a business number belonging to Fieler, Mueller and Associates - a firm of attorneys. Further research showed Mueller's residential address as 57 Linzerstrasse, near to the Schonbrunn Palace.

CHAPTER 8

On Monday afternoon, Silke took the U4 Metro line to the stop closest to the Schonbrunn Palace. From the station, it was less than 300 metres to Linzerstrasse. For her first visit, she had decided that she would walk slowly past number 57. There was a cold wind blowing but Silke knew that her shivering was caused by fear. Her heart seemed to be beating inside a hollow chest as she approached the house. It was a palatial home, set in at least half an acre of manicured gardens surrounded by a two-metre-high wrought iron fence. The main gate, also wrought iron, was topped with gilt coat of arms.

'Oh my goodness,' Silke said to herself. 'If this is the home of my baby, then she is so lucky.'

Silke was over-awed by the size and elegance of the building. She said in a whisper, 'Hello Odett. My darling, do you know I am so close? I want to hold you, that is all I want.'

111

The Crooked Star

Silke crossed the road and headed back to the train station, her stomach churning and with tears streaming down her cheeks. She now knew that she had to see her baby.

The following day Silke left work early and returned to Linzerstrasse. She was torn in half. She wanted to see the baby but she also wanted to avoid the intense pain and suffering she knew such a meeting would bring. At number 55 she hesitated and almost turned back, but something urged her on. She slowed her pace and as she walked past the huge gate, she saw a young child some thirty metres away. To the right of the gate there was a tall hedge almost as high as the fence. Silke used the hedge to conceal herself from the house. When she bent down, she could see a little girl dressed in a colourful, floral dress. She had short blonde hair. She willed her to turn around so that she could see the young child's face. Then without thinking, Silke shouted out, 'Hello.' The little girl looked up, not sure who was calling out. She waved her hand.

Silke waved back and beckoned her with hand. She could see the child was hesitant, so she waved again. Again, the child waved back and then as if drawn by a magnet, she hopped and skipped close to where Silke was standing.

'Hello. What is your name?'

The little girl just looked at Silke without saying anything. She had big blue eyes, a rosebud mouth and fine, blonde hair. Then she raised her hand and showed Silke the tiny white flower she had picked out of the grass.

'Please can I have that flower?' Silke pleaded. The little girl came forward and passed it though the fence. Silke took the flower and at the same time stroked her arm. She had touched her baby for the first time.

'Olivia! Where are you?' The shrill voice came from a side entrance of the house. Silke could see a portly woman, dressed in a pinafore.

The little girl turned and ran towards the house.

113

Olivia and not Odett, thought Silke but still a lovely name. She didn't want to be caught kneeling alongside the fence so she hurried away, filled with a mix of emotions. She kissed the fingers on the hand that had touched her baby. She then gently placed the flower in a tissue and decided she would press it and look at it every day.

Over the next few months she made two to three clandestine visits every week to 57 Linzerstrasse.

CHAPTER 9

Reinhard arrived at his office early the following morning. He immediately switched on his computer and opened the mail from Eicke. It was terse and to the point – Bruges Diamonds, Schupstraat 9, Antwerp. Reinhard decided that he would fly to Belgium the following day. He then composed a number of e-mails. The first one he sent to the four senior Heads of Department, advising that he would out of the office for an undisclosed period, and that he was to be given an exception report each evening via e-mail. He sent another e-mail to his secretary asking her to book him a flight to Brussels. Inwardly, he was worried as to what his trip to Antwerp would reveal. Another mail was sent to Schmidt at the Vienna branch, asking for the mobile numbers of Novak and Silke. He then telephoned Inge and arranged to meet for breakfast at a small cafe near the university. He checked his in-tray and quickly went through the documents and papers, signing those that required it and discarding those that were purely informational. At 08:15 he left the office and drove to his rendezvous with Inge.

Inge was already seated at a window table with a cup of coffee in front of her. Reinhard bent down and kissed her on the cheek.

'I am sorry about this, but the bank has a crisis that I personally have to attend to. How are you?'

'As you see me - happy and neglected. You missed a very good concert. So tell me about the crisis. For a moment, I thought it involved the bitch.'

Reinhard smiled. She always referred to his wife as 'the bitch'.

'This is a genuine problem. I won't give you a long explanation, except to say that someone has hacked into the bank's computer and we have received a veiled threat. I am taking it very seriously and that is why I was in Vienna yesterday and I will be in Antwerp tomorrow. I am really sorry that I missed the concert.'

'It wasn't important, but it did highlight the futility of our relationship. Reinhard, I don't want to add to your worries but I have done a lot of thinking. My whole personality is not geared to playing surreptitious games and

116

having to make changes to my schedule because 'the bitch' has arranged a dinner party or whatever. We are adults and you must go your way, and I will go mine.'

'Inge, Inge! What the bloody hell are you talking about? I didn't manufacture this problem!'

'It goes beyond this current problem, and well you know it. This is not the first time this has happened. I can never see you from Friday to Monday, when all normal people are going out. I cannot take it anymore, plus your bullshit about leaving 'the bitch.' Don't raise your eyebrows – 'bitch' is the word you use as well!'

Reinhard shook his head, 'It is a little more complicated than you make out. What about Eva? I have to have her best interests in mind as well. I cannot just say tomorrow; okay I am free. No more marriage. No more daughter. Life's a little more complicated than that. You are lucky, there is just you.'

'So now it's Eva. My life has to be put on hold because of your daughter. Do you know how many children there are in a divorced situation? More than forty percent. If you really wanted to leave your wife, you could make a very satisfactory arrangement for Eva, especially with your money. You can't fool me.'

'I need a cup of coffee!' Reinhard beckoned to a waitress. 'I cannot believe what I have walked into this morning. I am not happy in this dreadful marriage of mine, and you have been the one sane and solid anchor that I have had. I want to be with you, and I can only promise that things will work out in time.'

'Reinhard, psycho-analysing you is not difficult. You have some serious weaknesses in your character. Perhaps you had a strong mother, and this is why you allow yourself to be dominated by 'the bitch'. You don't have the courage to leave her, and Eva is just a convenient cloak to hide behind. Perhaps you do like me, but you want to keep your Garmisch house intact and have a compliant little pied-a-terre arrangement in Munich. Two convenient and separate compartments but that situation never works out quite the way people wish. Your deception is wrong for her and for me and ultimately wrong for you and Eva as well. That is why I am getting out of this mess.'

'Inge, I am so shocked that I am going to leave now and trust that you will soon come to your senses.' With that Reinhard abruptly stood up just as his coffee arrived and strode out of the cafe, angrily.

Inge had a wry smile on her face as she watched him depart.

* * * *

Hermann had not slept well for the past two nights, as haunting thoughts crawled out in the dark and swirled around in his mind. How he envied Blondi whose only dreams involved chasing rabbits. Several times during the night he looked at her with envy, as she slept at the foot of his bed. He put on his dressing gown and made his way to the wine cellar with Blondi following closely behind. He descended the short stairway leading to the locked door, which he opened with a code. He switched on the lights and realised that it had been several months since he had last been down here. Despite the ventilation system, it had a dusty, musty smell. He shuddered as the cold hit him. In the centre of the cellar, there was an old oak table with three chairs. The table was covered in a fine layer of dust. He looked around the walls which had wine racks from floor to ceiling. It was one of the finest wine collections in Germany, with every bottle catalogued in an old-fashioned card system.

Hermann walked over to rack number ten in the middle of the room and pulled at it. It opened smoothly and silently, revealing another locked door. It too had a number keyboard. It opened after a code was punched in. Hermann put his hand around the door and flipped a switch. The room was lit up instantly. It was even mustier than the wine cellar. Blondi sat down and rubbed her nose with her paw. The room was the width of the house and about five metres in length. Hermann sat down and looked at the shrine he had painstakingly created. It was in honour of his father, rather than the Nazi period. A large photograph of a man in a SS uniform dominated the one wall. It was captioned: Reinhard Tristan Eugen Heydrich 1904-1942. The face was narrow, in line with the genetic trait of the Heydrichs. The image revealed a slightly aquiline nose and a full mouth, with just the hint of an arrogant grin. Hermann looked at the photograph of his father, and he could see himself at the same age and also the uncanny likeness of his son, Reinhard. The gallery of photographs included some of Heydrich with the luminaries of the Third Reich - Hitler; Goering; Goebbels and Himmler. There was also the well-known photo of Heydrich, triumphantly mounting the steps of his grand Prague headquarters. His father's uniform was on display on a store mannequin in one corner and in another corner, the swastika flag hung limply from a pole. It was the same flag that had covered his father's coffin.

Hermann went over and dusted the shoulders of the uniform with his hand before sitting down on the single chair in the room. He had always believed that if the fortunes of the Third Reich had turned out differently, his father would have been the logical successor to Hitler, as Fuhrer. He was in awe of his father. The ultimate power over life and death that his father had possessed filled him with fascination and envy. He had this same power over rabbits that he often shot in the fields but that was as far as it went for him. He continued to sit in the shrine for almost an hour before finally going back upstairs.

The Crooked Star

CHAPTER 10

There was no direct flight so Reinhard flew to Brussel-Zaventem Airport where he rented a car and drove to Antwerp. He managed to find a parking garage in a central part of the city and with the aid of the GPS on his mobile phone, he found Schupstraat with ease. Halfway down the street he came to number 9. He was surprised to find that Bruges Diamonds was a non-descript shop with just a single display window. It was certainly very unlike some of the glamorous diamond merchants nearby, with their glittering window displays and plush interiors. Reinhard hesitated outside the shop, not sure how he would approach the enquiry. He walked on, pretending to look at the other window displays, while deciding on a strategy. Finally, he plucked up enough courage to return to the shop.

He entered and saw a short, balding man behind the counter.

124

'Good morning. How may I help you?' the man enquired in German.

'How do you know I am German?' enquired Reinhard.

'I don't really, but you have a Lufthansa tag on your briefcase.'

'You are very observant,' said Reinhard, pleased that the ice had been broken with some humour. 'Actually I am looking for someone a lot older than yourself who owned this shop maybe forty years ago.'

'That would be my father, and he still owns it, although he hardly ever comes in now. I am sure I can help you.'

'I don't think that will be possible. You see, I need to speak to your father about an event which took place here, in this shop in the early sixties. He may need some assistance in recalling the details. Is it possible for me to meet him?'

''He is old, but his mind is very clear. I am not sure he will want to see you, but I will phone him and see how he feels about such a meeting. Do you have a business card?'

The young man went to an office at the back of the shop. Reinhard could hear mumbled sounds but was unable to make out the language spoken.

He returned and said smilingly, 'Mr. Heinrich, to my surprise, my father has agreed to meet you at his house. At first, he said he was reluctant but when I told him you were about forty years of age, he agreed. He dislikes any German who is of an age where he could have been involved in the war. I must warn you that he may bring up the subject of the holocaust.'

'Thank you. I will treat your father with sensitivity. I do not know your name or that of your father'.'

'Mayer - I am Albert and my father is Otto. Mr. Heinrich, the house is quite a distance from here and you will need to take a taxi. Shall I call one for you?'

Reinhard thanked him and after writing down the address, went outside to wait for the taxi, which arrived within a few minutes.

Otto Mayer's house was situated on the outskirts of the city, near the Park Schidehof. It was an early 20th century, dark-brick house, surrounded by a high wall. As he rang the bell, Reinhard noticed the CCTV camera aimed at the gate.

'Please come in,' announced an elderly female voice. Reinhard pushed open the gate and walked up the pathway to the front door. The garden was overgrown and had obviously not received much attention for some time.

The conifers, which lined the path, reduced the amount of light getting to the house, giving it a dark, eerie look. A grey cat, sitting on a wicker chair on the veranda, silently observed him as he approached the front door.

'I am Mrs. Mayer. You have come to see my husband? Please follow me.'

Reinhard followed the woman, who walked slowly, aided by a cane walking stick.

The house, like the garden, was also dark and forbidding. The staircase was made of dark wood as was the furniture in the entrance hall. It was an old person's home both in sight and smell. They entered a room which was obviously a library, judging by the floor to ceiling shelves containing row upon row of books. Mr. Mayer was seated behind a large desk that was empty save for a writing pad, an old-fashioned ink stand and somewhat incongruously, a laptop computer.

Reinhard put out his hand in greeting but this was ignored by the old man who pointed to a chair.

'Please sit down Mr. Heinrich. My son tells me you have come from Germany to ask me to recall some event from the past.'

'Thank you for seeing me. Not really an event but a transaction that took place in 1960. You bought some diamonds and jewellery from two men. Like me, they came from Germany.'

The old man smiled at him. It was a derisive smile rather than a friendly one.

'I buy and sell diamonds. That is my business. Why should I remember one particular transaction fifty years ago? Is there a special reason why I should remember?

Was there something special about the items? Perhaps they were stolen?'

'I know nothing about the provenance of the jewellery, and I suppose it was foolish of me to consider that you would be able to recollect buying some items that long ago. I am sorry if I have interrupted you.'

'You are lying,' said Mr. Mayer, looking directly into Reinhard's eyes.

'Why do you say that? I have apologised for coming here.'

'I say that because I looked at your face, just as I looked at a face fifty years ago. It was narrow, arrogant and cruel. You cannot get away from your genes. I can see Heydrich's bloodline in your Teutonic looks just as I saw it in your father's face five decades ago. That day and that face is etched into my memory.'

Reinhard was visibly shocked by the sudden hostile attack he was under from Mayer. It was totally unexpected. He had come on this mission purely as an exploratory exercise to glean if there could be any connection between the e-mails and the sale of the jewellery, all those many years ago. He was now unsure as to which direction he should take.

'You didn't come here to ask me about what should have been a normal business transaction. You came because of the origin of those items. Admit it.'

'I do admit that,' confirmed Reinhard, who had decided not to cover up. 'I can assure you, however, that I did not know about the original ownership of any jewellery until a few days ago. You can see my age. I am not part of the Nazi period in my country's history. I do not condone it and would never glorify it. I would like to ask you some questions related to the transaction, and I would like to

131

offer to repay you for the amount you paid for the jewellery, including an interest factor of course.'

Mayer stood up and walked over to the large door of a safe. It was unlocked. He fumbled around and produced a small wooden box. He returned to the desk and opened the box.

'Every single item that I bought that day is still here. Let me tell you why. When your father and Eicke came into my shop, I went into a state of shock. For a moment, I thought it was Reinhard Heydrich looking at me. The resemblance was so strong. Eicke, I did not recognise and I only found out his father's background at a later stage through the Simon Wiesenthal organisation. I looked at the items they presented, and I was so keen to get rid of those two men that I made up a figure there and then. They accepted it and left. Later when I examined the jewellery in more detail, I came across a gold band with a fine inscription on the back.' He extracted a gold ring out of the box and held it up for Reinhard to see.

'The inscription reads: Sophie Mayer 20.4.1933. I thought to myself that Mayer is a fairly common name, as is Sophie. Could it just be a co-incidence that my father's sister was also Sophie? I didn't want to believe that, because along with all of my family, she perished in the gas ovens. Perhaps I was touching something she had worn? I can't explain how I agonised over the contents of this box and in particular this gold band.'

Reinhard was breathing heavily and was unsure as to what he could say at this juncture.

'I put the box away and it was many weeks later before I could bring myself to look at the ring once more. I decided to do some research and went to Prague, which is where my family had lived for many generations. Fortunately, Prague was one of the few major cities in that part of Europe that did not suffer any major

133

bombardments. All the records were still intact. I was able to re-build my family history, going back four generations. I came up with some blanks regarding my Aunt Sophie, for the date on the ring was not her birthday. Her birthday was 8 November 1913. Then one day I went to the offices of Aktualne newspaper. In their archives I looked up the issue of the 20th April 1933. Under personal notices I came across an engagement announcement of Sophie Mayer to Jakob Shaffer. This was definitely my aunt. This was her engagement ring.' Mayer hesitated to allow the significance of his statement to sink in. Then he continued, 'Jakob was German and a member of the communist party. He was arrested in 1934 and sent to the Dachau Camp. I then knew that the jewels sold to me by the two Germans, one of whom was the spitting image of Heydrich, were blood jewels. The irony of that date is that it was Hitler's 44th birthday and the year he became Chancellor.'

Reinhard had difficulty looking directly at Mayer, who was staring intently at him.

'Who was that man who came to me with a box of jewels? The man who looked like Heydrich, and who are you Mr. Heinrich?'

'My name is Heinrich. My father's name is Heinrich, but my grandfather's name was Heydrich. It was my father who came to you with the box. He had no direct connection to the box which surfaced years after the war. I truly do not know anything about the nature and origin of any of the items in the box. If there is any indication that they were acquired in an illegal or dubious way, I am prepared to pay the owners or their rightful heirs' suitable compensation.'

'Mr. Heinrich I only agreed to meet with you once my son had given me his estimation of your age. At around forty years of age, you could not have been alive during that murderous period in your country's history. While I do not accept that your date of birth makes you blameless for the sins of your forebears, it does mean that you had no direct connection to the atrocities of the Third Reich.'

'That is a little unfair do you not think?' responded Reinhard. 'I am two generations removed from the war. I am not one who denies the Holocaust or the many atrocities that occurred then, but I have to say I do not see myself responsible for something which took place well before my birth. It would be the equivalent of blaming a modern-day Frenchman for something committed by Napoleon.'

Mayer looked at the box and then at Reinhard.

'There have been many atrocities in history, and I have no doubt there will be more in the future. None will ever equal what Germany did with the human abattoirs it established under Hitler. They tried and almost succeeded in eliminating an entire people from the face of the earth. Germany and every generation of Germans following the war will have to live with an eternal guilt. It will be written on their foreheads like the mark of the devil. Of course this is unfair and there will be many kind and wonderful people in your country who will not be deserving of this burden, but that is how it is. The sins of the father... in this case, the sins of the Fuhrer.'

He is correct, thought Reinhard. The crooked star will shine down on Germany until the end of time.

'I mentioned compensation earlier on. Could you possibly assist me with this?' Reinhard was starting to realise that the unexpected onslaught had taken him off-track, and he needed to steer the conversation away from the purely emotional to something more concrete.

'Compensation? Who would you give compensation to? My family were all butchered and I certainly would never accept any money.' He put his hand in the box and drew out an assortment of brooches and stones. 'Look at these. Who do they belong to? No one will ever know. Each one could have a terrible tale attached to

137

it. This is a box of blood and tears. In a way, it represents humanity and history. That is why I never sold it on. Can you even begin to imagine the feeling of hopelessness and despair those people must have felt, as the cattle trucks carried them to some unknown destination? They lost complete control of their lives.'

'The Nazi period was a terrible period in my country's history,' said Reinhard leaning forward. He could feel perspiration forming on his forehead but he knew it would be a display of weakness if he wiped it away. 'Because of my family connection to the upper echelons of the Party, I have tried desperately to find out what drives people to blindly follow someone fuelling the fires of hatred, to the extent that all human feelings are obliterated and replaced with barbarism. I have great difficulty putting myself in that place and time. I cannot come up with a rational answer.'

'You are correct - it is difficult to imagine what it must have felt like to become nothing. If you demonise a people or group and reduce them to the status of an animal or insect, then exterminating them becomes easy. If there is a cockroach over there,' Mayer pointed to the wall, 'you can either stamp on it or you can spray it with an insecticide. What feelings of guilt and remorse will you have as you look back at the dead body of the cockroach? None. In our minds, a cockroach is not deserving of life. That is what the Nazis did. They reduced my people and others that they wanted to exterminate to the level of a cockroach. How else can a soldier take the butt of his rifle and bash in the head of a baby because it is crying? How is it possible for someone to herd a group of innocent people, including children, into a gas chamber and then afterwards go and have lunch?'

Mayer put his hand in the box and pulled out the ring again.

'What agony and suffering did Sophie go through? What about my father and mother and my sisters? Soon these individual tales of suffering will disappear like a mist under the heat of the sun and then we will just have statistics. It is difficult to measure pain and suffering in statistics. You mentioned Napoleon a short while ago. Did you know that four million people were killed in the various wars and expeditions during Napoleon's eleven-year reign? Do you feel any emotion about that number? I doubt it, but I hope you can imagine and feel the pain and utter anguish of the mother whose baby's head was bashed in by the rifle-butt of a German soldier. I know I can. What did she go through as she watched the life disappear from a tiny baby - blood all over her arms?' Mayer cradled his arms as if he too had blood on them. 'I can feel it now, but I feel nothing for the four million killed in Napoleon's reign!'

Reinhard was regretting that he had made this visit. He was being assailed by Mayer's relentless diatribe,

140

however, he was not going to attempt to defend himself or the actions of his forefathers. This would be futile and would only lead to further rhetorical questions and attacks.

'I understand your feelings and even your hatred. Perhaps I too would have had the same emotions if our roles were reversed. I would like to think not, but who can say unless one has suffered in the same way. You recognised the facial likeness that my father shared with his father and of course, I can see it in myself as well, but how did you find out that he was accompanied by someone called Eicke?'

'As I said, I was helped by the Simon Wiesenthal Institute. I do not wish to go into any detail. Suffice to say that his father was also a notorious killer. You still haven't told me exactly why you have come to see me.'

Reinhard could tell that the old man was lying but thought it would be fruitless to continue with this line of questioning.

141

'My father received a curious e-mail,' said Reinhard deciding to twist the truth slightly. 'It mentioned Antwerp. After a chat with him, I felt some light may be thrown on this cryptic message if I spoke to you.'

'I cannot help you as I didn't send any e-mail to your father. I am starting to feel tired, and perhaps it is time for us to end this meeting.'

'May I have your e-mail address so that we can keep in contact if something new should arise?' asked Reinhard.

'No. I do not think that is wise or necessary. In fact, I do not want to have any contact with you again,' replied Mayer bluntly.

'As you wish,' said Reinhard, standing up. 'This has been a traumatic meeting for both of us. I will leave you with one thought and that is, that not all Germans are evil. I do not believe that cruelty and evil are genetically transferred, or are built into the blood of a particular people.'

Mayer shook his head, 'I am not convinced that you are entirely correct. After all, your forebears branded all Jews as sly thieves, rapists and child molesters. They believed every single Jew was so innately bad that they needed to be exterminated, right from the grandparents down to the little children.'

'The situation that prevailed in the period between the two wars, led to nationalism and racism that was narrowly tribal in its outlook.' Reinhard said as he resumed his seat. He continued, 'the Nazis took that to the extreme, as it was useful for other political ends. Not every German was a Nazi. Not every German was involved in atrocities. I do not have any of the tendencies that my Grandfather obviously had.'

'When I see Germans,' said Mayer, with a scowl on his face, 'even those like you who are two generations

143

removed from the Nazis, I can see certain national traits - some that are good and some that are bad. There is that strong work ethic and a desire for order and obedience to authority which runs through Germanic people. It was these traits that enabled your country to come out of the ashes of destruction and rebuild the Germany of today. That is very admirable,' Mayer hesitated for a moment and then continued, 'but it was also those very traits that Hitler manipulated and twisted to an evil end. It is plain to see, in general terms, how Germans are different to Italians, for example. There are also Jewish traits that have been with us for centuries and persist today. In our desire to protect our identity, as a minority, we work to overachieve and this lays us open to envious hatred. Yes, there is no getting away from it, that there are definite national and racial behavioural patterns that set us apart.'

Reinhard decided to intervene at this point, 'Sadly, you and I will never be able to find common ground. Your hatred and bigotry are too great. I bid you good-bye.' He stood up once again, turned and walked away. He felt empty and drained.

Otto Mayer had no expression on his face as he watched Reinhard depart from the room. He looked down at his hands and saw that they were shaking.

Once outside, Reinhard made two calls, the first to the taxi company to send a cab and the second to Bruges Diamonds.

He dialled the number of the shop. 'Mr. Mayer. I had an interesting visit with your father, and I thank you for arranging it. He gave me his e-mail address which I omitted to write down. May I ask you to please give it to me again?' He wrote the address in a leather-bound notebook.

Albert Mayer smiled to himself as he dialled his father's phone number.

'I have just had a call from the German. How did the meeting go?'

'He lied about the e-mails mentioning Antwerp. I think we have got him worried. At first, I felt a twinge of regret, because he seems like a decent German, but what the hell, he is after all the grandson of the man who set the holocaust in motion. The bloodline must also suffer. I want you to contact Mr. K and set the plan into action.'

CHAPTER 11

Novak and Silke had a short meeting at the office and decided that Novak would concentrate on tracing the break-in at the bank while Silke continued with the investigation of Adolf Eicke's computer.

Silke took a taxi to the Grinzing district. She went up to the door of Eicke's house and knocked loudly. After what seemed a long wait, it was finally opened by Eicke, who looked a little surprised to see an attractive young girl smiling at him.

'Do come in,' he said, opening the door wider. 'Actually, I was expecting the young man with the strange accent.'

'Oh, you mean Novak. Sorry, but he is not available today so you will have to put up with me. I apologise if I ask some of the same questions he may have asked the other day.'

'You are welcome and you are a definite improvement,' said Eicke admiring her trim, young figure. 'Follow me and I will take you through to my study. I will be outside in the garden, taking advantage of the sun after the heavy rain yesterday. Call me if you need me.'

'Thanks, I will do that,' said Silke, sitting down at the desk in front of the open laptop.

She spent the next hour and a bit going through all the relevant files, looking for the entry made by the hacker. She was unable to establish how or where the Norton firewall had been broken. She was sitting back looking at the ceiling, when Eicke walked in with two cups of coffee and a ham sandwich.

'My wife made you a snack and some coffee. Well, have you managed to unravel who the mystery intruder is?' Eicke placed the coffee and the sandwich on the desk and sat down opposite Silke.

'You are correct about a mystery. There is no evidence of an illegal hack. It appears that whoever got into your computer had your password. Is that possible? Who has access to it?'

'Absolutely no one but myself, and now you and the Serb. In fact, when you have finished with your investigation, I am going to change it.'

'Look, a good hacker will be able to trace your password, but usually they prefer to go in via the back door, and I can see no evidence of that.'

'Unfortunately, I can offer no explanation. My knowledge of computers is just enough to enable me to do basic functions like Word and Outlook Explorer.' Eicke sat back and sipped at his coffee.

'Is that you in the uniform?' enquired Silke, pointing to a photograph on the wall.

'That was my father. He was an Obergruppenfuhrer in the SS. One of the most successful, I might add, until his untimely death on the Russian front.'

'Is success in the army measured by the number of deaths you achieve?' asked Silke sarcastically.

'Yes, it probably is the way success is measured in a war. If one has only lived during a period of peace, as no doubt you have, then it is difficult to understand that killing is the way of all beings in this world. All the animals on this planet, and I include humans, want to dominate. The strong subjugate the weak and killing is one of the means to an end. Do I shock you?'

'No,' Silke replied, 'I am here today because I know how to survive. I know a lot about domination, about people trying to impose their will on others. I could easily kill to secure my survival but not meaningless, wanton killing.'

'What about revenge. That is also a powerful factor that drives us. Hate trumps love every time.'

'I need to think about that. I want my life, going forward, to have more love than hate in it.' Silke closed the laptop. 'Well there is not much more that I can do here, so I will leave you in peace.'

'You are welcome to come back or to contact me whenever you wish. At my age, I don't have too many appointments.' He smiled at her as he stood up and left the study.

Silke drank the rest of her coffee and put the sandwich in a tissue. She placed it in her computer bag. She then inserted an instruction into the computer that would give her access to it wherever she was, provided it was switched on.

* * * *

Reinhard had spoken to Otto Siller and requested that either Novak or Silke should spend a few days in Munich so that he could be directly involved in certain aspects of the investigation. Otto decided to send Silke, as Novak was working at the bank's Vienna branch and needed more time to do his trace.

The following day Silke caught the early train from Vienna to Munich. She was surrounded mainly by businessmen in sombre suits who were either reading a business newspaper or tapping away at portable computers. Silke put on a set of headphones, sat back and looked at the scenery shooting past her window. The Bauhaus music made her completely oblivious to the activity in the train carriage. On arrival at Munich's Hauptbahnhof, she went outside the terminal and took a taxi to the offices of AH Bank.

She was expected at the bank and a secretary, with a disapproving look on her face, showed her into Reinhard's office. She caused a bit of a stir as she walked past the bank of glass-fronted offices that housed the administration staff.

Reinhard stood up and extended his hand, 'Ah, Miss. Kotter! Come in and take a seat. How was your trip this morning?'

'Full of stuffy, self-important businessmen.' She sat down and placed the cabin bag next to her.

Reinhard bent over and looked at her bag.

'Is that really big enough for all your things for a few days?' he enquired.

153

'This is all I take on a two-week holiday.'

Reinhard thought about the number of suitcases his wife took when they went away, even for a week end, and just shrugged his shoulders.

'I have decided to give you some confidential background information, without which it will be difficult for you to complete your task.' He handed her copies of the two e-mails that Eicke had received and gave her some details related to the formation of the bank, without directly disclosing that the funding had come from stolen Jewish articles.

'I have just returned from Antwerp, where I was able to see the man with whom my father and Mr. Eicke had dealings. He is very anti-German and I can understand this to a certain extent, however, there was something that he was withholding from me, but I cannot put my finger on it. I have his e-mail address, and I thought that perhaps you could somehow hack into his computer. What do you think?'

'Firstly, it is a pity I did not have this information yesterday when I visited Mr. Eicke. I was looking for evidence of the hacking on his computer, but there was nothing. I didn't look through his e-mails, but I can do so now. I should also be able to look into the computer in Antwerp and now that I know what I am looking for, it will make my job easier.'

'I know I don't have to repeat that all of this is very sensitive and confidentiality is vital.'

Silke looked at him with a scornful expression.

'I can tell there is a Nazi connection here, and that doesn't worry me. I don't even know who my father is or my grandfather, for that matter. Perhaps it was Adolf Hitler himself. I don't give a shit! You don't have to worry about

155

confidentiality with me, but you do know that hacking is illegal?'

Reinhardt nodded. He couldn't help admiring this feisty young girl with her rebellious exterior. If only he could be that direct.

'We have arranged for you to use a private office, which is, in fact, right next door to mine. Here is the e-mail address of Otto Mayer. You may come to my office whenever you need to discuss anything. My secretary will show you where the important things are, such as the coffee machine.'

It was after 4 o'clock when Reinhard checked his watch and decided to see what progress Silke had made.

'My goodness Miss. Kotter, you are an industrious bee. Have you had any success?'

'I have built up a small file for you,' she said, pointing to a plastic folder. 'And please call me Silke. I am not big on formality.'

'Very well. Look, it is after four so why don't you pack up, and I will take you to the hotel we have arranged for you. I will wait for you next door.'

It was just a short drive from the Bank's offices to the Art Hotel, which was situated near the Hauptbahnhof. Reinhard gave Silke a brief, tourist guide orientation as they drove through the old section of Munich, and when she told him this was her first visit to the city; he offered to give her a proper guided tour before she left.

'Perhaps we can have coffee at the hotel and discuss what you have achieved today,' suggested Reinhard, as he drove into the hotel's garage.

'I will have one of those cocktails,' said Silke as they sat down in the Lavendel Bar.

Reinhard ordered the drinks. 'Can you can give me a précis of what you have uncovered and then we can sit back and enjoy our drinks.'

'Well, I managed to break into Mayer's computer.'

'How the hell did you do that so quickly?' asked a surprised Reinhard.

'I sent him an e-mail with an attachment. I had to entice him to open it. I waited for at least three hours, and then he finally fell into the trap. The attachment had a roving bug that embedded itself in his hard drive, and it wasn't difficult to decipher his password. I have looked at some of his mail going back a month. He seems to have a lot of correspondence. Some of it is in a foreign language which I will need translated. The ones in German which I considered important, I have printed off and I will give you this folder to study. For me the most important was this one.' She pulled out a sheet of paper from the plastic folder and gave it to Reinhard.

The message said: *'RH visited me today.'* Reinhard blanched when he saw the recipient was Adolf Eicke.

'So, Mr. Eicke is playing some kind of game with me!'

'As I mentioned, I thought it was strange that his computer had absolutely no sign of an illegal entry. I will now look through his mailbox and see if that reveals anything unusual.'

'Silke, this whole thing is not making any sense. Why would a former shareholder and a large account holder, play silly games like this? I am in a very difficult position. I must think how best to confront him, but first I need you to look at his mail. I am very impressed with you and your ability to hack into computers so quickly. Maybe, there is a job for you in Munich?'

'Somehow, I don't think I fit into the bank's mould, judging by the people I met today,' said Silke laughing.

'Perhaps we need some modernising. Would it be rude of me to ask why such a young person like yourself has such a forceful personality?'

When Silke switched her identity, she built up a new persona and a background story. She wanted it to be very difficult for anyone to corroborate any information she may reveal.

'Forceful? Since I have been on my own I have realised that if you are meek then there are those who will take advantage of you and others that will try to crush you. They tried to crush me and break my spirit. In order to survive I had to fight.

'When you say 'they' who do you mean?' asked Reinhard.

'I never had a father and my mother died when I was young, very young. 'They' are the people who made the laws related to orphans. 'They' are also the people who

160

carry out the law and hide behind it. The foster home system in my country is disgusting. There are people who take you in for the money the state will pay them, not because they like children. In fact, they hate them. Can you understand what it is like to be surrounded by hate? All I had was a little doll to hug at night and to cry on. I still have that doll. My mind has huge periods of my life that are blocked off. I cannot face them, they are unspeakable. They sometimes haunt me in my dreams over which I have no control.'

Reinhard's thoughts went to his daughter Eva. He could see Silke as a young child, like Eva, crying at night. He sighed deeply and gulped down a large mouthful of his drink.

'I had a vision of my daughter as you spoke and what you have just said fills me with intense sadness.'

'Mr. Heinrich, I am not looking for sympathy. I only wanted to give you a background as to why I seem to be this way. I don't respect convention and authority, that's all. In your position, I am sure it will be difficult for you to contemplate what life in the gutter is like. What abuse is like when you are too small to defend yourself.'

'You are correct in that I have had no experience of a rough, tough life. I think somehow, I am the worse off for it. If life confronts you with a struggle, you can capitulate and become a bum, or you can rise to the challenge and fight it. When you win against all odds, you achieve a sense of purity and victory. My character has been weakened by my easy life. I have never fought for anything, and as a result I have never achieved anything.'

'You are the CEO of a bank, so that is a unique achievement.'

'Not really,' Reinhard said, shaking his head. 'I am not convinced that without my name, I would be in this position. So, are you essentially self-taught then?'

'I did go to school but not to university which I regret. A lot of my knowledge comes from private reading and study.'

'What did you study or read?'

'Astronomy, philosophy, scientific subjects and of course computers. I thought that if I read enough I would understand the meaning of life.'

'Did you?'

'Not completely but I came to the realisation that life is a private and personal matter. Each one of us has his own meaning as to what life is all about, and they are all valid. There are many who cannot see any meaning at all. They are the drop-outs and they become alcoholics or drug addicts or simply commit suicide. I have a great thirst for knowledge, and I want to experience the whole of human endeavour, be it music or the arts or science. I want to gulp it all down.'

The Crooked Star

'Has religion played any part in your life?'
Reinhard was beginning to enjoy her free spirit and
recognised what was missing in his life.

'My upbringing included a lot of religion, much of
it forced. A lot of religion seems to clash with modern-day
science. I can understand, for example, how Darwin came
to the conclusions he did with his theory of evolution, but
there are some flaws and gaps in it as well. We are also
asked to accept certain precepts on a belief basis as well. If
man is truly descended from apes, then in accordance with
Darwin's ideas of evolutionary improvement, surely we
should have kept the superior aspects of the apes, like
strength and agility, while developing our large brain? If
you buy into the survival of the fittest idea, then why has
man of all the animals set about providing for the survival
of the weakest? Our legal system and the police, doctors,
dentist, judges and prisons are all there to ensure that the
strong do not subdue the weak. This is totally at odds with
Darwin. Also, we must be the only species hell-bent on

destroying our environment and the whole world with it. I somehow believe that it is possible to have evolution and a creator. We are a crazy species and do not obey traditional laws and theories.'

'My goodness Silke you are so amazing for someone of your age and your background. I think you could achieve great things given the right opportunity. If you won't work at the bank, then perhaps I could sponsor you at University. We will discuss that in the near future. In the meantime, let me get you another drink, and then I have to leave you, I'm afraid.'

Reinhard went up to the bar and ordered a second round of drinks. As he turned to return to the table, he came face to face with Inge.

'My God, Inge, what are you doing here?' Reinhard could feel he was blushing.

'I should ask the same question of you. At least, I am not here with a teenage slut. It didn't take you long to find someone else.'

'Come on Inge, that girl works for an IT company, and she has been seconded to us for an investigation. We need to talk. Can we meet after I have finished this drink?'

'Sorry, but I am otherwise engaged, and what I said the other day stands. There is no change. Now go to your glamourous companion. She is starting to stare at us.'

Reinhard took the drinks to the table, swearing under his breath.

'A lover's tiff or was that your wife?' Silke smiled knowingly.

'You are quite astute for a young person. That is not my wife, but a long-standing friend, Inge. It is too complicated to discuss. Where were we when I got up?'

'I think you offered me a job at the bank, which I rejected, and a chance to study at university. Seriously, the next step is for me to farm around the mailbox of Mr. Eicke as well as Mayer's.'

'Yes, yes, you must continue, and we will meet tomorrow.'

Reinhard was now clearly preoccupied with his confrontation with Inge. He finished his drink quickly, made his apologies and left Silke at the table with her unfinished drink.

Reinhard walked past the reception area and peered into the restaurant. He spotted Inge at a table with three men and a woman. She had her back to him. He paused for a few seconds, thought briefly about trying to get her attention, but changed his mind and walked down to the garage.

CHAPTER 12

On the drive back home, Reinhard tossed ideas back and forth in his mind, trying to achieve some semblance of order and logic to the jumble of information he had collected over the last few days. Adolf Eicke's apparent lying added a curved ball and would need to be investigated. 'Why the hell do I have to have this nonsense thrust on me?' he thought to himself? 'Three bloody old men still fighting the Second World War.' He walked into the house and sure enough, the first one to greet him was Eva, who threw herself at him. As he lifted her up he gave her a kiss on her cheek.

'What has my little squirrel done today?'

'I am not a squirrel. Today I played with Blondi, who bit the ball, and it went down. Please get me a new one, Daddy.'

'Of course you can have a new one, my little darling,' Reinhard said as he put her down and noticed that Sabine had walked into the entrance hall. She gave him a peck on the cheek.

'I can smell drink on you. Where have you been?'

'I have just dropped off the IT investigator at the Art hotel and felt obliged to have a quick drink. Is it important?'

'Yes, it is,' she snapped back. 'You seem to be in some sort of a whirlwind. I don't know from one day to the next where you will be or when you will be at home!'

'I am sorry, but this e-mail problem is getting out of hand, and I can see myself having to get more and more involved.'

'You haven't forgotten the concert in London, have you?' Sabine glared at him.

'Right now, I don't know if I can attend. I will do my very best to come along,' Reinhard replied, and then hoping to change the subject, he commented, 'I can't smell anything being cooked for dinner.'

'That is because we are dining in Grainau, at my favourite restaurant. Mrs. Meier is staying on to look after Eva.'

Going out to a restaurant was the last thing Reinhard needed, but he knew if he showed any dissent, it would end in an acrimonious tirade, so once more he relented. Under normal circumstances he would have been pleased to go along to Grainau, where Sabine's favourite restaurant was situated in the Waxenstein Hotel. The big floor to ceiling windows afforded lovely views across the village to the Alps, and the food was excellent.

They were greeted like long lost friends by the maître d'hôtel, who knew that he was always assured of a generous tip at the end of the evening. The Heinrich's were, after all, the most affluent inhabitants in the area.

'I have reserved our best table for you,' he said, as he pulled back Sabine's chair.

'Thank you, Guenther,' she said, aware that the other guests in the restaurant were now looking her way.

The Maître d'hôtel handed Reinhard the wine list, but before he could open it, Sabine ordered a bottle of Les Gentilles Pierres 2004.

171

'Why did you order a French wine?' enquired Reinhard. 'What is wrong with our wines?'

'Don't be ridiculous,' she retorted, 'where will you find a good German red?'

Reinhard shook his head slightly, but this would be his only form of opposition. He proceeded to open the menu. He knew what he felt like, but wanted Sabine to decide first, in case she wanted the same dish. He would then deliberately order something different.

She looked up from the menu. 'By the way, I received a strange e-mail today.'

'What do mean by strange?' said Reinhard, suddenly enervated.

'It said something like - 'hello Heydrich, we know who you are.'

Reinhard slammed down his menu. 'Why the bloody hell didn't you tell me this when we were at the house! This is related to the bank's problem!'

Sabine was shocked by the uncharacteristic outburst from her husband.

'Don't you dare to speak to me like that. You can see the e-mail when we get home. It's just a few stupid words.'

'It may not be stupid. I think we should go home right now.'

'You are behaving like a fool. We have come for dinner and we are not going anywhere.'

Reinhard put his hands against the top of his head and squeezed as hard as he could. He would love to have punched her right there and then. The conversation for the rest of the evening was constrained, with a large part of it being Sabine describing the problem she was having finding the best outfit for the London concert.

When they finally returned home, Reinhard looked at the e-mail and saw that the sender had used an anonymous Hotmail address. He decided he would take Sabine's laptop to the bank the following day for Silke to analyse. He sent a message to her mobile phone.

* * * *

When Silke arrived at the bank the following day, Reinhard gave her Sabine's laptop and a printout of the e-mail message.

Silke handed him a typed page. On it were listed several dates and a transcript of related e-mails.

'I managed to get into Eicke's mailbox last night and I went back three months. It was mostly a lot of rubbish to family and friends but there were three that were sent to Otto Mayer. The only in-coming message he received from Mayer was the one I gave you yesterday.'

Reinhard looked at the sheet of paper.

July 5th - Confirm our meeting tomorrow at 1. Regards A.

July 10th – Met him yesterday. Next stage. Regards A.

July 12th - He should contact you. Regards A.

'So, there! This confirms that there is definitely something between the two of them. I just cannot see the point of it. Can you get back into Eicke's mail and look around July 5th and see if he made any flight or other arrangement regarding the meeting he mentions?'

'I can do that, but I can only get in if he has opened his computer, and he doesn't keep it on all day unfortunately.'

'We will speak later, once you have made contact. Thanks for your help, Silke.' Reinhard smiled at her, and she felt pleased that someone in the upper echelons of society could treat her so pleasantly. She was still sceptical regarding his sincerity, as most of her previous encounters with people in authority had always turned out to her detriment. The jury was still out with regard to Reinhard.

Later that day, Silke asked to see Reinhard in his office.

'I have come up with a blank on any bookings or arrangements Eicke may have made around the 5th. Perhaps they were done by telephone or maybe Mayer visited him. Then, on your wife's computer, the e-mail came from an anonymous Hotmail address. There is no easy way of tracing further back, and it is likely to lead to a dead end with an abandoned address.'

'So it looks like I will have to confront the old man, and that won't be a pleasant task,' said Reinhard as he bit his lower lip.

Just then his telephone rang.

'Hello. Yes, put her through. Hello Sabine.' There was a pause. 'What? How long has she been missing? Have you called the police? I am on my way.' Reinhard slammed down the phone and jumped up.

'My daughter and father are missing. I will speak to you later,' he said, grabbing his coat and shouting an instruction to his secretary as he ran out of the office.

CHAPTER 13

When he was still a few hundred metres from the property, Reinhard could see flashing blue lights indicating that the police had arrived.

He jumped out of the car and ran over to where his wife was talking to two uniformed policemen.

'Any news?' he shouted.

'Good afternoon, I am Sergeant Bauer,' said the taller of the two policemen. 'This is Patrolman Braun. We are here in response to a call from Mrs Heinrich regarding your daughter and her grandfather who appear to be missing.'

'Should we not organise a search party?' asked Reinhard, who was clearly in a very anxious state.

'Before we do that we need to establish some facts and get an understanding of the situation, otherwise we will be running around like chickens without heads. These are the notes I have made from your wife's statement. Your daughter visited your father's house around ten this morning. She was due back at twelve for her lunch, but didn't appear. At approximately 12:30 your wife phoned Mr. Heinrich, your father, but got no reply. She went across to the house and found the front door unlocked. There was no response to her calling so she went inside. She then heard the dog barking and found it locked in the downstairs lavatory. We received the call from Mrs Heinrich at 12:50.'

'Yes, yes,' said Reinhard impatiently. 'We can't just stand here. Let's do something.'

'We understand your anxiety, but I can assure you that the two of them are most likely to be out walking somewhere. Tell me, does your father suffer from memory loss?'

'Absolutely not! He has all his mental faculties and a very good memory.'

179

'Well then, I am going to ask you to take me to your father's house along the path your daughter would have taken.'

Reinhard went ahead followed by the two policemen, with Sabine bringing up the rear. As they approached the house Blondi started barking_and when they opened the door, she growled and barked even louder. Reinhard bent down to pat her. She recognised him but she was very wary of the policemen.

'My colleague and I will walk around the house. Can you please do the same and tell me if you notice if anything has been disturbed or removed.'

This cursory inspection took about fifteen minutes, after which they gathered in the kitchen. The Sergeant spoke first.

'At first glance there does not appear to be any disturbance. Did either of you notice anything?'

Sabine shook her head negatively.

'Nothing appears to be out of place,' replied Reinhard. 'I looked in the garage. His car is there, although he never drives it himself anymore. By the way, Sabine, I didn't see Guenther and his wife and their cottage is locked.'

'This is the day they have off each week,' she replied.

The Sergeant wrote some notes in a wire-bound book.

'From my experience, I want you to know that I don't think anything horrible has happened. Soon they will come walking in from the fields. But to put your minds at rest, I am going to suggest that you phone your neighbours and ask if anyone has seen them. We will walk around the rest of your property. If they haven't returned by, let's see, five o'clock, then we will institute a wider search and bring in tracker dogs. Does that make you feel better?'

'Not really,' said Reinhard, pulling his wife by the arm.

Once outside he said to her, 'Hurry back to the house. I am going to phone the helicopter service in Garmisch and get them out here. We can't wait for those arse-holes. If we wait until five o'clock, it doesn't give us many hours of daylight to search if we need to do so. We cannot take this matter lightly; we need to start the search immediately!'

'Reinhard, I am going out of my mind. Please don't let anything happen to Eva.'

They watched the police car leave and then went inside. Reinhard contacted the helicopter company in Garmisch. They confirmed that they could have one of their aircraft available within thirty minutes. He gave them the GPS co-ordinates for the house.

'Sabine, I am sure there has to be a sensible, rational explanation to this disappearance. Perhaps they have gone walking - you know how my father loves rambling.'

'Then why aren't they back?' cried Sabine. 'Perhaps your father is lying injured somewhere. I don't want to even think about it. You must find them.'

'I am going to wait outside for the helicopter,' said Reinhard walking outside.

Reinhard scoured the skies in the direction of Garmisch and then suddenly he heard the sound of a helicopter. He ran over to a patch of lawn, frantically waving his handkerchief in the air. The helicopter slowed down and banked towards the house. It made a slow descent, creating a small dust storm as it landed on the grass. Reinhard bent low and ran to the side of the craft, where a door was opened. The pilot helped him on board.

It was very noisy as Reinhard shouted instructions to the pilot. He was given a set of headphones to put on so they could communicate more easily with one another.

The Heinrich property was a parcel of farmland about ten acres in extent and was surrounded on three sides by smaller farms. The valley ran from the village of Grainau to the town of Garmisch. There were towering mountains on either side, heavily wooded with trees on the higher slopes, and lush green pastures on the lower slopes. The helicopter flew in a grid pattern at 300 metres in altitude, which afforded excellent views. The pilot handed Reinhard a pair of binoculars. With the exception of the wooded area, it would have been easy to see a white-haired adult with a four-year-old girl. They scanned the ground as they flew over it. There were cows grazing in fields, two cyclists and a few people out walking. Each time they came upon a cluster of houses, the pilot followed the course of the road. Reinhard could see people in their gardens. Some looked up and waved, unaware of the nature of the flight.

After forty minutes in the air, Reinhard telephoned his wife and told her to instruct the police to begin the search with the tracker dogs.

As the helicopter landed, Sabine came running out of the house. Reinhard thanked the pilot and went over to where Sabine was waiting. She put her arms around him and burst into tears.

'We must find her,' she said, in between her sobbing. 'Please do something Reinhard.'

'We will find her, that is for certain. Where the bloody hell has my father taken her? We combed the area, but it is not possible to see someone if they are sitting under a tree. We have to get a search party on the ground. Did you speak to that policeman?'

'He said they would be here within the hour. I have phoned all the neighbours but no one has seen or heard anything. Some have offered to come over and help with the search.'

Reinhard waved to the pilot as he took off and with his arm still around Sabine they went inside the house, leaving the front door open.

When anxiety is at its highest, all waiting periods seem extended and agonising. Reinhard and Sabine paced aimlessly around the house. The tension was slightly broken by two telephone calls, one from Sabine's mother, who wanted to fly down to Munich but was persuaded by Sabine to wait until after the police search. The other call was from a neighbour who had spotted an elderly man in the main road at Grainau, but the description of a short, stout man did not fit that of Reinhard's father, who was over six feet tall and slim.

They both rushed outside as the first of four police vehicles arrived. One was a 4x4 all - terrain vehicle, with three German Shepherd dogs in the back section. Twelve policemen alighted from the vehicles. Sergeant Bauer, who had been there earlier, and approached Reinhard and Sabine.

'Mr. Heinrich, we are ready to commence the search of the area. Can you please give me a piece of your daughter's clothing, preferably unwashed, and if you have something belonging to your father, that will also help. I can tell you that a senior officer from the detective division, Inspector Bosch, will be here shortly. He will need to interview both of you to make a written report, so please be clear on the information you give – the more detail we have the better.'

Reinhard nodded. 'I went up in a helicopter for about an hour, but saw absolutely nothing. Some of our neighbours have offered to help with the search.'

'We have twelve men which should be sufficient. We have a map of the area, and we will work in a grid pattern. I would prefer it if you would stay here and speak to Inspector Bosch when he arrives.' He turned around. 'In fact, that is him arriving now.'

The unmarked car pulled in beside the police vehicles. A bespectacled man in his early fifties got out and walked over to Bauer.

'Inspector, may I introduce Mr. and Mrs. Heinrich.'

'Good afternoon. I am Inspector Georg Bosch. I am sorry to hear about your missing daughter and father.' He shook hands with both of them. 'At the outset, this appears to be a case of missing or lost people. Firstly, the police will conduct a thorough search of the property and surrounding countryside. I am confident that they will find your father and daughter soon. I will, however, need to ask you some questions. Is it possible we can sit down somewhere?'

'Of course,' replied Reinhard, leading the way into the house.

Inspector Bosch seated himself opposite Reinhard and his wife and removed an Apple iPad from its black cover. 'I apologise if some of these questions have already been asked by one of my colleagues. I will be looking at it from a different angle.'

Georg Bosch was fifty-two years of age and had been a policeman all his working life, initially in the uniformed division and for the last twenty years as a plain clothes detective. He had passed all the police degree examinations and had studied psychology privately, as he felt a large part of any detective work involves analysing people and their motives. Five years earlier he had

189

achieved recognition in the Munich area, when he solved a spree of murders of foreign students.

Bosch went through all the usual questions related to the movements of Eva and Hermann that morning. The properties had separate entrances and the row of trees that divided them, meant that there was no clear view from one to the other. Sabine said that Eva had gone over to her grandfather at around ten o'clock as she did most days. She usually played there for between one and two hours. Sabine had been busy in the house, including lengthy telephone conversations with friends, and had not heard any unusual sounds. Reinhard indicated that it was highly unlikely that his father would have gone too far, as he walked with some difficulty.

'Is there any possible reason why someone would have fetched them?' enquired Inspector Bosch.

'I cannot think of anyone,' replied Reinhard looking at Sabine for confirmation. 'For the last few years, since my mother died, my father has kept to himself.'

'He would never take Eva off the property without telling me first.' said Sabine.

'Well then, is there any reason why we should consider foul play?' asked Bosch looking up from his iPad.

'No,' said Reinhard emphatically, concerned that Sabine might blurt out something about the e-mails. She avoided his eyes and stared at the floor.

'There is very little evidence to base our investigation on and at this stage it appears that foul play need not be considered. I will leave you now and join the search parties. Please let me assure you, that in my experience there is always an explanation for disappearances like this, and I am confident they will soon return. I will see you before I leave.'

Inspector Bosch stood up and walked towards the door, dialling a number on his mobile phone.

After the door had closed, Sabine turned to her husband and said, 'Why didn't you mention the e-mails? What if there is a connection?'

'I don't think there is a connection,' replied Reinhard abruptly, 'and I am investigating them right now. You know I want to keep it private. If there is a connection, then of course we will have to inform the police.'

It was getting late and the light was fading, when there was a knock on the door. Sergeant Bauer and Inspector Bosch were standing there.

Bosch was the first to speak, 'I am afraid we haven't been successful. The men have scoured a large area, well beyond your property. The dogs did not pick up any scents. We have contacted local emergency services and hospitals, also with no success.'

Sabine started crying and Reinhard looked distressed.

'What happens next, please tell me?' pleaded Reinhard anxiously.

'We will put out alerts across Bavaria. I will need recent photographs of your daughter and father, and these will also be issued to all police stations. Because of the circumstances--an old man who cannot walk far and whose car is still in the garage-- I am going to escalate this to the next level. I have to warn you that the press could get hold of this and come around here. We would prefer it for the police to release any information publicly, so rather say nothing to them.'

'Isn't there something that can be done tonight?' implored Sabine.

'As you can see it is too dark to go stumbling through the fields. The helicopter search and our ground search should have uncovered something, even a trail. There is nothing to suggest that they are in the vicinity of your property. Mrs. Heinrich, you discounted the possibility that someone may have taken them off the property. After a certain period of time we have to look at other possibilities as well. Here is my card. Do not hesitate to contact me if anything comes up during the night. Good night to both of you.'

Reinhard closed the door behind the policemen and turned to Sabine and took her in his arms.

'How are we going to get through this night?' his voice was cracked and raspy.

'I have all these dreadful thoughts going through my mind. Is she sitting somewhere, shivering in the cold? I can see her crying. Please God don't let her be harmed.' Sabine burst into tears.

194

'Come through to the kitchen. I am going to make some coffee,' said Reinhard as he ushered Sabine into the kitchen. He switched on the kettle and put some instant coffee granules into two mugs.

Sabina looked at him with swollen, reddened eyes, 'I still think you are wrong not to have told the police about the strange e-mails. What if there is a connection?'

'I agree there could be a connection, and I will be spending all my time looking into it. We have an IT expert seconded to us. She is staying at a hotel in Munich. If I draw blanks and if Eva is not back within two days, I will give the police all the information we have. Right now, I believe we can act a lot quicker than the police. You saw them. They are not that interested. Here drink this.' Reinhard handed her the coffee, which she cradled in her hands.

'Reinhard, I am completely drained, and I have this feeling that something dreadful has happened. I think it is

195

because I feel so helpless. I feel I should be walking around the streets and in the forests looking for them.'

'I feel the same way. My mind is racing. Never before have I felt such utter despair. I am no longer in control.' He started sobbing uncontrollably.

* * * *

Sergeant Bauer accepted a lift with Bosch. As they drove off he asked, 'What is your take on this case? They own a bank and must be filthy rich, so kidnapping has to be a possibility.'

'I have heard of their name and seen them on the social pages. If it is a kidnapping, then we can expect a ransom note or some communication soon. I am not convinced they are telling us everything. You know how I love to look out for small clues and nuances. My success has always come from some insignificant detail. When I

196

was speaking to them and asked if there could be foul play, the husband replied rapidly and his wife looked at the floor, avoiding my eyes when I looked in her direction. Maybe it is nothing, but I will keep it at the back of my mind. Why would he want to dismiss foul play so vehemently? Tomorrow will be the critical point.'

'I agree,' said Bauer, 'and quite honestly, after the search we conducted and the helicopter search that Heinrich was involved in, I cannot believe that an old man and a four-year-old girl could have got far enough on foot, for us to have missed them. We managed to lift some tyre prints at a sandy patch near the house. We will see if they match any of the cars on the estate, including that of the servant who returns tomorrow.'

A light rain began to fall, so Bosch switched the windscreen wipers on intermittent. He looked at the clock on the dashboard and saw that it was 22:22. He pushed a button on his mobile phone, which was in a hands-free device on the windscreen and a few seconds later there was a ringing tone as it connected with his home.

'Hello,' said a female voice.

'Hello, sweetie. I am on the road and should be home within forty minutes. What can I expect on the table tonight?'

'Fuck all. You are bloody late so your food is on the kitchen floor.' The voice was slurred and Bosch winced.

'I have Sergeant Bauer sitting next to me,' replied Bosch, feeling a little embarrassed.

'Fuck him too.'

Bosch terminated the call and shook his head dejectedly. It was well known among his colleagues that his partner had a serious drinking problem.

The Crooked Star

Georg Bosch was divorced from his first wife and for the past four years had been living with Anna-Marie, who was six years his junior. Initially, she had proven to be a calming influence after a tempestuous marriage and a financially devastating divorce which had left him living in a sparsely-furnished, one bedroom apartment. He had started drinking every night after the divorce, and even though he could see the negative effect it was having on his job and his two daughters, he was unable to stop. He knew he wasn't an alcoholic in the true meaning of the affliction, but nevertheless, he drank himself to sleep most nights. He once joked that he slept more often on the couch than in his bed.

George first met Anna-Marie when he had been called out to a hostage situation at an all-night food store. The hostage taker had been seriously wounded by the police in a shootout, and Bosch had driven to the Bogenhausen hospital hoping to interview the man who was suspected of having links to a terrorist organisation.

On arrival at the hospital, Bosch had been told by the night duty nurse that the hostage taker had been declared dead on arrival. Bosch swore and then immediately apologised. The nurse, Anna-Marie, laughed and told him she had heard worse. She invited him to join her for a cup of coffee in her office. She was in her mid-forties and still had a trim figure, which she attributed to the extensive walking around the large hospital her which her position necessitated. She had very smooth skin and a mouth that always seemed to be smiling. Her husband had died the previous year from cancer, and although she never mentioned it to anyone, she was still in mourning. When Bosch phoned her the next day, offering to reciprocate her offer of coffee the previous evening, she initially refused. A week later he called in person at the hospital with two tickets to a concert. She hesitated at first but then decided to accept. The relationship developed very slowly at first, as there would be two or three refusals to one acceptance of any proposed meeting. It was another year before she

200

finally moved in with Bosch, but not before he had rented a much more acceptable apartment than his post-divorce one had been. At first, she hid her drinking problem from everyone, including Bosch. His work often kept him out late at night, and he would usually arrive home to find her sound asleep, unaware that it was an alcohol induced sleep.

He came home one day to find her in tears. She had been dismissed from the hospital. She claimed it was victimisation because she had spurned advances from a senior medical official. Bosch decided to confront the hospital authorities and was shocked when he was given a private meeting with the Chief Superintendant. It transpired that Anna-Marie had given a patient the wrong drip, resulting in a near fatal incident. Colleagues had noticed that her speech was slurred and she had been given a breathalyzer test which she failed. A disciplinary enquiry found her guilty of gross misconduct and she was dismissed.

CHAPTER 14

Inspector Bosch arrived at his office just after seven a.m. on Sunday morning and immediately telephoned the Heinrich household to see if there had been any further news of the missing grandfather and their daughter. He told them that he would be forming a task force, which he personally would head, to carry on the investigation. He could hear the utter desperation in Reinhard's voice.

He typed out the salient pieces of information he had gathered the previous day, together with photographs of the two missing people. He arranged for the photographs to be put into the police data base and circulated throughout Bavaria.

Hauptkommissar Schmidt agreed to come in for a short while so that he could be briefed on the situation in Garmisch, which fell under his jurisdiction. At 8 o'clock, Bosch went to his superior's office and handed him a copy of the notes he had made.

Schmidt looked at the notes and shrugged, 'The Heinrichs are important people in the community and they are wealthy, so why is there no ransom note? Maybe one will arrive today. Initially, take two officers to join you and if it is required we can bring in the Federal Police as well. Keep me well-informed because the media vultures will be onto this before the day is over.'

Bosch had a big whiteboard in his office, and he set it up with some notes and the two photos. He then called in the two junior detectives allocated to him, August Keller and Birgit Hoffman.

'My apologies for ruining your weekend, but criminals don't operate only during office hours. From

203

today, you can stop whatever you are working on as you have been assigned to me. In front of you are some notes that I have made, which will bring you up to speed. On the board to my right, you will see two photographs and a map of a farm area near Garmisch.' Bosch swivelled around in his chair in the direction of the whiteboard. He continued, 'I have made a call to Mr. Heinrich, and the case has gone from missing persons to kidnapping. Please read my notes while I make a call.'

The two detectives read the two-page summary Bosch had made from his visit the previous day, while Bosch called the local Garmisch police station.

He put down the phone.

'As I said, Mr. Heinrich confirmed a few minutes ago that his father and his daughter have not returned or been found. It then clearly looks like a kidnapping. Do you have any questions about this case?'

Birgit Hoffman was the first to respond.

'Statistics show that where kidnappings are for political or financial gain, there is always a demand either immediately or within twenty-four hours. Nothing has been received yet.'

'What conclusion would you draw from that?' asked Bosch.

'Perhaps a revenge killing?' she replied.

'And what do you think?' asked Bosch, looking at August Keller.

'Well, I agree with my colleague but are we not being too premature in thinking it is not still a missing persons case?'

Bosch smiled, 'The old man is eighty. The young girl is four. The old man's car is still in the garage. How far do you think they could have walked - maximum two or three kilometres? We covered three times that last night, and you saw in the notes that a helicopter was also called in.'

Keller wasn't giving up. 'What if someone picked them up? They could be anywhere now.'

Bosch smiled again. He liked sparring with rookie detectives. 'I accept what you say, and we need to use the media to see if anyone picked them up. However, if we don't escalate this case, and it is a kidnapping, and we lose several vital days, then we will end up with egg on our face. This is a high profile family. What did they teach you at college about the first forty-eight hours?'

The two young detectives nodded their heads in unison and waited for Bosch to continue.

'This is what I propose. We will go to the Heinrich estate right away. I have already advised them and they are waiting for us. I need to speak to them again, as I have a feeling that I wasn't given the full story yesterday. I need you two to contact the neighbours and check if any vehicles were seen in the area, that were not the usual ones. In small communities, people notice anything that is not the norm - strangers walking around or a strange car cruising the streets. Right now, we have zero leads. I suggest you requisition side arms and meet me at my car in fifteen minutes.'

CHAPTER 15

Bosch drove up to the house and saw that Reinhard and Sabine were standing at the open front door. He jumped out of the driver's seat and shook their hands. He took one look at their reddened, bloated eyes, and he knew that they had suffered terribly during the night. One of the tasks he hated most, was dealing with parents whose children had been killed or injured, or in this case, missing. This was only the second time in his career that he had investigated a child kidnapping. In the previous case, an estranged father kidnapped his seven-year old son. He led the police on a manhunt all over Germany and had finally killed himself and his son when he was cornered in a warehouse in Hamburg. The case had a terrible emotional effect on Bosch, and he feared that this could be a repeat case.

Bosch and the two detectives followed Reinhard and Sabine inside the house.

'May I introduce my colleagues who will be assisting me in this investigation -Detectives Keller and Hoffman.'

When everyone was seated, he continued. 'We have escalated this investigation to a kidnapping status. Obviously, when we look at a kidnapping versus a missing person scenario, we adopt a different technique, and we ask different questions.'

'Are we only looking at three policemen for this investigation?' asked Reinhard.

'No, not at all. We represent the front line and your link to the police system. Right now, photographs of your father and daughter are being e-mailed to police around the country, including border staff at airports and harbours. Interpol will be alerted and the Garmisch station is having posters printed, which you will see at strategic points in this district. I can assure you this has all been done with the utmost speed.'

'What different questions would you like to pose? We are ready.'

'Firstly, can you confirm that all the cars that are usually based on this property are present?'

Reinhard nodded in the affirmative.

'We will need to take more tyre impressions. We will also need to interview your father's manservant and his wife. I am going to ask my colleagues to go ahead and do these tasks while we have a further chat. They have a map of the property.' The young detectives excused themselves and Bosch continued, 'Kidnappings fall into several, clearly-defined categories. One, a demand for money. Two, a political demand. Three, for revenge. Four, for psychological reasons such as torture. Five, family kidnappings usually after a divorce. Six, Tiger kidnappings, these are to force someone to reveal something like a pin number. Seven, female and child abductions into the sex trade. We can eliminate some right away. In my experience as a policeman, money, alcohol, drugs and sex are the motivators for just about all crime committed. You are obviously wealthy, so we have to look at the money angle or could it be abduction, like the famous Maddy case in Portugal?'

'Please don't say that,' shouted Sabine, 'they still haven't found that beautiful little girl.'

'The fact that they have taken her grandfather as well reduces that possibility but does not entirely eliminate it. Do you know of any reason someone might be looking for revenge either against you or your father?'

'Nothing I can think of,' said Reinhard, shaking his head. Once again Bosch picked up an almost imperceptible grimace on Sabine's face as her husband replied.

'I mentioned Tiger kidnappings, where people are kidnapped to force them to reveal the whereabouts of something or to open a safe. Do you know if your father kept large sums of money or other valuables somewhere - in a safety deposit box in Liechtenstein, for example?'

'Of course, I cannot be absolutely certain, but I have never been told of anything like that. He does have an enormously expensive wine collection in his cellar, but it is not easily transportable.'

'Exactly,' agreed Bosch. 'If we do not get a demand letter or communication within the next few hours, we will have to work along the lines of revenge, tiger or psycho. I cannot emphasise strongly enough that you must rack your brains for the slightest clue, and you must not withhold anything from the police, no matter how sensitive or embarrassing it might be.' He looked directly at Sabine. There was silence in the room.

'There is something you are not telling me, Mrs. Heinrich,' said Bosch directly.

'What nonsense is this?' shouted Reinhard. 'How dare you make accusations like that?'

Sabine started crying, and Bosch threw up his hands.

'I apologise, but I know in traumatic situations like this, the mind is in such turmoil that it forgets many things. I have to make sure that I have all the facts. Right now, we do not have much to help us progress with this case.'

Reinhard put his arm around his wife, preferring that she cry rather than blurt out anything about the e-mails.

Bosch stood up, 'I am going to see if my colleagues have made any progress. Do you wish to join me?'

As the trio walked across the field and through the row of trees that separated the properties, they were approached by Detective Keller.

'Well, what have you found so far?' asked Bosch.

'There is a set of tyre tracks, which does not belong to any of the cars on the property. We will get a positive identification. We have interviewed Mr. and Mrs. Braun and they say that no visitors have been to the house for

213

weeks. But there is something I want you to see in the cellar. Keller led the way as they entered the house and went down the stairs leading to the cellar. He walked past a row of wine racks against the far wall.

'I noticed one section of the shelving was jutting out, and then I realised it was a door. Fortunately, it was open as it has a digital keypad lock.' Keller pushed it open and stood aside for those behind him to enter. He followed and switched on a light. For the second time the inner sanctum had been breached.

'That is a Nazi flag,' he said, pointing to the flag hanging limply from a flagpole in the one corner of the cellar, 'and over here is something else.'

'Oh no, that is Eva's teddy bear!' Sabine shouted. She bent down and picked up the small toy bear.

'Please put it down, Mrs Heinrich,' instructed Bosch. 'It may contain some evidence.' Then he turned to Reinhard, 'What can you tell me about this room?'

'Absolutely nothing about this particular room,' replied Reinhard with a shocked expression on his face. 'I haven't been down in the wine cellar in years, and I knew nothing about a secret room. But I suppose this is the appropriate time to tell you that my grandfather was Reinhard Heydrich, the notorious Nazi. After the war, we changed our name.'

Bosch looked annoyed, 'I think you should have told us this sooner. It could have a bearing on your missing family. There could be neo-Nazis involved.'

'I don't think so,' retorted Reinhard. 'We are looking at 1942! What the hell has that got to do with the 21st century?'

'There are still neo-Nazi movements all over Europe. Just look at what happened with Norway and Anders Breivik recently.' He turned towards Detective Keller, 'Get forensics here right away.'

As they left the house, two cars followed by a white van pulled up outside the gate. A man carrying a professional video camera on his shoulder came up to the gate and a woman holding a microphone started waving her hands.

Bosch was the first to react, 'The media circus has arrived!'

'Tell them to go way,' shouted Sabine.

'Calm down. We need them to get the message out to the widest possible audience,' said Bosch, holding up his hand. 'I will speak to them but either you or your husband should also be prepared to say a few words. Trust me, this can help us.'

216

Bosch walked up to the gate, 'Good morning. I am Inspector Bosch and as you no doubt already know, we are investigating the disappearance of Mr. Heinrich Senior and a four-year-old child, his grand-daughter Eva.'

The women thrust her microphone closer to him. 'Tell me Inspector; is this just a missing persons' case?'

'After our initial investigation, we are now looking at the possibility of foul play. We have very little evidence at this stage and would appreciate any assistance your viewers could give us. If anyone in Garmisch or the Grainau area has seen a strange car or anything suspicious, could they please contact their nearest police station. We are busy setting up a control room in Garmisch as we speak.' Bosch dug into his briefcase and pulled out two photographs, which he held up to the camera. 'If you contact the control room, you will be given enlarged photographs. Mr. Heinrich is eighty years of age, about 182 centimetres in height and of a slim build. Young Eva is four years old, with blonde hair in pigtails. She is wearing a red dress with white and green flowers.'

'Can we speak to the parents, please?' asked the TV woman.

Bosch beckoned to Reinhard to come forward.

'We are desperate to find our daughter and my father. We appeal to all members of the public to please keep a look-out for them.' His lips started quivering, which is something TV newsreels love showing.

'Have you received a ransom note yet? Will you be offering a reward?'

'No and yes. Of course, we have no problem offering a reward.'

Bosch stepped forward, 'I am sure you can see how distraught the family is. Can I ask you to leave it at that until we convene an official press conference, hopefully later today?'

218

'Mrs.Heinrich,' shouted the TV woman, 'how are you coping? Say a few words.'

Sabine turned away and hurried inside the house, followed by Reinhard and Bosch.

'I know these people can seem like vultures, but they can also be very useful in cases like this when we need even the smallest lead. In today's high tech world, the television and the press can reach a wide audience far more quickly than we can.' He waited for Sabine to stop sobbing. 'I would like to ask you once again to let me have any information that may be pertinent to this investigation. Even if you think it is unimportant let me be the judge of that. The fact that your grandfather was Reinhard Heydrich could be significant.' He paused, hoping that Sabine might offer some information. 'I am going to leave you for a while, however, you have my mobile number and can contact me anytime, day or night.'

'Thank you, Detective Bosch,' said Reinhard. 'We appreciate your concern and the efforts of the police force. We hope it won't take too long to find Eva and my Dad.' Reinhard shook his hand and accompanied him to the door.

As soon as the door was closed, Sabine started crying once more.

'What are you planning to do, Reinhard. Please God help us.'

'I am going to Vienna. I am going to confront bloody Eicke, who, I am convinced is involved in some way. Please explain to your mother when she comes, that I could not wait for her arrival.'

Reinhard then made two calls, one to a company at Munich airport that rented out private business jets and the other to Silke, telling her to meet him at the Jetair desk in the Departures Hall. Jetair confirmed that they would have a Citation X ready to depart within two hours.

Reinhard rushed upstairs and packed a weekend bag with some clothes and his laptop. Downstairs he found Sabine curled up in a foetal position in a chair.

'I have to go. I will do everything, and I mean everything, to get Eva back. Stay in contact with me.' He bent down and kissed her. 'Your mother should be here soon but in the meantime, you could ask Hermann to come over and look after you. It will be alright. '

Reinhard looked back at Sabine as he closed the door. In his heart and mind, he was beginning to doubt that it would be alright.

CHAPTER 16

The Crooked Star

Reinhard and Silke sat opposite one another in the sleek new Citation X. Silke was overawed by the experience and had to be reminded by Reinhard to fasten her seat belt. The Citation X is one of the fastest business jets available and operates just below the sound barrier. It takes off in a very steep climb, pushing its occupants deep into the plush seats. Silke was clearly enthralled by it all. She could hardly believe such luxury could exist, and she determined right then and there, that she would aim for the stars and lift herself out of the hand-to-mouth existence that was presently her lifestyle.

As the plane levelled off, Reinhard leaned towards Silke and started to bring her up-to-date on the latest events and information.

'I believe we have, at the most, forty-eight hours to establish what has happened, before I am forced to give the police all the information I have, including the e-mails that started it all. I am going to need you to be at my side because of all the internet intricacies. Are you comfortable with that?'

'Yes of course. I have no roots or personal commitments, so you can count on me. The office knows that I am with you. Also I think I can get used to this lifestyle.'

Reinhard smiled weakly, 'Thank you. I will see that you are personally compensated at the end of this nightmare. Now, you have established a connection between Eicke and Mayer in Antwerp. Our first port of call will be to Adolf Eicke. I will insist, by brute force if necessary, that he comes clean with us. You must simply take over his computer when we are there and extract anything which is relevant. I am struggling to find any rational reason behind this kidnapping. It just doesn't make sense.'

The Citation X received permission to land, and the pilot brought it down in a sharp descent then levelled out and made a smooth landing. Reinhard went straight to the Sixt desk, signed one document and was handed the keys to a Mercedes S-class. Thirty minutes later, they arrived in the Grinzing district and pulled up outside the home of Adolf Eicke.

Reinhard rang the bell and the intercom was answered by a woman, who said she would see if she could find Mr. Eicke. Reinhard assumed that she was a housemaid. The intercom buzzed, and the gate swung open. A young woman opened the front door and indicated that they should wait in the entrance hall.

Reinhard looked through an open door that led into what was obviously a large lounge. The walls were a bright sand colour and he could see a number of paintings that had been placed at different levels, all with ornate gilt framing. He recalled hearing that Eicke had a penchant for purchasing expensive paintings, mostly impressionists.

225

One of the paintings was almost certainly a Sisley that he had acquired at a Christies' auction some years before.

A clearly annoyed Adolf Eicke then emerged from the sitting room.

'What is the meaning of an unannounced visit?' he asked, not bothering with any greetings or niceties.

'My apologies, Mr. Eicke, but when you hear my news, I am sure you will understand the need for my sudden unscheduled visit. You know Miss Kotter?'

'Yes, yes. Come inside.' snapped Eicke impatiently. He turned and walked into the sitting room, followed by Silke and Reinhard.

'Mr. Eicke, my daughter and my father have disappeared and I fear they may have been kidnapped. I believe you can help us with some information.'

'My God! I did not know about any kidnapping. When did this happen?'

226

'Two days ago. I believe that you may know something about this – what do you know about it?'

'Don't you bloody understand? This is the first I have heard about it. Why are you coming here and making insinuations?' Eicke had raised his voice, and his face had reddened.

'After I visited Mayer in Antwerp, he contacted you. I believe there is a connection between the kidnapping and Mayer and you.'

'How do you know there has been any communication between Mayer and myself? Oh yes, of course, it is your young computer lady here. She has, how do you say it - hacked into my computer? Well, this is bullshit, total bullshit I tell you!'

'Well then, you won't mind if Miss Kotter looks at your computer now?'

Eicke stood up, 'Get out of my house immediately,' he shouted. 'Get out or I will call the police.'

'Keep quiet, you stupid old man. You are welcome to call the police.' Reinhard shouted in return and then paused and decided to chance his arm with an exaggerated claim. 'We have enough proof to link you positively to the disappearance of Eva and my father. It would be in your best interest to take us to your computer right away.'

The ruse seemed to have worked, as the flustered Eicke turned on his heels and walked towards his office, followed by Reinhard and Silke.

Eicke slumped into a chair and pointed to his laptop.

'Go ahead. I am sure you know my password.' Then turning to Reinhard, he said, 'Mr. Heinrich, I want you to know that I have no knowledge, whatsoever, about the kidnapping, and I have had no involvement in it.'

'Then why have you been contacting Mr. Otto Mayer in Antwerp?'

Eicke seemed startled by the accusation.

'I am shocked by the news of the kidnapping. Something has gone terribly wrong here. I can tell you that I did see Mayer on two occasions recently and I gave him information about the stolen Jewish jewellery. For the past few years since I left the bank, I have been brooding about how your father cheated me and how he then simply ignored me. It grew inside me like a cancer, and I thought I would shit on his parade, by forcing him to give away massive reparations to save the bank.' Eicke started taking in deep breaths and covered his face with his hands.

'Hurry up with your story. We are running out of time,' shouted Reinhard.

'We concocted the e-mails and then Mayer was going to send some people around to get your father to pay over money to a foundation in Israel. That was all. I don't know how this has escalated, and if it even relates to the kidnapping. I am very sorry for you. It appears to have a totally different direction from the original intent.'

Reinhard asked, 'Was there anything in your conversations that could give us a clue as to where they might be? Why did they have to kidnap them? It doesn't add up.'

'I have just come across an e-mail from you to Mayer in which you mention a trunk. What is that about?' asked Silke excitedly.

Eicke looked at Reinhard, knowing they had agreed to keep this a secret between them.

'It is alright. Silke has most of the information related to the early days. This is an emergency and I had to tell her. You can go ahead.'

'The trunk was an old army trunk that housed the jewellery and some papers. Your father kept it locked inside a cellar under his house. Do you know about the secret cellar behind all the wines?'

'I only learned about it a short while ago.' said Reinhard.

'I do not wish to discuss this in front of this young lady. Let us rather go next door.'

Eicke struggled to his feet and led Reinhard into an adjoining room. He closed the door firmly behind him.

Eicke sat down.

'There were only five of us who knew of its existence. The other three, like us, were the sons of prominent Nazis. Well, the old trunk was kept there along with some old Nazi memorabilia. I told Mayer about it. He wanted to see if it contained any other items. I told him that there were only papers in it. He thought they could shed some light on the Holocaust. Maybe they contained Swiss bank account numbers of Jews killed in the war.'

'Tell me about the other three men.'

'There was Frederick Muller, whose father was Heinrich Muller. Josef Daleuge, son of Kurt Daleuge and Erich Koch's son, Wolfgang Koch. You have to understand that when we started the bank, we used whatever contacts we had, and I suppose we specialised in moving money around for Nazis living in exile. Many were still being searched for and needed to move around. They required safe havens for their money. The five of us would meet in your father's wine cellar, and then we would go into the secret room at the back, which was in effect a shrine to our parents.'

'Where are these men now?' asked Reinhard.

'Josef Daleuge died some two years ago. Frederick Muller moved back to Berlin after the re-unification. I believe he has terminal cancer. Wolfgang Koch lives in your neck of the woods, north east of Munich. There is absolutely no reason why they would be involved in any kidnapping.'

'When I last spoke to my father, he informed me that he had disposed of the trunk some time ago, but he didn't say where. Mr. Eicke, you have to phone Mayer right away. He has to tell you what is going on. I will pay a ransom. Anything! I will see if I can contact Koch.'

Eicke pulled off a Post It page, and dialled a number. Reinhard stood next to him.

Eicke asked if he could speak to Mayer and then enquired if he had a mobile phone where he could be contacted. He put down the phone and turned to Reinhard.

'That was Mayer's wife. She says he has gone with his son to a health spa. She doesn't know where and they have no mobile phones with them. It seems very strange.'

Reinhard sat down opposite Eicke.

'I am going to ask you to tell me everything you know about Mayer and his son and the three neo-Nazis you used to meet with. I want to know your involvement. If you are in anyway involved with this kidnapping, you are in serious trouble. If you are not, then you must help me.'

The old man looked at him, and it was obvious that he was extremely agitated. His breathing was clearly audible.

'I have had absolutely nothing to do with the kidnapping, this you must understand. I have explained about my dealings with Mayer. I did mention the papers in a trunk. As I said, Mayer thought they could contain details of Swiss bank accounts belonging to the_concentration camp victims. I never saw the trunk or the papers. All your father told me was that everything was in some sort of code. All Koch was interested in was finding some clue as to the whereabouts of the missing amber panels. I am sure you are aware of the famous panels that disappeared from Russia during the war.'

'Do you think the Mayers could have escalated the extortion scheme, hoping that by kidnapping my father and daughter, they would get access to what they think are bank account numbers.'

'I don't know,' replied Eicke, wringing his hands. 'Perhaps, but I am totally unaware of it. I will do everything to help you.'

'And the neo-Nazis- what about them?' enquired Reinhard.

'Firstly, none of us are neo-Nazis. There are no shaven-headed, tattooed people amongst us. I don't know

235

if you know it but Wolfgang's father, Erich Koch, was involved in the looting of the Amber Room at Tsarskoe Selo Palace on the outskirts of Leningrad. The amber panels disappeared in the dying days of the war and have never been found. Several times he asked your father if there was any information from his father, as to the whereabouts of this treasure. Apparently, Wolfgang was allowed to visit his father in the Polish prison where he was serving a life sentence. It was, I think, 1986 and the doctors felt that Erich Koch was at a terminal stage. He said his father was almost incoherent and mumbled about the Amber Room panels. The name Heinz Heydrich came up - he was your great uncle. Your father confirmed that all the papers he had, were in some sort of code and there was nothing that mentioned the Amber Room as such. I do know that Wolfgang Koch met with Otto Mayer.'

'Well that could open a line of investigation. You said he lives north-east of Munich. Do you know exactly where?'

'Yes, but I will look it up just to make sure.'

Eicke paged through an old telephone index book.

'Here it is. 21 Karl Theodor Strasse, Passau. He has a splendid house on the river. Here is his telephone number.'

Reinhard copied the address and telephone number in his notebook, then turned to Eicke and said, 'I think we should allow Miss Kotter to join us now. Shall I fetch her?'

'Go ahead,' replied Eicke.

Reinhard opened the door and called Silke. He handed her the piece of paper with Koch's details.

'Please see if we can arrange a meeting with this gentleman - maybe even tomorrow. I think we need to sort out all this confusing information we keep coming across.'

Silke nodded and sat next to Reinhard. He turned to her and said, 'In addition to the Mayers in Antwerp, we now have another suspect, in the man whose name is on the paper I have just given you. Apparently, his father stole the famous Amber Room Panels in Russia during the war. They have never been discovered and they are priceless. Some people think that information related to them, could have been in the damn box. This box is a true curse. What was that children's story? Pandora's box. Well this is it. Shit!'

'Could there be a connection between the Mayers and this man?' enquired Silke, tentatively.

'I am hoping Mr. Eicke will enlighten us,' replied Reinhard. He then turned back to face Eicke. 'Well?'

'I am afraid that this could be the case.' Eicke's head drooped as he stared at the desk. 'I omitted to tell you that I took Wolfgang into my confidence about my plan to get, let's call it, revenge. He seemed eager to be part of the plan and accompanied me on my last trip to Antwerp. I truly do not know if he subsequently contacted Mayer or made any arrangements with him. Shall I 'phone him now?'

'No don't do that. We will contact him. I have to ask you not to contact anyone in this regard if indeed, you are innocent as you claim. Please confirm your agreement.'

'I agree,' said Eicke, nodding his head slowly

'For my benefit, can I ask you to tell me how this plan you had with the Mayers was to proceed? What exact goal did you have in mind?' asked Silke.

Eicke was clearly annoyed at being questioned by a young girl, whom he felt was beneath his station.

'I think I have already explained it. By using veiled threats concerning the bank's Nazi connection, we would force Mr. Heinrich to pay a large chunk of his wealth over to the Jews. There was no hint of any kidnapping. I was not going to be involved, only Mayer and Koch.'

Reinhard stared directly at Eicke.

'I have no choice but to accept what you have told me. I must emphasise the importance of your not contacting any of these people. You could be considered an accessory to a double kidnapping.'

'As I said, kidnapping never came into it, I can assure you. You have my word that I will not contact anyone.' Eicke looked very distraught and kept wringing his hands.

'We must go as we are running out of time. Good day Mr. Eicke. We will be in touch,' said Reinhard as he turned abruptly and walked out of the room followed by Silke, who didn't even have enough time to fasten her computer case.

As he drove off, he turned to Silke and said, 'I cannot believe that Eicke seems to have orchestrated this whole thing, out of a desire to get revenge for some shareholding dispute. But why the kidnapping?'

'As I see it,' said Silke, 'Eicke was just looking for revenge. It was blackmail but not for personal gain. There seem to be others involved who have different motives. Your father has told you that he disposed of the trunk and presumably the contents as well. Perhaps these other people believe, that by kidnapping him, he will reveal its whereabouts.'

'Why Eva?' asked Reinhard.

'Maybe to blackmail you. I agree that there are a lot of things that don't add up. We need to dig further.'

'Please, please help me Silke. We don't have much time,' pleaded Reinhard.

CHAPTER 17

The Crooked Star

Willy Koch was seated at the Erdinger Weiss Bier Bar, situated just outside the Arrivals Hall at Munich Airport's Terminal 1. He had arranged to meet Otto Mayer and his son Albert, who were flying in from Belgium. He was feeling slightly nervous, and the fact that he had arrived almost an hour before the flight arrival time, made it worse. He had walked around the Arrivals Hall and then taken a seat at the bar and ordered coffee and a sandwich. Trying to make himself appear what he considered inconspicuous, he had read through the four-page menu several times. His eyes caught a man staring at him, so he picked up the menu once again and summoned the waitress. This time he ordered a beer.

Wilhelm Koch, or Willy as he preferred to be called, was the son of Wolfgang Koch, who in turn was the son of the Nazi, Erich Koch. Erich Koch had been the Reichskommissar for the Ukraine. Although his father Wolfgang, only experienced the Nazi era as a child, he nevertheless enjoyed the fruits of his father's ill-gotten gains. He was able with the assistance of AH Bank, to move some of his father's looted fortune to secure investment sites around the world. He was a quietly-spoken man who had become very mellow as he got older. Willy was born in the prosperous post-war period and seemed to have inherited some of his grandfather's odd genes. They say that certain genetic traits can jump a generation. He revelled in his family's Nazi background. His anti-social behaviour as a teenager led him into conflict with the authorities, and he was arrested at the age of twenty when a gang, of which Willy was a member, was accused of killing a Turkish *gastarbeite*r. Willy was seen bending over the prostrate body of the victim and strangling him. Wolfgang Koch used his money and influence to get the charge against Willy dropped after an eyewitness and certain vital evidence linking him to the crime, mysteriously disappeared, however, this was not before he was sent for a psychiatric evaluation. The report, which was never published, indicated that Willy was a borderline psychopath. He was seen as very likeable and charming but also cunning and manipulative. His egocentricity was linked to his privileged background but the psychiatrist also found that he did not show any internal restraint or sense of responsibility for his actions. The report recommended that he should undergo further psychiatric evaluation. This never took place. Several years later, Willy again came to the attention of the police when he reported his wife to be missing. All searches for her proved fruitless, including a private search, paid for by Willy. No connection was made to his earlier encounter with the police. Willy then joined the Green Party and was able to convince everyone that he was an example of the new German generation. At first, Willy didn't want to get involved with the Mayers and only agreed reluctantly when his father explained the potential size of the fortune that awaited them, if the missing Amber Room Panels could be found.

Willy drank his beer slowly and checked his watch. He calculated that if the plane was on time and allowing for thirty minutes for the passengers to disembark, then the Mayers should be arriving soon. He had a description of the two men, and he moved his chair slightly so that he could observe the people coming through the revolving glass doors. He took another sip of his beer, looked up and saw an old man shuffling through the door, followed by a slightly-taller younger man. They stopped and looked around the beer garden as if expecting to be met. Willy raised his hand in a tentative way. The younger man acknowledged him and directed the older man in the direction of Willy's table.

Willy stood up. He was at least ten centimetres taller than either of them, with a much bigger build. The younger man spoke first, 'I am Albert and this is my father Otto.' He held out his hand in greeting.

'Pleased to meet you. I am Willy.' They had previously agreed to use only first names. The old man sat down before Willy could offer his hand.

'My father, Wolfgang, whom you know, does not feel well today, which is why he isn't here. I will take you to our rendezvous hotel where you will meet him. Before we depart can I order you a drink or something to eat?'

Otto Mayer shook his head, and his son replied, 'Thank you, but we had some food and drink on the flight.'

'In that case I will settle my account, and then we can leave.'

Once they had left the airport and were on the E52 motorway to Bad Reichenhall, Willy addressed Otto Mayer, who was seated in the back of the car.

'My father told me about your background and I am truly sorry that you and your family had to endure what must have been sheer hell.'

'Well your father also told me about you and your political inclinations, so I am pleased that maybe your country can start back on a new road to civilization.'

'I was surprised to hear that you had chosen Bad Reichenhall as the base camp, as the area has many connections with Hitler.'

'There are Nazi connections throughout Germany,' the old man replied. 'I liked the idea of the salt treatments for some of my ailments, which is why I chose the place. I just hope no old ghosts come along at night.'

'I am sure that won't happen,' chuckled Willy. 'You will find that it has a very beautiful setting. My father has produced some plans for us to look at, once you are settled in. In the meantime, enjoy the scenery of our beautiful Bavaria.'

Bad Reichenhall is a lovely spa town situated in the Chiengauer Alp region in southern Bavaria, close to the

Austrian town of Salzburg. It lies in a basin, circled by high mountain peaks. For centuries, it has been a slate producing area and this has resulted in a number of spas opening, offering brine treatments for arthritis and respiratory ailments.

Willy drove into the grounds of the impressive Hotel Amber Rezidenz, and pulled up outside the front door. The accommodation they had arranged consisted of two penthouse suites for the older men and standard rooms for the sons. It had been booked and paid for through a travel agency using false names. The suites were equipped with Wi-Fi computer connections and from here they would be able to follow the operation in Grainau about 50 kilometres to the east. A concierge brought along a luggage trolley, and Willy went ahead to the reception.

'As my father explained to you, all you have to do is sign these forms,' informed Willy, handing them each a form. The information has been completed. Otto, you are

248

in penthouse number 3 on the top floor and Albert you have room 32 on the third floor, which is next to mine. The plan is that we will meet in Suite One on the same floor as your penthouse, Otto, after you have freshened up.'

About an hour later, the Mayers were ushered into penthouse Suite one. A desk had been placed in the middle of the lounge section and four chairs were arranged around it.

Wolfgang Koch eased himself out of his chair and approached Otto Mayer. The two men shook hands. Wolfgang was smiling, but Otto remained impassive.

'Welcome,' beamed Wolfgang, hoping to break the ice. 'As I understand it, this is your first visit to Germany. What is your first impression?'

Otto Mayer carefully placed a notebook in front of him. 'The most difficult part for me was actually stepping onto German soil. I once made a vow that it was something

I would never do, but if it benefits some of the victims of the Nazi period, then I am comfortable breaking it. Driving along the road here, it was a strange, surreal experience. Everything is clean and orderly. The natural surroundings are beautiful and the few Germans I have encountered at the airport and here at the hotel seem pleasant and helpful. I keep asking myself - where are the Germans who murdered my people? Is it possible for a whole nation to have undergone this amazing metamorphosis? You have to excuse me, but I am feeling very emotional right now.'

'Otto, we have discussed this before and my son here is possibly the best example of how this nation has changed. He doesn't believe that Germany should have any armed forces or nuclear power stations. Certainly, his grandfather was a Nazi official. What if your grandfather had been a serial killer? Should we look at you differently?'

'I am looking forward to the salt treatment for my lungs,' said Otto, changing the subject of discussion.

'Well then, shall we look at the plans? Willy, please spread out the map of Garmisch,' instructed Wolfgang, grateful that the Nazi discussion was over, at least for the moment.

Willy spread out the map which had a number of circles and lines drawn on it. Wolfgang proceeded to outline the plan, which was for Willy and Albert to approach the house on the following day when Hermann's staff would be away and to coerce the old man into handing over the trunk. Wolfgang knew the layout of the house, including the basement rooms. He had drawn a sketch of the property showing the various rooms and exits. A few days earlier, Willy had booked into a small local hotel and using the pretence of being a hiker, had found a good hiding place near to the Adlerhorst estate. Using a powerful pair of binoculars, he was able watch the comings and goings of the residents, which he carefully noted.

Albert Mayer looked up from the map.

'I think it is very important that we have a plan B and a good exit strategy. What if the trunk is not in the house but at another location? If we have to drive him to another location, then we have to remove the stockings from our faces, and we could then be recognised.'

'Good thinking,' replied Wolfgang. 'I think the trunk is in the secret basement room, but if it has been removed, we can either force him to tell us where it is or as you say, take him along with you to make sure that it is there. From Willy's observation, Frau Heinrich, his daughter-in-law, seems to go out, somewhere around ten and returns at about midday. She has a maid who seems to spend the whole day in the house. The ideal time will be between, say ten thirty and eleven thirty. That gives us a window of about one hour, which should be sufficient. If you have to take the old man, then put him in the boot so that he can't see your faces, however, it would be preferable to leave him behind. You will need to tie him up so that he can't raise the alarm.'

'I don't want to be party to any violence,' said Otto.

Wolfgang shook his head, 'I don't think that violence will be necessary after we tell Hermann that we know that his bank helped people like Klaus Barbie and Eichmann. I have to say that I think Eicke's idea of getting Heinrich to pay blackmail money, is not a good one. That can become very risky business.'

'I too have misgivings about that. For my part, I would rather just secure information on the bank accounts. I feel that is more legitimate. Then it is agreed that we just concentrate on the trunk.'

Everyone nodded in agreement.

They had acquired four prepaid mobile phones and acknowledged that contact with the base at the hotel would be via short, text messages. After a further run through, it was confirmed that the plan would be executed the following morning. Wolfgang suggested a celebratory drink, which was declined by Otto, who wanted to retire to his room. Willy and Albert decided to go to Albert's room to 'fine tune' their plan and consider any eventualities which could occur.

CHAPTER 18

The following day, after breakfast and without any obvious fuss, Albert and Willy left the hotel and headed in the direction of Garmisch-Partenkirchen. Willy took the road that passed Bad Tolz and meandered along the scenic drive to Garmisch. The GPS directed them to the gates of Adlerhorst. There were two gates, set about forty metres apart. Wolfgang had instructed them to take the second gate, which led directly to Hermann's house. They drove in slowly to minimise the engine noise and glided to a stop outside the front door. As they got out they could hear a small dog barking. They pulled stockings over their faces, and Willy knocked on the door, gun in hand. After what seemed like a long time the door opened and Hermann stepped forward.

'What the hell is this?' he shouted and stepped back inside. He started closing the door, but Willy was too fast for him. He pushed the door open with such force that Hermann was sent sprawling onto the floor. He was grabbed by his arms, and the gun was pushed in his face. Just then Blondi rushed into the room and with her loudest growl, she lunged at Albert and bit him on his thigh. He screamed and kicked out at Blondi, who was coming back for a second bite. Fearing his dog would get injured, Hermann shouted, 'Stop Blondi, stop.' This seemed to have the desired effect and Blondi just issued a low growling sound. Albert let go of Hermann and grabbed Blondi, who went berserk, snapping, kicking and growling.

256

Albert threw the dog into the downstairs toilet and shut the door, but not before she could sink her sharp teeth into his hand.

'What do you want? Leave me alone,' shouted Hermann, as he ripped his arm out of Willy's grip. Both Albert and Willy pointed their guns at the old man.

'Shut up you silly old bugger and if you do as we say, no harm will come to you.' Willy pointed his gun in the direction of the dining room. 'Sit down over there and don't do anything stupid.'

Hermann glared at them, his chest heaving from the drama of the last few minutes. 'Alright, no fucking around. You have in your possession an old trunk going back to the war years. Give it to us and we will go right away.' Willy waved his gun to emphasise the seriousness of the threat.

'That trunk is no longer here. I disposed of it years ago. It is finished, gone - not here. Now go away.'

'Don't fuck with us. It is here in your basement. Take us to the basement.'

Just then Eva walked in carrying her small teddy bear. She had just woken from a sleep and looked a little dismayed at seeing the two visitors.

'Granddad, what was all that shouting about?'

'Oh shit. Who is this?' demanded Albert.

'This is my granddaughter. Please don't harm her. Please let her go back to her house.'

'You must be mad! So that she can get her mother to call the police. Nobody is leaving this house!'

Eva ran up and put her hands around her grandfather's leg and just then Blondi started barking.

'Where is Blondi?' Eva asked.

'Enough of this shit. Take us to the basement,' said Willy as he stood up, followed by Albert.

258

Eva held onto her grandfather's hand as he led them to the stairway that led down to the basement.

Hermann pointed his hand, 'There you have it. This is my basement wine cellar.'

'Open the secret door,' demanded Willy. 'We know about it.'

Hermann took a long look at Willy's disguised face. Through the fine mesh of the stocking, he thought he recognised the features of the man facing him. Only five people knew of the existence of the back room, however, he thought, is it possible one of them had betrayed him and revealed its existence to an accomplice? He was younger than the five who knew of the room, but could he be related. It was the voice that suddenly had a familiar tone to it.

'Hurry, you old bastard,' shouted Willy, more out of nervousness than anger.

Hermann's hand was shaking as he pulled at the wine rack which swung open revealing a door. He punched four numbers into the digital lock and opened the door. He stepped into the room and switched on the light. Eva was still clinging to his trousers.

'Fucking hell, what is this?' exclaimed Willy, as he entered the shrine.

Albert grimaced as he came in. 'I feel like I have entered Hitler's bunker.'

'Okay, where is the bloody trunk?'

'I told you I no longer have it.'

With that Willy swung his right hand which held the gun, against Hermann's cheek, immediately drawing blood from his thin wrinkled skin. Eva screamed.

'Shut up,' Willy shouted at the little girl.

'Do what you like to me but let her go. She is just a little child. Please I beg you,' pleaded Hermann, as the blood ran in a small rivulet onto his neck and shirt collar.

Albert raised his hand, 'Where is the trunk? Tell us and we will leave you and your granddaughter alone. You have to hurry.'

Hermann looked at him and then at Eva, who was shaking and gripping his leg.

'I disposed of the trunk, and you are welcome to have it if it can still be found after all this time. There is nothing of value in it. What more can I tell you?'

'Where did you dispose of it?'

'I took it to Sassen Island on the Eibsee. It is a small island, and I walked into the interior and dug a hole and buried the trunk. That was a few years ago.'

Willy and Albert looked at one another. Willy was the first to speak, 'He will have to take us there. We can't go around digging holes all over a bloody island.' He turned to Hermann, 'Come on, you and the little girl are going with us to this Sassen Island. Where do you keep your tools?'

'I have already begged you to leave the child. She doesn't know anything about what is going on. She is only four years old.'

'She won't be harmed if you do as we ask. She cannot go home now as she will just cause us trouble. Where can we get a spade? What are the directions?'

'There is one in the garden at the side of the house,' Hermann bent down and hugged Eva. There were tears running down his cheeks, mingling with congealed blood on the one side of his face. 'Go in the direction of Grainau. Just before the church there is a road marked Eibsee. It is a direct road but you will need to rent a boat to get to the island.'

Willy led the way with Albert bringing up the rear. He opened the boot of the Audi Q5 SUV and helped Hermann and Eva into it. Before he closed it, he looked inside, 'We will release the back seat so that you will have plenty of air,' he said, trying to be reassuring. Eva sobbed quietly and buried her head in her grandfather's stomach. Albert swung the spade onto the back seat of the car.

They drove slowly out of the estate and onto the road leading to Grainau.

Inside the boot, Hermann cradled Eva in his arms. 'Don't worry little darling. I will get us out of this,' he whispered. 'I want you to remember a word. It is a name - Koch. Say it for me - Koch.'

'Koch,' she said and then she started sobbing.

'Please say it once more.'

'Koch,' she whispered through her sobs.

'Remember, you have to tell your father and mother this name - Koch.'

It was a short drive to Grainau and then onto the road to the Eibsee. It is a beautiful, clear lake with almost luminous, alpine-green water. It is situated about 200 metres above Grainau and the rack-railway that wends its way upwards and into the Zugspitze, runs alongside it. At the one end there is a hotel and nearby on another bank, several jetties jut out into the water and it is here that one can hire a boat. It is busy over the weekends and during holidays, but today it was quiet with just a few ramblers in the nearby woods and no one on the lake.

Willy stopped the vehicle and stepped outside, in order to orientate himself. He could see the boats for hire and he followed the shoreline of the lake. He saw that past the hotel there was another parking area which was deserted.

The Crooked Star

He instructed Albert to rent a boat and bring it around to the parking area on the far side. Albert walked across to the boat hire kiosk while Willy drove around the back of the hotel to the parking ground, which was situated about five hundred metres further on. He stopped in the far corner and looked around to confirm that it was empty. He decided not to open the boot until Albert had brought the boat alongside the parking ground. He checked the digital clock in the car. It was now an hour since they had first arrived at Hermann's house. Within the next hour, it was a distinct possibility that Mrs Heinrich would raise an alarm when she returned home. Then he saw a boat slowly coming towards him. He cursed quietly to himself. It was a big pedalo.

As Albert directed the pedalo onto the shore, Willy shouted, 'What the hell is this?'

'It was either this or a rowing boat,' Albert replied, jumping onto the land and dragging the boat a little way so that it wouldn't float away. 'Let's get the spade and open the boot.'

Willy and Albert pulled on their stockings and Willy, brandishing his gun in one hand, opened the boot.

'Get out,' he grunted.

Hermann lifted Eva onto the ground and then wearily dragged his body out of the boot. He was trying to imagine exactly what they were hoping to get out of the trunk. There were just worthless codes in it, and it was now sixty years or more since they were typed. But his main worry was for his granddaughter. He would wait for an opportune moment and then grab the gun from one of them. He needed to be careful lest Eva, who was clinging onto him like a leech, ended up in the firing line.

They were ushered onto the pedalo, with Hermann and Eva made to sit in the front seat while Willy and Albert sat behind them and pedalled.

266

'Don't try anything silly or brave,' warned Willy. 'We have our guns trained on you.'

Hermann turned slightly and addressed them, 'What circus are you from?'

'Shut up and enjoy the view. Which is Sassen Island?'

Hermann pointed to the island directly in front of them. After pedalling for about fifteen minutes, they arrived at the island. Willy decided to take the pedalo to the far side of the island where they would be hidden from the hotel and the boat hire people. They found a suitable spot. Willy and Albert jumped into the shallow water and waved Hermann and Eva off the boat. They dragged the boat onto the land and tied it firmly to a tree with a rope.

'Well old man, get your memory going and point out where the trunk is buried.' goaded Willy.

'I will first have to get my bearings. I don't think I started off at this point, and I didn't count exact steps like some pirate hiding his treasure chest. I simply walked into the trees and dug a hole. I have to think.'

'Well hurry up, we haven't got all day,' said Albert, sounding impatient and checking his watch.

Hermann walked to the water's edge trying to recall where he had beached the boat those several years ago. Eva kept at his side all the time, her eyes wide with fear. Hermann walked about twenty paces to the left of where the pedalo was secured and then moved into the tree line, followed closely by the two gunmen. Then he started walking into the interior of the island. He stopped beside a tree that had been blackened by a lightning strike.

'This is a likely spot,' he said, turning to the two men.

'Dig,' said Willy, handing Hermann the spade.

Hermann gave him a withering look and took the spade. He started to dig. He remembered that he had buried the trunk just over half a metre deep. He couldn't see signs of any previous digging, which over the years would have been covered by dead leaves and pine needles. He dug a test hole down to just under a metre, then another nearby and another which also revealed nothing. He then moved to the other side of the tree and continued digging. The sweat was pouring from him, and every now and then he had to stop to gasp for breath, but he was determined not to show any weakness to the two gunmen whom he now despised.

He stood up and said, 'Wrong tree. I am going to try the next one.'

Using his foot, he pushed the spade into the ground and pulled up a mound of earth. His heart was pounding in his chest. His breathing became shallower and more rapid. The hole produced nothing but sand and pine cones. The next hole was also fruitless. He moved onto a new one, and he could feel the sweat dripping from his forehead and onto his hands as he bent over the spade. A tight band was encircling his chest. He felt dizzy and a blackness came over him. He fell heavily to the ground. Eva screamed. Albert rushed forward and turned Hermann on his side. The lifeless eyes stared ahead. Albert put his hands on the carotid artery on his neck, but there was no pulse and his skin was damp.

'He's dead,' Albert shouted. Eva fell on top of her grandfather, sobbing.

'Get up, granddad. Get up!' she cried. Willy pulled her up and pushed her aside. She was screaming hysterically.

Willy bent over the lifeless body. He took Hermann by the shoulders and shook him as if by some miracle that action would bring Hermann back to life. He looked up at Albert.

'Take the girl to the boat and tell her to stay there - and no noise from her.'

Albert lifted Eva in his arms and carried her to the pedalo. He put her into a front seat. He was shaking and nervous.

'You must sit here until we come back. Do you understand?'

'I want my mommy,' she screamed.

'Please don't cry. You will see mommy soon.'

He hurried back to Willy, not knowing what their plan would be now. These circumstances had not been considered and they would have to reconsider their moves quickly and carefully. The last thing they needed was a dead body on their hands.

When he returned he saw that Willy had already started extending the hole that Hermann had started digging.

'There is no trunk here, so we must make this into a grave for the old man. Help me push him in.'

The two men dragged Hermann's body and pushed it into the hole, which wasn't quite long enough so they folded his legs. Willy covered the body with sand and patted it down. Now he too was sweating from the exertion, but he immediately moved to the next tree and started digging. After another three unsuccessful attempts, he hit something solid. He then began to dig feverishly, and soon he could see the top of an old trunk.

'Look,' he shouted, 'it's the bloody trunk. The old bastard was so close.'

He dug around the sides and was able to move it from side to side. Albert bent down and the two of them pulled the trunk free. It was covered in mud and sand and was still locked.

'There is no time to open it now. We are running out of time.'

'Do you think we need to keep these masks on now that the old man is gone?' asked Albert.

'No, the little girl won't recognise us. Let's go.' They ripped off their masks and each held a handle of the trunk. They ran back to the pedalo and were relieved to find that Eva was still there.

They lifted the trunk onto the back seat, and Willy got on next to it. Albert pushed the boat into the water and jumped in next to Eva, who was curled up in a foetal position. Willy typed out a text message- *have box Hermann died from heart attack we have granddaughter with us.* The reply came back almost immediately - *proceed to cottage.*

They pedalled back quickly to the parking ground. Willy carried the trunk to the car and placed it in the boot while Albert carried the sobbing Eva and put her on the back seat. Albert pedalled the boat back to the jetty and waited for Willy to pick him up.

They travelled in silence. Eva would break out in uncontrollable fits of crying and Albert would try to console her.

'Tell her to shut up,' Willy said angrily, but this only made her cry even more.

They arrived at the cottage in Oberaudorf where Wolfgang and Otto were waiting. Willy closed the door behind him and put the trunk on a table while Albert put Eva on a chair. He gave her a packet of crisps, which she refused to accept.

Otto was the first to speak.

'This is a huge mess. I said specifically, no violence, and now what have we got - a kidnapping and a dead person. This is going to lead to so much trouble.'

'Tell us exactly what happened,' demanded Wolfgang.

'It didn't go according to plan because the bloody trunk wasn't at the house. The silly old bugger buried it on an island in the middle of a lake. We didn't kill him. He died of a heart attack.'

'He died during a kidnapping,' said Otto angrily,' that is the problem. The police will be swarming around his house by now. We will be implicated in what is now a serious crime.'

'Wait,' said Wolfgang, holding up his hand. 'It has gone wrong but we have to remain calm and work out what we have to do to ensure no one can implicate us. Is there any evidence pointing to any of us?'

'None whatsoever,' responded Willy confidently. 'The only witness is her.' He pointed to Eva who had fallen asleep on the chair from the sheer exhaustion of her crying. 'We must get rid of her right away.'

'I don't like the sound of that remark,' Albert interjected. 'No violence. All we do is drop her off at a safe place where she can be found.'

'Open the trunk,' instructed Wolfgang.

Willy took the ice pick which was hanging from the front door and proceeded to force the padlock open. Eventually, the leather which was badly decayed ripped apart and Willy opened the lid. Everyone looked in at the seemingly empty trunk. Then Willy pulled out a black notebook.

Willy dug around the trunk, probing with the ice pick, but there was absolutely nothing else.

Otto Mayer took the book from Willy. He examined it slowly and carefully with the precision of a jeweller. The pages were discoloured but the lists of numbers were still legible.

'I can't be sure,' he said, 'but these could be bank account numbers. Today, the bank could be anywhere, but in the thirties and forties, it is very likely that they belonged to banks in Switzerland. It was the country of choice then.'

'Well you have what you came for,' said Wolfgang Koch sounding dejected. 'We have failed. Perhaps the panels will never be found. Gentlemen, events have not turned out as planned. This was intended to be a visit to an old man, coupled with some lightweight, blackmail suggestions. Nothing else. We now have a double kidnapping and a dead person. This could be bloody serious for all of us. We have to make new plans.'

'As I see it,' said Albert, taking the pages from his father, 'there are four items that we have to consider. One, there is a dead body on the island. Two, we have a little

277

girl. Three, the contents in the trunk. Four, where should each of us go now?'

'Right, let's look at the four points. Of course, there could be more than four. Number one - we did not kill the old man. He obviously died of a heart attack. We have to assume that his body will be discovered one day. Maybe a week; maybe a month? It's anyone's guess.'

'Let us not be complacent,' interrupted Otto Mayer. 'We could still be charged with causing his death. More like culpable homicide and we hid the body. I don't like it.'

'That point needs further discussion,' continued Willy, pointing his hand at Eva who was still sound asleep, curled up on the chair. 'Point two. The granddaughter. This was never part of our plan. How do we handle this one? Perhaps...' he drew his hand across his neck.

'She could be a bargaining chip if things get tough,' suggested Wolfgang Koch.

'No, no, please,' implored Otto Mayer, 'we are not a bunch of insane criminals. Albert made it absolutely clear - no violence. My son and I are here to redress an historical wrong. We cannot have blood on our hands or act like barbarians. She is maybe three or four years old and won't be able to identify us.'

Albert raised his hand, 'I agree. We must drop her off at a place where she can be found. First thing tomorrow morning we will do it. Please, no harm must come to her. Is everyone agreed on that? Do you all agree?'

They all nodded, except for Willy, who continued, 'We must dispose of the trunk. You have your papers,' he said turning to Albert. 'We are empty-handed, but that doesn't matter. Then your last point is where we all go. After we dump the girl and the trunk, I am considering taking a flight to Mallorca for a ten-day break.'

'I will take these numbers to Zurich,' said Albert, holding aloft the pages from the trunk, 'and see what I can find out about them. It will be a long and difficult task as the Swiss banks are not keen to admit their involvement in strange wartime accounts.'

'I intend to stay right here for a few days,' said Wolfgang Koch. 'What about you, Mr. Mayer?'

'I enjoyed my stay at the spa. I think I will fly to Luxembourg and then take a taxi to Mondorf where they have a very nice thermal spa. This is where I told my wife I would be. I am feeling very tired and I am worried about the potential outcome.'

'That settles it,' said Wolfgang Koch. 'Tomorrow Willy will take you to Munich airport, from where you can go your different ways. I suggest that you give me your mobile phones so that they can be destroyed. From tomorrow, there will be no contact between us. I mean the two families of course. Now I had the foresight to buy food, including some cookies for the girl.'

Otto Mayer stared at the floor, 'Oh my God. I see only disaster ahead.'

CHAPTER 19

The following day they were ready to leave by seven o'clock in the morning. Eva was handed a packet of biscuits, which she clung on to. She had stopped crying, but had not uttered a single word. It had been decided that they would drop her off in a field near Rosenheim, which was en route to Munich. They drove through the town and took a minor road going north. A few kilometres outside of the town, they saw a farm road that led to a copse, which shielded them from the view of a house about three hundred metres away. There was smoke coming out of a chimney, so they knew somebody was inside. Albert carried Eva out of the car and placed her on the ground. He pointed to the house which was partially visible through the trees.

'When we leave, you must go to that house. Do you understand?'

Eva looked at him without acknowledging that she understood. Willy was waving frantically, so Albert gave one last look at the frightened little girl and walked back to the car.

The Crooked Star

Eva watched them drive away and just sat there holding her packet of sweet biscuits. Then she slowly stood up, dusted her dress, which was quite crumpled by now and started to walk in the direction of the house. After about five minutes she came to a gate which she tried to open, but the latch was too tight. Just then a German Shepherd rushed up to the gate, barking ferociously. Eva backed away and started running down the path. The farmhouse door opened and a woman appeared, looked around and then closed the door again. Eva went back to the trees where she had been left initially. She started to cry. Tears ran down her dusty cheeks causing muddy splodges to appear. Still clinging to her biscuits she walked towards the road. Only the occasional car or van came by. She got to the side of the road and sat down again. It was on a corner and unless someone in a car was deliberately looking at the side of the road, she could easily be missed. Three cars sped past her, creating a wind that blew her blonde hair. Then suddenly a car braked sharply and stopped about fifty metres from her. The car reversed until it was near her, and a woman got out of the passenger side and went up to her.

'Where is your mother? Are you lost? Is that your house up there?' she pointed at the farmhouse.

Eva just looked at her and said nothing. The driver of the car, also a woman, got out and came over.

'I don't know what is wrong,' said the first woman. 'She hasn't said a word. We can't leave her here. It is too dangerous!'

'Perhaps she belongs to that house over there. Put her in the car and I will drive up there.'

The two women drove up to the house and were also greeted by the boisterous dog. A woman came out of the house and approached them. They explained the position and she also tried to get Eva to respond. The farmhouse lady, whose name was Ingrid Lang, agreed to

284

take Eva to the Rosenheim police after they explained that they were hurrying to an appointment. She took her inside, poured her a glass of milk and opened Eva's packet of biscuits. Eva drank the milk and ate two biscuits but despite all her coaxing efforts, she refused to utter a single word.

At the Rosenheim police station, Ingrid Lang was sent to the office of a social worker, who knelt beside Eva and also tried unsuccessfully to get her to speak. Eva was given some old toys that were in a box and a torn book about the story of a lost duckling. Later, she was given lunch and at around five o'clock the social worker was getting worried that no one had reported a missing child, so she went to the station commander as paperwork would now have to be completed and a home found for her. Captain Brenner, the station commander jumped up,

'My God,' he shouted, 'I have just remembered. A child was kidnapped in Garmisch. There is a fax here with a photo. Quick take me to her.'

They rushed down the passage and when he saw her, it was immediately apparent she was the missing child. A call was put through to the Munich police who had issued the notice.

'

CHAPTER 20

The jet took off in a steep ascent from the Vienna airport runway. Almost immediately it banked to starboard heading in the direction of Munich.

Reinhard caught Silke's eye as she turned her gaze from the window.

'I am still concerned that we have nothing concrete to work on. My mind is spiralling and I feel completely out of control.'

'I disagree,' said Silke. 'We have a lot of disconnected information which we must now thread together somehow. I will work on it as we fly.' She opened her computer case and removed her laptop.

'We will land around four o'clock. I want to go straight to Passau to see this Koch person - about an hour's drive, I estimate.'

Silke nodded, 'Then after that, we should set up a meeting with the detectives. I don't think you should do this on your own anymore. I will prepare all the information we have collected, and you must decide what you will tell them.' Silke looked relieved when the flight attendant came with some sandwiches and coffee. She was starving but felt she couldn't discuss this with Reinhard, who didn't seem to require any sustenance.

After about ten minutes Silke looked up from her computer.

'I have added this morning's information, and I now have a diagram with all our known data. Have a look,' she said as she handed him the computer.

Reinhard looked at the screen. Silke had put names and place-names in a circle and joined some of them with dots. The names were R.Heinrich; S.Heinrich; E.Heinrich; H.Heinrich – Garmisch; Mayer-Antwerp; Eicke-Vienna; Koch-Passau; Inge-Munich. In the notes, she listed the various e-mails and comments by Eicke.

After a while, Reinhard looked up from the computer.

'I suppose we do have some useful leads here. One thing, I do not want Inge's name mentioned. I can absolutely vouch that she is innocent. I think you must remove her name.'

'A woman scorned?' questioned Silke.

'How did you find out her name?' Reinhard looked bemused.

'You mentioned it in the hotel bar in Munich.'

'You certainly don't miss anything. Please delete it.' He put his head back and closed his eyes. How can one's life, he thought, get into such a complicated mess so quickly? He could feel his stomach tightening as visions of Eva flashed before him. Please God look after her. Please.

'You see how I have joined Eicke with Mayer and Koch,' said Silke pointing to the computer screen. 'We know for certain that Eicke and Mayer were involved in some sort of conspiracy and now we have Eicke pointing a finger at Koch. Later today we will hopefully have a clearer picture of his involvement, if any.'

'I still cannot accept that my father's life-long friend and co-owner of the bank could have been party to something as terrible as this.'

'The human mind, unlike that of our animal cousins, is capable of great cruelty,' said Silke.

Reinhard nodded in agreement. The sound of the engines altered as the pilot throttled back and reduced speed as he approached Munich airport. The fasten seat belt light came on and he and Silke sat back in their seats as the aircraft descended.

It only took them a few minutes to get through arrivals and into the car park building. Reinhard set the GPS, built into the dashboard of the BMW, and drove out of the airport. With a bit of luck, they would be in Passau within an hour. The roads were relatively clear that day and soon the GPS voice was saying 'You have reached your destination.'

Known as Dreiflussestadt or City of Three Rivers, Passau is at the junction of three rivers. It is here that the Danube is joined by the rivers Inn and Ilz. The city dates back to Roman times and is essentially a university town.

The original Institute of Catholic Studies, founded in 1622, was expanded into a full university in the late 1970s, giving it a distinctively youthful feel.

Number 21 Karl Theodor Strasse was a large house, from the turn of the 20th century. It was in an elevated position on the bank of the Danube. Reinhard opened the gate and proceeded up the path, followed by Silke. He rang the doorbell and could hear that it was working. He waited for a courteous time before pressing it again. When there was still no reply, he walked around the side of the house and banged on a window. A man appeared from the back of the house dressed in dirty clothes and Wellington boots.

'There is no one here today. I can't help you. This is my gardening day.'

'Do you know where Mr. Koch is?' enquired Reinhard.

'He phoned me two days ago to say he would be away for a few days. That's all I know. He asked me to continue with my gardening work while he is away.'

'Do you have any idea where he has gone?'

'I think I said that's all I know.' He turned abruptly and walked away.

'Pig,' muttered Heinrich to himself. He turned to Silke and said, 'I think we should see if a neighbour can help us instead.'

They went next door and were greeted by a young woman pushing a baby in a pram.

Reinhard introduced himself and asked if she knew anything as to the whereabouts of Wolfgang Koch. She said that she had seen Koch leave the house the previous day carrying a suitcase. He got into a white Audi. She didn't recognise the driver who sat in the vehicle while

Koch put his suitcase in the boot. Reinhard thanked her and he and Silke got back into their car.

'I think you are correct. We have to contact the police. Here is Bosch's card. Please give him a ring and see where we can meet. Silke phoned the direct number listed on the card and got straight through to Bosch. She spoke for a short while then switched off the phone. 'He says he will meet us at your house in two hours time. Shall I go over the notes once more with you to make sure I haven't omitted anything?'

'No I am satisfied with everything you have put down. I have said this before. You seem a lot more mature than your years. I am very impressed with you. Have the past few days changed anything in your life?'

'I don't ever want to be mature. I have never trusted anyone and this situation you are in, confirms that people are basically bad.'

294

'All people?' queried Reinhard.

'Yes, almost all. We are all self-seeking hypocrites and liars. If only we could see the private thoughts of those around us, then we would know the true person. People hide their true thoughts and feelings. Some are thoughts of hate; some of lust; some of derision; others of cruelty and torture. We secretly wish bad luck or even disaster or death on people, but when we face them, we utter lies and deceitful remarks designed to hide our true feelings. The only living thing I will ever trust is a dog.'

'Silke! That is such a negative view of the world. What about my love for Eva? I realise that if I say that I love my wife, you will immediately, and correctly, shove Inge in my face. Look, I know you have been mistreated at a vulnerable age but perhaps when this is over, I will be able to show you a different side to some people. When I think about the type of people who have kidnapped my father and daughter, then I too despair of humanity.'

The Crooked Star

'In my short life I have come into contact not only with evil foster parents but also with horrible social workers and the police. Even the people I work with. They seem like nice guys and can be fun, but when it comes to handing out money or a bonus, then the vulture emerges. I once saw a programme on TV of vultures eating a kill. They jump and fight and try to get the best bits for themselves - to hell with sharing or fairness. Humans are no different; they just hide their vulturity behind a cloak of false decency.'

'Vulturity. I think you have just invented a word. Very apt,' said Reinhard, smiling slightly for the first time in days. 'Where in your opinion does this leave the human race?'

Silke looked at the passing scenery, which was so beautiful to her eyes as until recently had only seen city streets and walls. She desperately wanted to immerse herself in the quietness and beauty of the fields and the tall mountains. She imagined herself lying in a field of grass surrounded by small wild flowers, looking up to the mountains and the sky. Even the clouds seemed lovely. 'I have studied the vulturity of man, if I may use my funny word again. All mankind has wanted since time began, was to have control over his fellow beings - the strong subjugating the weak. Even today, look at what the Chinese do to the Tibetans or the Americans to the Islamists. Man also wants to control everything around him - the animals, the sea and the environment. He is driven to play God and as science has given him powerful tools of control, he can now do so. Sadly, he cannot see any value in trees and animals and insects, so he destroys them, and unwittingly, he is orchestrating his own demise. I believe we have passed the point of no return. This is our last century. I say good riddance.'

'Oh my goodness, you are making me depressed, but I can see a lot of truth in what you have just said.'

As Reinhard pulled into the estate, he saw that Bosch's car was already there. The sun was starting to set, and the last two days now seemed like two weeks to Reinhard. They went inside the house and could hear Bosch and his two assistants talking to Sabine. As Reinhard entered Sabine jumped up and threw her arms around him.

'Please give me some news,' she cried.

Reinhard patted her on her back, 'Let me sit down. We have a lot to discuss. I am going to ask Silke to do the debriefing as she has it all on her computer. Firstly, Detective Bosch, I want to ask if the police have anything new to report.'

Georg Bosch looked at his own netbook computer.

'Well, we have escalated this nationally and internationally through Europol. We have identified the tyre tracks as belonging to a large SUV or 4 x 4. We also have a tiny blood sample which was found outside the downstairs toilet which may have come from the little dog biting one of the perpetrators - we know there are two of them from the shoe prints outside the front door. We are working on a shoe identity. Hopefully, the blood sample will yield DNA evidence. A resident in Grainau, who was walking in the main street at around eleven that morning, says he saw a White Audi Q5 or Q7 driving up the street - this ties in with the tracks we found. He thinks there were two men in it but no elderly man or a little girl. We are checking the car register for all Audi Q5 and Q7 vehicles registered initially in Bavaria. That is where we are at the moment. I look forward to hearing what you can bring to the table.'

Reinhard nodded to Silke, who opened her computer. She then proceeded to explain the findings she and Reinhard had made. She went through the main points in her usual succinct manner. Sabine sat impassively with her arms folded throughout the proceedings, while Bosch and his assistants made a few notes.

After Silke had concluded her report, she asked if there were any questions.

'I would like a copy of the report please,' Bosch requested. 'I have to say that you have made some significant findings, however, I think, Mr. Heinrich, that you have acted in an irresponsible way trying to do this on your own. Our resources are more sophisticated than yours and the delay in giving us this information could be significant.'

Reinhard was clearly annoyed at being admonished by a lowly policeman.

'Your initial response was to my mind too slow and ineffective. Now you have the facts, how are you going to apprehend this Koch man?'

'Based on what you have now told us, we will put out search warrants for Mr. Koch, and we will contact the Belgian authorities and get them to start looking for Mr. Otto Mayer. We will also consider questioning Mr. Eicke and possibly extraditing him from Austria.'

'In my opinion, Mr. Eicke should take a back seat. We know that he doesn't have my father or daughter, and I tend to believe him when he says that did not play a role in the kidnapping.'

Bosch stood up and walked into the entrance hall. He made a call on his mobile phone.

When he returned he said, 'The police in Passau will be at Koch's house within a few minutes. As soon as I have returned to Munich, I will contact the Belgian police. Cross-border requests, even in the EU, require a lot more paperwork and red tape. You can contact me at any time and please, if you have any further information, I would like to hear about it immediately.'

'Don't worry. I will see that it happens,' said Sabine, speaking for the first time. 'Please tell me what you think the chances are of rescuing Eva?'

'I was concerned with the absence of a ransom note or any communication from the perpetrators but with this latest information about the Nazi trunk, I am more hopeful we can resolve this very soon,' said Bosch, standing up, followed by his two assistants. As he was about to leave his mobile phone rang.

'They have found Eva,' he shouted, 'she is at the Rosenheim police station.'

Sabine started sobbing. Reinhard jumped up excitedly while Silke punched the air.

'We will go there immediately. Follow me,' commanded Bosch, 'I will use my blue light.'

'This is the best news I have ever had,' said Reinhard, his eyes filling with tears.

CHAPTER 21

The police car and the BMW pulled up outside the police station in Rosenheim. Bosch was the first one inside, followed by Reinhard, Sabine and the others. Bosch held up his police identity card and asked to be taken to Eva, who was still in the social worker's office.

Sabine rushed into the office. As soon as she saw Eva sitting forlornly on a small chair with a book in her hand, she fell to her knees next to her and put her arms around her.

'My little darling. Are you alright?' she said between loud sobbing. Reinhard cradled both of them in his arms. Eva started crying as well but did not say a word.

'Well, well! This is a happy ending,' said Captain Brenner. 'You must be relieved,' he said turning to Bosch.

'This is fantastic,' replied Bosch, 'but we still have to find the grandfather.'

Silke stood close by and seeing the sad, dirty little girl, brought back memories of her childhood, memories she tried to block away but which somehow seemed to reappear in her dreams and nightmares.

The social worker went over to Reinhard and Sabine.

'Your daughter has been examined by a doctor and other than some minor scratches, she is fine physically. She obviously has been severely traumatised and I recommend that you get her to a child psychologist as it is best not to let whatever has happened, fester in her young mind.'

Reinhard had tears in his eyes, 'I want to thank everyone here for everything you have done, and I would like the name of whoever found her. I think we should leave as Eva needs a lot of care and attention right now, not to mention a good bath. Thank you, thank you.'

'We will arrange for someone to take Miss Kotter back to Munich. Mr. and Mrs. Heinrich, I am so pleased that young Eva is safe and sound. Of course we will need to speak soon but today is just for you to cuddle your daughter.'

After having an obligatory coffee and a police chat, Bosch asked for the name and contact details of the person who had delivered Eva to the police station.

He rang the number, and it was answered by a woman who confirmed that her name was Ingrid Lang, and that she had taken Eva to the police station. She said however, that she was not the one who had found her. The driver of the car that had stopped, had told her that the young girl had been sitting at the side of the road, where her farm road intersected it. Bosch thanked her and informed her that police investigators would be despatched as soon as possible.

Bosch turned to Brenner and asked if he would get a forensics task force together, to comb the area thoroughly for any clues that might lead to the identification of the perpetrators. Brenner agreed and went to the detective section at the rear of the building to muster the required team.

Bosch shook his head and said to Keller and Hoffmann, 'I hope you have nothing on tonight. It could be a late night.' Then he remembered. 'I had better phone my wife.'

Less than an hour later, a police convoy consisting of two vans loaded with forensic equipment, a marked police car and the unmarked car of Bosch, arrived at the farm of Ingrid Lang. She had tied the dog up but this didn't stop him tugging at his chain, barking and growling furiously. Although it was now nine o'clock, there was still sufficient light for the investigation to begin. In addition, they had brought powerful searchlights, should they need to work after dark.

Bosch went over to Ingrid Lang and introduced himself.

'Mrs. Lang, may I ask you a few questions please? The young girl you brought to the police station had been kidnapped, so I am sure you will understand the seriousness of this investigation.'

'I think I heard about it on the news. Wasn't there a grandfather involved?'

Bosch nodded, 'Yes and he is still missing. We believe we may find some vital clues where Eva was found. Do you live alone?'

'No, my husband is away at an agricultural fair, and my daughter is at the university in Munich. Alone for a few days, I suppose, would be correct.'

'Can I ask you to please let me have, in chronological order, the events related to the finding of Eva, the young girl?'

Ingrid Lang described the arrival of the car with the two women and Eva and then her subsequent trip to the police station.

'Not much to tell really,' she said. 'Wait. I remember Brutus barking at about seven-thirty this morning. I went outside but there was no one there. He is not a dog that barks for no reason, which concerned me, but then I forgot about it.'

'Thank you. That could be significant. I will go now and brief the team. Bosch walked over to where Brenner and the forensic team were gathered.

'Right guys, the young girl could have been dropped off here as early as seven-thirty this morning. Now, she must have arrived in a vehicle. Did it park on the roadside or did it go off-road? We are fortunate in that today it was dry, so there could still be tyre tracks, footprints or anything else. The car that drove her up to the farm gate was apparently a VW Golf. I was also informed that no other vehicles were here today except Mrs. Lang's Renault van. I will be here with Captain Brenner should you need me. You know what to do. Call me if you spot something of importance.'

The men were joined by Bosch's assistants and split up into three teams. They started their systematic search. They had put on sterile white overalls which covered them from head to foot, to reduce any contamination of the investigation site.

'Do you think we will find anything of importance here?' enquired Brenner.

'One never knows, but I have learnt over the years that often something which appears insignificant, can provide vital clues. Thoroughness is the detective's best weapon. Tonight we can only hope.'

Brenner's walkie-talkie crackled. 'They have found recent tyre tracks off the dirt road in the direction of the trees,' he said. 'Shall we go and have a look?'

They walked up the path to the trees. Bosch went down on his knees and looked at the parallel tracks that veered off the dirt road. Other tracks showed where the vehicle had reversed and returned to the road.

'We must take casts and have them identified. They are very wide and look to my eye like the ones where the kidnapping took place. I obviously can't be certain, but they are definitely not a standard car size. Well done, guys.'

The tyre tracks stopped near the tree line, and adult-sized footprints went from the tyre tracks to the tree. Smaller prints led away from the tree but then disappeared when they reached the grass. Bosch was pacing up and down, trying to build the scene in his mind. He could imagine a car driving off the road to the copse and someone getting out, presumably carrying Eva. She had been put down next to the tree, and the vehicle had then left. Perhaps they could establish which direction the vehicle had taken, if the tracks hadn't become too intertwined. He then started planning the necessary actions to be taken the following day. He would need to contact the police in Passau. It would be great, he thought, if Eva would just tell them what had happened. Maybe he should call on the Heinrich's to update them?

It was almost midnight when the forensic team leader joined Bosch and Brenner in one of the vans, where they were having a hot cup of coffee provided by Ingrid Lang.

'I think that is about all we can do tonight. We have photographed tyre tracks and footprints and taken impressions. We have collected a number of small items, which may or may not be connected. Oh, by the way, both the tyre tracks seem to indicate that the vehicle came from the direction of Rosenheim and returned in that direction too.'

Bosch thanked the men from Rosenheim for their invaluable assistance and he and his two colleagues headed back to Munich. After dropping them at the police headquarters, he went home, hoping that his wife would be in a sound, alcohol-induced sleep. He opened the door quietly, took off his shoes and went through to the bedroom. As he opened the door to the bathroom, the sleeping figure sat up in bed.

'Is that you Georg?'

'Sorry I am late. We found the missing girl in Rosenheim.'

'Come and talk to me. I have been on my own all day and night.'

'Darling, I am so exhausted. Please wait until breakfast and I will tell you the whole story.'

There was no response, so he had a shower and within a few minutes, he too was asleep.

CHAPTER 22

It was early morning and Reinhard was awoken by a scratching on the door. He got up and as he opened the door, Blondi rushed in and jumped on the bed. She went straight to Eva, who had spent the night nestled between her parents, and started licking her face. Eva, who was half asleep, suddenly shouted out, 'Blondi!' This was the first word she had uttered since leaving the island. She hugged

314

the dog and Sabine had to restrain Blondi, who was beside herself with canine joy.

'Did you hear that Reinhard?' asked Sabine, who had started crying. She hugged Eva and once again Blondi jumped all over them. 'My darling, are you happy to be back home?' Eva just looked at her and it was obvious she had once again entered her silent world.

Later, just after eight, the phone rang. Reinhard answered it. It was Bosch wanting to know how Eva was, and if he could visit and see if any information could be gleaned from her. When he heard that Eva was still refusing to speak, he suggested that he should bring along a child psychologist. Reinhard agreed on condition that it would be very low-key and must cease if it appeared to cause any stress.

Bosch telephoned his wife, as he recalled that the hospital where she had previously worked had a psychiatric ward.

The response was so different to her usual bi-polar behaviour that Bosch was taken aback.

'Leave it with me and I will get someone to contact you,' she said. She was so pleased to be needed.

Twenty minutes later, Bosch received a call from a well-spoken person who introduced himself as Doctor Krueger, a psychiatrist specialising in children with problems. He explained that although he had a busy schedule, he could rearrange some of his appointments to allow him to visit Eva that morning. He elected to drive himself to the Heinrich's estate.

They arrived within ten minutes of each another. Bosch had waited for him and before going inside, he gave Dr Krueger a brief background to the kidnapping, as well as the previous day's events.

Bosch and Dr Krueger then went inside and were taken through to the lounge. Dr Krueger sat directly opposite Sabine and Reinhard. Eva sat on the floor holding onto her mother's leg. He made no attempt at this stage to engage with Eva, wanting her to first get used to his presence and to see that he presented no danger to her.

Dr Krueger sat back and in a calm, well-modulated voice said, 'Now first let me give you some general descriptions of the effects of shock and trauma, particularly in children. It is very common for emotional traumatic events to cause temporary amnesia; a disorder called dissociative amnesia. This happens frequently to people who have been involved in war situations or earthquakes. Many soldiers suffer from it. There are many other associated reactions, one being speech loss. In a young child wanting to block out an event, a defence mechanism they can hide behind, is to stop speaking. The need is to get away from the experience, to build defences and to become less vulnerable. It is the classic case of denial.'

'How long can this go on for?' Sabine asked.

'There is no hard-and-fast rule, and it depends on a number of factors. Generally, with a young child, it will be of a temporary nature. There are instances where there have been long-term learning difficulties, however, this is rare. We have to give her back her self-confidence. She has to feel safe, and the true healer is love. She is fortunate in that she has returned to her parents. There are many instances in war zones where a young child is the sole survivor, and then the healing process takes much longer - some of the scars are there forever. Tell me, has Eva not said a word since you were reunited?'

'Only one word,' said Reinhard. 'When my father's dog jumped on the bed this morning, she called out her name, Blondi.'

'Hmm, that is interesting. Animals can often play an important part in the recuperative process. Hello Eva. Is it alright if I call you Eva?'

Eva looked at him but made no response.

318

'Look I have a small sucker. Do you want to try it?' Krueger pulled out a round sucker from his coat pocket.

Eva buried her head behind her mother's legs.

'Is it possible to fetch the dog?' Krueger asked, addressing Reinhard. Reinhard stood up and left the room. 'I know something that you do like,' continued Dr. Krueger.

Reinhard carried a wriggling Blondi into the room and put her down next to Eva. She immediately pulled the dog towards her.

'What is your dog's name?' asked Krueger. 'No name? Can I give him a name? Let's see, what about Silly?'

'His name is Blondi,' said Eva defiantly.

'Blondi? What a lovely name. Do you love Blondi?'

She nodded.

'Does Blondi love you?'

Eva nodded again. Then she started crying.

'I am tired,' she said quietly. This was her first sentence.

Krueger smiled, 'That is enough for now. I think perhaps we have found the key in Blondi. Inspector Bosch, I don't think this is the right time to ask Eva anything about the ordeal she has been through. She needs reassurance, and this is best provided by her parents and her dog. I am confident that she will make a speedy recovery. If you will excuse me, I think I should leave now. I need to get back to the hospital. Good-bye Eva and Blondi, see you soon.'

Eva looked away and tugged at her mother's dress.

Reinhard escorted Dr. Krueger to the door. He spoke quietly to Reinhard.

'Eva needs a lot of care and encouragement now. I realise that she could have important information regarding the kidnapping but don't try to probe too soon or too aggressively. Here is my card. Should Eva begin to open up on the problem, please call me immediately as we need to approach this with great care. We do not want her to slip back into silence but it is a very precarious situation once she starts talking.'

Reinhard thanked him and shook his hand. He returned to the lounge where Bosch and Sabine were in conversation and Eva was playing with Blondi.

'Detective Bosch, we are really so grateful to you for finding Eva and feel that this is half of our problem solved. However, my father is still missing and this is obviously just as important to us.'

'We now have a good body of clues and evidence to work with, so I am feeling more confident. Little Eva no doubt holds the key to this mystery, but we will have to wait. If she says anything, even something insignificant, you must let me know right away. Now, unfortunately, I need to get back to my desk so please excuse me.'

*****

Once he was back at the Munich police headquarters, Bosch updated his whiteboard with the latest information and then called a meeting. In addition to his two assigned staff, the Area Commander, Dieter Hess and the Head of Forensics, Karl Friederich were also invited.

As soon as everyone was seated, Bosch began the meeting.

'We have had a major breakthrough in the Heinrich kidnapping. There will be a press conference in an hour and we need to discuss what information we wish to reveal, but more importantly we need to find Mr Heinrich. Young Eva Heinrich was taken to the Rosenheim police station yesterday, after a passing motorist spotted her on the side of a minor road on the outskirts of Rosenheim. I have to acknowledge that we played no part in her discovery, but I believe we are starting to build up enough information to enable us to conclude this investigation. If you look at the information to date,' he said pointing to the board, 'you will see that I have connected a number of people and incidents.' The diagram was very similar to the one given to him by Silke.

'Adolf Eicke, a former partner of Hermann Heinrich is a key player in our investigation,' he continued, pointing to the name on the board. 'It seems he concocted some sort of blackmail scheme with a Jewish jeweller in Antwerp, known as Otto Mayer. This is a very strange combination because Hermann Heinrich's father is none other than Heydrich, one of Hitler's top aides. I trust you youngsters have heard of Heydrich. That is why I have written 'neo-Nazi' next to Hermann's name with a connecting line to Adolf Eicke. Eicke is a German citizen who resides in Vienna. In addition to this Nazi puzzle,

Eicke told Reinhard Heinrich that yet another possible neo-Nazi, Wolfgang Koch was involved. He lives in Passau, and I have asked our colleagues there to check him out, however, he is not at home at present - a neighbour saw him leaving with a suitcase two days ago.'

'This sounds very complicated to me,' remarked Dieter Hess. 'Are these people really neo-Nazis as we know them and why would neo-Nazis get involved with a Jew in Holland? Strange bedfellows to say the least!'

'Yes indeed,' replied Bosch. 'At this point I am calling them neo-Nazis because of their backgrounds. Perhaps they are not. I have to say that I am not convinced that Reinhard Heinrich has told us all he knows. He is holding back on certain information. Why? I do not know. I have warned him several times about this aspect. I suspect there are still some skeletons that will come out of their cupboards. In order for us to proceed, we need to question Adolf Eicke. Then we need to trace Mayer and

Koch, and we need to find the old man as soon as possible. If you look at the map of Bavaria, we are dealing with a small area within a radius of roughly one hour's drive from Munich, with Garmisch to the south and Rosenheim to the east. I am convinced that this is where we will find Hermann Heinrich.'

'Why do you think they released the girl and not her grandfather?' asked Hess.

'My guess would be that they weren't expecting her to be at the house when they arrived. They then dumped her, as it would be difficult holding a young child. Maybe they still need the old man for whatever reason prompted the kidnapping in the first place.'

'That would indicate that we are not dealing with violent criminals, some of whom would not have thought twice about killing her,' observed Hoffmann.

'Let's hope that is the case, especially for the old man, who is obviously still being held because they haven't got what they want from him. I would like to allocate some tasks. Karl, can you contact your opposite number in Rosenheim and see what forensic evidence was collected last night. Hoffmann, can you continue to track Koch - get hold of the Passau people or even go there. We have to find him. Keller, I want you to see how far the Belgian police have got in tracing Mayer. If things get sticky with them, then perhaps Captain Hess will assist you. I am going to phone the Vienna police and get myself there as soon as possible. Oh, Hoffmann, can you also maintain contact with the Heinrich's, in case the little girl has said something useful.'

Turning to Captain Hess he said. 'Shall we discuss the press conference?'

'What about the young woman we met at the Heinrich's?' asked Hoffmann. 'What was her name? Kotter?'

'I don't think we need amateur sleuths. She and Reinhard Heinrich have caused enough of a delay already.'

CHAPTER 23

When they were alone once again, Reinhard and Sabine spent time playing with Eva and Blondi. It was very apparent that a strong bond existed between the little girl and the dog. Gradually, Eva was starting to laugh and

327

giggle, and she must have wondered why she was getting so smothered in hugs and kisses. Her cold mother was transformed into a doting, loving woman who could play and romp around the floor, even if it meant that her hairstyle would be in disarray. Eva, with Blondi's assistance, decided to make the most of it. For a while, just a short while, she could put aside the memories of her nightmare.

After about an hour of play, Reinhard made two phone calls. The first was to a security company who were requested to provide a 24 hour armed presence at the house. The second call was to Silke waiting at the Art Hotel in Munich. She confirmed that she had been working for several hours and had established that Adolf Eicke hadn't sent any e-mails to Mayer or anyone else since they visited him. She explained how she had gone into the land registry sites in the state of Bavaria. Under the name of Wolfgang Koch, only one property was registered - that was the one in Passau. She had dug deeper and found that

Koch and his son Wilhelm, had a number of directorships in investment companies that included property, finance and a restaurant. The property portfolio listed a total of three investments which were in the hands of an international letting agency. One was a penthouse in Berlin, another a ski lodge in Oberaudorf, and the third was a chalet on a hillside overlooking the bay at Andratz in Mallorca. The restaurant was in Passau. Silke felt that Koch could be hiding at one of his investment properties. She agreed to contact the rental company to see if any of the properties were available to rent. They concluded their conversation and Reinhard rejoined Sabine and Eva in the lounge. Eva, exhausted by all the activity, started falling asleep. Sabine propped her up against a cushion, and Blondi snuggled up next to her.

'Who was that second call to?' enquired Sabine, trying to tidy her hair with her hands.

'I phoned Silke. She has unearthed some more information. I am amazed at her ability with a computer.'

'I don't like her,' Sabine said abruptly.

'What reason can you have for disliking her?' questioned Reinhard. 'She has done more work than the bloody police!'

'She is a twenty-year-old upstart and full of herself. She has a funny accent, probably some low class Austrian one.'

'Oh come on, Sabine. You can't judge someone purely, by their accent. She doesn't sound low class to me.'

'Now you are defending her. I suppose you fancy her because she is from the gutter.'

'Sabine this is nonsense. She is young enough to be my daughter, besides we need her expertise if we are to find my father. Please, don't be destructive, especially at this time. Let us be happy Eva is here, but we also need to find my father.'

'Alright, I hear what you say but I am watching you.'

Just then the phone rang. It was Silke.

'I have made contact with the rental agent. The property in Mallorca is fully booked for the next nine weeks. The Berlin penthouse will be available only from next week but the lodge in Oberaudorf is available now. I think we should go there, however, you need to tell Bosch.'

'I agree,' said Reinhard. 'I will be at the hotel within the hour. Please wait for me outside.'

He went back and told Sabine of the latest developments. 'Unfortunately, I will have to go to Oberaudorf right now, as this could be a very positive lead that Silke has unearthed.'

'Why not let the police handle it,' responded Sabine, sounding slightly annoyed.

'They are too slow and we need to act quickly.'

He bent down and kissed her and Eva, grabbing a wind-cheater jacket from the hat-stand as he hurried to his car.

As he drove at a high speed on the motorway to Munich, he realised that he was experiencing a strangely, conflicting emotional experience. There was the euphoria at having found Eva, but this was coupled with the gnawing fear and doubt as to his father's whereabouts. He kept asking himself how his well-ordered life was now in such chaos. He had lost control of it and was being dragged along by influences beyond his control. As he approached the outskirts of the city, the traffic slowed considerably and then came to a halt. After being at a standstill for over five minutes he reset the GPS requesting an alternate route. He made a sharp u-turn and followed the new instructions.

He saw an anxious Silke pacing up and down on the pavement outside the hotel. He pulled up with a slight screech and Silke jumped in the car. She gave Reinhard the address in Oberaudorf which he entered into the GPS. A moment later a reassuring female voice said, 'In one hundred metres turn left.'

Reinhard phoned Bosch and told him about the findings Silke had made with regard to Koch. He was clearly very annoyed because he obviously felt Reinhard was once again acting on his own. Bosch insisted that he should only approach Koch if accompanied by a police officer. He said that he would arrange for someone from the Rosenheim police to meet them . A few minutes later a call came through to Reinhard. It was from Capt. Brenner, who advised Reinhard that he would meet them at Koch's house. Reinhard gave him the address and smiled at Silke, who had heard the blue tooth conversation.

Reinhard obeyed all the GPS instructions and pulled up at the address in Oberaudorf as the voice said, 'You have reached your destination.' He saw the police car parked a discrete distance away. He flashed his lights, and the driver's door opened.

The air was much cooler up in the mountains even though it was July. It was also very quiet, as this was essentially a winter resort. The few people who came to the resort to hike would have started their walks much earlier than this.

Reinhard and Silke got out and greeted Capt. Brenner. 'So we meet again. How is your daughter, Mr Heinrich?'

'She is fine, thank you. Now hopefully we can find my father and get those responsible for this awful deed into prison.'

'Inspector Bosch gave me a short briefing, and I understand you have a suspicion that Koch is somehow involved. We have no hard evidence at this stage, and so we have to be very careful. As the police, we are allowed to interrogate him but he has every right to object to the presence of you and the young lady. Sorry, I have forgotten your name.'

'Silke. Silke Kotter,'

'Let us see then if he is here, and we will play it by ear,' continued Capt. Brenner.

Brenner led the way up the short path to the door and knocked loudly.

Silke wondered if policemen generally knocked louder than other people. They could hear noises inside and then the door was flung open.

'Yes?' said Wolfgang Koch. He looked straight at the police ID badge that Brenner held up to his face.

'Police. We would like to come in as we have a few questions to ask you.'

'In connection with what?' Koch responded abruptly.

'May we please come in, and I will explain,'

Koch stood aside and the three entered. Koch gestured to the couches placed in the centre of the room. It was very untidy, with newspapers strewn about and several dirty coffee cups on the table.

Brenner began, 'Perhaps you have seen all the publicity concerning the kidnapping of a young girl and her grandfather. Fortunately, the young girl is safe, but our search for the grandfather and the perpetrators continues.'

'What has this got to do with me?' Koch asked, his eyes revealing his anger.

'We have information that you knew the victim, Mr. Hermann Heinrich. We thought you could assist us.'

'The last time I met that gentleman was at least five years ago. I cannot help you.'

'I would then like to ask you a few questions. When did you arrive at this address?'

'I don't want to answer any questions. In fact, you don't have any right to be in my house.'

'We can either question you here, or if you refuse, and it is your right to do so, I can instruct you to come to the police station for questioning. That is my right as an investigating officer. Which will it be?'

Koch took a deep breath and sighed, 'What exactly do you want to know?'

'How long have you been here?'

'This is the third day.'

'Who else has been here with you?'

'I have been here completely alone, as you can see I am on my own.'

'What was your relationship with Mr. Hermann Heinrich?'

'We were friends. Our fathers were comrades in the war.'

'When was the last time you saw him?'

Koch punched his hand, 'I have already told you. About five years ago, but I don't know the exact date. I have had nothing to do with his disappearance.'

'No one is implying that, Mr. Koch. We do, however, have to investigate all avenues. Will you allow us to search this house?'

'Certainly not! Not without a search warrant.' Koch was obviously buying time.

Brenner stood up, followed by Silke and Reinhard. 'Very well then, that will be all for the time being. We could come back for further questioning. Here is my card should you wish to tell me anything further. Goodbye.'

Koch slammed the door after they left and collapsed onto the couch. His mind was in a whirl. How could they have got here so quickly he asked himself? He went to a cupboard and poured himself a whisky to steady his nerves. Why the hell did they have to kidnap Hermann, the bloody fools. He had to be careful how he communicated with the others. He would go to an internet cafe, he decided. Then there would be no trace of his communications.

Brenner told Reinhard to follow him to Rosenheim so that they could have a discussion at the police station.

'I don't like the look of him. What is your impression of Koch?' Reinhard asked Silke, as he pulled in behind Brenner's car.

'His anger suggests that he knows more than he is prepared to admit to. I happened to notice four pizza boxes on the kitchen counter. That seems a lot of pizza for someone on his own.'

'That was very observant of you,' said Reinhard. 'Perhaps you should pass that information on to Brenner.'

Reinhard parked outside the Rosenheim police station and went inside with Silke. Brenner was waiting in the entrance and ushered them into his office.

'That man is hiding something, which is why he became so aggressive,' he suggested.

'What can the police do?' asked Reinhard.

'I will get a search warrant, and we can be back there in two hours. If he is guilty, this could pressurise him, but first I will need to let Bosch know, as this is his case. Mr. Heinrich, I am impressed by your detective work even though my colleague, Bosch, is not all that happy with it.'

'Not mine,' said Reinhard. 'All praise should go to Miss Kotter, who by the way spotted four pizza boxes in the kitchen which suggests that there were other people at the cottage.' Reinhard gave her a smile and continued, 'I thank you for joining us, as I can see we would not have got past the front door without you. Please can I ask you to keep us informed if the search should reveal anything? I am extremely worried about my father as he takes tablets for his blood pressure, and he will get very ill without them.'

'I am not completely up-to-date with the investigation, but it appears that pieces are starting to fit into the jigsaw. You may see a conclusion sooner than you realise. Why don't you go home now, and I will keep you informed if we make a breakthrough at Koch's house?'

As they drove off Reinhard turned to Silke. 'Why don't we stop at a roadside restaurant for something to eat? I am sure you must be as hungry as I am.'

'Actually I am,' replied Silke. 'I missed breakfast at the hotel this morning. I saw a nice garden restaurant on the way down here, about ten minutes before Rosenheim.'

When Silke spotted it, she called out and Reinhard pulled into the parking area. It had a backdrop of trees and because of its elevated position, there were lovely views over the valley.

They sat down at a table alongside a window. After reading the menu and placing their order, Reinhard turned to Silke.

'I know I have said this many times in the past few days. You are a remarkable person, and I have to thank you for the tireless effort you are putting into solving my terrible predicament. What is it that drives you so?'

Silke was slightly embarrassed by the compliment.

'Where I come from, my very survival has been because I am driven, as you call it. I have become emotionally and personally involved with the kidnapping. I suppose I am also driven by revenge. I am determined to catch whoever did this. How can someone make Eva suffer? What has that child done to anyone?'

'I think I know where you are coming from. I too want to see justice done for what they have put my family and I through.'

'I have to admit that I enjoy being ahead of the police and seeing their annoyance. I hate people in authority. If you give people any kind of power, sooner or later they abuse it. I also hate seeing cruelty to animals. As a species, we have used our brainpower to dominate the rest of the animal world. I often lie awake at night thinking about the suffering that animals have to go through at the hands of man - it can make me cry. We have abused this

343

power in the most horrible fashion, even to animals we have domesticated and who give us unconditional love. All over the world, children are also being treated cruelly. In fact, cruelty in its many forms and guises is built into our genes.'

'You have very strong views Silke. I like that. There is not a lot of grey in you, just high definition white and black. I have just had a thought. Perhaps you will allow me to adopt you.'

Silke laughed, 'With no opposition from your wife? I can see she doesn't think much of me, with my home-based hairdo versus her manicured blonde. It would have to be our secret.'

Reinhard smiled and sat back as the food was placed before them on the table. He found something very appealing in this unusual girl sitting opposite him. She was attractive, in an East European Slavic way rather than the Teutonic looks of his wife, but it was her mind, courage and determination that he found magnetic. She was the street fighter that he wasn't.

'Getting back to our case, Silke, what can we do to solve the rest of this bloody mystery quickly?'

'As I see it, there are three main culprits that we know of - Eicke, Mayer and now Koch. Three old men, none of whom would be capable of carrying out a kidnapping. That tells us that there must be accomplices or people who were commissioned to do the dirty work. Eicke, if we believe him, was on the periphery, so let's leave him out of the equation for now. We know that both Mayer and Koch left home at about the same time. We have found Koch but not Mayer. I need to see if I can find any link between the two of them over the past week. As you know, I can still get into Mayer's computer. Maybe I will have another look . What if Mayer is also in this part of the world? Could it be under his own name or an assumed one? There is a lot of work for me to do today. Hmm. This schnitzel is lovely.'

On the journey back to Munich, Silke worked on her laptop while Reinhard made several calls to people at the bank.

Reinhard dropped Silke off at the hotel. He then went to AH Bank before heading home. They agreed that he would contact her the following day, to see what other information she may have been able to glean from her hacking.

CHAPTER 24

Wolfgang Koch parked his car in a metered parking area in Rosenheim. He had never been to an internet cafe before and hoped he would be able to manage. He knew how to use his own computer and to send e-mails, but now he wanted to make a clandestine connection with several people. As he turned the corner, he noticed a narrow shopfront with flashing lights announcing that it was an internet cafe. It offered cheap calls to Turkey and a few other destinations. He walked past the shop, as he was still in a very nervous state and unsure of what he needed to do. He crossed the road and sat on a bench that was situated in front of a small floral display. He did not want to act impulsively, as he needed to collect his thoughts. He had received no communication from the other three, so he could not contact them yet. Sending an e-mail or a text message could be courting trouble as he didn't know what the police had discovered. The best person to speak to would be Adolf Eicke, who had started all this trouble and was now sitting pretty in Vienna, blissfully unaware of the volcano that was about to erupt. He pulled a telephone index out of his pocket and looked up Adolf Eicke's name. He saw that next to his name he had a telephone number; a mobile phone number and an e-mail address. A quick telephone call from the internet cafe would be his best option, he decided. He walked back across the road and entered the shop.

He asked the Turk who was sitting behind a dirty counter, if he could make a phone call to Austria. The Turk pointed to a row of telephones. Bar stools had been placed in front of each phone and on either side, someone had erected ineffective privacy boards, which were covered in numbers and strange lettering. Koch picked up the phone and gave it a thorough rub with a tissue, hopefully wiping away most of the immigrant germs that had been placed there by lonely people, wanting to hear the voices of relatives and friends in faraway lands.

He dialled the number shown in his telephone book. It was answered by Eicke.

'Adolf, Wolfgang here. I must be quick. The police have just been to see me. We must meet.'

'What the hell is going on? Hermann's son was also here. Would it be possible for you to come to Vienna?'

'I can do anything. This is an emergency.'

'Right then, I am going to give you the number of my housekeeper's mobile. We will use her for contact. When you have landed, contact her, and she will give you directions. Have you got a pen? The number is 076 2298767. Let me know which flight you are on. Good-bye.'

Koch paid for the call and returned to his car. Once he had arrived back at the cottage, he contacted his travel agent and asked for the next flight to Vienna, plus accommodation for one night. He had just completed a hurried packing of some clothes, toiletries and medications into a bag, when the travel agent phoned to confirm his travel arrangements. The flight was scheduled to depart in four hours' time. A booking had been arranged at the Meridian Hotel, situated on the Opernring in the Altstadt. He phoned for a taxi, deciding to leave his car at the cottage. He didn't mind driving along country roads or in small towns, but he felt he wasn't confident driving around airports and cities.

As soon as he had been booked onto the flight, he sent a text message to Eicke's housekeeper giving his arrival time.

Koch was seated at a window in the small business class section of the plane. He looked out of the window but he was so preoccupied with his thoughts, that he wasn't aware of what he was looking at. How could everything have gone so horribly wrong? He meant no harm to Hermann with whom he had enjoyed a friendship going back decades. Now he was dead. He was too old to have this level of stress and worry. He focused his eyes and saw that they were coming into land at the airport on the outskirts Vienna.

*****

Wolfgang Koch only had a cabin bag with him, so he proceeded through to the Arrivals Hall with little delay. He switched on his phone, and a beep indicated that he had a message. "Meet at 3 pm, Cafe Frauenhuber, Himmelpfortgasse 6". Koch went out of the airport building and hailed a taxi. He sat back in the comfort of the leather seats with a deep sigh as the events of the day had exhausted him.

Vienna is famous for its coffee houses, many of which are like history books. Mozart, Strauss, Freud and even Hitler frequented them. Some catered for the bourgeoisie, others for the aristocracy and at the bottom of the pile, there were coffee houses that were only frequented by Marxists, Trotskyites and an assortment of left-wing revolutionaries. Cafe Frauenhuber attracted artists and actors and looked like a cellar with its sweeping arches and dark wood-panelling. It claimed to have a history going back to 1824. Eicke had chosen it because it had some alcove seating where one could sit in seclusion, thus making it ideal for private conversation.

Adolf Eicke had arrived before Koch and was seated in a quiet part of the coffee house in a small alcove. He had a cup of coffee next to him and a house newspaper. All the coffee houses have several copies of the daily newspapers, which clients can read at leisure. There is never any pressure to leave, such as one feels at Starbucks. Wolfgang Koch spotted Eicke and went over and sat down opposite him. They made no show of greeting one another.

'A coffee for you?' asked Eicke, putting the newspaper on the chair next to him.

'A coffee for now, but later I will need something stronger. Adolf, I am too old for this bullshit. It has all gone wrong. The whole bloody thing has blown up in our faces.'

He proceeded to explain how Hermann and his granddaughter were taken to a lake to find the trunk, and how he had died of a heart attack. He told of the release of Eva and the arrival of the police. Koch kept questioning how the police could have connected him so quickly.

'I think the problem lies with Hermann's son, Reinhard and some strange IT private eye he has employed. She is getting in everywhere. This woman is dangerous,' said Koch pointing his finger at Eicke.

Eicke nodded in agreement. 'But first let me tell you about the visit by Reinhard and the woman, her name is Silke Kotter by the way. She infiltrated my computer and perhaps Mayer's as well. They said they had enough evidence to implicate me in the kidnapping. I was confused as I knew nothing about any kidnapping and in my confusion, I think I mentioned the meetings we used to have at Hermann's house before he became a recluse. Your name and Mullers came up. I can only think that Reinhard and this girl have gone against their word and contacted the police. How the hell did it escalate from a simple blackmail to a double kidnapping and a death? Somebody, and I presume that it is your son and Mayer's idiotic judgement, has got us into this shit.'

'Maybe that is true,' said Koch gritting his teeth to keep his voice down, 'but some arsehole gave my name to Hermann's son, and now the cat is out of the bag. From now on, we all have to have the same story - do you understand?' He waited for Eicke to confirm with a gesture that he understood and then continued. 'There can be no direct connection to the kidnapping for either you or me. Do not offer any further information and this meeting never took place. I don't care about Mayer's son, as long as he doesn't implicate Willy. Willy must lie low and let the police run around chasing their tails.'

'That is all very well,' said Eicke, 'but have you considered that there could be circumstantial evidence linking you, Mayer and me. Something I think they call, conspiracy to commit a crime. I don't think you realise how wrong this has gone. Why - because of a lack of planning? If this had played out correctly, we could have got what we wanted from Hermann, and he would not have been able to go to the police because of the bank's background.'

'Recriminations will not help us now. We have to see how we can minimise the danger. You think this Silke Kotter, that was her name, represents the biggest threat?'

'I am only saying that because she seems to be able to break into computers, and she seems bright, even if she does look very young.'

'That's weird, what does she look like?' asked Koch.

'She looks Hungarian or Russian with those high cheek bones. Very striking features. She is working for Hermann's son, Reinhard.'

'Bloody hell! I am sure she was at the cottage with the policeman from Rosenheim. There was another man there as well. Could it have been Hermann's son? Yes, yes, now I can see the Heydrich resemblance. Shit, shit so they were there. No names were given. Why was I so stupid? Does she work for the bank?'

'No, she gave me a card the first time. IT Wache, I think the company is called. They are based in Vienna.' Koch's phone beeped once. He checked it and saw a number and Willy's name.

'That was Willy. He wants to make contact.'

'Why don't you get back to the hotel and contact Willy? Perhaps it is time for me to die soon.' Eicke looked tired and worn out like a lion who has decided that it is time for him to walk away from the pride and find a quiet, permanent resting place.

'I feel exactly the same as you do. I am staying at the Le Meridien Hotel. Why don't we go there for a meal and a change of conversation topic? It will do us good to reminisce about the good old days, rather than dwell on the mess we are in.'

Eicke nodded in agreement.

CHAPTER 26

Willy Koch arrived at the modern airport in Palma Mallorca. There were several agents situated in the Arrivals Hall, offering accommodation and car hire. By the time he had got to the fourth desk, he was starting to become concerned as there appeared to be no accommodation available on the island. It was July, and a long weekend was coming up. He saw a man dropping a parcel of tourist guides at the official information desk, so he approached him and asked if he knew of any available accommodation on the island.

The man recognised Willy's German accent and addressed him in German.

'Well it is my good fortune to have found a German. Walter Schmidt,' said Willy, shaking his hand and using the first false name that came to mind.

'Andrew Egan. Actually, I am English but I lived and worked in Germany for several years, so I speak a little German. I can tell you now that you won't find it easy to get accommodation over the next ten days. How well do you know the island?'

'This is my first visit,' lied Willy.

'I live in the north of the island, in Alcudia and I think I can fix you up with something. One of the advertisers in my guide has an apartment which he rents out, and I think that it may be available. Do you have a car or do you want to come with me?'

'May I come with you as I wasn't planning on moving around,' said Willy with a big beaming smile. 'Just parking off in one place and soaking up the sun. I have heard that Alcudia has some great beaches. I can't tell you how grateful I am.'

The road from the airport to Alcudia in the north, skirts around Palma and joins a motorway running through the centre of the island, passing through olive and almond groves. It bypasses the towns of Santa Maria and Inca and ends up in Alcudia, which is a somewhat nondescript town that thrives on the hordes of cheap package holidaymakers that arrive each summer, largely from Britain. One road, in particular, Avenida Pedro Mas y Rues, is known to the locals as 'The Greasy Mile'. It is home to most of the cheap, all-inclusive hotels in the north of the island. These in turn are surrounded by bars and restaurants that make it seem like Blackpool on the Med. Union Jacks flutter outside pubs and restaurants, with names like Linnekers, Winston, and Lady Diana, all trying to entice punters by offering non-stop television featuring Coronation Street and all the Premier League football matches. Many of the tourists who come to this part of the island do not even go to the beach, preferring instead to sit in a pub from ten in the morning to midnight, watching the television while binge drinking on watered-down Spanish beer or plonk wine.

It was here that Andrew drove to a small restaurant called the Foxes Den. The owner had an apartment in the grounds of the house they rented. Willy waited in the car, but he could see on Andrew's face when he returned, that he was not going to be in luck.

'No luck there. I tell you what,' said Andrew as he got in the car again, 'I am going to take you to my house where I will make a few phone calls and if the worst comes to the worst, you can doss down in my second bedroom. Normally, I wouldn't do this, but we seem to have so much in common, that I am sure it will be mutually acceptable.'

'Andrew, I will insist on paying you, and tonight I would like to invite you to enjoy a meal with me. I looked at your guide, and this Restaurant Boy looks like a good place. I would like to taste some typically Mallorcan food. What do you think?'

'A very good place indeed and surprisingly it is German-owned. They have the best steaks in town as well as traditional Mallorcan fare.'

Willy used his charm to good effect on Andrew. He felt even more secure now that he was staying in relative anonymity. He would wait until the following day before contacting his father.

The conversation that evening was relaxed. Willy invented a story about his work in various charities in Germany and even hinted that he could be interested in getting involved in Andrew's publishing company, with promotions to German tourist agencies. This caused some animated conversation as Andrew was hoping to find additional finance in order to grow the business. Willy almost slipped up several times when Andrew addressed him as Walter, and he didn't respond. At least once,

362

Andrew raised his eyebrows but assumed it was related to a language difficulty.

*****

The following day, Willy explained that he had left his mobile phone in Germany and asked if it would be alright if he arranged for his father to phone him on Andrew's landline. He used Andrew's mobile to send the number. In the early part of the evening, the phone rang and Andrew indicated that it was for Willy. Andrew went upstairs to give him privacy. His father was calling from yet another internet cafe. He explained in detail what had happened since Willy had left - how they had been betrayed by Eicke and how a young girl had uncovered evidence against them. Willy made notes and asked his father to get more information on Silke Kotter. Willy suggested that maybe he should return to Germany, but his father was insistent that he should stay on in Mallorca for at least another week.

Willy was shaken by the call, and the news that the police were onto them already. He went upstairs to his bedroom and surprised Andrew, who had Willy's passport in his hand.

'Why are you looking at my passport, Andrew? I didn't think you were like this.'

Andrew's eyes widened 'I only came in here to tidy up,' he stammered, 'and your passport was lying on top of the desk.'

'Don't fucking lie, Andrew, it was inside my bag,' shouted Willy angrily.

'Listen, I am not interested in your bloody passport,' said Andrew throwing it on the bed. 'Anyway, your name is not Walter Schmidt. Perhaps you should leave. In fact, leave right now. You are obviously not who

364

you say you are and what else are you hiding besides your real name?'

Andrew was five foot seven and Willy was six foot two. Andrew only had a split second to see the palm of Willy's big fist approaching the side of his neck. The heavy blow caused the blood in the carotid artery, to momentarily stop flowing to his brain. He collapsed onto the floor. Willy bent down and tightened his hands around Andrew's neck and strangled him, just as he had strangled his wife and the Turkish migrant. He looked at the body lying on the carpeted floor and felt no emotion whatsoever.

Willy then went downstairs and partially emptied the chest freezer which was in a small room adjoining the kitchen. He then returned to the bedroom and dragged Andrew's body down the stairs and into the kitchen. He lifted the body into the freezer but found it wouldn't fit so he removed some more food items and eventually managed to close the lid. He placed some of the freezer items in the fridge and the balance he left lying on the kitchen floor.

Willy sat down in the lounge and started planning what he would say if anyone enquired after Andrew. He recalled from a conversation they'd had the previous evening, that Andrew had relatives in England. That would be the story he decided – an unexpected visit, something to do with the illness of a family member, perhaps a visit to his brother in England. No one would expect a German visitor to have more details than that.

He was able to calmly dismiss the murder and was completely relaxed as he walked to the Playa de Muro beach nearby. He had to collect his thoughts about something more pressing than worrying about Andrew's demise.

As he sat on a bench overlooking the calm waters of the Bay of Alcudia, one name his father had given him kept appearing before him - Silke Kotter. He didn't know her or anything about her - what she looked like; where she lived. He would find out, and he would make her disappear. He decided he would stay just a few more days in Mallorca, and then he would slip back into Germany. He wouldn't use airlines as they require photo IDs and their manifests are easily checked. No, he would take a ferry to France and then a train into Germany. If the authorities checked thoroughly enough, they would conclude he was still in Mallorca. He was pleased that he had been able to devise this plan so quickly, that his face broke out in a big smile. He stood up and started walking along the promenade. Earlier on, he had spotted what looked like a five-star hotel, so he headed in that direction. It was the Grand Palace de Muro, a large, four-storied hotel, built in the neo-classical style. Its outstanding feature was the impressive atrium, with huge glass windows that stretched up the full height of the building, providing a panoramic view over the sea and the beach as you entered the hotel.

He walked into the air-conditioned atmosphere and enquired as to the whereabouts of the restaurant. He was informed that there were three, and he chose the one with an Italian sounding name. He was shown to a table which had a pleasant sea view. It was still early, and the restaurant was relatively empty. To his left, a woman also sat alone at a table. She was reading a Kindle e-reader. When she looked up, Willy nodded and smiled at her. She returned the greeting.

'I hope you won't think I am being too forward, but I am fascinated by the device you are reading. Is that one of these new tablets?'

'Not quite a tablet but it is a Kindle reader.' She had a cultured English voice originating from south-eastern England. 'I have downloaded a number of books to keep me occupied while I am on holiday. This is a lot easier than carrying four or five books.'

Willy got up and went over to her table, 'May I have a look at it? Electronics never cease to amaze me.'

She handed the Kindle to him. 'Please sit down and I'll explain it to you.'

Willy sat opposite her while she explained some of the functions of the reader. She seemed pleased that a good-looking man had shown such an interest in her. Willy asked if he could share her table over lunch to which she readily agreed.

'My name is Andrew Egan, and I am over here on holiday from Germany. What is your name?'

'Angela,' she replied. 'You have an English name but a German accent.'

'My father was in the British Army based in Germany. He married my mother who is German, and I suppose he decided to continue living in Germany after he left the army,' he explained effortlessly, without losing a beat. He was such an accomplished liar.

He then went on a charm offensive, 'What is a beautiful woman like you doing on holiday alone in Mallorca?'

'I am recovering from a motor accident, and I thought I would get away from the so-called English summer. It has been particularly unpleasant this year. My husband was unable to get away from the bank.'

Willy, on hearing she had a husband, decided to abandon any thoughts about attempting a seduction and thought his afternoon could be more fruitfully spent making plans for his return to Germany and the elimination of certain people.

Willy enjoyed her company and the wine made him feel mellow. At the conclusion of the lunch he paid for both lunches and then excused himself. He indicated he had a prior arrangement to meet a fellow German at a bar in the harbour.

CHAPTER 27

The Crooked Star

The media interest started waning when it was announced that Eva had been found unharmed. They had turned this into another Maddie story, but fortunately this one had a happy ending, except for the missing grandfather. Reinhard had decided that he would continue, with the aid of Silke, trying to trace his father and to bring the perpetrators to book. Silke had discussed this with her colleagues and they agreed that she should stay as long as required. After hearing how dangerous it seemed, Novak offered to let her have the use of a small assassin's pistol he had acquired while in the army in Serbia. It could easily be concealed in the palm of a hand and held four .22 bullets. It was purely for close range and to be effective, the shots would have to be to the head. He arranged for a friend, who was visiting Germany, to drop it off with Silke.

Silke told Reinhard that she would continue working with him as long as he required her services. He explained that until his father had been found, and the criminals caught, he wanted to continue hiring her. He offered to open a bank account and deposit an interim bonus of fifty thousand Euros. He even suggested that she could have the use of one of the cars from the bank's pool. Silke didn't need much convincing and agreed on the spot.

She then set about gathering her thoughts and collating the facts yet again. She was actually enjoying the detective work she found herself doing and thought that perhaps it was her lifestyle after running away from home, where she had mastered various survival techniques that gave her the edge. She also had a strong sense of justice, even it was somewhat unorthodox. Before she could start, she wrote down €50 000 at the top of her notepad. It was such an enormous amount, that she needed to study the number carefully; to convince herself that it was true. She had never known financial security on this scale. Then she scratched it out with several strokes from her pen and started to write the kidnapping facts in the chronological order in which they had presented themselves. Sometimes, when one looks at facts from a different angle, a previously hidden clue emerges. This is what she was hoping for.

Her mobile phone rang. It was Reinhard.

'Bosch has just contacted me,' he said excitedly. 'He was making arrangements to visit Eicke in Vienna, when he was informed that he had died. It looks like suicide.'

'That is a pity,' replied Silke. 'I never felt he had told us everything he knew, and now he is gone. Some revenge for you, I imagine.'

'Not really. I knew him well and at one time he was a great friend to my parents. I know he acted badly and may even have set these events in motion, but somehow I feel he was misguided and in his mind harboured some old feelings of hurt. I can't believe he wanted to actually harm my father and daughter.'

'One day we will find out the truth, but for now we have to find your father. I want to visit Mr. Koch's cottage again and I am going to try to get into Mayer's computer. Do you want to come with me?'

'I think you should go alone. Please be careful and talk to Brenner or Bosch before you go. Sabine and I have asked Dr Krueger to come over and see if we can get Eva to give us any more information. She is much more relaxed and is even saying a few words.'

'Eva is such an important piece in this puzzle. It saddens me to see how traumatised she has been. No child on Earth deserves that. Perhaps we can talk later. Give Eva a hug from me.'

'Will do, and look after yourself.'

Silke pulled the computer closer and started her trawling operation into Otto Mayer's computer. She was surprised to find it was switched on but there was no evident activity. The inbox of his e-mail was empty as was the sent box and the deleted box. He had obviously decided to delete a lot of files, but Silke would be able to retrieve them from the rubbish bins that existed in the bowels of every computer. She couldn't believe her eyes when an electronic airline ticket popped up. It was for a flight from Amsterdam to Munich with an open-ended return. Then she noticed a second one for Albert Mayer for the same flight. So father and son had arrived in Munich a day before the kidnapping. This was too good to be true. Maybe they had stayed over at Koch's ski cottage? She was unable to find any other pertinent information. She decided that she would mention this find to Bosch, as the police were better equipped to trace if the Mayers had made any hotel bookings in the area. Before she did that, she decided that she would make an unannounced visit to the Koch ski cottage.

Silke contacted Reinhard's secretary and made arrangements to fetch a car from the bank. After the luxury of Reinhard's seven series BMW, she was slightly disappointed to find that the secretary had arranged for her to use a Volvo S40. However, she soon found the Swedish car was far from ordinary and had a good turn of speed, not that she felt confident about assessing this aspect. She had never owned a car and had mainly driven friends' vehicles and then usually at night, when she was the only sober one able to drive them home. She remembered the route to Koch's cottage and in less than an hour, she had parked a short way from the house.

Her plan was to search through the garbage bin, to try to ascertain whether Koch was telling the truth about having been alone at the house. She went up the path that led to the front door. She could see a window slightly ajar and music was coming from inside. She wanted to get to the rear of the house where she assumed the garbage bin would be situated, without being seen. She walked around to the side of the house and stopped, as she now had to walk past a window. It was quite low and not easy to crouch under. She crept up to it and peeped in. It looked like a bedroom, and as she could see no one inside, she held her breath and scurried past. Then she negotiated a second bedroom window without being seen.

There were two bins at the back of the house. She shook the first one - it seemed to be empty. Not so the second. She prepared herself for the smelly, dirty task ahead and opened the lid. It was about half full. She started unpacking the rubbish. There were four pizza take-out boxes, presumably the same ones she had spotted in the kitchen on her previous visit. She noted that they were all large ones. She retrieved some tied up plastic bags and opened them to examine the contents. The first one contained rotting peels and unused pieces of tomato and carrots. The second one had an overpowering smell and it looked like the scrapings from plates. She recognised bits of pizza as well some bones. At the bottom, there were two folded newspapers and a screwed-up piece of paper. Silke smoothed it out. Someone had written a long international number and the name 'willy' without a capital letter. She put it in her pocket. She was beginning to feel nervous, so she started repacking the rubbish into the bin. Before she could close it, the back door opened and Koch stepped out with a plastic bag in his hand. He was startled to find someone there and then instant recognition took place.

'I know you,' he said throwing the bag on the floor. 'What are you doing trespassing on my property?'

'I can explain,' said Silke closing the lid. She couldn't believe that she had been caught red-handed.

'Don't give me bullshit, you bitch. You and Heinrich were here with that policeman yesterday. Let me see what he has to say about this.' With that he lunged forward and grabbed Silke's arm.

She knew she was stronger than him. She clamped her hand over his wrist and applied downward pressure. He shouted and let go.

379

'I am calling the police. I will have you charged,' Koch screamed at the top of his voice.

Silke held up her hand, 'Let me explain. I am working for Mr. Heinrich. We have found his daughter, and we are now looking for his father, a former friend of yours. I did not believe your story about being here alone, so I have rummaged through your rubbish. It was wrong, and I apologise. The four large pizza boxes tell me that you had company. I think your son Wilhelm was here.'

'He is entitled to come and go whenever he wishes.' Koch had calmed down and was now concerned as to exactly what Silke had uncovered. 'If you don't leave in one minute, I will sound the alarm to get the police here. In fact, I am reporting this to the police in any event. I will lay charges against you. Now get off my property.'

Silke turned on her heels and walked away without looking back. She cursed under her breath at getting caught, but she felt it had been worthwhile, as she had proven circumstantially at least, that Koch had lied to the police about being alone all the time he had been at the house. She was expecting Bosch to come down heavily on her for acting on her own.

Silke returned to the apartment in Munich. It was very smartly furnished, possibly the choice of his mistress, she thought. It was on the third floor and overlooked the Alter Botanical Garden. To Silke, this was another aspect of unimagined luxury into which this project had plunged her. It was as if she had died and gone straight to heaven.

Silke pulled out the note she had recovered from the bin and looked at the number 0034971237999. 0034 was the international dialing code for Spain. She googled international telephone codes. This revealed that the 971 was the area code for the island of Mallorca. She decided to dial the number to see who would answer. After eight rings, a recorded message clicked on – "Hi, this is Andrew. I am not available so please leave a message and contact number. Thank you." This was followed by a long beep at which point Silke replaced the receiver. She thought it was strange for the message to be in English. She knew from her earlier investigation into Koch's affairs, that he owned property in Mallorca, but why would the telephone message be in English. Who was Andrew? She decided that she would see if she could get an address connected to the number in Mallorca. She would then contact Reinhard and maybe Bosch.

Silke maintained that her earlier assumption that the three old men, Eicke, Koch and Mayer, were unlikely to have got personally involved in a physical thing like a kidnapping, was correct. They would have used younger help. Otto Mayer flew into Munich with his son and Koch's son Wilhelm was at the cottage. Could it be that they decided to involve their sons - far better from a security perspective than involving outside parties. Eicke was dead and Koch's whereabouts was known to the police. The missing links were the Mayers and Koch's son.

382

As Wilhelm Koch was a company director, she could access some information on him, and she had other sources, including the new social media.

Thirty minutes later, Silke had drawn up a fairly comprehensive biography of Willy. Born in 1970 and like his father, he too lived in Passau. He listed skiing, travel and cars as his main leisure activities. Photos on Facebook showed him on a beach with a dark-haired girl and in a ski outfit with a blonde, as well as inebriated at several parties. He was evidently a popular man.

Silke decided to establish if the Mayers or Wilhelm Koch had taken any flights out of Munich. Most major airlines and travel agents use a central reservations system called Amadeus. While it is password protected and has a number of security checkpoints, the fact that it is used by so many people makes it open to illegal access. Silke had the operator password of a Turkish Airlines employee. If she tried to access it while he was active, then alarm bells would ring. She went into the system and typed in the Mayer's details which she had from their e-tickets. Their flight details came up immediately. Otto Mayer had taken a return flight to Amsterdam, and Albert Mayer had gone to Zurich. They departed within a few hours of one another. Why Zurich, Silke asked herself? She pondered this for a while and was on the point of closing the computer, when she entered the name "Wilhelm Wolfgang Koch." She wasn't expecting anything to come up. Then it came on the screen. On the same day as the Mayers departed, he took an Air Berlin flight to Palma de Mallorca. It was a one-way ticket. That explained the Mallorcan telephone number she had discovered in the rubbish bin. Silke couldn't believe her luck. She was building up a wad of information, not all of it making sense.

Now that she had even more evidence to add, she started re-organising her fact chart. Against her better judgement, she decided to contact Inspector Bosch and to reveal the latest information she had uncovered.

Bosch listened to what she had to say without interrupting her. He knew that successful detectives are usually good listeners. He then asked her to come down to the police station to present the information in person.

Bosch arranged for his two assigned assistants, Keller and Hoffman to be present at the meeting. When he mentioned it in passing to his boss, Dieter Hess, he also decided to attend but only as an observer, he indicated diplomatically.

Silke greeted everyone and shook Dieter Hess' hand.

'In England, I believe there is a female detective invented by Agatha Christie. I can't remember her name, but I know she is a funny old lady. Miss Kotter is Austria's version, but of course, she is very young as you can see.' Bosch smiled at his introduction and then continued, 'Our Viennese PI has uncovered some more information that could be useful in bringing this case to a successful conclusion. I want you to listen to what she has to say and also to ask questions and offer criticism. Over to you Miss Kotter.'

Silke looked at the whiteboard and saw a copy of her fact wheel, which she had given to Bosch. A slight smile appeared on her face.

'I would like to plug in my computer to your projector. That way, you can follow what I have uncovered.'

She had a list of the latest information which she projected onto the screen.

- Adolf Eicke - suicide
- Wolfgang Koch - presently at a cottage in Oberaudorf.
- Otto Mayer- returned to Belgium - present whereabouts unknown.

- Albert Mayer - flew to Zurich - whereabouts unknown

- Wilhelm Koch - flew to Mallorca - whereabouts unknown.

- Mallorca telephone number - telephone unanswered. Address: 40 Ctra Arta de Muro

- Answering machine mentions a name 'Andrew' in English.

'Now, this is purely my supposition. Based on the confession of Mr. Eicke, who implicated both Mr. Mayer senior and Mr. Koch senior, and taking into account their respective ages, they must have had younger accomplices. I believe these were the sons of the two gentlemen, namely Wilhelm Koch and Albert Mayer. To my mind, they are the culprits.'

'I can follow that line of reasoning,' said Bosch, looking at the projection on the wall, 'but where is Mr. Heinrich senior? Has he been hidden somewhere in

Oberaudorf? Has he been killed and his body hidden? If only Eva would tell us.'

Birgitt Hoffman raised her hand as if asking permission to speak. Bosch nodded at her.

'Tell me, how did you obtain this telephone number?' she asked in a brusque manner.

'I found it in a rubbish bin at Mr. Koch's cottage in Oberaudorf,' replied Silke.

'So, you had permission to go into his rubbish?'

'Not exactly, I helped myself.' Silke had been anticipating this question, nevertheless she said 'bitch' under her breath.

'Herr Hess, this is the problem one has with amateur PIs,' Birgitta remarked pointedly, turning to Dieter Hess. 'As we know from police training, illegally obtained evidence can be rejected in court and how much contamination of other evidence has now taken place at

Mr. Koch's house?' It was very clear that Birgitta Hoffman looked on the younger woman with a fair measure of disdain, coupled with a dose of envy.

Bosch answered, 'On two occasions, Miss Kotter has produced some very useful leads - the first time when she and Mr. Heinrich had information that they withheld from us and the second time, these new leads here. I am pleased that Miss Kotter has come forward as soon as this but it would have been much more useful if she had let us go to Mr. Koch's cottage ourselves for a thorough investigation of the property.'

Silke could feel anger welling up inside her, 'Then why haven't you done so? You now need to trace the two Mayers and Wilhelm Koch.'

Bosch smiled at the jibe. 'It may surprise you to know that the Belgian police have been to Mayer's home in Antwerp, where his wife maintains he is at a spa somewhere in Europe. We now need to involve both the

389

Swiss authorities and the Spanish. This is turning into a complicated international investigation. I don't want to dampen your enthusiasm, but I also don't want you interfering in legitimate police work.' Birgitta grinned as Bosch said this. Silke stared at Bosch and decided not to respond, as her acerbic wit would only further alienate the sensitive police.

'Miss Kotter,' said Dieter Hess, trying to defuse the tense situation that had obviously developed, 'we need all the help we can get from members of the public and the media. Without them, our job would be immeasurably more difficult. Please understand that for various operational and legal requirements, there is a dividing line beyond which only the police and associated organisations can operate. Blurring that line can cause chaos. We do appreciate everything you have discovered to date. Perhaps you would consider taking a job in the police force in the future?'

'I don't think so,' replied Silke, unplugging her computer. 'Good luck and I hope you find Mr. Heinrich soon.' She stalked arrogantly out of the room.

After she had closed the door behind her, Bosch looked at everyone at the table.

'I hope we have not been too rude to Miss Kotter. I didn't want to say this in front of her, but she has been much more successful in this case than we have. I am going to give you my ideas and then everyone can throw theirs into the pot, and we can start doing some real detective work.'

He opened a writing pad and scribbled a few notes.

'Koch's rubbish has revealed some snippets of information. Eva Heinrich was found near Rosenheim. Koch is staying, not at his house in Passau, but in a cottage in Oberaudorf, which is near Rosenheim.' He stood up and went over to a map of Bavaria.

391

'Look,' he said making a circle on the map with his finger. 'This is a very small area, and as I have said before, I believe it is here that we will find Heinrich or his body. I propose that we get search warrants for Koch's house in Passau, the cottage in Oberaudorf and his son's house in Passau too. We should use three teams and search the properties simultaneously.'

No one, not even Dieter Hess, wanted to add anything or question this decision, so the meeting was closed.

Bosch then called in a secretary to type the requests for search warrants to be issued. It would be a mere formality now that they had sufficient evidence pointing in the direction of the Kochs. He phoned the duty officer and arranged for the manpower to be organised for the searches. Finally, he contacted Brenner in Rosenheim.

CHAPTER 28

As soon as she got into her car, Silke contacted Reinhard and told him about her reception at the police station. He was angry and suggested she should come out to Garmisch so that they could look at developing their own strategy. He told her that Dr Krueger was busy playing and talking with Eva.

When Silke arrived at the Heinrich house, she was greeted by Sabine. She was surprised at the warm reception she received.

'Dr Krueger is playing some games with Eva. Even Blondi is involved,' said Sabine, obviously pleased with the progress her daughter was making. 'Come to the lounge where Reinhard is sitting. I will arrange for some coffee.' Reinhard was poring over a family photo album and abruptly closed it as Silke entered. He was looking very dejected.

'I understand Eva is making rapid progress,' said Silke as she sat down.

'Yes, if only we could find my father now. I have this dreadful feeling that he is dead. I contacted his doctor, and he is worried that if he doesn't have his hyper-tension medication, he could suffer a heart attack or a stroke from the rising blood pressure. I feel so helpless. Please go through what you have uncovered again as I didn't absorb it in on the phone earlier.'

Silke went over her latest discoveries and her theory about the two sons being the direct perpetrators.

394

'Tell me Silke, who will be easier to find, Wilhelm Koch or Albert Mayer?'

Silke thought for a while, 'Perhaps Koch. He is on an island, and we know he and his father have a property there. If we trace him there, we will have to ask the German police to assist us. The local police in Mallorca are not going to detain him on the flimsy evidence we have.'

'Have you ever been to Mallorca?' asked Reinhard.

Silke smiled, 'I have never seen the sea.'

'Oh, my goodness. Then why don't we make a quick visit to the island? It is only a two-hour flight from Munich on Air Berlin. I hope I am not being too impulsive, but like you, I feel that this Koch fellow is key to the kidnapping. I am sure we will be able to get a flight tomorrow. Is that alright with you?'

'Of course,' Silke replied quickly, hoping she didn't sound too enthusiastic.

'Shall we go and see what progress Dr Krueger has made?' said Reinhard standing up.

Sabine was sitting with Dr Krueger in the second sitting room. Eva and Blondi were both asleep on a big cushion on the floor, which was strewn with dolls, toys and pieces of paper that the dog had torn up.

'I apologise for the state of your lounge,' said Dr Krueger standing up and shaking Silke's hand. 'Good to see you again, Miss Kotter.'

'I have just been telling your wife,' he said turning to Reinhard, 'about the progress I have made. I have to say that it goes way beyond anything I expected at this early stage. Using this toy car, Eva showed me how she and her grandfather travelled in the boot. She doesn't want to say where they went and changes the subject if I press her. We have to be very careful about the pace we adopt - go too quickly and she could retreat into her safety zone of no memory. I have developed a fun game that slowly allows her to relive some of the traumatic events, but not in a frightening way. She tires easily so that is all I can do today. I am actually on a short leave period for this week, but I am so fascinated by your daughter's terrible experience, that I would like to suggest that I come again tomorrow, perhaps a little earlier than today.'

'That sounds like an excellent idea. We are very pleased to have someone like you devote this time to Eva. I may not be here but of course Sabine will.'

* * * *

Six police vehicles left Munich headquarters. They split into twos and headed in three directions. They were armed with search warrants and included in each team were forensic experts. Bosch had decided to go to Oberaudorf where he hoped to still find Koch at the cottage.

Bosch pulled up outside the cottage in Oberaudorf and the police van parked directly behind him. He went straight up to the door and banged on it. He could hear some soft classical music coming from inside and then the door opened. Wolfgang Koch stood at the door with a cleaning cloth in his hand. He had anticipated the police visit and had set about wiping down every possible place where any fingerprints could be found.

'I have a warrant to search this place,' announced Bosch, waving a paper at Koch.

Koch stepped aside and Bosch, followed by three policemen, followed him. 'We will be searching this house and we will be questioning you in connection with the kidnapping of Mr Hermann Heinrich and his granddaughter. You are not under arrest but I must tell you, that your house in Passau is also subject to a search warrant and is being searched right now. If there is no one there, then a locksmith will be used to gain entry. The same applies to your son's house in Passau.'

'This is quite ridiculous,' sneered Koch. 'Go ahead and make a fool of yourself.'

Bosch walked into the kitchen and saw that everything had been meticulously cleaned.

'You are a very good cleaner for someone of your age. Was there something you wanted to cover up?'

'Since when is being clean a cover-up?' retorted Koch.

'I would like to ask you some further questions. We can do it here in the comfort of your house, or we can go down to the police station.'

'We can do it here, but I first wish to call my lawyer.'

Bosch nodded, and Koch went into one of the bedrooms.

'Rubbish bin empty,' called a voice through the door.

Koch returned and sat at the dining room table opposite Bosch, who had already taken a seat.

'Fire away and waste some time. Have you not got something more worthwhile to occupy your time?'

'We will find out if it is a waste of time.' Bosch opened a pad. 'At this stage this is not a formal interview, but nevertheless, we can use information collected here in court. Tell me, when was the last time you saw Mr. Otto Mayer and Mr. Albert Mayer?'

The question had caught Koch by surprise, and he needed to buy some time.

'Mmm, let me see. That would be about a month ago in Antwerp.'

400

'Why did you see them in Antwerp?' probed Bosch.

'I went to look at some jewellery.'

'It seems a long way to go to look at jewellery! What is wrong with Hemmerle in Munich? They used to supply the Bavarian Court.'

'That may well be the case, but for me, Antwerp is the place for diamonds.'

Bosch looked directly into Koch's eyes, 'These two gentlemen were in Munich earlier this week. Did you not meet up with them?'

Koch was becoming a little agitated. He didn't know how much Bosch knew, or if he was on a fishing expedition.

'No,' he replied, rubbing his hands together to remove the dampness.

'Not even a phone call?'

'No.'

'Where is your son, Wilhelm?'

'Willy is on holiday in the Med. I don't know exactly where.'

'What if I said Mallorca?'

'We both go there several times a year, so it is very possible. Willy is an independent adult who doesn't have to report to me about his movements. I am sorry that I can't help you. Now I have a question for you. Why did that interfering young girl come and rummage through my garbage? That is trespassing.' Koch's voice was loud and angry, as he hoped to use attack as a defence strategy.

'She does not work for the police. She has connections with Mr. Reinhard Heinrich. You may lodge a complaint with the police at Rosenheim if you feel so inclined. I understand you have cleared away the rubbish

402

even though it is not the collection day?' Bosch didn't really have any idea which was the rubbish collection day.

'It was getting full, so I took it to the dump. Is there anything wrong with that?' responded Koch.

'You don't have to be on the defensive all the time. We are going to leave you now, but I have a funny feeling this won't be our last meeting.' Bosch stood up and let his gaze wander around the room. He walked slowly to the door.

Once outside, Bosch asked the forensic team to take the fingerprint evidence to headquarters and to co-ordinate the findings with that of the other two teams. He then made a call to his boss, Dieter Hess, in which he explained that he had deliberately had a short interview with Koch. He wanted to leave him worried and guessing - hopefully this would encourage him to make contact with his co-conspirators. Approval for surveillance and phone tapping had already been arranged.

Koch watched the police leave and was aching to contact Willy, but he was worried about the possibility of his phones being tapped. He would wait for Willy to contact him, he decided.

CHAPTER 29

It was a warm clear morning in Mallorca, with temperatures in the thirties predicted for later in the day. Willy Koch was boarding the early ferry from Alcudia to Menorca and from there he would catch a connecting ferry to Nice. It was peak season, and the ferry queue was long.

Overhead, planes were flying in hordes of tourists wanting to change the colour of their skins from pasty white to various shades of bronze.

As the flight from Munich left mainland Europe near Genoa, Silke had her first view of the sea from the window of the plane. The blue was different to that of the lakes in Austria, and it stretched all the way to the horizon. She was fascinated by the white wakes left by the fishing boats returning to port with their early morning catch. Her heart beat faster as she took in the beauty of this sea that was truly liquid history. She longed to be down at sea level and to be able to walk slowly into the sea's embrace - to smell it and to feel it and then to dive into it. More than any other sea or ocean, the Mediterranean casts a spell on all who see it.

Reinhard and Silke landed at the airport in Palma and went to the Sixt car rental desk, to collect the car they had booked a few hours earlier.

Reinhard knew Mallorca well, having spent many holidays here, mainly on the west coast in the affluent area around Andratx. He drove out of the city and took the main highway from Palma to the North of the island.

Carretera Arta is the main road linking Puerto de Alcudia and Can Picafort. Reinhard located the address that Silke had found from her directory enquiries, without much difficulty. The house which was in the name of Andrew Egan, was a neat townhouse with a small front garden. Reinhard rang the bell on the gate post. There was no reply, so he opened the gate and went up to the front door. He knocked loudly. There was still no reply so he and Silke walked around the side of the house. All the curtains were closed, and the carport was empty. They cupped their hands together and tried peering into the windows wherever there was a small gap in the curtains, but this revealed nothing at all. Silke went back to the front door and knocked again. She tried the handle, and found that the door was unlocked. She opened it slightly and shouted 'Hello' several times.

Reinhard looked at her and shrugged his shoulders, 'I don't think we can go in there,' he cautioned.

'What happens if the wind opens the door?' asked Silke, pushing it wide open.

Reinhard shook his head and peeped in. The interior was dark, lit only by the light entering from the open door. He felt along the wall and found a light switch. It was a small entrance hall. He could see rooms to the left and to the right and a stairway leading to the upper floor. He stepped inside followed by Silke. They took turns to shout 'hello' and when it was apparent that the house was empty, they nervously walked into the first room which was a lounge. A number of books and magazines were scattered on a table. A small alcove had been turned into an office, with a laptop computer and a printer on a small desk. It was eerily quiet. They went into the second room which was a dining room and from here a stairway led upstairs. Silke climbed the stairs and found there were two bedrooms and a bathroom on the upper floor. Both bedrooms looked as if they had recently been used. The bigger bedroom of the two had a powerful shortwave radio on a bedside table and an air conditioner that was still running. She went back downstairs to the kitchen where Reinhard had gone to investigate. She looked around for evidence as to how recently it had been used. There was a frying pan on top of the cooker. She lifted the pan and noticed that there was still some uncongealed fat in it.

'Reinhard, my guess is that someone made breakfast here this morning.' She tilted the pan to show him how the fat was still slightly runny.

'I think we should leave then. We don't want to be caught in here,' said Reinhard, starting to move to the passage.

Silke went into the scullery next to the kitchen and called out.

'Come and look here quickly.'

The floor of the scullery was covered with packets of what should have been frozen vegetables. A box of ice-cream was lying on its side, with liquid ice-cream in a puddle around it.

'What the hell has happened here?' shouted Reinhard, surveying the floor.

Silke tiptoed past the goods on the floor and lifted the lid of the freezer. She let out a scream and let the lid slam down.

'There is someone in the freezer,' she screamed. 'Quick let's get out of here.'

She ran out of the room, and out of the house followed by Reinhard.

'Who do you think it is?' asked Reinhard, visibly shaken.

'I don't know, but it was like one of those scary movies. Shit, that was the biggest fright I have had in a long time. Do we call the police or just leave? I think we will have to call the police as there is a neighbour watching us.'

'I agree. We have nothing to hide. I just hope we won't be delayed by this.'

Reinhard waved at the neighbour and walked to the wall separating the two properties.

'Buenos dias. Hablo Ingles, Aleman,' Reinhard was trying out his pidgin Spanish, which wasn't nearly as fluent as his English and French.

'I am German,' the elderly woman replied in German. 'Are you looking for Andrew? He is not here at present as he has gone over to England. In fact, he has a

German friend staying here at the moment. He may not be in, as I heard the car leaving very early this morning.'

'Is this the friend who is staying here,' asked Silke, producing two photographs she had printed off Facebook.

The elderly woman put on her spectacles and studied the photographs. Eventually, she nodded and said, 'Yes, that is him. I think he said his name was Walter. Do you wish to wait at my house until he returns? I like hearing about Germany.'

'Thank you, we will come in, but first we want you to please telephone the police. Don't be alarmed but there is a dead person in the house.' Reinhard avoided mentioning the freezer part so as not to alarm her unnecessarily. Even so, she was clearly shocked.

It took the first police car about thirty minutes to arrive, and this was followed in quick succession by a car from the Guardia Civil. Reinhard asked the German woman, whose name was Kristina, to act as an interpreter for them. Her twenty-five years on the island and a Spanish husband meant she was fluent in the local Catalan dialect.

Silke led the way into the house and through to the scullery, where she stood back and pointed to the freezer. A policeman opened the lid and let out an exclamation. Other officers squeezed in to have a look. An animated discussion took place among them, and several calls were made. A junior policeman went to a car and returned with a roll of red and white hazard tape which he proceeded to put across the front and side gates. Distant sirens became louder as several police cars and an ambulance converged on the scene. Through Kristina, Reinhard learned that they would have to accompany the police to the Alcudia police headquarters to make a statement. Another member of the Guardia Civil then arrived. The extra braid on his uniform indicated his seniority. He approached Reinhard and Silke and when he learnt that they didn't speak Spanish, he switched to passable English.

'This is a very serious matter. I am going to ask one of the officers to accompany you in your car to our headquarters. I trust that you will find this acceptable.'

'Certainly. It has to be okay,' replied Reinhard.

Reinhard and Silke got back into their hired car together with an officer. They followed the police car with its flashing blue lights.

At the Guardia Civil headquarters, they were ushered into a small office and offered coffee.

'I think we must tell them everything we know.' Reinhard spoke in a hushed voice to Silke. 'All we did was find a body. We don't even know whose body it is.'

'My guess,' said Silke, 'is that it is the body of this Andrew person, however, we don't know for certain. If Wilhelm Koch is behind this, then what kind of monster are we dealing with?'

413

'I must say I am glad we didn't walk into him at the house. Maybe then, there would have been two more bodies in the freezer?'

Just then Captain Nadal walked in and sat down at the desk. He was a dark- complexioned man in his early forties. He had a ready smile on his clean-shaven face.

'Before you ask,' he said smiling, 'I am not related to Rafa, our famous tennis player and I do not have his money. He does, however, live only about half an hour from here in the town of Manacor.'

He continued, 'Regarding the body in the freezer, well we have a name for the victim. He is an Englishman, Andrew Egan, who is resident here on the island. The next door neighbour, who is sadly in a state of shock, identified him. Apparently, there is a visitor from Germany staying with him. All the neighbour knows is that his name is Walter, and we are obviously hoping to speak to him.'

'His name is not Walter,' said Silke, pulling out the photographs and handing them to the policeman. 'It is Wilhelm Koch, from Passau in Germany. The police in Germany are trying to locate him and there is a warrant out for his arrest with Europol.'

'Very interesting. Now I have to ask where you two fit into this picture. What were you doing at Mr. Egan's house?'

Reinhard replied, 'It is a complicated story. You see, my daughter and father were kidnapped from our home in Germany a few days ago. We have subsequently recovered my daughter, but my father remains missing. We believe that this Wilhelm Koch could shed some light on the investigation. It was established that he had flown to Mallorca. All we had was a telephone number and an address, so Miss Kotter and I decided to come here to see if we could find and talk to Koch.'

'I would have thought your police authorities could have handled this matter on your behalf,' said Nadal sarcastically. 'So where does the unfortunate Mr. Egan fit into this?'

'We haven't any idea. We do know that Mr. Koch had some investment property over here, so perhaps that is the connection.'

'If you think that Koch is involved in your kidnapping case, do you think he is involved in this murder? What can you tell me about him?'

'We know nothing about him. His father was a friend of my father. To go back to your earlier question - the German police are fully informed of all the information we have. I just cannot wait for all the red tape, so we are doing a parallel search for my father. I can give you the contact details of Inspector Bosch of the Munich police.' Reinhard took out his wallet and handed Bosch's business card to Nadal, who noted down the details and handed back the card.

'How did you get into Egan's house?' Nadal asked abruptly.

Silke replied, 'The door was unlocked and when I gave it a push, it just opened. We called and when there was no reply, we entered and were alerted by the freezer food on the floor. It was then that we found the body. We immediately contacted the police.'

Nadal looked at both of them without commenting. He then wrote on his note pad.

'What you did was trespassing but it did result in your finding the body, so I am sure that it will be overlooked. I am still not happy with your story about what seems to be a private vendetta. What exactly did you intend to do with this Mr. Koch you came looking for?'

Reinhard said, 'We are not exactly on a private mission as we are informing the police whenever we come across any important evidence. We have reason to believe that Mr. Koch could help us in the search for my father.'

'If, as you seem to indicate, this man is implicated in a kidnapping and could now possibly have something to do with a murder, are you not being foolish in not involving our police force?'

'We were concerned that we did not have enough concrete evidence to convince the police here to start an investigation,' replied Reinhard. 'As you can see,' he continued, 'at the first sign of trouble we called you.'

'That was a sensible thing to do. Please understand that you are material witnesses and even possible suspects at this stage, so you will not be allowed to leave the island until you have been cleared. We will need to draw up a statement for both of you to sign.'

418

'Oh no! Please! Other than reporting the finding of the body, we have had nothing to do with this incident.'

'Perhaps, but we may need to question you further. You will have to leave your passports with me. Do you require accommodation?'

'I know the island,' replied Reinhard, 'I have been here many times.'

'Let me have your mobile numbers and it is important that you inform me where you will be staying. I would like to keep these photographs of Koch, if you don't mind.'

* * * *

It was late afternoon when the ferry arrived in Nice. Willy was feeling weary after the long sea voyage and would have preferred to have spent the night there, but as he was planning to catch a train to Munich, he decided against it. At the railway station, he found a public telephone and called the landline at the cottage. His father answered after just two rings.

'I am in France. I will be back tomorrow. Will phone then.' He hoped that the brief call would be understood by his father. He would book into a hotel in Munich the following day and arrange to meet his father.

It was a long journey with two changes, and Willy was absolutely exhausted when he finally reached his destination at Munich station. He went to the Tourist

Information office and was given the name of a pension near Gartner Platz, close to the Staatstheater. He took a taxi to a point two streets away and walked the final short distance to the pension. At the railway station, he had purchased a basic Nokia mobile phone. He assembled the phone and once again contacted his father. He arranged that they would meet at a coffee bar at the Staatstheater, and he asked him to bring along as much cash as he could arrange at short notice.

Willy found a quiet table at the coffee bar and ordered himself a strong Espresso. He sat drinking his coffee, confident that he had left no trail in Mallorca. In fact, he believed that even when the body was discovered, the police would be conducting a fruitless search for the murderer all over the island. There was no way he could be connected to the murder. He smiled when his father entered the coffee bar. Wolfgang sat down and looked around nervously.

'Don't be worried,' said Willy trying to be reassuring, 'I am still in Mallorca.'

'Yes, maybe, but that young, interfering bitch seems to be everywhere. Willy I am worried. This thing has gone horribly wrong, and I feel responsible. All I wanted was to find out the whereabouts of the panels and this is the shit we find ourselves in. First, a policeman came to the cottage, accompanied by two people that I now know were Heinrich's son and this woman Kotter. Then a whole group of police arrived with a search warrant and searched the cottage from top to bottom. They said they were going to search our houses in Passau. I hope there is nothing there to link you to the crime. Even if we didn't kill Hermann, we are still involved in a kidnapping.'

'You are not involved - just the Jew and myself. We can put the blame on him. You must sow the seeds with the police the next time you see them. Say that it was a conspiracy between Eicke and the Mayers. Leave the rest with me, I can handle it. Beyond that, all you do is deny everything and say nothing. Do you understand? The police and this girl are just clutching at straws from information that old fool Eicke gave them. Now give me all the information you have on this girl.'

Willy wrote down all the details on Silke that his father had collected from Eicke. This was mainly the name of the company she worked at, her surname, the registration number of the car she had used when he caught her on the property and a description which didn't get beyond 'tallish, slim with blonde hair.'

Willy then handed his father a sheet of paper with nine numbers on it, against which each had a description.

'Let me explain,' said Willy. 'When I contact you, I will just give you a number, nothing else. Next to the number on the page is the message. For example, number 2 says meet me down the street, left. So whether you are here or at your house or wherever, you must pretend you are taking a walk. You go left when you exit, and I will be waiting for you at some suitable point. I made up the messages on the train trip. This is just in case someone is tapping your phone. It is better if you don't know where I am staying. I left my car at the airport, can you please fetch it? Here are the keys and the ticket. I know it is in section D. Move it to the long term parking where it won't arouse suspicion for at least a few weeks. Now only in an absolute emergency must you leave a message at this number. I will put my phone on once a day to check if there are messages.'

After some small talk, they left the coffee bar. Willy was determined to start building up his information base on Silke.

His first call once he got back to the pension was to find the number of IT Wache in Vienna. He dialled the number and asked for Silke. He was told by a woman who answered the phone that she was in Germany and her return date was unknown. He persisted and was given her mobile phone number. He then tried to see if she was listed in the Vienna telephone directory and came up with three S. Kotters. He would have to do some elimination work, so he decided to see if he could get any information out of AH Bank, as it appeared she was working for Reinhard Heinrich. When he asked for her by name, the receptionist said that she had never heard of her. He gave a brief description, and he was then put through to Reinhard's secretary who said that Silke was away with Mr. Heinrich but refused to divulge any further information. Willy tried all his charm, saying that it was Silke's birthday and that he just wanted to wish her. The secretary then said it would not be possible as she was in Mallorca. He cursed as he disconnected the call. What the bloody hell was that bitch doing in Mallorca? Could she have somehow picked up his trail? How could that be possible, he wondered? He had purchased the ticket at the airport. He had used a credit card but there was no way she could access such information.

* * * *

Reinhard had booked them into the Boatel Hotel in Puerto Alcudia. The hotel has one of the best positions in the town, being situated on a promontory next to the yacht harbour. After checking in, Reinhard took Silke to the hotel shop where they bought extra clothing for their unexpected delay on the island. He also persuaded her to buy a bikini so that she could have her first swim in the sea. Silke, who had developed a distrust of most people but especially men, felt herself warming to Reinhard. She sometimes found herself looking at him and thinking that here was someone who could really be the caring father figure she had never known. Then she would steel herself and think of something else.

'Why don't you give me an hour or two to make some calls and then perhaps we can meet for a swim,' suggested Reinhard.

Silke agreed and after putting her purchases in her room, she decided to take a short walk to familiarise herself with the harbour nearby. The Boatel Hotel is linked to the yacht basin by a long pier. Silke was amazed at the size and grandeur of some of the yachts moored in the harbour. Who can afford such luxury she questioned – possibly Reinhard she concluded. Once she got onto the main boardwalk, she immediately saw the contrast to the opulence on the pier. Tacky restaurants interspersed by even tackier curio shops and sleazy pubs, made up Alcudia's port area. It was apparent that the target market was mass tourism, brought over on budget airlines.

Silke read some of the menus which are placed on lecterns outside each restaurant. Spanish cuisine was noticeably absent; with the ubiquitous pizza appearing on all the menus, even if the name of the establishment was clearly not Italian.

Silke walked past the harbour and came to a point where it opens into the Bay of Alcudia. She sat on a rock and took in the beauty of her surroundings - the Mediterranean had grasped her in its embrace. She looked at the intense blue of the water and watched as it gently lapped against the rock. Water, the sea in particular, often induces a deep sense of introspection in many people. Silke looked at the gentle ebb and flow of the sea and in her wildest dreams she could not have imagined such natural beauty. It was alive. The dervish-like activities of the past days had completely overwhelmed her senses. In some ways, it brought her terrible recent past back into focus. She was still fighting to distance herself from the disturbing thoughts that crept into her consciousness each and every day. She could hear the muffled voices in the adjoining room where her new born baby was being snatched away from her. She wanted the memories to be pushed into the deepest recesses of her brain where they could be forcibly restrained. She desperately wanted her child reunited with her. She lost all sense of time until suddenly she looked at her watch and realised that she needed to return to the hotel.

She found Reinhard waiting for her near the swimming pool. She waved at him and rushed up to her room to change into the bikini he had bought.

The hotel doesn't have much of a beach but there is a strip of sand from where one can slip into the sea for a swim. Reinhard ran into the water and called back for Silke to join him. She shrugged off the towel, and he was amazed to see what a lovely figure she had. She had slim hips and shapely legs. There was not an ounce of fat on her he observed.

She approached the water gingerly, going in up to her ankles. Reinhard had swum closer to her and suddenly splashed water on her and pulled her into the sea. She screamed with both fear and delight.

'It is so salty,' she shouted, 'and so warm.' She propelled herself forward into the deeper water.

'So, you can swim,' said Reinhard, coming up alongside her.

'Of course, but I have only been in fresh water. This is fantastic. I could spend a whole day here. Thank you so much.' She felt the urge to hug him but was unsure of his reaction, so she swam away instead. She continued swimming even though Reinhard had got out of the water and was sitting on a lounger provided by the hotel for its guests. When she finally emerged from the sea, he stood up and wrapped a towel around her and gave her back a brisk rub. Her make-up had come off, and he could see a different person.

That evening Reinhard decided that they should eat in the hotel restaurant which overlooked an infinity pool, across the bay of Alcudia to the main beach. It is a beautiful sight on a warm, calm evening. As the sun started to set, the sea became like a pond with slowly-changing colours. The luminescent blue gradually darkened and streaks of red formed on the horizon, before it all went black. Reinhard had persuaded Silke to buy a full-length, white shift, and even he was impressed with how glamorous she looked when he called for her. She had put on slightly more make-up than usual, but as it was evening it seemed perfect.

'My God, but you look beautiful,' he said as they walked to the stairway. She was embarrassed by the compliment and gave a false laugh to dismiss his comment.

They sat at a table next to a window, giving them a wide view of the bay. Reinhard could see Silke taking it all in like a child in a toy shop at Christmas. He loved to watch Eva in similar circumstances when she was confronted by something new. He thought it must be wonderful to be so in awe, at seeing something lovely for the first time. He recalled his first visit to Venice and even Paris and how he had absorbed all the beauty those cities offered. He still felt the same way about the Alps, but so much of the world was just ordinary to him now. At times like this he regretted that his privileged position had made him so blasé.

'By the way, I spoke to Detective Nadal. He says they have confirmed that the man had been strangled, and that Koch is the prime suspect. They have put out alerts at the airport and the ferry stations. It is not easy to get off an island, so my guess is that he has gone into hiding. Nadal wants to see us tomorrow, and then we are free to go. Oh, and he has spoken to Bosch, who is apparently as mad as a snake with us, for going off on our own again.' Reinhard burst out laughing and Silke joined in.

'I have provisionally booked our return flight for midday. Don't look so disappointed.'

Silke pouted, 'I know we have to go, but I have just experienced the best few hours of my entire life. I understand we are in the middle of a tragedy for you, so I appreciate that you have allowed me to experience such joy.'

Reinhard held her hand, 'You are like a daughter to me. I owe you so much.'

'I was hoping you would say mistress. However, I suppose somebody else has beaten me to it.' Silke couldn't believe what she had said. She held her hands to her face. 'I am so sorry! I shouldn't have said that.'

'Come on, Silke. I would love to have you as a lover if it wasn't for the 25-year age difference - stop being so negative about yourself.' He wagged a finger at her in a mock display of recrimination. 'Now we will have some wine to celebrate your introduction to the sea.'

'To Aphrodite, the Goddess of the Sea,' said Reinhard, smiling as he and Silke clinked glasses.

Silke smiled at the Freudian slip, for she knew that Aphrodite was not the Goddess of the Sea but the Goddess of Love.

CHAPTER 29

Dr Krueger came over to the estate early in the morning, as he had arranged with Sabine the previous day. Eva ran up to him and greeted him with a hug. It was obvious that in a short time he had gained her trust. Although she associated him with games and fun, he was confident that she would slowly be able to reveal more of what had taken place - perhaps only in an indirect way. He needed to be careful and not expose raw nerve endings that her childlike mind still found too terrible to verbalise.

'Right Eva, I have another game today. See this big board. It is a map, and we are going to have a lot of fun getting lost. Where is Blondi?'

'He is having his food. I have finished all of mine. Shall I get mommy to fetch Blondi?'

'Let him finish his food first. I am going to lay this board on the floor.'

Dr Krueger had taken a big piece of cardboard and with cut-outs from several magazines, as well as some drawings, he had produced a composite of various scenes. Some were urban with buildings and others more rural with trees, mountains and rivers.

'Eva, you have to sit on the floor next to me,' Dr. Krueger beckoned to her to sit on a cushion he had placed on the floor. 'Now with this game, you have to drive the car and at certain points you will get a reward of a sweet.'

Eva clapped her hands in delight.

435

'This is where our journey starts,' said Krueger, placing the toy car next to a house. 'This looks like your house.'

Eva nodded in agreement.

'Do you see all the roads leading away from the house? You are the driver so you must say where we are going today.'

Eva studied the map looking carefully at the various options. 'I want to go to the mountain.'

Dr. Krueger pushed the little car in the direction.

'Look, there is a cross near the mountain. You have won a sweet.'

Eva clapped her hands again and squealed in delight.

After a few more car journeys, Krueger left the map and he and Eva played with Blondi, getting her to retrieve a rubber ball. This resulted in some unruly behaviour.

Sabine, who was watching from a distance, thought it was as if nothing had ever happened to her daughter.

After an hour, both Eva and Dr. Krueger needed a rest. She fell asleep on the couch and Dr Kruger sat down with Sabine.

'I think I am getting somewhere. We drove all over the map in the little car I am using. She chose the path the car would take, but she flatly refused to go near the photograph of a lake. Is there a lake in this area?'

'We have plenty of lakes. The nearest one is the Eibsee, just beyond Grainau. Then of course there is Plansee and Welchensee. Those are our nearest ones and further afield there are numerous lakes. Do you think she was taken to a lake? What about Chiemsee, near Rosenheim, where she was found?'

'That now opens up a vast investigation, as it is unlikely that she will be able to pinpoint a specific lake. It was so apparent that the image of a lake made her frightened, that there has to be something in it. Perhaps when she wakes up, we could take a drive to the three lakes you mentioned. It is a long shot but it could produce some results. We have to do this gently so as not to cause her to clam up again. It must be a continuation of our game.'

Sabine drove, while Krueger sat in the back seat with Eva, relaxing her with a game of recognising passing bits of scenery. They pulled up at the restaurant at the Eibsee, and as soon as they got out, Eva clung onto her mother and insisted on being carried. They went to the water's edge but Eva refused to join Dr. Krueger in throwing stones into the water. A pedal boat went by with a woman and two young children in it. Krueger asked Eva if she wanted to go for a boat ride. She started screaming.

They walked away from the lakeside and at a kiosk Sabine bought Eva an ice-cream. She had calmed down but she wouldn't move anywhere without having her mother close by.

The visit to the Eibsee had clearly traumatised her and at the next two lakes, she flatly refused to get out of the vehicle. On the return journey, Krueger managed to pacify her and when they returned to the house, she appeared to have regained her normal self-composure once again.

'I will give Inspector Bosch a report on today's findings, which are very intriguing. It is obvious that Eva associates the lake and boats with the traumatic experience she has had. I cannot push her anymore at this stage. She has been amazing, but she simply needs to play for the next few days and get back to her normal routine. If you don't mind, I would like to phone you each day to discuss her progress. After seeing her reaction at the lakes today, I would like to ask you to watch out for any regression that may occur.'

Eva stood next to her mother and waved goodbye as Dr Krueger drove away.

* * * *

As soon as Bosch received Krueger's report, he asked a forensic expert and his two junior detectives to join him. They headed down to the Eibsee in Bosch's car. He believed that detectives have to absorb all the evidence and facts, even though usually seem disconnected. One then has to use gut feel to start unravelling the loose ends - that is why he always said that age improves detectives. He had seen and heard a lot in his career and he had been through much personally, so when he had a gut feel, he listened to it. He now had one about the lake at the base of the Zugspitze.

'I have been informed that there is not much at the lake,' he said, addressing the two detectives as they approached their destination, 'only a hotel, a restaurant and a boat hire. We must question anyone who may have been there or seen anything on the day of the kidnapping - anything out of the ordinary, but especially if they saw an old man and a young girl. Where did they see them? Who were they with? Where did they go? Anything suspicious. What the hell am I telling you this for? You learnt all this in college. You have your photographs of the old man, and the little girl but in any case, this has had extensive coverage on TV and in the papers. If we draw a blank, then there are two more lakes in the area which we will need to investigate.'

Bosch chose the hotel, Keller the restaurant and Birgit Hoffmann went to the boat rental.

The Crooked Star

No one at the hotel or restaurant could recall seeing an old man with a young girl or anything that aroused their suspicions. Hoffmann initially received a similar response from the young man in charge of the boat-hire office. Then he recalled a foreign man who had rented a pedal boat that day. He said that he had thought it strange at the time, that a middle-aged person would do so on his own. He noticed the boat heading south to the section of the lake left of the hotel. Later, he saw that several other people were on board, but it was too far for him to recognise anyone. They seemed to be heading in the direction of the main island. The boat was only returned two hours later, which in itself was unusual, as most people only hire them for thirty minutes.

Bosch sat on a bench with his colleagues. They decided that it would be worthwhile to reconnoitre the islands. Bosch went over to the lifesavers' office and they agreed for a lifesaver to accompany the policemen in one of their rubber ducks.

The lifesaver beached the rubber duck on the first island and everyone clambered off. The undergrowth was thick and reached into the water, except for the small patch where they had pulled in. Bosch spotted that something had been dragged into the undergrowth. It must have been recent, he concluded, as the plants hadn't yet recovered. The drag marks went far into the bushes. Bosch asked the lifeguard if people went onto the islands. He informed him that it wasn't allowed, as they were the duck breeding grounds. They spread out slightly and started searching for any clues of recent activity. It had rained the previous evening, making the ground soggy underfoot and any footprints had been obliterated. Bosch was not confident that they would find anything worthwhile on this muddy island.

Just then Keller shouted that he had come across what appeared to be a recently broken branch. They rushed over to him. He pushed the branch aside which revealed the recently disturbed mound of earth.

443

Bosch asked the lifeguard to radio the base and have someone bring a spade across to the island.

As soon as the spade arrived Keller started digging into the soft sand and soon saw that it was just an empty hole. They saw further disturbed patches and Keller dug into these as well, but to no avail. At this point the lifeguard offered to take over the digging task to relieve Keller, who by now was sweating profusely.

He pushed the spade into the ground and it hit against something solid. He scraped away some of the soil and Bosch shouted, 'Stop! That is a human head!' They all gathered around the hole. It was clearly the top of a human head. Grey hair matted with mud could be seen.

'Phone HQ and get a full crime scene team out here right away,' instructed Bosch. 'This could be the old man. I think we should wait until everyone is here with the correct equipment. Also, we need contamination suits so that we don't disturb the crime scene, which is why we should go and wait at the boat.'

Bosch didn't join the others at the boat but stood a short distance away and looked across the lake. How terrible, he thought, that such an idyllic place could be defiled by a murder. He took in the view. The lake was still and rising above it into the heavens was the majestic mountain that dominated the skyline. A duck glided by, barely breaking the water. Bosch tracked its movement until it disappeared from view on the other side of the small island - nature at peace, but mankind in turmoil.

CHAPTER 30

As soon as they entered the arrivals hall at Munich airport, Reinhard switched on his phone and a series of beeps indicated that he had messages. He saw that Sabine, Bosch and his secretary had left messages for him.

He phoned Sabine first. She informed him that a body had been discovered on an island on the Eibsee and that he would be required to identify it. He sat down at the nearest seat and told Silke the news. He was having difficulty holding back tears. The message from Bosch asked him to call the police headquarters. He telephoned Bosch, who confirmed the news and asked if Reinhard could come to his office.

Reinhard said very little on the drive into the centre of Munich, while Silke worked on her laptop.

They were taken through to the Commander's office where Bosch was already seated.

'It is a bitter-sweet victory,' said Dieter Hess. 'You have your daughter back in your hands but sadly, we believe your father is no longer with us. There is a strong resemblance to the photographs we have. The case is not closed, and it won't be until we have the perpetrators behind bars. We haven't established the cause of your father's death, but we are treating it as a murder and kidnapping case which is as serious as it gets. The entire Federal Police Force is looking for the prime suspect, Wilhelm Koch and we have initiated international warrants for Albert Mayer as well. We have searched Koch's property and those of his father. I am waiting for the full report.' Hess hesitated and then continued, 'I am afraid that you will be required to identify the body.'

He opened a file that was on his desk. 'The Belgian police, as you already know, have interviewed the wife of

Otto Mayer. It says here that she is a frail woman, possibly suffering from dementia and doesn't know the whereabouts of her husband and son. She mentions a health spa. Then also, we have contacted the Swiss police. They confirm that Koch arrived on a flight from Munich and after that they have no further information. They will also institute a search for him. Now, Inspector Bosch has some questions for you.'

Bosch looked first at Reinhard and then at Silke.

'This is not the time to have yet another discussion about your involvement in private investigations. You know my feelings on the matter. I have received a report from the Guardia Civil in Mallorca. The Spanish police are keeping an eye on all possible exit routes from the island. Would you tell me from your side what happened?'

Silke took the initiative, much to the obvious annoyance of Bosch, and proceeded to give precise details of what they had found in Mallorca. It was difficult to fault her logical and rational description of the events.

Bosch finished some notes he was writing and said, 'If Koch is indeed involved in the murder of this person in Mallorca, and if he is also involved in the kidnapping and possible murder here, then we are dealing with a dangerous man. I am going to see if he has had any prior brushes with the law.'

'I think his father knows more than he is saying,' said Silke. 'In fact, I think he and Eicke, in Vienna, were intricately linked in the kidnapping. What a pity Eicke committed suicide.'

'We are going to bring Mr. Koch senior in for formal questioning, which will increase the pressure on him. I presume you will be going back to Vienna,' said Bosch, directing his last comment at Silke.

The Crooked Star

'I may retain Miss Kotter's services for a short while yet,' replied Reinhard, on her behalf.

* * * *

As Reinhard pulled up outside the apartment where Silke was staying, she leant over and gave him a kiss on the cheek, 'I am so sorry about your father. I hope you can get your life back to normal again soon. Let me know when you want me to leave.'

'Please not yet. I would like you to stay for a day or two longer, as I wish to go through your notes with you, to finalise everything. I just need some time to come to terms with my father's death.'

That evening, after playing with Eva and talking to Sabine, Reinhard went down to his bench in the garden and once again looked into the clear night sky. He wondered if the crooked star was satisfied with the disaster that had befallen the descendants of the Butcher of Prague,

Reinhard Heydrich. Even innocent Eva had suffered! Where would it end?

The following day he met Silke at the apartment. He was feeling subdued but in a strange way, relieved that the ordeal was finally over, even if the culprits still needed to be caught.

'Well Silke, what a time we have had! You took it all in your stride, and your brilliant mind made up for the ineptitude of the authorities. I will never forget you, and even if you won't come and work at the bank, I want us to stay in touch.'

Silke was hoping he wouldn't bring up the night she had spent in his bedroom in Mallorca.

'I have learnt a lot during this short period, and I have had some life-changing experiences. I will certainly stay in touch,' she said sadly.

451

'Today I am going to deposit into your bank account another fifty thousand Euros. Spend it wisely.'

'Please, that is too much money,' protested Silke. 'You have already paid for my services and given me a big bonus. I cannot accept it.'

'No arguments please,' said Reinhard, brushing aside her protests. 'As my adopted daughter, and I trust you don't mind me calling you that, I want you to have a small jumpstart to your young life. I think I should go now. I am feeling very emotional. If you contact my secretary, she will arrange your flight to Vienna.'

She followed him to the door, 'May I give my adopted father a hug?' They held one another for a while before Silke broke away and left the room.

As she closed the door she began to cry uncontrollably.

CHAPTER 31

Willy sat in his bedroom in the pension, scribbling

on a piece of paper. He was collating the information he

had on Silke. He then wrote the initials RH and drew an

arrow through them. He must also die, he said to himself.

He figured that he would have a few days grace, while the

Spanish police searched in vain all over Mallorca. After

that, he would need to alter his appearance. He went into

the bathroom and looked at himself in the mirror. He had

long, blonde hair that was greying at the temples. His shaven face was large and bloated from his excessive lifestyle. He could grow a moustache, he thought, and cover the gray hair with hair dye. Spectacles would complete the change. Instead of staying at hotels or pensions, where he could attract attention, he would rent a holiday apartment, paying in advance with cash.

He returned to his notes and added what he knew about Reinhard. He had been at his house in Grainau, so he had an idea of the layout and he knew where he worked. He would have to devise a strategy to get rid of his two adversaries. It had to be done soon if he was to make it look like the Jew was involved. Then suddenly a brilliant idea came into his mind. He stood up and punched the air with excitement.

A few hours later, he had booked out of the pension and was sitting in a train en route to Zurich. Fortunately, Luxembourg only has one spa resort town so it was relatively easy for Willy to contact Otto Mayer. After explaining that he needed to speak to Albert urgently, Mayer gave him the new mobile number that his son had acquired in Switzerland. He sat back, completely relaxed now that his grand plan was finally being put into action. The direct train journey to Zurich takes four hours and goes through some of Europe's loveliest scenery, as it passes through Kempten and then Bregenz on Lake Constance, before arriving at Zurich Hauptbahnhof. Willy noticed a chart dangling from the train carriage window sill. It indicated the complete Swiss railway network. He studied it for a while and with his usual method of flying by the seat of his pants, he chose a town called Eglisau, north of Zurich. He decided to do a quick investigation to see if would suit his plans. Just before the train arrived, he phoned Albert who seemed shocked to hear his voice. He explained that he would be in Zurich within the next two hours and that he needed to see him as a matter of extreme urgency. Albert suggested that Willy should come to his hotel, the Adlerhof, which was a few hundred metres from the station. He gave Willy his room number and brief directions.

At the station, Willy bought a return ticket to Eglisau. The ticket attendant informed him that there was a train every two hours and the journey took just thirty-one minutes.

He only had to wait a few minutes before the train arrived on line S5. The ticketing official had been perfectly accurate, with the train arriving in Eglisau exactly thirty-one minutes later. Willy walked out of the station and saw that he was in Bahnstrasse. He walked a short way down the road and came to an open area where he could see the Rhine River below, intersecting the town; it appeared that the main part of the small town was on the other side of the river. He looked back and saw the bridge going across the river. He decided to walk away along Rheinsfeldstrasse. It was a typically pretty Swiss town - clean streets and tidy gardens. Willy wondered how it was that all Swiss towns looked so picture perfect. The road he was on turned away from the river so he took a side path which led into a farming area. On the hill sloping towards the Rhine he noticed neat rows of vines stretching into the distance. He came across a wooden shed piled high with logs, obviously for heating in the winter months and a few hundred metres further on he could see a large house with a number of outbuildings on either side of it. He made a mental note of the layout of the area and turned and walked back in the direction of the railway station. He continued onto the bridge which he crossed over and then proceeded along the other bank of the river. He had only walked for about five minutes when he came across a house with a 'pension' sign above the front door. This is perfect he thought and retraced his steps back to the station.

After the short journey back to Zurich, Willy bought a newspaper and a bottle of Coca Cola at a kiosk in the station and then followed Albert's instructions, which took him across the river and along Limmatquai. The Adlerhof is a small hotel and fortunately for Willy, there was no one at the reception. He walked swiftly past the desk, holding the newspaper against his face, in case there were hidden CCTV cameras. He mounted the staircase and went to the second floor, where assumed Room 216 would be situated. He knocked and almost immediately Albert opened the door and ushered him in. They shook hands.

'I thought the plan was for us not to communicate with one another?' enquired Albert.

'Yes, it was, but suddenly things have started getting really hot. Heinrich's son and a young private investigator, at least that is what I think she is, have uncovered a lot of our movements. They followed me to Mallorca, and they are onto your trail here in Zurich. What have you been doing so far with your numbers?'

'It has been very difficult, as I haven't been able to get beyond low level managers at the bank. This is going to take a long time. You cannot believe how secretive these people are. They are like brick walls. I am going to need a lot more time than I initially anticipated. I am also considering giving this information to the Israeli authorities as they will have more clout than I have.'

'That is your best solution, Albert. In the meantime, you need to get away from this hotel. You have been here too long already. I am convinced that these bastards will be onto this address in no time.'

'Do you really think so?' remarked Albert going up to the table. 'There is a kettle here and some coffee. Would you like some?'

'Yes, thank you,' replied Willy. 'There is a little town not far from here called Eglisau. It is very quiet and on the train line. Why don't we go up there and hang out for a day or two? I will get my father to give us the latest police information on the search for you.'

459

'Eglisau. Do you know the place?'

'Of course, I stayed there a few years ago,' lied Willy. 'It is a lovely place and there is still time for us to catch a train there. Don't worry about the coffee. You go and book out and I will see you at the station. If you stay here much longer you will be arrested. Why do you think I rushed here to find you?'

'Okay, you go ahead. I will need to pack and book out. You have made me so bloody nervous now.'

Willy walked back to the station where he bought the two tickets to Eglisau.

For his plan to work, he needed Albert to disappear. He realised that it would not be that easy to make that happen. Eglisau seemed an ideal place for him to carry out his plan for Albert's demise.

Albert arrived twenty minutes later, pulling his suitcase. He looked nervous and gaunt, as if he had not eaten much in the past few days.

Willy went up to him with a big smile on his face. 'Don't look so worried, Albert, you are in good hands with me. I will discuss our strategy later this evening over a bottle of good wine.'

Willy was concerned that someone at the Eglisau station would recognise that he had been there two hours earlier, so when they alighted from the train, he lowered his head, hoping this would make him less recognisable. Willy and Albert were the only ones to get off the train at Eglisau and save for a railway official, the station was deserted. They walked along the same route Willy had taken earlier, following the path alongside the river. Clouds covered the sky, darkening the dusk and reducing visibility.

'Are you sure we are going in the correct direction,' asked Albert, who was having difficulty pulling his suitcase over the rough path. This looks like bloody farmland,' he protested.

'Not far to go,' replied Willy. 'Only another few hundred yards before we come to the hotel. You can see the lights up ahead,' he said, pointing to the farmhouse.

His mind was racing. He had to act quickly if he was going to kill Albert. They were approaching the shed filled with logs of wood that he had selected earlier on. This is it, Willy said to himself. He removed the Coke bottle from his pocket and fell slightly behind Albert. As they reached the end of the shed, he smashed the bottle onto the side of Albert's head. Albert let out a loud groan and crumpled to the ground. Willy bent down hitting him repeatedly on the head. He tightened his hands around Albert's neck and squeezed tightly until he was convinced that he was dead. He looked at the body on the ground and quickly checked to see if they were still alone. There was no one about, so he dragged the body into the back of the shed which was open on two sides. He started removing logs of wood and had soon made an opening in the pile. He found a sheet of heavy-duty, black plastic which was used for rain protection. Before wrapping Albert in the sheeting, he rifled through his pockets and found a mobile phone, a wallet and a passport which he slipped into his coat pocket.

He pushed the body into the space he had made and placed logs around it until it was completely sealed. He took the excess logs and made a small stack at the opposite side of the shed. In all likelihood, the wood would only be used from October or November onwards and so the probability of any discovery for the next couple of months was remote. He could now become Albert Mayer, except he didn't resemble him - Albert was dark-haired and thin faced. Just another minor problem to overcome, he thought. He knew of people who could do a photo swop on the Belgian passport. He wasn't worried about the language problem as long as he stayed out of Holland or Belgium. Everyone knew that the Belgians and the Dutch were the best linguists in Europe and that many spoke fluent German, so he could easily get away with being Albert and speaking German.

Willy did his best to tidy himself after all the effort he had put into the concealment of the body and returned to the main road where he approached the pension which he had found earlier. It was closed, but he noticed a light on in the second floor. He rang the bell and an irate woman opened the window and asked what he wanted at this late hour. Willy apologised and in his usual charming manner, managed to coax the landlady into opening the door. Within a few minutes, he had her laughing at his joke about getting lost and walking into a bush, in order to explain his ruffled appearance. He booked in as A. Mayer.

The room, like most accommodation in Switzerland, was clean and comfortable. Willy walked over to the window, outside of which there was the usual window box filled with red and pink flowers. It was dark outside and across the street, lights glowed in the upstairs rooms of a house. Only Willy knew what dreadful secrets the dark hill on the opposite bank concealed.

He sat down on the bed and rationalised that Albert had to die if he, Willy, was to be free. His grandfather would have agreed with that logic, especially since Albert was a Jew. He smiled to himself as he undressed and went into the bathroom, where he had a long and refreshing shower.

CHAPTER 32

Wolfgang Koch arrived at the Munich police headquarters accompanied by his lawyer, Thomas Bahr, with whom he had dealings spanning several decades. They were taken to an interview room which was equipped with video and recording equipment.

Bosch introduced himself and asked Koch and his lawyer to identify themselves.   'Is my client going to be charged?' demanded Bahr.

'This is a formal investigative and questioning meeting. We have no intention right now of charging Mr. Koch but in any investigation, everything is on the table. Some of the questions may already have been put to your client, but they need to be repeated for the record. Do you have any other questions before we begin?'

Both men shook their heads. Bahr placed his own tape recorder on the table.

'As you already know, we are investigating the double kidnapping of Hermann Heinrich and his granddaughter, Eva, and the possible murder of Mr. Heinrich. Mr. Koch, when did you last meet a man called Otto Mayer, who resides in Antwerp?'

'I told you the last time that it was about a month ago.'

'What contact, if any, via telephone or the internet have you had with him since that meeting?'

'None.'

'You said that your son was in Mallorca. Is he still there?'

''I think I said that he was somewhere in the Mediterranean.'

'Are you aware that the authorities wish to question your son in connection with a murder on the island of Mallorca?'

Koch was visibly shaken by the news of the murder. 'I don't know what you are talking about – this is absolute bullshit. My son is not a murderer.'

Then Bahr intervened, 'Is this now an enquiry about an alleged murder in a foreign country? If so, I will advise my client not to answer this line of questioning.'

'Tell me,' shouted Koch, 'why have you not had Europol arrest Mayer and his son? They are the ones you should be questioning.'

'I think you should leave Mr Koch's son out of this questioning session.' Bahr added.

Bosch hated lawyers who thought they were so much more intelligent than the police. He usually treated them with contempt.

'I just thought that Mr Koch might want to know that his son is an international fugitive. We also wish to question him, but I think it is obvious that your client knows nothing about the murder in Mallorca.' Bosch rested his chin on his cupped hands, waiting for the silence to have maximum effect before continuing. 'Mr Koch, we have proof that you were in contact with the late Mr Eicke, that both of you went to Belgium. Mr Eicke confessed to Mr Heinrich junior and to Miss Kotter, that the two of you were intending to blackmail Hermann Heinrich. What part did you play in this?'

'Do not answer that question,' intervened Bahr. Then turning back to Bosch he said, 'That is hearsay and the man who is supposed to have said it is dead.'

'What is more,' shouted Koch, 'your Miss Kotter is guilty of trespassing on my property.'

'She is not my Miss Kotter,' responded Bosch, 'and if you wish to lay a complaint or charge against her,

470

please, you are entitled to do so. I am going to need to take a set of fingerprints for our records. It is most important that you should inform me should your son, Willy, contact you. Also, if you have any evidence linking Mayer and his son to the kidnapping, then you should present this to the police.'

Bosch knew there was no chance of Koch responding to either request. He stood up to indicate that the interview was over.

'I think I should express my feelings,' said Bahr, as he also stood up, 'that there is a fine line between police investigation and police harassment.'

Bosch just smiled at him. He returned to his office and asked Keller and Hofmann to join him.

'I have just upset Koch and his lawyer, which is a good thing. If what Eicke told Heinrich is true, then both the Kochs and the Mayers are key to this enquiry. What is the latest information from either Switzerland or Belgium?'

Keller was the first to respond, 'Nothing further from the Belgian authorities, except that they managed to get photos of both Mayer senior and junior and have circulated these to their border posts, as well as Europol. They also indicated that it would be necessary for someone from here to be present, when they finally get to interview Mayer. The Zurich police are still sifting through hotel records, and the Spanish police in Mallorca have lost all trace of Wilhelm Koch but they are confident that he hasn't left the island.'

'Personally I have no confidence in the Spanish police. There is something about the Mediterranean climate that makes people relax too much. It is great for a holiday but I couldn't work in an environment like that. Have either of you ever been to the Balearic Islands?'

'I went to Turkey last year,' replied Birgit, 'and I can confirm that there is chaos everywhere. Nothing works properly. As you say, you can forgive that attitude when you are on vacation.'

'I will never understand why we let so many Turks into our country,' said Bosch, getting onto his favourite anti-Turk stance. 'My father worked his fingers to the bone after the war and then along came the next generation that thought it was beneath them to sweep the streets or collect rubbish, so they brought in the Turkish hordes. What they couldn't achieve with their armies a few centuries ago, they have now achieved with their street sweepers. We Germans are such short-sighted fools!'

Bosch cleared his throat, 'I want you to check with forensics to see if they have found anything from our raids. Koch's fingerprints will now be on record. Wait here while I contact the coroner's office to see if they have completed the autopsy on Heinrich's body.'

Bosch then dialled through to the senior Coroner. He listened and made a few notes.

'That is interesting,' he said putting down the phone. 'I am told that there is no sign of any wound or trauma that would indicate he was murdered. They are suggesting heart failure, but are still waiting for the toxicology report, in case some poisonous substance was in his body. We should have their full report in two days.'

'So, does that mean we can't charge the kidnappers with murder?' asked Keller.

'That depends on the degree of murder. If it can be shown that he died because the kidnapping denied him access to vital medication, then we can still charge them with culpability towards his death. We will then have to rely on medical experts. It is amazing what they can come up with these days. It boils down to the two families, Koch and Mayer, and we now need to show they were directly involved. We can do it, and we have all the police facilities to assist us. You know what to do so let's do it.'

CHAPTER 33

Silke arrived back at her small apartment in Vienna. She kept thinking that she had awoken from a dream – a dream in which she had been transported into a world of luxury and indulgence, the like of which she could never have imagined would happen to her. She had decided not to tell anyone at work about the money Reinhard had given her, as they could feel she should share it. The company had

476

received a lot of money for the project, but she argued, this was a personal present to her from Reinhard. She still had trouble contemplating what one hundred thousand Euro could buy. She would definitely not waste it, but she would spoil herself with a one-week holiday somewhere in the Mediterranean - she simply had to swim in the sea again. She would also buy herself a small car and maybe some clothes, and she wanted to study for a university degree. She put an estimate of twenty-five thousand Euro on the spend, with the balance being invested.

When she walked into the IT Wache office, she was greeted by a round of clapping. Almost single-handedly, she had raised the company's finances tenfold. They had received a confirmation e-mail from Reinhard himself, thanking them and advising that the agreed bonus would be paid into their account later that week. Silke was told about the celebration they were going to have that evening. It was made to sound like a booze party that would certainly burn the midnight oil.

Silke eventually sat down at her desk and wondered if she was going to be able to settle back into what now appeared to be a boring, monotonous routine. She wasn't convinced that her partners believed her when she told them about flying in a private business jet or going to Mallorca for two days. It still seemed like a dream, and already it was starting to seem as if it had happened a long time ago. Her friend Anna, who had acted as a locum while Silke was away, mentioned to her that a persistent man had phoned and asked to speak to her. She told Silke that she had given him her mobile number.

'Well no one has contacted me. Did he leave a name and contact number?'

'I didn't think to ask,' replied Anna sheepishly, 'but I am sure it is not important if he hasn't contacted you.'

'Roughly what time was the last call?'

Anna thought for a few seconds, 'About four o'clock. I know because I wanted to leave early to get to a lecture on that day, and I took the call as I was packing up. Do you think it could be important?'

'One never knows,' replied Silke, making a note of the time. She could trace the number through their telephone company who provided a record of incoming and outgoing calls on a monthly basis.

*****

The following morning, Silke arrived home after two in the morning, her head pounding from all the alcohol she had consumed, first at a restaurant and then at a noisy club. Although she wasn't in full control of her faculties, she felt nervous walking up the quiet stairway to her apartment. She wasn't normally a scared person so she put this aberration down to her recent experiences involving a murder and a kidnapping. She cursed the fact that she hadn't left a light on in the entrance hall. She listened at the door, opened it quickly and switched on the light. She looked around the apartment and was barely able to undress and get into bed before the full narcotic effects of the drink took away her consciousness.

CHAPTER 34

After the flight from Munich to Amsterdam, Bosch caught the high-speed train to Antwerp. He sat back in the warm carriage as the train sped along the monotonous route, reading his notes as he drank the uninspiring coffee which was served up in a polystyrene mug. He had received a call the previous day from the Belgian authorities, informing him that Otto Mayer had returned home. The Belgian police had visited Otto and he had agreed to come to the police station to be interviewed.

It was a miserable day, with a dark, heavy layer of cloud turning everything grey. Intermittent squalls of rain added to the misery. Bosch fastened his anorak to the top button as he walked along the platform to the information sign where he was to be met. Waiting for him was the senior detective in charge of the investigation, Jan deVries. They shook hands and greeted one another warmly, although they had never met before. It seems that policemen share some sort of special camaraderie, even across international borders.

On the short trip to the police headquarters, Bosch gave deVries a summary of the evidence they had, linking Mayer and his son to the kidnapping. That they knew about the flights to and from Munich and the statement by Koch, incriminating Albert Mayer, as well as the comments Eicke had made to Heinrich. deVries listened intently and finally commented, that while the evidence was largely circumstantial, it certainly was enough to warrant questioning the old man and to establish the whereabouts of his son.

Otto Mayer was escorted into a small room. After a few minutes, Bosch and deVries entered and sat opposite him. deVries explained the protocol surrounding the questioning and introduced Bosch. A tape recorder was started.

The initial questions concerned some mundane facts for the tape recording, including names and addresses.

'Where were you on the 19th and 20th of this month?' asked deVries with his first probing question.

Mayer was afraid that they could have uncovered his flight details, so he decided to tell a partial truth, 'I went to Munich on business and then I returned and booked into a spa in Luxembourg.'

'Where is your son Albert? He is not at his home or the business. He appears to have been away for a while.'

'He is in Zurich on business.'

'Where is he staying in Zurich?' continued deVries. He could see that Mayer was only giving short, concise answers, which is not what interrogators like. The more a person speaks, the greater the likelihood that they will make mistakes or reveal something interesting.

'I don't know,' answered Mayer.

'Well then, when did you last hear from him?'

'Let me see,' said Mayer looking at his watch, 'at least three days ago.'

deVries turned to Bosch, 'Is there anything you would like to ask?'

'Thank you,' replied Bosch. 'Mr. Mayer, where did you stay when you were in Munich?'

Otto Mayer realised that he couldn't mention Bad Reichenhall, as they had used false names, and he couldn't lie about being at another hotel, as this could soon be established as a lie. 'I stayed with a friend at his house.'

'Would you kindly give me your friend's name and address?'

Mayer hesitated, 'I do not wish to go any further with this questioning. I would like to see my lawyer first.'

'You know, Mr. Mayer,' said deVries, leaning forward so that he was in Mayer's face, 'you are perfectly entitled to do so, but in my experience, whenever people need to 'consult their lawyer', it is because they have something to hide. Isn't that so Inspector Bosch?'

'Exactly so,' responded Bosch. 'Mr Mayer, we are putting together a lot of information regarding the kidnapping of Mr Heinrich and his granddaughter and the subsequent murder of Mr Heinrich. It is interesting and of concern that your name, and that of your son Albert, keep coming up.'

The old man was starting to shake slightly, 'I need some water please.'

deVries poured him a glass of water from a jug on the table, which he drank rapidly.

'Wofgang Koch has pointed a finger at you and your son, as the kidnappers,' Bosch said, resting his chin on his hands and stared intently at Mayer.

'He is a Nazi just like his father. Who will believe people like that?' shouted Mayer.

'You stayed with Koch and planned the kidnapping while you were there.' Bosch was now turning questions into accusations.

'I don't know what you are talking about,' said Mayer, whose mind was now in a turmoil, as he did not know what the police had actually established.

485

'Of course you do.' Bosch was suddenly adopting an aggressive tone. 'We have proof of your movements.'

'I do not kidnap people.'

'Then what were you doing at Koch's cottage in Oberaudorf,' shouted Bosch.

Mayer closed his eyes. He realised that the police had obviously uncovered enough details of the plot, which had enabled them to identify him.

'I played no part in any kidnapping. I went there purely to obtain bank account numbers of Jewish victims of the Holocaust. If there was any kidnapping, then it was Koch and his son who arranged it.' Mayer was breathing rapidly and deVries was worried that the old man was going to collapse.

'Mr Mayer, please accept my recommendation. Write out a statement detailing everything that happened in Germany. By all means have your lawyer present.'

Mayer nodded his head indicating that he would comply. 'I don't need a lawyer,' he said feebly.

'We will leave you alone now. There is a telephone on the table behind you if you wish to use it, and here is a pad and a pen.'

DeVries took Bosch through to his office where he poured him a cup of coffee from a flask on his desk.

'Well what are your thoughts?' asked deVries.

'I am glad I came. He is clearly a worried man and he was very evasive as to his whereabouts in Munich, which is why I decided to confront him. I don't actually know if he stayed with Koch, but I think we can take that as a confirmation now. As I mentioned to you in the car coming here, I firmly believe that the two missing sons are the key to this crime. We have got permission to tap Koch's phones. Is it possible for you to do the same here on Mayer's phone?'

'It is not easy. We have to apply and show strong reasons that we believe a crime has been committed or is about to be. We may have enough solid evidence here, but it is still fifty-fifty. I certainly don't think we have enough to arrest Mayer. We need some positive evidence linking him - you know DNA or fingerprints or even documentary evidence.'

'We have raided the three homes belonging to Koch and his son, and we are also conducting a forensic search at the site where the old man was found buried. I am hoping that something will come from of all of this. Then we are hoping to get a forensic report from Mallorca, but there may be no link as such, except that Wilhelm Koch is possibly involved in both. Right now, we have the two parties each trying to implicate the other. That is perfect, and we must use this apparent fallout to our advantage. Oh yes, we are also awaiting information from the Swiss police as to where Albert Mayer is staying. We will try to get him arrested by Europol. We may need your help in this.'

'I can see we will have to maintain contact for some time,' said deVries smiling. 'This certainly has a wide-ranging European aspect to it, which as you know, brings all sorts of problems with it. Being in the EU doesn't mean freedom of movement for us police. The red tape is ridiculous. I have been waiting for one year to extradite a Serbian in London on a drug-dealing charge, and I have a watertight case. The law, in trying to protect the innocent, actually aids the clever criminal and his highly paid legal team. Look at Strauss-Kahn in France. He simply shrugs off all charges like a Teflon frying pan.'

'It is so frustrating. I have heard this is what has driven the Rio police to send out death squads at night, not that I am advocating that here,' said Bosch to laughter from deVries.

'As soon as the statement is ready I will send you a copy,' said deVries. 'Can I buy you something to eat? There is actually a very good bistro at the train station.'

'That sounds good,' said Bosch. 'This has been a useful interview, as I have now been able to speak to Mayer and Koch, both of whom were implicated by Eicke. Unfortunately, it is their missing sons who hold the key to this crime but it is always satisfying when an investigation starts to narrow down to just one or two suspects. Thank you for inviting me. Perhaps one day I will be able to reciprocate.'

* * * *

Willy caught the early train to Vienna. He paid for the ticket with cash. He was wearing a pair of number-one spectacles which he had purchased at a pharmacy. He had chosen a black-rimmed pair, as they were better as a disguise than the light coloured or rimless ones. He had also trimmed his long hair, covered the grey with dye and was allowing his new moustache to grow. It would need another week to be effective, he thought. He was quite pleased with the transformation and felt he looked a lot younger. He was confident that if he eliminated just two more people, he would be untouchable. He was toying with the idea of moving to another country, perhaps Australia or Canada. Even South America was a possibility, as there were still some sizeable German communities there. He sat back as the train glided silently on its way to Vienna. His mind was conjuring up what life would be like in a foreign land. What about Turkey or Thailand, he wondered?

Trains from Germany arrive at the Westbahnhof in Vienna, which was undergoing extensive renovations. Willy went to the tourist information office and was given a list of budget accommodation. He felt more secure at the low-cost end, as they tend to turn a blind eye to formalities like identification, and prefer being paid in cash. He chose a pension in Tell Gasse, which was a short walk from the station. It was a slightly run-down part of town but Willy was pleased that there was a cyber-cafe across the street.

He had the address of IT Wache where Silke worked, and three phone numbers of people with the name S. Kotter. After checking into the pension, he accepted under the circumstances that that the room was certainly not up to the usual four or five-star status to which he was accustomed. It was clean, he thought, and it did have en-suite facilities.

Willy went across to the cyber-cafe and tried to phone the three numbers he had. He could eliminate the first one, as it turned out that this S. Kotter was a man. The second one had an answering message with a female voice. No mention was made of the first name, as the message merely asked the caller to leave their telephone number and name and gave a promise to return the call. The third number just rang and rang. Assuming Silke had a listed number, then it had to be one of these two. Willy looked up the numbers in a directory the cyber-cafe gave him. He cursed when he consulted his map and found they were on opposite sides of the city. Willy decided that he would first investigate the office where Silke worked and then go to the two addresses he now had.

Vienna has a tramway network that goes back to 1865 and is one of the features of the city. Sadly, it is said to be under threat from the underground system, which is undergoing continuous expansion. The citizens of Vienna, who affectionately call their trams, 'Bims', after the sound of the bell, are unlikely to let them disappear completely without a fight. Willy climbed onto a number 18 that would take him close to Berggasse where Silke worked. By studying his city map, he had a vague idea where to alight.

He walked about two hundred metres until he came to the non-descript building where Silke's company had their offices. He found a vantage point where he could wait and observe everyone who entered and left the building. Willy only had the skimpy description his father had given him. Nevertheless, he felt that she sounded different enough, with her high cheek bones, for him to be able to spot her. Within a few minutes after five o'clock, people started emerging from the building. Willy scanned each woman as she stepped onto the pavement. It was no easy task, as they often came out two or three abreast, so he wasn't able to get a good look at their faces. There was a short break of several minutes when no one emerged and then two men walked out, accompanied by a young woman. The men went in one direction, and woman went the opposite way, waving good-bye as they parted. She certainly had high cheek bones so Willy decided that this had to be Silke, and proceeded to follow her at a safe distance. She turned a corner and joined a queue at a tram stop. Willy also joined it, separated from her by two other people.

The Crooked Star

The tram arrived and Willy saw that it was almost full. He squeezed on and found himself standing directly behind Silke. She had inserted earphones into her ears and was obviously listening to her favourite music completely oblivious that she was being followed. The tram rattled along, the brakes squeaking at each stop as some people got off and others got on. This was the afternoon rush hour, a ritual repeated in all the cities of the world, with the human ants scurrying along predetermined tracks.

The tram came to a stop, and Silke pushed her way to the back door and jumped off. Willy had to force open the doors as they closed on him and just managed to get off in time to see Silke disappearing into a crowd of pedestrians. Then suddenly he lost sight of her. He looked up and down and was unable to trace her in the sea of people. He noticed a wide entrance leading into a shopping mall, and he realised that he would have great difficulty picking her up again. He was pleased that he had accomplished most of his objective that day. She obviously

495

lived in this part of Vienna and that eliminated the other S. Kotter. If she had a landline, then her address would definitely be the last of the three names. He decided to wait until dark before doing a closer reconnoitre. He found a quiet coffee lounge where he could while away a couple of hours. The problem he encountered was, that at this time of the year it stays light until at least ten o'clock. Afterwards, he went to a small bookshop and browsed through arbitrary books and magazines before going to a restaurant, where he tried to eat as slowly as possible, willing the time to pass faster.

He finally decided to walk in the direction of the address he had found in the telephone directory. It was a suburb catering for students and low-income families. The apartment buildings had all been built in the immediate post-war period and mirrored the austerity of that time - they were functional and ugly. Trees planted on the pavement softened the Spartan architecture to a degree, but it still remained a faceless and somewhat soulless place.

The Crooked Star

Willy found the apartment building quite easily. It was four storeys high and had a glass door at the entrance. There was a bank of buzzers on the wall next to the door. He dropped a letter addressed to Silke into the post box next to the door. Before leaving Munich he had posted a similar letter to Reinhard. Willy presumed 47 would be on the fourth floor. He then went to the other side of the street. Almost all the apartments that were on. He looked up at the fourth floor and wondered which one would be her apartment. He would be back but first he needed to lay some false trails implicating Albert Mayer.

Willy made his way across Vienna using the trams once again. He purchased a take-away consisting of sausages, sauerkraut and two beers from a dubious-looking restaurant near his pension.

As he sat on the lumpy bed, he tried to think his way through the strategy he would use to gain entry into Silke's apartment. The front entrance would be easy to get through. The challenge to entering her apartment would be the front door. If it was simply a Yale type lock, then he would have no problem, however, if she had installed a more sophisticated locking device such as a deadbolt or a digital lock, then he could have a problem.

He took out the wallet he had removed from Albert Mayer's pocket and spread the contents on the bed. He counted the notes. There were 250 Swiss Francs and 180 Euros, three credit cards and what looked like a loyalty card. He found five business cards with Albert's name, plus a card bearing the name of a diamond wholesaling company in Antwerp. There were also a number of receipts, including one from the Hotel Adlerhof.

Willy thought it would help his plan if he left behind the card from the diamond wholesalers. Even a stupid policeman would make the connection between it and Albert Mayer. He threw away half of the food he had purchased into a small rubbish bin in the bathroom and drank the beers. He was quite pleased with his planned deception. It was starting to look fool proof.

CHAPTER 35

Bosch had returned the previous evening from Antwerp, to find his wife as drunk as a lord. She had sworn off alcohol the previous week and was taking an active interest in the Heinrich kidnapping case. She had even arranged for Krueger, the psychiatrist, to visit young Eva. Georg Bosch was so pleased, that he gave her several hundred Euros with which to spoil herself. They had enjoyed dinner in an expensive restaurant and he was so proud of her when she chose to have a fruit juice with her meal. He was convinced this was a turning point. Sadly, this was not the case.

He detected a burnt-food smell coming from the kitchen. Whatever was in the pot on the stove had turned into a black, cremated lump. He switched off the stove and opened all the windows to get rid of the smoke. He returned to the bedroom where Anna-Marie was lying across the bed. She hadn't even bothered to remove her shoes. He shouted her name but there was no response, just drunken snoring. He shook her violently until she came around, still in an alcoholic haze. He then reacted incorrectly by shouting at her and telling her she could have caused a fire. She started swearing at him, so he walked out of the apartment and went to a nearby fast-food outlet, where he sat fuming over a plate of Spaghetti Bolognaise.

The following day, he arrived at the office in a foul mood. He went straight to the dispensing machine and poured himself a black coffee. He needed something to calm himself before he called a meeting. Two faxed reports were on his desk, one from the Zurich police and the other from deVries in Antwerp. He read them and immediately summoned his two assistants.

He gave them a brief summary of the interrogation of Mayer and then read the two faxes to them. The one from deVries was a copy of the statement that Mayer had made. It was a partial confession in that he said his son went to see Hermann Heinrich, in order to get hold of a box they thought could contain Swiss bank account numbers belonging to Jewish victims during the Nazi rule. Any subsequent kidnapping, he claimed, was entirely the work of Wilhelm Koch and his father. deVries added a notation that Mayer had been charged with conspiracy to commit a crime and had been released on bail.

The second fax was a report from the Zurich police, confirming that they had traced Albert Mayer to the

Adlerhof Hotel where he had booked in under his own name. They confirmed that before they could interview him, he had already checked out of the hotel. They had no positive information of his whereabouts or that he had left Switzerland.

'Perhaps we have to have another meeting with Koch,' said Bosch, setting aside the fax messages. 'We can do it at his residence. Will one of you set it up? The noose is tightening but sometimes, just as you think you are closing in, the fates take over and you end up at another dead-end. You two will soon get to know all the frustrations of this job. You are looking at your future career and I am counting the years to retirement.'

'Please don't retire yet,' said Birgit. 'We still have a lot to learn from you.'

* * * * *

Birgit, who had agreed to contact Koch, was surprised at his willingness to attend another meeting. She was advised that he had returned to his house in Passau, and the meeting was confirmed for later that morning.

Koch arranged for his lawyer, Bahr to be present, and he set up the table in the dining room with a tape recorder, as Bahr had recommended.

Bosch decided to attend the meeting alone.

After the usual greetings, Bosch opened the meeting, 'Mr. Koch, I can tell you that I have just returned from Antwerp where I was present at an official police enquiry. This enquiry included an interrogation of Mr. Otto Mayer. He has issued a statement in which he claims that he stayed with you when he was in Germany a few days ago, at the very time of the kidnapping. You have denied this. I am here to sort out all the conflicting accounts we now have.'

Bahr responded, 'My client would like to issue a formal statement. He has tried to recall all the incidents leading up to the arrival of the Mayers and their subsequent departure. I want to point out my client's advanced age and that his memory is sometimes not what it should be. We can get medical proof of this.' Bahr handed Bosch a single page which he read.

'So,' said Bosch putting the statement down, 'you claim here that the plot was hatched by the Mayers, and that you and your son were accidently implicated in it.'

'Yes,' replied Koch. 'I believe that the Mayers are anti-German Nazi hunters, possibly working for Mossad. They claimed that they were looking for Swiss Bank account numbers that Jews had in the forties. Now tell me why I, or my son for that matter, would be concerned about Jewish bank accounts. I believe they wanted to kill Hermann because his father was Heydrich. I was also very scared of them. They are out for revenge, even if it goes back generations.'

'There is still the question of why you helped them and let them stay at your ski cottage,' remarked Bosch.

'My friend Eicke, who sadly felt the need to commit suicide, asked me to help them. He was directly involved with the Mayers. I don't know the details. Find Mayer's son and you solve your case.'

Bosch smiled, 'We will find him, but I have to tell you, that while I accept that most of what you say could be true, nevertheless, you have unwittingly involved yourself in a serious crime.'

'I think you will find,' said Bahr, 'that a court will agree that it is possible to have someone stay at your residence without being aware of the commission of crime they are involved in. Criminals do not go around telling everyone of their plans.'

'I accept that, but I am still undecided as to what role Mr Koch's son played in this crime. All we know about his whereabouts is that he arrived on the island of Mallorca a few days ago and then disappeared into thin air. A body was found at the place where he was last known to be staying and...'

'I am sure there is a perfectly good explanation,' interjected Koch. 'Willy and I have some investment property on the island and he has friends there as well. He loves travelling and may even be in Sardinia or the Greek islands.'

'Are you able to give me the names of his friends on Mallorca?' asked Bosch.

'I haven't the faintest idea who they are. I personally do not have any friends there.'

'If Albert Mayer is behind the kidnapping as you claim, did he act alone or was Willy an accomplice?'

'You would have to ask Willy that. What I saw indicated that Mayer acted alone.'

'Did the lake, Eibsee, come into any of the conversations you had with the Mayers?'

'Not that I can recall. I obviously know the Eibsee, which is at the base of the Zugspitze. No mention was made of it.'

'Did Albert Mayer use either your car or Willy's?' asked Bosch.

'I can only speak for myself, and the answer is a definite no. Please, I am starting to feel a little tired.'

'Mr. Koch, I will leave you for now. I thank you for your frank discussion, but I have to warn you that you are not entirely off the hook, so to speak. I may need to contact you again.'

'My client is willing to co-operate within the bounds of the law.' said Bahr, shaking Bosch's hand.

507

On the return journey to Munich, Bosch mulled over the short interview he had just completed with Koch. He tried to work out why Koch had changed from his earlier aggressive stance, to this more compliant one. What made him change his mind? He knew that the missing Albert Mayer was a key figure, as was the missing Willy. His instinct told him that Willy was somehow involved with the murder in Mallorca, but what was the connection? How does it fit in? The story about the Jewish Swiss bank accounts was plausible, he thought. There seemed to be an on-going battle between the Jewish relatives of those killed in the war and the Swiss banking authorities. Perhaps he should contact Silke and discuss it with her, in view of the clever way she found and analysed all the evidence. He had a sneaking admiration for her detective work, although he would never admit this to anyone.

CHAPTER 36

As Silke got to the front door of the building, she realised that she hadn't checked the mailbox the previous evening. She opened the door and there were two letters in her box, one for someone else and one for her. She put the letter in her handbag and hurried outside to catch her tram to work. When she arrived at the office she sat down at her desk with a cup of coffee and then remembered the letter. She didn't recognise the handwriting and noticed there was no stamp or postmark, so presumably it had been hand-delivered. As she opened the note, she became visibly nervous. It read – 'I am going to get you, you Jewish-hating Nazi bitch.' She read it several times and even looked inside the envelope a second time, to see if there was anything else inside.

'Novak,' she called out as he had walked within earshot, 'look at this letter that was put in my post box yesterday.'

She handed him the letter.

'Shit, this could be serious,' he said, returning the note, 'especially in view of the investigation you have just done. You will have to go to the police, but before you do that, I think we should show it to the others.'

After reading the note, they all agreed that she should contact the police both in Vienna and Munich, where the main investigation was taking place. Silke thought she should contact Reinhard as well.

Her first call was to Bosch's office, only to be told that he was out. She left a message for him to contact her on her mobile. She then phoned Reinhard, who was delighted to hear from her so soon after she had left Germany. Like everyone else, he advised her to go to the police and he immediately offered her the use of the apartment in Munich, as it would be a 'safer address' he suggested. She thanked him and said she would consider the offer if it appeared that she was in serious danger.

Anna called in at the office later in the day to collect her pay for the period she had worked as a locum for Silke. She looked at the note and offered to stay at the apartment with Silke. Initially Silke scoffed at the suggestion but after some persistent persuasion by Anna, she relented, as she had been drained by the events of the past few days, especially after finding the body in the freezer. The killers and the kidnappers were still on the loose, and she could not be certain that somehow the killer or killers knew about her connection to Reinhard. She needed some company and reassurance.

On her way home that evening Silke stopped off at a Spar grocery store and bought some extra provisions, now that Anna would be staying with her. Anna was waiting outside the block of apartments when Silke arrived at the front door, carrying several parcels. She gave her a hug and grabbed a parcel.

'I see you have taken the one with the wine in it,' joked Silke, as she unlocked the door.

'I think we may need some Dutch courage, and anyway, I want to relax with a glass of wine and hear about your adventures.'

After heating two ready-cooked meals in the microwave, Silke spent the rest of the evening recalling her involvement with the kidnapping. She admitted that she did not have a camera with her and all she had were a few pictures she had taken in Mallorca with her mobile phone. It was nearly midnight when the two bottles of wine they had emptied, finally made them realise how tired they were.

Anna checked that the front door was locked and then climbed into her make-shift bed on the couch and fell into a dead sleep. She was so sound asleep that she didn't hear the scraping of a credit card pushing open the lock of the front door. The door opened slowly and silently.

Willy sneaked into the apartment and stood very still in the entrance hall. He listened for any sign that the noise, when opening the door, had disturbed Silke. He had on very thin, latex, medical gloves and dark clothing. He pulled a ski mask over his face. Then he remembered the card, which he took out of his pocket and threw on the floor near the front door. He waited, listening carefully for any tell-tale sound. All he could detect was some heavy breathing and so he advanced into the lounge, taking slow measured steps. The curtains hadn't been fully drawn, resulting in a thin shaft of light filtering in from the streetlamps. He stopped suddenly. The breathing he had heard was coming from the couch. What was Silke doing sleeping on the couch, he wondered? He pulled the small claw-hammer from his pocket. He had a choice of either smashing her head in as she slept, or waking her and terrorising her before he killed her. For some fun, he decided to do the latter. He shook the sleeping body. Anna sat up, startled, expecting to see Silke. She looked up at a man bending over her saying, 'Wake up Silke, you bitch.'

'Help!' screamed Anna at the top of her voice.

Silke woke up in a disoriented state, grabbed the revolver from under her pillow and threw open the door of the living room. In the dim light, she could see the outline of a man. Willy was also startled to see that there were two people in the apartment. He raised the hammer and brought it down on Anna, who raised both arms in an attempt to protect herself. The hammer struck her left arm and she felt an intense pain. A loud bang echoed in the room as Silke fired the revolver in the general direction of the intruder. Willy turned and fled out of the apartment and down the stairs. He had jammed some paper in the front door, allowing for an easy escape into the streets of Vienna.

Silke switched on the lights and saw Anna clutching her arm, which was already beginning to swell. She had been struck halfway between the wrist and the elbow.

'I can't move my hand,' she cried. 'Silke what is happening? This is like a nightmare.'

'Don't move. First, we must get you to a hospital, and then we can call the police. I am sure this is in connection with that letter I received.' Silke rushed over and banged the door shut.

Anna started sobbing loudly. Silke came and sat next to her while she phoned for an ambulance, followed by a call to the police emergency number. In less than fifteen minutes, both the ambulance service and the police arrived. The medics confirmed that it looked like a broken arm. They told Silke to stay with the police, as Anna's injury was not life-threatening and that she would be returned to the apartment in a few hours.

* * * *

Willy had been completely surprised when the gun had been fired at him. The bullet had missed him and struck the wall. He cursed himself for his short sightedness that had resulted in a miscalculation of the potential danger posed by Silke. She was obviously a tougher character than he realised, and he would have to rethink his strategy for dealing with her. Why did she have someone sleeping on the couch, he asked himself? What kind of woman has a gun? Over and over he cursed himself and questioned the potential danger of Silke.

As he left her building, he kept close to the wall, as there was an overhang that partially hid him from view. He was worried that the loud bang from the gun would have woken the neighbours. He peered up at the building and saw that lights had been turned on in three units, in addition to Silke's apartment. He increased his stride but avoided running. Running late at night would only attract attention. The streets were deserted, however he realised that even if he saw a taxi, it would be dangerous to hail it, as this would be one of the first checks the police would make. He would have to walk all the way to his accommodation and he would need to avoid the main thoroughfares. He could hear sirens in the distance and assumed that Silke had called the police.

CHAPTER 37

At eight the following morning, Bosch sat down at his desk and saw a message to contact Silke Kotter.

Before he could dial her number, a call came through. It was from Reinhard Heinrich.

'Inspector Bosch, good morning. I felt it best that I should inform you that I have received a threatening letter. Let me read it to you:

For its participation in the Genocide, your family is eternally cursed. I am going to eradicate the Heydrich lineage from the face of the earth.'

Bosch interrupted, 'I don't like the sound of this. Please avoid contaminating the letter or envelope. I have to tell you that in all high-profile cases, one gets what I call loony letters or phone calls. This is slightly different because as far as I know, there has been no connection in the media between yourself and the name Heydrich. The comments in this note lead me to believe it could be from Albert Mayer.'

Reinhard confirmed that he had carefully replaced the note in the envelope and would drop it off at Bosch's office on his way to work. He also told Bosch that his wife would be taking Eva to Hannover, where they would both stay with her mother for a short while. He would continue to keep the 24-hour security presence at the property in Grainau.

Bosch then dialled Silke.

'Good morning Miss Kotter, Inspector Bosch. How may I help you?'

'Thank you for returning my call, Inspector. Unfortunately, the morning is not good. Yesterday I phoned you to inform you of a note, which I think is connected to the kidnapping. Then last night an intruder broke into my apartment and injured a friend who was staying with me. I believe it was me he was after.'

'This is very serious. I have to tell you that Mr. Heinrich informed me a few minutes ago that he too has received a threatening letter. Your life could be in danger. May I ask you to scan the note and e-mail it to me. I am also going to contact the police in Vienna so that we can co-ordinate our efforts to track down the intruder, as it seems that one of our suspects is currently in your city.'

'Thank you, Inspector. I spoke to Mr Heinrich yesterday and I may take up his offer to return to Munich.'

'Excellent, and if you do, I would like to spend some time comparing notes, as we have quite a lot of new information from both Mr. Mayer and Mr. Koch - the seniors that is, as both their sons are still missing. I have to say that I think one of them may have been your intruder.'

Silke agreed to contact Bosch, if and when she returned to Munich.

An ambulance returned Anna to the apartment. She was still in her night attire, and her plastered arm was in a sling. They hugged one another.

'They said it was a clean break so there shouldn't be any complications,' Anna informed Silke through tears and nose blowing. 'To think I came here to protect you! What did the police say?'

'Firstly, you did protect me, as I am convinced I was the intended victim. I told the police that he had fired a gun as he ran off. We must keep to that story as I don't have a license for it. I hid the gun in the fridge and I kicked the empty cartridge near the door. The police are so useless. Even though I told them about the note, they maintained it was just a random burglary gone wrong. There should be someone coming here to take fingerprints, so try to avoid touching too many things, especially the door knob. I spoke to Reinhard yesterday, and I am thinking of taking some leave and going to Munich. What will you do?'

'I am going back home where my mother can look after me, but I can still do another locum for you, as I only go back to my studies in a months' time.'

'That is kind of you, Anna. We are also not that busy at work, you know how it is at this time of the year. Perhaps they can give you a call if it gets hectic. I think I will only be away for ten days at the most. Hopefully, they will have captured this lunatic by then. Now listen to me, your injury and getting better must be your top priority.'

CHAPTER 38

Silke took the mid-afternoon flight to Munich. She had taped two toothpaste tubes to the gun and put her case into the hold. As arranged, Reinhard was waiting for her at the arrivals hall and as soon as they met, they embraced one another warmly.

'I didn't think I would see you so soon,' said Reinhard, as they walked to the car park. 'I am feeling so terrible that by getting you involved in my problems, your life is now in danger. I too have received a threatening note but thank heaven, Sabine and Eva are safely in Hannover with her mother.' Reinhard somehow felt more secure now that Silke was back. He couldn't understand why he should feel this way about a young girl, but he did.

'Here is the key to the apartment. You can stay there as long as you like and you can phone my secretary to arrange a vehicle whenever you need one. Before I take you to the apartment however, Bosch has asked us to come to his office. Is that alright with you?'

'Of course,' replied Silke, as she got into the car. 'I have already had a conversation with him and he actually sounded quite human. I think he is hoping we can collaborate on the case, which is fine with me. I have done a bit of research and developed some theories which I would like to discuss with him.

Bosch smiled and greeted them warmly when they walked into his office. He had copies of both notes on his desk.

'Well, well,' he said, leaning back in his chair. 'It seems as if your family is still being targeted, Mr. Heinrich, and Miss Kotter is also included. Our forensics department is looking at your note right now.'

Silke reached into her bag and handed over the note she had received. Bosch used a pair of tweezers to pry it out of the envelope.

'Thank you. I will pass this onto them as well. Hmm, similar anti-Nazi sentiments I see.'

'Does this not point to Albert Mayer being the culprit as we discussed earlier?' suggested Reinhard.

'Well that was my first reaction as well. We really don't know much about Wilhelm Koch's political leanings but his grandfather was a famous Nazi General. Based on that, one would not normally associate him with those sentiments. What do you think Miss Kotter?'

Silke hesitated before speaking. She didn't want to appear to always have an opposing viewpoint and come across as an arrogant know-all.

'It is very possible it is Mayer. My thinking is that it could also have been left there to disguise who the real culprit is. As I see it, we have two principal suspects, namely Albert Mayer and Wilhelm Koch. There could be others we don't even know about but let us stick with these two for now. I spent some time this morning searching the internet on mainstream engines and some minor ones as well and I have to say that there is very little to be found on Mayer, except that he has a degree from the University of Antwerp. Other than that, he is a non-entity but Koch is a different story.'

Silke opened her laptop.

'In 1986, five men were arrested after a Turkish man was killed in the streets of Passau. A newspaper article lists their names, and one is Wilhelm Koch. After that, there is no further mention in any newspaper. Perhaps you will have better luck by checking the police records at the time. Then in 2002, in the same newspaper there was a small article regarding the disappearance of Angela Koch, twenty-seven-year-old wife of Wilhelm Koch. Again there was no further mention. Perhaps you can follow up that one as well.'

'That is most interesting. You have an uncanny knack of finding small bits of information. It's a pity I missed out on the computer revolution.'

Bosch phoned through to August Keller and instructed him to check the police records on the two incidents which Silke had uncovered.

'Miss Kotter, there are three possibilities concerning your intruder. He could be either Koch, or Mayer, or just an arbitrary burglar. Now, you were within a few metres of him. Can you give me a description of the man?'

'I am rather embarrassed to say, that in the confusion of having been woken out of a deep sleep and with the darkness in the room, I didn't get to see his face. I seem to recall that it appeared as if he might have had a mask over his face. I am certain that I wouldn't recognise him if he were in this room now.'

'In the darkness, it would have been difficult to see distinguishing facial features even without a mask, but perhaps you can remember some overall physical aspects, regarding height or size.'

Silke thought carefully for a while before answering, 'I have black-out curtains because of the street lighting and I have to say that all I can recall is a dark form. My friend was screaming and my adrenaline was pumping. It happened so quickly.'

'I understand,' said Bosch. 'Perhaps you can ask your friend if she noticed anything that could be significant. Even with a mask on, one can sometimes calculate the size and shape of the head. Hopefully the police in Vienna will have done a forensics check on your apartment. I will see if we can make contact with them. Please leave me your address in Vienna before you go.'

Silke wrote her address on the back of a business card and handed it to Bosch.

Bosch continued, 'Now I will tell you about the interviews I had with Otto Mayer and Wolfgang Koch, but first I must swear you to secrecy as I don't want to compromise an on-going investigation.'

Bosch did a précis of the two meetings and also mentioned the police reports from Zurich and Mallorca.

'To summarise,' he said, 'we have two missing men who could still be in Switzerland or Mallorca, or they could be anywhere. Wilhelm has definitely not flown out of Mallorca according to the Spanish police. As you know, the Schengen Convention has made border crossings within the area almost undetectable, which is why one or both of our suspects could be here in Germany or even Vienna where someone entered your property, Miss Kotter.'

'I believe,' said Reinhard, 'that they must have acted together when they kidnapped my daughter and father. Could they still be together and are now targeting my family and Miss Kotter?'

'The information we received from the boat hire man at the Eibsee, is that a foreign man, let us say this was Mayer, rented a boat. He was later seen with several people on board the boat going to the island. Now this does indicate that more than one person was involved, which makes sense. Are they still together? I don't know.'

'If we look at the interviews you had with the two fathers,' said Silke, 'then it seems that they have had a disagreement. Without detailed knowledge of the two personalities, I am inclined to think that Albert Mayer is less likely to be the violent one.'

'The difficulty with criminology,' said Bosch interrupting Silke, 'is that profiling only works fifty percent of the time. With certain crimes, such as serial killing, the finding, especially in the States, is that often the killer is not your stereotype, violent individual as portrayed

531

in B-grade movies, but rather a quiet, unassuming citizen. His neighbours and friends are often shocked when the truth comes out. So I hear what you are saying, but we must be careful not to exclude Mayer at this point.'

'I think one of them is a psycho case, and that he is now targeting Mr. Heinrich and me for whatever twisted reasons he may have.' Silke had a gut feel that the person they should be looking for was Willy Koch, but she didn't wish to confront Bosch while he still had Albert Mayer in his sights.

Just then the telephone rang. Bosch answered it and other than the odd grunt, didn't comment but he made rapid notes. He thanked the caller and looked up at Reinhard and Silke.

'That was Keller. It seems all the records for the past fifty years have been digitised which is why he could retrieve the information so quickly. You are indeed correct, Miss Kotter. In 1986, Wilhelm Koch, along with several other young men, was taken into questioning regarding the death of a Turkish worker. Evidence from an eye-witness resulted in the presiding judge requesting a psychiatric assessment of two of the accused. Koch was seen by a forensic psychiatrist by the name of...' he hesitated as he tried to read his own hand writing, 'I think it looks like Angemeier. It appears then, that at the next court hearing, the eyewitness who was also a Turk disappeared and the charges were dropped. This is why it didn't come up as a red flag item when we initially checked for a criminal record. There is also a police report on the disappearance of Willy Koch's wife. The missing person's case is still open. A sighting was apparently made of her in Thailand, which is most likely why it was not pursued. It would seem that officially he is still married to her. This is a very strange man indeed.'

'May I suggest,' asked Silke, 'that you should perhaps speak to the psychiatrist whom Koch consulted?'

'A very good idea. Miss Kotter, if I may also suggest, I would like you to accompany me to my meeting with the psychiatrist. I will make it official and appoint you as a civilian expert. This is quite normal, as we use all sorts of people, including clairvoyants, although I have personally never used one.' He laughed at his last comment.

Silke was taken aback by the sudden turnaround by Bosch.

'I would find that most interesting,' she said quietly.

Reinhard smiled. He could see how she had blossomed in such a short time. He acknowledged that she had a brilliant mind and was largely self-taught, but there were times when he could see she had a troubled mind that hid secrets from her past. Bosch asked Keller to establish whether Angemeier was still practising in the area and to set up an appointment with him.

* * * *

Silke had only just finished unpacking her small suitcase when her mobile phone rang. It was Bosch, advising her that they had traced Professor Angemeier and he would fetch her for the meeting within half an hour. It gave her little time to prepare for the meeting. She sat down and made a list of possible questions she would put to the psychiatrist. Picking up her laptop, she went downstairs to wait for Bosch.

In the car, Bosch explained to her that Angemeier was now Professor Angemeier at the Munich University, but as they were closed for the summer vacation, he had agreed to meet them at his private residence. Bosch was also able to inform her that the police in Vienna had recovered a bullet that had lodged in the wall of the apartment. It was a .22. They also had some shoeprints to work on and had found a business card belonging to someone called Hersov, from a diamond company in Antwerp.

'Things are starting to point quite strongly in the direction of Albert Mayer,' commented Bosch, as they arrived outside Professor Angemeier's house.

Angemeier, who was now in his early sixties, lived in a large house a short distance from the University. The garden followed a classic, formal design, with a central pathway along which there were two rows of manicured shrubs. It was more a green garden, as there was an absence of any colour, save for two standard rose trees on either side of the steps leading to the house. Angemeier lived there with his demanding wife and a simpleton twenty-year-old son, who enjoyed playing a set of drums most of the day.

Professor Angemeier was of medium height and slightly built. He had short-cropped grey hair. After the introductions, he ushered them into a large study. The bookshelves were so full that some books had been put into neat piles on the floor.

'Your man, Keller, told me briefly what you were coming to see me about. When I joined the university, I brought all my files here. You see, I also write books and need to refer to specific cases from time to time. I looked up the file on Wilhelm Koch. To be truthful, I had no recollection of this case, however, when I read the file, I could understand why. You see, I only had one session with him but now my memory cells are working overtime and some things are returning. How can I help you?'

'Let me fill you in on some background,' said Bosch. 'We are still involved in an investigation concerning the kidnapping of a Mr. Heinrich and his granddaughter. I am sure you will have seen it in the media.'

Angemeier nodded, 'Yes, in fact, I have met the son on one or two occasions at the university. Sorry, please carry on.'

'Among others, Mr. Koch is linked to the kidnappings and we would like to question him, which is why we thought you could possibly add to the profile we are constructing. We understand that you once interviewed him professionally in connection with a street murder. In addition, his wife went missing in 2002 and has never been found.'

'As I said, I only have one session to go on, but I will do my best to help. The information I am able to give you will not jeopardise the doctor-client relationship. It took place over twenty years ago and is not directly related to the case on which you are working.'

'May I add one snippet of information?' asked Silke. 'I was in Mallorca with Mr. Reinhard Heinrich recently and we came across the body of a local man. We think Koch had been staying in the house where the murdered man was found. He was certainly on the island at the time and the police have not been able to trace him.'

'Oh, my goodness. That is interesting, very interesting. As I talk, I will be referring to my notes but please interrupt me with any questions you may have. Wilhelm - I see he asked me to call him Willy, was a charming young man. He smiled a lot during the interview and tried to move attention from himself, by asking me about some of the photographs I had on my wall at the time. In fact, two of them are behind you.'

Silke and Bosch both turned at the same time. The one photograph had been taken in Venice. It showed a row of gondolas tethered to anchor poles and in the mist, the Rialto Bridge could be seen. The other photograph was obviously taken in the Greek Islands, from a boat approaching the harbour at Mykonos. It showed the familiar blue and white buildings lapped by the sea. Both were very typical tourist photographs.

Angemeier continued, 'Willy was cunning and manipulative. He spoke about going hunting and explained that he liked to wound the animal initially and then finish it off at close quarters. I underlined that part in my notes. Cruelty not only meant nothing to him, but he seemed to enjoy it. Animal cruelty in young people often turns nasty in later life. I could tell that he was trying to conceal his true psyche or inner-self, through conviviality. Without him realising it, I could deduce from the responses I received, that he had no feelings for his parents. I wrote a side note,' Angemeier turned the page slightly so that he read the note more easily, 'cold, distant, no concern for family or friends. At that very early stage in my discussion with him, I was already seeing someone with an anti-social *or even psychopathic* personality disorder.'

'Why was there only one session?' asked Bosch. 'It almost seems like he slipped through the net.'

'I was acting on a court instruction. At the time, I was contracted to the state of Bavaria. If I can remember correctly, I set up a subsequent appointment for a week or so later. This was cancelled as the charges against him were dropped. I was so busy working for the authorities at that time, that I simply filed the report and today is the first time I have revisited it. How many suspects have you interviewed only to let them go, and then they pop up sometime in the future, having committed a crime that maybe you could have prevented? I agree the net is not fine enough.'

Silke spoke, 'Professor, I understand that you can only give us a vague assessment of Willy, but perhaps you could extrapolate from what you know about him and build up a psychological portrait, of how he could be today.'

Angemeier looked at the ceiling and pursed his lips, 'Of course I can take what little information I have, as well as what you have just told me, and give you a number of possible avenues someone like Willy could have taken. Largely conjecture I must point out.'

'Every little bit would help us because we are fearful, that if he is the man behind the kidnappings, he may still have violent plans.'

'Very well. In general terms, imagine if you can, not having a conscience, no feelings of remorse or guilt, no concern for the well-being of friends, family and even strangers. No internal struggles or sense of responsibility about any action you have taken. Add to this the ability to conceal from other people that you are an aberration, since all of humanity assumes that conscience is universal. In other words, you are completely free of normal restraints, which gives you carte blanche to do as you please. Psychologically, you are not human. Cleckley summed it up perfectly with the title of the book he wrote - The Mask of Sanity.' Angemeier looked again at the ceiling.

He continued, 'We tend to think only in terms of violent psychopathy, whereas we are not commonly aware of the larger number of non-violent sociopaths among us. These are not blatant lawbreakers, but they are often those who can lie with impunity or spread malicious false rumours. They are also characterised by not having any feelings of guilt or remorse. Do you know how many innocent people were arrested during the Nazi era, purely on the basis of someone giving the Gestapo anonymous, false information?'

'What about revenge?' asked Silke. 'Mr. Heinrich and I have both received death threats.'

'Revenge for some act either real or perceived, is often the trigger that sets these people on their path of destruction. If we assume that Willy was the mastermind behind the kidnapping, then he could quite easily conjure up a justification to harm you. He could see you as a threat, perhaps getting too close for comfort. Psychopaths can do bizarre and self-destructive things because consequences that would fill the ordinary man with embarrassment or guilt, simply do not affect them. I would be very careful if you have received a death threat from our friend Willy.'

'Miss Kotter has already moved to a new address,' informed Bosch. 'Tell me, how would you go about finding someone like Willy, if indeed he is a psychopath?'

Angemeier smiled, 'I am not a police detective, but if I were, I would try to put myself into his mind. What would be my next move if my name was Willy? How would I disguise myself? How arrogant would I be? How would I frighten my intended victims? How could I get close to them without being exposed?'

'Do you think someone like that would act alone or with someone else?' asked Silke. 'Also from the information we have, the events in Willy's life are far apart. For example, the incident with the Turk was twenty years ago, then four years later, the disappearance of his wife and now the murder in Mallorca. Is this a likely scenario?'

'Generally speaking, these people act alone but there are many documented cases where they use surrogates - usually someone they have some form of control over. With regard to the time scale you have mentioned, that is also not unusual. When a series of murders happen over a short period, we immediately use the term serial killer, but these so-called serial events can equally be spaced over years. I am sorry I can't be more specific than I have been but the data base is rather flimsy. Inspector Bosch, I would like to suggest that you start looking for the body of Willy's missing wife. From what you have told me, she could have been one of his victims.'

'It is a strange co-incidence,' replied Bosch, 'but that was a thought that came to my mind as you were

545

talking a few moments ago. I will set that in motion as soon as we leave here. I want to thank you for giving us your time on your vacation. The profile you have constructed will be most useful.'

As they left, Angemeier called after Silke, 'Be very careful.'

CHAPTER 39

Willy slept through until eleven in the morning. The previous evening's activities which included a break-in, being shot at and a three hour walk across Vienna had totally exhausted him. After showering, he decided to get something to eat as he had missed the breakfast at the pension. He sat down at a quiet cafe in a narrow side-street close by. He needed to rethink his strategy, as he hadn't taken into account that Silke was armed with a pistol.

547

He believed he had achieved part of his plan with the two notes he had delivered to Silke and Reinhard, which hopefully pointed the finger of suspicion in the direction of Albert. This would probably intensify the search for Albert, he thought, and leave him relatively free. He cursed his luck that he had been so unsuccessful the previous evening but now, more than ever, he was determined to annihilate the two people who constituted his prime enemies. The events of the previous evening only intensified his desire for retribution. He then let his mind wander as he started planning where he would go skiing at the end of the year, when all this trouble was behind him. He loved the après-ski scene with its socialising and womanising. There were always many beautiful women available for a good time in the ski resorts. Not a single thought crossed his mind about the killing of Albert in Switzerland or Andrew in Mallorca, and he never had any thoughts about his wife lying in the grave he had dug in a forest one night, all those years ago. None of these people existed in his brain.

Willy decided that he would leave Silke alone for a while and concentrate on Reinhard. She would be on high alert after the previous evening's encounter, and he felt more comfortable when he had the element of surprise on his side.

He returned to the pension where he checked out and then caught a tram to the Westbahnhof station. He bought a first-class ticket to Munich. It was a direct, high-speed train and the timetable showed he would be there at 5 in the evening.

A copy of the Suddeutsche Zeitung, a local Munich newspaper, was lying on the seat opposite, left there possibly by someone who had travelled on the train from Munich to Vienna earlier that day.

He scanned through the paper, not finding much of interest him, as so many of the articles related to the Greek economic crisis for which Willy had no sympathy. He saw the Greeks as a lazy, useless nation who weren't able to manage their silly little economy - they were now holding out their hands like the beggar nations of Africa. Why should hard-working Germans have to rescue an indolent bunch of people, was the argument he always put forward. Let them eat baklava. His eye caught an advertisement in the classified section: *A private sale of a motor-bike, in excellent condition, only five hundred Euros.* He tore the advertisement out of the paper and put it in his pocket. He needed transport, as it would be unwise to use his own car, which was still parked at the airport. Here was an opportunity to buy a motor-bike privately, and he was sure he would be able to remain anonymous, paying cash. He also made a note of two self-catering apartments which were advertised. The train glided along the rails silently, thanks to the extra-long tracks and the excellent sound insulation in the modern European trains. He was soon lulled into a state of semi-sleep. He closed his eyes and his mind starting working out a new plan. He decided that he would spend some time observing both where Reinhard worked and lived. He knew that his house, which was in a very secluded area, could easily be investigated. He would have to be careful not to be seen by the young girl. She was now the only one who could recognise him. Maybe they were stupid not to have got rid of her too, he thought. His mind rambled on and then he fell asleep only waking up when he heard the announcement that they had arrived in Munich.

At the station, he phoned the number listed against the motorbike advertisement. The bike was still available and he made arrangements to view it within the hour. He wrote down the address and went outside to the taxi rank.

The taxi driver stopped outside the address he had been given. It was a neat, suburban house. The front door was opened by a sprightly old man as soon as Willy walked through the garden gate. He greeted Willy and directed him to a spotlessly-clean garage where the 1978 BMW R80 was standing in a corner. It was painted black and looked in showroom condition. Willy thought it was the perfect size and the 800cc motor would be fast enough for his requirements. He handed over the ten fifty Euro notes, and the owner took him inside to do the paperwork. Without sitting down, Willy explained that he wanted to get a permanent address first before they finalised the paperwork, which he claimed he would have within a week. He asked if the paperwork could be delayed until then. The man agreed readily but insisted on giving him a receipt, so Willy handed him Albert's passport. He looked at the passport and muttered something about Belgium, to which Willy grunted in return. He then handed Willy the keys to the bike and they shook hands.

At first, he rode cautiously, as he hadn't been on a motorbike for some years but after practising by, going around the same street a few times, he became more relaxed and confident. He was amazed at how quickly the skill required for riding a bicycle or motor bike returns, even after many years.

Willy drove to one of the self-catering apartments listed in the newspaper. It was in a small but neat, three-story block of apartments. He phoned the owner who agreed to meet him and show him the apartment. It was a bed-sitter, with a tiny kitchenette and a small bathroom. It was basic but comfortable enough for one person. Willy paid the deposit and a month's rent in cash and didn't ask for a receipt, which seemed to please the owner. He now had a place to stay as well as transport. He was confident that no one knew his whereabouts and a motorbike was a lot more anonymous than a car, even more so if one wears a full helmet.

Willy had noticed a small shopping complex nearby and decided to walk there, as he could carry more this way than on the bike. He purchased some basic provisions and some extra clothing. He had been surviving with only a few items of clothing and underwear. He also bought a pair of binoculars at a camera shop. Then he checked his watch and saw there was still enough time and light for him to drive down to Garmisch and survey the Heinrich residence. It was also an opportunity to get more practice riding the motorbike.

Willy found that he was comfortable travelling at 120 kilometres per hour on the motorway, but he realised that at this speed, the wind-chill factor made it slightly unpleasant. He would need to buy a leather jacket and gloves the following day. He enjoyed the sense of freedom a bike gives one on an open road, and the old bike was steady and powerful beneath him. It confirmed just how well it had been maintained.

He drove through the town of Garmisch and onto the Grainau road, slowing down so as not to attract attention. It was almost six o'clock, and people were arriving home. He took the country road that went past Adlerhorst. He slowed right down to a crawl and looked over the fence. Two cars were parked in the driveway, a big silver BMW 7 Series and a small white Opel, which he thought to be Reinhard's wife's car. The door of the house was closed and there was no sign of anyone. He continued to the second gate and saw the house where he and Albert had carried out the kidnapping. He drove off the road and into a clump of trees, where he hid the bike from view. He decided to approach the property from Hermann Heinrich's side, as he was certain this would present fewer problems. He climbed over the fence and walked carefully along the perimeter. If anyone approached him, he would say he was bird watching and the binoculars hanging around his neck would give credence to that. As he got closer to the house, he heard up a sound. It sounded like a radio or a television, and then he saw a woman walk out of the small cottage behind the main house. He had completely forgotten about

555

the staff that the old man employed. He would have to give the cottage a wide berth, which would involve hugging the fence until he was out of sight of the cottage. He eventually came to the side of Reinhard's house. Willy realised that he didn't know what had become of the cheeky little dog that had bitten Albert. Was he at the cottage or with Reinhard? They should have killed it at the time of the kidnapping, and he wouldn't have that to worry about now. He could see the BMW and with the binoculars, he could read the number plate. He scribbled the number on the back of his hand. He surveyed the house through the binoculars, noting where all the doors and windows were situated. Drain pipes at the rear of the house offered convenient access to the upper level, where people often feel comfortable leaving windows ajar in the summer. Willy was a bit concerned that there was no sign of Reinhard or his family, but he was satisfied with the reconnaissance he had conducted. This time, the planning would be more professional than his previous attempt in Vienna.

Once he was back at the apartment, he made sketches of the property. He had paced out the approximate distances and indicated on the sketch possible entrance and exit routes. He was worried that the two servants were still on the property and he would like to have known where the dog was being kept. He sat back with a beer and a microwave dinner he had warmed and felt very satisfied with his proposed plan. Tomorrow he would try to find out what Reinhard's movements were during the day. He wanted to establish the level of security where Reinhard parked his car. Soon he would be rid of two enemies.

* * * *

Less than a kilometre away, Silke was also settling down to a microwave dinner. She had gone into Otto Mayer's e-mails but had found nothing to suggest that he

557

had received any communication from his son. After she had eaten, she made a phone call to Anna to see how she was recovering after the ordeal with the intruder. She then went back to work on her laptop. She decided to hack into Wolfgang Koch's computer. While scrolling through his e-mails, she noticed that he received electronic bank statements. She opened the first one which was from Deutsche Bank. She whistled when she saw the large balance in the account. She scrolled down the items and came across an amount of 5000 Euros that had been withdrawn in cash. In today's so-called cashless society, this is a large amount for anyone to withdraw, and she thought she should make Bosch and Reinhard aware of it. She dialled Reinhard's number immediately.

Reinhard agreed with her that it was an inordinately large amount of cash and that Bosch should be informed. He explained that he had several important meetings the following day but would like to catch up with her to discuss the meeting with Professor Angemeier. They set a time for five the following evening at the apartment.

On her computer, Silke typed in two names, Albert and Willy. She decided to follow Angemeir's lead and call him Willy instead of the more ponderous Wilhelm. Below each name, she typed in their movements as she knew them and other bits of information. She wanted to see if any pattern existed. She could see that the trail for Albert ended at a hotel in Zurich, but with Switzerland now part of the Schengen Agreement, it would be easy for him to slip back into the rest of Western Europe completely unnoticed. Willy's trail went cold at Andrew Egan's house in Mallorca. The airports officials would have required either a passport or a photo identification document. Of course, he could have travelled under the name of Andrew Egan. She would have to look into that possibility. The only other way off the island was by boat or ferry. Did the Koch's own a boat which they kept there? What records do the ferry companies keep of their passengers?

The Crooked Star

* * * *

The next day, Willy rode to the offices of AH Bank. Across the road from the bank and directly opposite the entrance to the parking garage, he found a small bakery which had six tables, three inside and three on the pavement. Willy ordered a coffee and a bun, settling down with a complimentary newspaper at a pavement table. He watched as the cars of the bank employees entered through the automatic gates. The flow of cars stopped just before nine and then he noticed the silver BMW drive in. The registration number matched the one he had taken from the car the previous evening. Willy paid his bill to the cashier and walked across the road. He proceeded at a slow pace past the garage entrance. He saw a CCTV camera pointed at the gate. It was encased in a smoked-glass dome, which usually indicated that it could swivel around and cover a 180-degree view. He walked around the block and came down the opposite side to the bank. He spotted another camera covering that side and a further two keeping watch on the main entrance. The exterior of the bank was well protected, and presumably the interior, including the parking garage, even more so.

Willy walked along Wildenmayer Strasse beside the river and then turned left into Prinzregenten Strasse. He crossed the street and went into Munich's famous Englischer Garten, which is one of the largest urban parks in the world. Near the Japanese Tea House, he found a bench in the shade of an old oak tree. A few young boys were playing a game of football on the path nearby and they were delighted when he kicked an errant ball that came his way. He stood up and joined in the game for a few minutes, switching effortlessly from planning a murder, to kicking a ball and laughing with the young boys. Children were generally fond of Willy but cats avoided him, almost as if they could detect evil.

Willy went back to his look-out point at midday, sitting at the same table he had occupied earlier. He noted all the cars that left the parking, presumably workers going home for lunch, who then returned an hour or so later, but there was no BMW 7 Series amongst them.

Once again he walked aimlessly around the city, spending some time in the sports department of a departmental store. He returned to the café at four o'clock, just as the cars were streaming out. Again there was no BMW. Willy began to think that perhaps Reinhard had slipped out when he wasn't there. He paid the bill and was about to leave, when the big silver car appeared at the gate and drove out. Fortunately for Willy, the afternoon traffic had built up. He managed to start the bike and pull into the line of cars - he found himself just four cars behind Reinhard, a perfect following distance. The traffic moved slowly so Willy could maintain his distance. Up ahead, he saw a traffic light. Willy was worried that he would get caught by the red light, so he pulled out and went down the side of the stationary cars until just one vehicle separated him from BMW. Reinhard drove through just as the lights were changing back to red and Willy came almost alongside him, before slipping back once more. Instead of taking the road that would have put him on the motorway to Garmisch, Reinhard took a left turn in the direction of the university. This road was not as busy, so Willy hung back and was taken by surprise when Reinhard slipped into an empty parking bay on the road. Willy had to drive past and pull his bike in between two cars further up the road. He watched as Reinhard hurried across the road into a block of apartments. He didn't ring the bell, so Willy assumed that Reinhard must have a remote electronic door release.

Willy had the problem that as it was still early, there would be no tell-tale sign of a light being switched on, to indicate which apartment Reinhard had entered. He went back to the bike and fetched the pair of binoculars he had put in the side pocket, over the rear wheel. He would have to be careful using them, as people in urban areas become very suspicious when they see someone using binoculars. Bird watching in a suburb of Munich, is not a common pastime however the binoculars were small and fitted easily into his pocket. He went back across the road and stood alongside Reinhard's car. He looked at the building and noticed that several of the apartments had windows that had been opened, indicating that someone was home. He saw a shadow at a window and pulled out the binoculars. He got a quick of the occupant - it was an elderly lady. This could be a long wait he thought, as he may have a better opportunity to identify Reinhard in the apartment after dark.

*****

Reinhard received a hug and a warm greeting from Silke as he entered the apartment.

'So just when we thought it was all over, we still find ourselves in this mess and intrigue,' said Reinhard, as he sat down.

Silke remained standing, 'I am afraid I can only offer you coffee or wine.'

'Wine please. I have had non-stop meetings today and at least eight cups of coffee. Do you know how toxic coffee is? I love the smell of it, but I am not convinced that it agrees with me.'

Silke went to the fridge and produced a bottle of white wine. She poured out two glasses of the low-priced wine and sat opposite Reinhard.

'Cheers, to a final solution,' she said, raising her glass.

'Not a good choice of phrase but I understand the sentiment, so cheers,' responded Reinhard.

Silke went through the salient points of the discussion she and Bosch had with Professor Angemeir.

'It is very frightening to think that we could be looking at a psychopathic killer with a grudge against the two of us,' remarked Reinhard. He paused and took a small sip of the wine before continuing, 'Tomorrow we will be having my father's funeral. It is a private family affair, but I would be pleased if you were there. Sabine will be arriving for the day with her parents. Eva will remain in Hannover with some friends of ours. You do not have to worry about your safety, as there will be two private security guards present.'

'I would like to attend. I have never been to a funeral before so I don't know what to expect.'

Reinhard laughed, 'There seem to be so many things you have never done. I just wish I could say the same, not that I am pleased I have experienced funerals.

They say that it brings closure and healing. I take it you have been to church?'

'I was forced to go to church when I was young. At the time, I wasn't convinced that the God who resided in this' big tall building', was concerned about me. I prayed and prayed for love. Nothing happened so I invented my own God. My God didn't have a big, fancy church with marble columns and all the ancient symbols and trimmings. He loved children, and he loved me. I prayed to him when I was walking to school, or in the dark. I especially loved the dark because that was when I felt closest to Him and while He didn't directly answer my prayers, He gave me hope and the strength to fight on. I can't recall ever crying, which concerns me in a way. I suppose meeting you has answered some of my prayers.'

'That is a lovely description of your personal religion and you are correct. We have taken the simplicity out of God and made religion complicated and ornate. I am glad to hear that I have helped you because you have helped me immensely. Now, I am going to suggest that we go out for an early meal. There is a quaint French bistro a short walk from here.'

*****

Willy had walked up and down the road, sometimes crossing over or removing his jacket so as not to appear too conspicuous to the residents. Then he saw a man and a young woman emerge from the building. He could see that the man was definitely Reinhard. He hid behind a tree and watched as they turned and walked away from him. He followed at a discrete distance and watched them enter a restaurant. Willy stayed on the opposite side of the street and saw them being seated at a table. He hadn't been able to get a full-frontal view at the woman; however, she did have high cheek bones and so he wondered if it could be Silke. He questioned why she was back in Munich.

568

He decided to take a chance and walk past the restaurant, which was empty except for two tables. He crossed the road and strode past the big windows of the bistro. He glanced sideways as he passed by. That is definitely Silke Kotter, he said to himself. She fitted the description his father had given him. Here she is having dinner with Reinhard - both of his enemies together. If only he had a gun, he could walk in there and shoot both of them, then get on his bike and disappear. The police would then run around looking for Albert. As this scenario was not possible, he would have to wait and be patient. Nevertheless, this had been a very successful day. He walked back to the apartment block and checked the list of residents. Only two had listed their names. He tried the first one and there was no reply. The second one, whose name was Steiner, answered.

'Sorry to trouble you, Mr. Steiner. I am looking for Mr. Heinrich. Do you perhaps know which apartment he is in.?'

'No,' came back the curt reply.

Willy shook his head and then he saw a small sign that indicated that the block was managed by a realty estate company. He made a note of the name and contact number.

* * * *

There had been no funeral announcements in the press, so Reinhard felt sure that there was no danger from either Albert or Willy. The security guards were dressed in dark suits and would have been inconspicuous, except for the fact that they kept well apart from the main body of mourners. Silke felt a little awkward surrounded by the well-dressed women, including Sabine, her mother and two sisters. She chose a pew two rows behind the family and noticed that she attracted a number of glances, as some family members turned around to get a glimpse of her. She could see Sabine giving a whispered explanation, which she thought would not be too complimentary.

Silke looked around the church, which was similar to the ones she had been to in Austria. Perhaps the Catholics only have one set of building plans she thought to herself, and mass-produced statues of Christ and the Virgin Mary. Why do they all look the same?

The service lasted almost an hour and Silke found herself standing in the entrance of the church where the family had gathered, to await directions to the luncheon that was booked at one of Munich's best restaurants, 'Tantris.'

Sabine came up to her and said, 'How nice of you to come to the funeral. Reinhard tells me you have been attacked at your home in Vienna. It is important that we catch these people soon, as I cannot go on living like this. I have not done any training for weeks.'

'Fortunately, I wasn't attacked directly but my friend was injured. There are two suspects and we know who they are, so it is only a matter of time before they are apprehended. Tell me how is Eva?'

'She appears to be back to normal, although she does ask after her grandfather from time to time, which I suppose is only natural as she saw him every day. Well, I must go and talk to the other people. I'm Sorry you are not joining us for lunch.'

Silke smiled, relieved that she had not been invited to a lunch where no doubt, the talk would be about their latest fashion acquisitions. She felt like an outcast in this rich and false society. Jogging in the streets of Vienna didn't come close to having a personal trainer.

Silke slipped away quietly without even saying goodbye to Reinhard, who was in an intense conversation with his father-in law.

* * * *

Willy arrived at the realty company whose sign said they managed the apartment block that Reinhard had entered the previous evening. Willy smiled and greeted the woman behind the counter. He noted that she was about his age and would therefore be susceptible to light hearted flirting.

'A lovely day and a lovely woman. What more can a man ask for?'

'How can I be of assistance?' she replied, returning the smile.

'I have to photograph some paintings at the apartment of a Mr. Heinrich. The address is Apartment Edelweiss but I do not know the actual apartment number. It is not listed in the phone book. Can the lovely lady please help me?' He leaned forward over the counter and while he appeared confident, he was actually aware that his request was so weak and stupid, that it was unlikely to convince anyone.

'I cannot divulge details like that, I'm afraid. But let me check it on my computer.' She tapped in some numbers. 'Yes, here it is. I have Mr Heinrich's business number. One moment and I will try and connect you.'

She rang the number and asked to be put through to Mr. Heinrich. 'Oh, I see. Mr Heinrich is at a funeral and cannot be contacted.'

She turned to Willy and said, 'You heard that, he is at a funeral and can't be contacted, so I am sorry but I cannot help you.'

Willy feigned disappointment, 'Just a number. Please, and then I can be on my way.'

She shook her head and shrugged, 'Twenty- two.'

574

Willy blew her a kiss as he turned and walked out of her office, smiling.

CHAPTER 40

It was a warm summer day at the start of the weekend. Reinhard had invited Silke to his house in Grainau, promising to take her to the peak of the Zugspitze. He had received a call from Sabine who claimed she was going out of her mind in Hannover and wanted to return home. Reinhard repeated some of the warnings Silke had relayed from her meeting with Professor Angemeir. He explained that with the two suspects still at large, he was concerned about any further danger, to Eva in particular. He knew that he would not be able to keep convincing Sabine, who objected to having her luxurious routine interrupted. Eva came on the line and gave him kisses over the phone. He was pleased that she seemed back to normal, although no one would know what fears she still harboured in her young mind and how they may affect her in later life.

Silke arrived just after 10 o'clock in one of the bank's cars. She was more confident driving now and on several occasions, pushed the small car up to 160 kms on the motorway, forcing cars into the slower lanes with her aggressive flashing of lights.

The security guard had been advised of her arrival by Reinhard and she was allowed to drive up to the front door, where Reinhard and Blondi were waiting for her.

Reinhard shook her hand and gave her a hug, while Blondi jumped up and down until Silke bent down and stroked her.

'Do you need to go to the bathroom,' enquired Reinhard, 'otherwise we should leave right away?'

The Crooked Star

It was a short drive to the station at Grainau, which is the starting point for the rack railway that goes to a midway point up the mountain. Reinhard deliberately sat on the left side of the wooden coach, as he did not want to look at the Eibsee which the train passes soon after leaving Grainau. After a few hundred metres, the train enters the bowels of the mountain and travels in the cool, dark atmosphere until it reaches its destination at a point roughly halfway up the mountain.

They emerged from the mountain and onto the sun terrace which was covered in snow, even at this time of the year. Initially the whiteness is blinding and it takes a while for one's eyes to adjust to the sudden brightness. Silke was amazed, for while it does snow in Vienna, the city is not part of the Austrian alpine system, being situated in a low-lying plateau and she had never before been surrounded by so many snow-covered peaks. Reinhard pointed out the peak of the Zugspitze that they would get to via a cable car. It is a mighty mountain and at 3000 metres, it towers over the surrounding peaks like a matriarch with her young. At the peak itself the views are even more spectacular, as the North face looks over a vast expanse of Bavaria, while the South face offers a vista into Austria.

As they sat on the sunny restaurant terrace, enjoying two bowls of goulash and glasses of beer, Reinhard looked wistfully over the scene below.

'My father loved coming up here. He would come up at least four times a year and one of my earliest memories is looking down on the beautiful scene below.'

'I am so sorry for you. I think that when a loved one is taken away by unnatural causes, it is always worse than the normal death which awaits all of us.'

'Yes, that is so. We have to stop whoever was responsible for my father's murder from carrying on their evil work. I am still not convinced about the ability of the police to find these culprits. Silke, you are back for a short while and so I am going to ask you to keep up with your investigative work. I will pay you.'

'I will only do it on condition that you do not pay me. You have been so generous to the point of embarrassing me, however, I have been doing some research, and when we return to the house perhaps we can go through it.'

'Excellent. Look down there,' said Reinhard, pointing into the valley below. 'That is where I live and often I sit in the garden, especially on a clear night and I look up here. Now I am up here looking down, I can't decide which is the best view. What I do know, is that from below there is a bright star situated close to this peak. I call it the crooked star.'

'Why the crooked star?' asked Silke.

'It is a star, which in my mind, is in the likeness of a swastika. It shines down on this country and in particular it shines down on the House of Heydrich. How can we expect to do what we did and still prosper? That would be so wrong and immoral. I am seriously considering selling my shares in the bank and giving the bulk of the proceeds to Jewish organisations. Sabine, I know, will kill me for this but if I can somehow extinguish that star, then perhaps Eva will not have to carry the genetic scourge throughout her life.'

'Reinhard, I think you are being very hard on yourself. Why should you suffer because of your grandfather? I don't know who my parents were let alone my grandfather. I would be very angry if my life had to be affected by some anonymous grandparent.'

'Did you not feel that fate had somehow dealt you some cruel cards that caused you to have to struggle?'

Silke looked at Reinhard and her immediate thoughts were, that although she liked him and saw him as a father she had never really known, he was still a weak pathetic figure who didn't realise how fortunate he was to have unlimited money and luxury.

'I didn't enjoy my early life. In fact, I hated it.' Silke paused, because she wasn't ready to divulge the details surrounding her changed identity and the child taken from her. Much of my education was heuristic in nature and my yearning never ceases. Do you know what I am going to do with some of the money you gave me? I am going to go to university. Reinhard you have to look at your life and work out why it is not fulfilling. No one else can do it for you and when you find the answer it may well be that you give away half of your money or it may be something else. Don't waste time. Rich people and poor people alike have a finite allocation and of all the things one may squander, time is the most precious.'

'The philosopher speaks again. If only I could take your mind and put it into my cranium I would be a happy man. For the first time in my life I really learned about my background especially going back two generations. It was a bitter-sweet education I have to admit but it was necessary.' He looked directly into Silke's eyes, 'I detect there is something that burns in your soul. Do you not want to know where you come from?' he asked.

'I do and I don't, 'Silke lied, 'But what if the information that I find hurts me even more than the lack of knowledge does now? Perhaps one day I will have the courage to look into the inner reaches of my soul.'

Reinhard checked his watch, 'Come we need to descend into the valley again and we need to look at your computer for clues that we can give useless Inspector Bosch.'

* * * *

The Crooked Star

Willy had gone along to 22, Apartment Edelweiss and after ensuring that no one was in the apartment, he went inside the building and up a flight of stairs to the first floor where he checked out the locking mechanism on the door. He was surprised to find that it was a simple Yale type which he would again be able to open with a credit card. He toyed with the idea of entering the apartment but dismissed it immediately, as his plan was to attack Reinhard and his family first. He went back to his self-catering apartment and prepared his kit for later that night. Earlier he had purchased a stun gun which he was charging. A torch, binoculars, and a claw hammer made up his lethal kit.

*****

It was sometime after five that evening, when Reinhard and Silke returned to the house. Reinhard took

Silke into the garden and down to where his bench was located.

'There,' he said pointing up to the peak towering in the distance, 'now you can see Zugspitze from below.'

Silke sat on the bench and gazed up at the mountain. Its majestic mass dominated the skyline. She could see why Reinhard felt the way he did about it. The mountain had some sort of magnetism, making it impossible not to look at it. Could it be possible for an inanimate object to have a soul, she wondered.

Reinhard sat down next to her, 'Later on when the stars come out, you will see the star I spoke to you about. It is a bright star to the left and slightly above the peak. I will show it to you later when it appears.'

'Your crooked star - perhaps we can hide it behind the mountain so that it no longer shines here.'

Once they were inside, Reinhard poured some drinks while Silke fetched her computer. As the battery was low, she plugged it in to recharge.

Silke explained, how she felt Willy could have left the island of Mallorca. He would have avoided the airport as a photo ID is required in all EU airports, so that only left the sea. The options would be a private boat or a commercial ferry. Then, in the case of Albert, if he was no longer in Switzerland he could simply have hopped on a train and gone into any of the four countries that surround it.

'It is my theory,' said Silke, 'that Albert has gone into hiding and that Willy has somehow made his way to the mainland and he is the one pursuing us, despite some of the evidence indicating the involvement of Albert Mayer. Willy is insane, but cleverly insane. I think we will catch him through his father. Why did his father withdraw five thousand Euros in cash? I believe it was to enable Willy to move around unseen. Today a credit card is almost like an instantaneous tag on your whereabouts. I am convinced he will contact his father and I am hoping to detect when he does.'

'So, you don't think Albert is also involved?'

'He was certainly involved with the kidnapping but when you look at Willy's psychological profile, he seems more likely to be the one targeting us. I could be wrong of course.'

'Despite the fact that I believe the police are thick-headed, I think you should advise Bosch about the cash withdrawal and your ideas on the ferry escape from Mallorca.'

'I intended to do that on Monday. At least I have now got a working relationship with the inspector. Look, the police move slowly but I think Bosch is quite shrewd.'

The Crooked Star

Silke looked at her watch, 'I am going to head back to Munich while there is still some light. I am not yet comfortable with night driving. Today was a very beautiful experience for me. I can see why you love living here and I am now torn between the Mediterranean and the Alps as my favourite place.'

'Silke, there is still so much more for you to see around the world, but your two favourite places would also be in my top five. Let us see if it is dark enough to see the star.'

They went outside and to Heinrich's disappointment, while it was dark enough, clouds had moved across the sky around the mountain obscuring the stars.

Silke gave a good-bye hoot as she drove out and headed for the road to Munich.

Reinhard went inside and walked through to the kitchen, wondering what he should cook for himself. He looked in the fridge but finally decided that a take-away pizza would be easier and possibly more enjoyable than any dish he could make. He phoned a pizzeria in Garmisch which did deliveries, and ordered two medium-sized pizzas, one for himself and one for the security guard.

Just then his mobile phone rang. It was Inge, his estranged mistress.

'Is it convenient to talk?' she enquired.

'I am alone at the house. Inge, I didn't expect to hear from you. How are you?'

'I am fine. I have been out of mind thinking about the terrible time you have been through. I am so sorry about your father, but getting Eva back must have been wonderful.'

'Yes it was. My whole life is in turmoil. My father actually died of a heart attack, which was no doubt brought about by the trauma caused by the kidnapping. That is why it is so important that we catch these bastards. Sabine and Eva are in Hannover and will stay there as long as the culprits are at large. What have you been doing lately?'

'Nothing much out of the ordinary. I went to Paris for two weeks but returned after one. Reinhard, I have really missed you.'

'You hurt me terribly, but the events of the past few weeks have overpowered all other emotions. I feel so drained, nevertheless, I too have missed you. Why don't we meet tomorrow? Are you still on holiday?'

'I am doing nothing tomorrow. Phone me at any time.'

'I will contact you. See you tomorrow.'

Reinhard put the phone down and switched on the television.

*****

Driving along the motorway, Silke didn't notice a black motorbike heading in the opposite direction.

Willy stopped about two hundred metres from the entrance to the Heinrich residence. He pulled the bike into the bushes and laid it on its side. It would be virtually impossible for any passing motorist to see it. He dangled the torch from his belt and put the head of the claw hammer into a side pocket of his trousers. He held the stun gun in his hand. He walked quietly along the grass verge, keeping close to the fence. He stopped suddenly when he saw a car parked next to the driveway. There was still enough light for him to make out a logo painted on the side of the car. An interior light was on and someone was sitting inside. Shit, he said under his breath. This had to be a security guard. He couldn't continue as planned, so he turned around and went back to where the bike lay. He sat down next to the bike pondering what his next move should be. He was aware of the problem he had encountered in Vienna and he didn't want a repeat of that. He needed to either distract the guard or to get close enough to him to disable him with the Tazer stun gun. He decided that he would pretend he was lost and get the guard to come over to the gate. It would have to be done quietly, so that no one in the house was aware of it.

He fiddled in the side pocket of his jacket and found a ballpoint pen. He needed some paper to write on. Where the hell would he get paper in the middle of a field? He felt in his pocket again and found the receipt he had been given when he purchased the stun gun, the back of which was blank. He scribbled an address on it and walked back in the direction from which he had just come. The guard was still inside the car. Willy held the note in his left hand and leant over the gate and said, 'Excuse me' but he didn't get a reaction so he shouted a little louder, 'Hello'.

This time the guard heard him and looked to the gate where Willy was waving a piece of paper. He got out of the car and walked towards Willy.

'I am looking for this address,' said Willy, holding the piece of paper in such a way that the guard would have to come closer, in order to read it. As the guard bent forward to read the false address, Willy's right hand shot out and he dug the end of the stun gun into his neck squeezing the trigger. The electrical charge caused the guard to fall to the ground immediately, his arms and legs shaking involuntarily. Willy jumped over the gate, dropped the stun gun on the ground and pulled out the hammer which was in his pocket and brought it down on the guard's head. He dragged the limp body across to the car and pushed it underneath. He looked around to see if the noise had alerted anyone but all was quiet.

Willy walked back to the gate to retrieve the stun gun and as he was about to continue towards the house, a car painted in the Italian national colours drove up to the gate. A young man, holding two pizza boxes, jumped out of the car and announced that he was here to deliver the order.

Willy took the boxes from the delivery man who asked for a payment of fourteen Euros. Willy pulled out his wallet and gave the man a twenty Euro note and told him to keep the change. He waited for the brightly coloured car to drive away. He could hardly believe his luck. Now he wouldn't have to break into the house. He returned to the car and dragged the guard's body from underneath it. He could hear some shallow breathing coming from the limp form. He stripped off the guard's green jacket and tried it on. It was a reasonable fit if he left the buttons undone. He dusted off the jacket, picked up the two pizza boxes and went up to the front door.

As he knocked on the door, he could hear Blondi barking and the sound of heavy footsteps approaching. He stood slightly to one side so that his face would be in the shadows. The door opened and Heinrich's line of vision went to the two pizza boxes.

'Thank you,' Heinrich said, reaching forward to grasp one of the boxes. 'One is for you, of course.'

As Reinhard took the top box, Willy dropped the bottom one onto the floor and pushed the stun gun at Heinrich's chest. Heinrich fell back shouting loudly. Willy wasn't sure that he had successfully managed to achieve a full electrical charge, so he bent down to try again. A blur of fur caught his eye, as Blondi attacked him, biting his hand. He dropped the stun gun and grabbed the dog with both hands. This time he was determined to kill it. Blondi twisted her head and her razor-sharp teeth dug into his wrist. Willy let out a shout and dropped the dog. He kicked out wildly at her, but Blondi saw it coming and darted away, barking furiously. Heinrich managed to get to his feet but Willy was at his side and threw him to the ground.

He pushed the stun gun into his neck and this time a direct charge went into Reinhard's body, causing violent convulsions. Willy wrenched the telephone cord out of the wall and tied Reinhard's hands behind his back. After a short while the convulsions stopped and Reinhard was able to talk.

'Who the hell are you?' he shouted, trying to sit up.

Willy pushed him down again and laughed.

'My name is Albert Mayer.'

'Don't lie. I have met Albert Mayer. You are not him. You must be Wolfgang Koch's son. You killed my father and kidnapped my daughter.'

'Shut up. You don't know what you are talking about. Albert Mayer and his father carried out the kidnapping. You thought you were clever hounding my father. Now look at you.'

Blondi was still growling and barking furiously. Willy tried to grab her but she ran around him and out the door. He ran after her but stopped after a few metres when he realised he was no match for her speed. Then he heard the sound of a mobile phone ringing. It was coming from the direction of the security guard's car. He cursed and ran back into the house, worried that the security company was trying to contact the guard. When he got back inside, Reinhard was nowhere to be seen.

Willy rushed from room to room in a panic and then he saw him at the top of the stairway. Reinhard, with his hands still tied behind his back, was pushing an alarm button with his nose. Suddenly a siren went off. Willy ran up the steps and threw Reinhard to the ground. He pulled out his bloodied claw hammer and brought it down on Reinhard's skull. Several blows rained down on Reinhard. A pool of blood formed around his head.

Willy bolted down the steps and ran to where he had hidden his bike. He had to get away before the police were alerted by the security company. He rode down to the main road and headed in the direction of Munich. He breathed in the cold night air and smiled to himself. Had he looked back, he would have seen the stars shining, as the cloud cover lifted. Reinhard's crooked star seemed brighter than usual that night.

CHAPTER 41

Once back at the apartment, Silke kicked off her shoes, poured herself a glass of wine and opened a packet of potato crisps. She had scanned through the television programmes and settled on an old movie, Lawrence of Arabia with Peter O'Toole in the leading role. It was an exceptionally long film and the German sub-titles added to the tedium. She fell asleep as Lawrence was attacking a

Turkish train with his ragtag Arab army. It was the persistent ringing of her mobile phone that awoke her. It was Bosch on the line, apologising for the late call.

'I am sorry to have to tell you this but the Garmisch police have just informed me that Reinhard appears to have been murdered. His private security guard is unconscious and on his way to hospital.'

'Oh my God, no,' shouted Silke into the phone. 'I was with him just a few hours ago. I can't believe this. I just can't believe it. We must catch these bastards.'

'That is why I am phoning you. You could be next on the killer's list. Do you want me to post a police car at your address?'

'That won't be necessary as no one knows this address.'

'It seems possible that you were the last person to see Mr Heinrich alive, so can I ask you to come into my office tomorrow to make a statement regarding your visit to his house.'

'I will be there first thing in the morning. I can't explain how shocked I am. I am devastated.'

As Silke put down the phone, she burst into tears. Here was the first person in her life she felt she could trust and now he was abruptly taken from her. She went to the front door and slid the chain into place - just as a precaution she said to herself. She thought about Eva and how at such a young age she would no longer have a father. Eva obviously wouldn't suffer financially but money can't bring back a parent. Silke hoped that Sabine would allow her to see Eva from time to time. Incoherent thoughts were bouncing around in her confused mind.

Silke realised that sleep wouldn't come easily that night, so she composed herself and started planning what she would do to protect herself. There was no way, she decided, that she would wait like a sitting duck for this nutcase to come along and murder her. That wasn't her style. She was a survivor and a fighter. She considered and rejected various methods, until she had narrowed it down to one workable scenario. She would lure Willy to a place where he could be captured or killed. She was still convinced that Wolfgang Koch was the key. She racked her brain as she sat in the chair looking at a blank television set. She closed her eyes for long periods, as this helped to focus her thinking. She got up several times to check the door or to investigate noises. Finally, at four a.m. she fell into a deep sleep.

When Silke arrived at the Munich police headquarters the following day, Bosch was expecting her and without even asking, he poured her a cup of strong coffee.

'I can see that neither of us slept much last night. After talking to you, I drove to the Heinrich house. It was terrible. We have a maniac on the loose. The security guard had been struck on the head and he was found underneath his car. His company jacket was lying in the driveway near the gate and Mr Heinrich's body was lying at the top of the stairway. It appears he had somehow managed to set off the security alarm. Two uneaten pizzas, still in their boxes, were lying near the front door.' He hesitated before continuing. 'Mr Heinrich had been violently bludgeoned and must have died almost immediately. Someone will check with the pizza company as to who ordered the pizzas. Another strange point is that there was no sign of the little dog, which is unusual. Was it there when you visited earlier on?'

'Yes, it was definitely there. The poor little creature has also been through an awful time, and I hope it hasn't been harmed in any way.'

Bosch handed Silke a pad and a ballpoint pen. 'I need you to write out a statement. Put down everything you can remember, especially if you noticed anything odd. Try to be accurate with times.'

'That won't be a problem, but I can assure you that everything seemed normal. Obviously, when I left in the early evening, there was a different security guard to the one who was on day shift when I first arrived, but that was all.'

'I have asked a senior officer from Hannover to break the news to Mrs. Heinrich. First was the funeral of the old man and now another family death. I am glad the task of telling her isn't mine. It is one of the aspects of this job that I truly hate.'

Silke wrote out her statement which ran to half a page and handed it to Bosch. He read it through noting some points.

'You left at 7:15p.m. and all was in order then. The next important time must be when the delivery of the pizzas took place. In the statement you say that you and Mr. Heinrich discussed some aspects you had uncovered. What were they, if I may ask?'

Silke replied, 'In fact, I was planning to contact you today. I think Willy left Mallorca by ferry. This should be checked out.' She had decided to delay mentioning the cash withdrawal made by Wolfgang Koch, until after she had seen him herself.

'Good point. We can ask the Spanish police to look at ferry records or maybe even CCTV footage, if they have something like that. We also shouldn't forget about Albert Mayer. I have a sneaky feeling he is still connected.'

Bosch put her statement into a folder.

'Thank you for coming in, Miss Kotter, I will keep you informed of any developments, but I must caution you to be very vigilant until we have apprehended these maniacs. You have my phone numbers, so if you feel you are in any danger, do not hesitate to call me. How long do you intend to stay in Germany?'

'I feel safe where I am staying at the moment, so I will be here at least until the end of the week. After that, who knows?'

'If my observation is correct, you and Mr. Heinrich seemed quite close. How are you taking this dreadful news?'

'Last night was horrible,' replied Silke, holding back tears that wanted to flow. 'When someone dies, a part of your life comes to a standstill. The rest goes on but one track halts. I see life like a series of parallel tracks and when all the tracks come to an end - you die.'

Bosch stood up and held out his hand to her, 'Be very vigilant.'

They shook hands and Silke walked out of Bosch's office, knowing that her next move could have disastrous consequences.

Now that Reinhard was dead, Silke had no idea how long she would be able to drive the bank's car, so she decided, without delay, to go from the police HQ to Passau and see if she could meet with Koch.

While she was driving, she was still thinking about how she could trap Willy into coming out into the open. It was unlikely that he would agree to meet at a rendezvous that was too public or from where he would have difficulty escaping. He would probably want to set the time and place for a meeting, but then again, she thought, he may refuse to meet her at all. If he really was a psychologically unstable, and it certainly seemed to be the case, then she would have to appeal to his arrogance. A plan was now slowly developing in her head.

The Crooked Star

As Silke got closer to her destination, she became acutely aware that she had reached a pivotal point in her life. She took a number of deep breaths to steady herself. She thought back to her cold and lonely childhood - the times when she had been so frightened and alone, surrounded by people she couldn't trust enough to confide in. Eva and even Blondi the dog must have lost all faith in mankind. She realised just how important trust is in a person's life. Reinhard had come closest to someone she felt she could close to and now he was gone - not just gone, but murdered. A strong sense of revenge welled up inside her, not only must she negate the danger facing her but she must also seek revenge for the killing, the unnecessary killing of Reinhard. What about Eva, she thought. What have they done to this defenceless, innocent child? She knew what it was like to stand and look up at a giant-like creature shouting at you. She had cowered many times when her father had admonished her, not in surrender, but out of fear of some eternal damnation that would await her if she showed any resistance. Each time it happened it was like fuel to the fire that burned in her soul. These murderers would not defeat her.

Silke slowed down as she approached the house and parked outside the property next door. She was feeling edgy, as she hadn't brought the small gun Novak had given her. She walked up to the gate, hesitating for a few seconds before opening it and walking up the short pathway to the front door.

She knocked twice and waited. Eventually it was opened and there was instant recognition from Koch.

'You are not the police. Get off my property,' he shouted, ready to slam the door in her face. Silke held up her hand.

'Please hear me out before you close the door.'

'Well...' replied Koch, opening the door wider.

'Mr. Koch, I have not come here to hound you but to offer my help. I have some information about Willy that I think you should be aware of. Please may I come in?'

Koch hesitated, unsure whether to believe her or not. Finally, he opened the door and stood aside for Silke to enter. He directed her into a small office and pointed to a chair.

'Well?' he said again, looking enquiringly at her.

Silke began, 'Mr. Reinhard Heinrich was murdered last night. It will no doubt be in all the media later today, but I can assure you it is the truth.' She hesitated to see if Koch would show any reaction, but he remained completely impassive.

Silke continued, 'Mr. Koch, you must agree that there is a thread linking the kidnapping of old Mr.Heinrich with this murder, the murder of his son Reinhard. There was also an unrelated murder in Mallorca at a place where we think Willy had been staying.'

Koch looked at Silke for a long time. He was very worried about his son. All those years ago, it had cost him a large sum of money to get a key witness to return to Turkey, so that Willy could go free. He was also aware of the rumours that were circulating when Willy's wife suddenly disappeared. He didn't like to contemplate it, but inwardly he was worried that he had a son who was a murderer. Despite everything, he would continue to protect him.

'What you say is all supposition.' He was trying to appear unconcerned but inwardly he was extremely worried. 'I am very sorry to hear about the death of Mr. Heinrich so soon after that of his father. His father was a good friend of mine. I have already told the police, several times in fact, that they need to find Otto Mayer and his son,

Albert. Then they will have the answer to all this nonsense.'

'The police have spoken to Mr. Mayer senior. His son, like your Willy, is also missing. I think you know where Willy is. I would like to talk to him. You see, I have found evidence linking Albert Mayer to certain events. I am convinced your son will find this evidence very useful.'

'Give me the evidence and if he contacts me, I will pass it onto him,' Koch said, pleased that some good news might be forthcoming.

'I need to discuss it directly with Willy,' Silke responded firmly. She noticed how he had suddenly perked up and shown some interest. Was this an indication that he knew more than he was saying?

'Why would you want to help my son, when you were working for Mr. Heinrich?'

'Firstly, Mr. Heinrich is now dead, and I don't want to see your son accused unjustly. You and Willy must decide if you want this information or not. I am going to leave you with my mobile number.'

'Where will you be?' asked Koch.

'Here and there. Maybe Germany, maybe Austria but I am free for the rest of the week. By the way, that was a lot of cash you gave Willy. What was it? Five thousand Euros?' Silke could see the shock on Koch's face as she dropped the last bombshell. She wanted him to know that she had confidential information.

'How do you know this? Have you been snooping around my house again? What you do is against the law. I don't know that I can trust you, and maybe I shouldn't be speaking to you. Please go now.' Koch stood up and walked to the door.

As Silke got to the door, she handed him a piece of paper.

'This is my phone number.'

Koch closed the door behind her without saying good-bye.

He went inside and sat down at the desk. He held his head in both hands. How something as straightforward as trying to locate some stolen panels could have led to a disaster of this magnitude, was beyond his comprehension, he kept saying to himself. He started looking for the number Willy had given him to use in an emergency. He searched through all the papers on top of the desk. He could feel a panic attack coming on. What if he had lost the bloody number? He went through the four drawers of the desk and then rechecked the top. He was feeling desperate. He went to the bedroom and looked everywhere. How much bad luck can a person have? he thought. He went back to the office, going down on his knees to look under the desk. He found two papers on the floor but not the one he was looking for. He could feel himself getting emotional. He walked past the bathroom and saw a pair of trousers lying across a washing basket. He felt in the pocket and there was the paper. He looked up to heaven and said a prayer, for his housekeeper would have washed them the following day and the number would have been lost. He sat down at the desk and typed a single word into his mobile phone - 'emergency' and entered the number Willy had given him. He pushed the 'send' button.

CHAPTER 42

Wolfgang Koch was going crazy with anxiety as he sat looking at his mobile phone. He checked it several times to see that it had a sufficient charge and a strong enough signal. A little after 6 p.m. the phone came to life with a double beep, indicating that a message had come through. His hand was shaking as he opened it. All it said was 'no.3- 8 p.m.'. He had forgotten that Willy had given him a code. With shaking hands, he started looking for yet another piece of paper. He was a lot luckier this time. He read the note Willy had left him. No 3 simply said - turn right and walk. He looked at his watch and saw that he would have to wait almost another two agonising hours.

At precisely 8 o'clock, he picked up his walking stick and stepped onto the pavement outside his house. He turned to the right and started walking down the street. On the opposite side, he noticed a couple also out for a stroll and further down the road, he saw two young boys doing wheelies on their bicycles, but no sign of Willy. He walked to the end of the street, looked back from where he had just come and then crossed over. Perhaps he was too early, so he checked his watch again. It was now six minutes past eight. Then suddenly someone emerged from behind a tree. It was Willy.

'Continue walking slowly. We are two people out for a stroll. I can't stay too long. What is the emergency?'

'That Silke Kotter woman was here earlier today. She says she has information you could find useful. Some of it relates to Albert. She also knows about the cash I withdrew for you. Do you know that Reinhard Heinrich was murdered yesterday?'

'It is all over the Munich papers this evening. I couldn't care less about him. That bitch is delving into everything. Tell me, how am I supposed to get this information?'

'Here is her phone number.' Wolfgang handed his son the note that Silke had given him. 'Now please tell me. Did you had anything to do with the death of Heinrich?'

'Of course not, father. It could be that bloody Albert. He and his father and your stupid friend Eicke got us into this shit of a mess. Now I have to try to sort it out. Turn up this road and hopefully it will lead me back to where I parked my bike.'

It was a smaller side road and had less street lighting, which made Willy feel more secure. He couldn't help thinking what a lovely evening it was. It was warm, with a light breeze. Birds were starting to gather at their nesting places in the trees, and their last chatter indicated they were jockeying for the best branches for the night. It was Willy's relaxed attitude that convinced his father that he could not have been involved in a murder the previous day.

'What plans do you have to sort out this 'shit' as you call it?'

'What plans do I have?' Willy repeated. 'That is easy. I will finally expose Albert, but because I could be seen as an accessory to the kidnapping, I will have to leave Germany until he is found guilty and imprisoned. Then I will clear my name.'

'You make it sound so simple. I just hope you can do it before I die. All of this stress has accelerated my demise. I could even drop dead tonight.'

'Father, you have nothing to worry about. Say very little to the police but keep mentioning Albert's name. Look, I think if we go down this lane, we will come to my bike. Please do not worry, as I have everything under control.'

They arrived at the bike. Willy put his arm around the old man's shoulders. In the fading light, he wasn't able to see the tears welling in his father's eyes.

'Willy, do you need more money?'

'Not yet. Take something to help you sleep tonight.'

Willy revved the engine and drove off. Wolfgang watched the red tail-light turning into the main road and disappearing from view. Tears ran down his face. Somehow he knew that he had seen his son for the last time. As he walked slowly back to his home, he thought back over his life. Yes, it had been successful from a material point of view, but he had witnessed how his father had languished and died in a foreign prison. His wife and daughter had died in a car crash, and now his son was on the run. He was really too old and frail to help him. Was it some kind of curse, he wondered? One that lets you think you are walking the road of achievement but then undermines you in such a way, that all you have is a bitter taste in your mouth - like a mirage.

Perhaps life is a mirage he said to himself. You imagine you have achieved something, only to find when you are close to dying, that it was just a worthless vapour. What if life is not real but just the imaginings of our minds?

* * * *

Willy waited until mid-morning of the following day before contacting Silke.

She answered her mobile phone after two rings.

'Hello, this is Albert Mayer. I understand you wish to talk to Willy Koch.'

'Yes, that is so,' replied Silke.

'Well then, you will need to follow these instructions, but please don't be stupid and have the police there because we will simply disappear. You must be at Rosenheim railway station at exactly four p.m. today. Buy a return ticket to Kufstein. Wait outside the information office on the station. Do you understand that?'

'I have written it down. I will be there.'

The call was disconnected and Silke let out a long breath. Was she being stupid she asked herself? Here she was walking into the wolf's lair. So Albert was alive and obviously working with Willy. Why Kufstein, she pondered? It was a small border town on the Austrian side.

Silke looked at her watch and saw that she had three hours to get to Rosenheim, so she needed to start her preparations for the meeting. She checked the battery power on her portable tape recorder. Then she rummaged through her suitcase and found the small gun. She took off the tee-shirt she was wearing and tied the gun to the label at the back. When she put the tee-shirt back on, she found that the neckline had pulled right up and was very uncomfortable. With much manoeuvring, she managed to relieve the downward pressure by taping the gun to the back of her neck with medical plaster. She checked in the mirror to make sure that it was not too obvious. Then she wrote a note on her mobile phone which she saved to drafts. It read – 'Call from Albert Mayer. Meeting arranged with Willy at Rosenheim/Kufstein; 4p.m. today'. If it all went wrong, she wanted the police to have some information, to assist them in their hunt for Willy and Albert.

She was feeling so nervous that she decided to leave right away, even though she had two hours to spare. On the road, she kept considering the idea of contacting Bosch, but what if that ruined it all. She could not live like some frightened bird sitting up in a tree, surrounded by predators. She had seen how fragile life is - how you could be alive one minute and dead the next - it was very frightening. She wanted to live and she had to see the Mediterranean again, perhaps even find a place to live nearby. Fear was competing with her resolve to continue but she was determined to overcome this. She knew she had to go through with it.

CHAPTER 43

There is only one railway station in Rosenheim which Silke found quite easily. She parked the car in an area to the side of the station and just before getting out, she decided to leave a note addressed to Inspector Bosch at Munich police HQ. She repeated the message she had put into her phone and left it next to the gear stick. Then she went into the contacts menu on her phone and linked Bosch's number to the speed dial, so that she would only need to press a single button for it to dial his number. She was beginning to think that she was becoming paranoid.

She walked into the railway station and looked around at the people, some of whom were hurrying by, while others were lounging around. It was strange, she thought, how railway stations always attract a good proportion of a town's low-life. Is it because railways stations offer anonymity and acceptability? She couldn't see anyone who looked like the photographs she had seen of Albert or Willy, so she decided to walk a short way into the town.

She returned to the station at fifteen minutes to four and purchased a return ticket to Kufstein as she had been directed. She stood outside the information office. At precisely 4 o'clock her phone beeped.

The message instructed her to proceed to Platform Two. She went onto the platform and looked around her. Two young couples were standing talking, and an elderly lady was sitting on a bench. An oriental looking man was reading a guide book.

The public-address system announced the arrival of a train on Platform Two. Her phone beeped again and this time the message told her to board the train. Silke got on the train and found an empty seat. She sat down and looked out of the window, to see if anyone else got on board but the platform was empty. The train accelerated rapidly and was soon at maximum speed. Silke looked around surreptitiously to see if she could recognise anyone. The elderly lady and the oriental man had got into a different coach. The high seat backs prevented her from seeing beyond two or three rows of seats, so she stood up and glanced quickly in both directions but still there was no one she recognised. Perhaps they were in disguise, she thought.

At the first stop, which was Nussdorf, no one left the train, and one man got on dressed in lederhosen and other Bavarian paraphernalia. The next stop was Oberaudorf, where the Koch's had their ski cottage. Silke could feel the train brakes being applied and just then her phone beeped. 'Get off' was all it read. As the train stopped, she stepped onto the platform. She looked around and saw a thick-set man alight from a coach further down. She walked slowly to the exit, waiting for another instruction, when the thick-set man almost touched her.

'Follow me,' he whispered, walking briskly ahead of her through the exit and into the street. She battled to keep up with his pace, staying about ten metres behind him. He crossed the street and turned up a side road. Silke realised she was being taken to the Koch cottage. It was too late to phone Bosch. She would have to wait for a more opportune time. They walked for about two hundred metres before he turned into a road that Silke remembered. She could see the cottage ahead of her. The man entered the gate to the cottage and walked up to the door. He stood aside to let Silke enter and then threw the baseball cap he was wearing onto a chair.

'We meet at last Silke Kotter. So, you are the one who has been hounding my old father.'

'You are not Albert Mayer. You are Willy Koch.'

'A very good observation, young lady. Now before we talk at all, I want you to hand me your mobile phone so that it can be switched off, and I also want you to hand me your gun.'

'I will happily switch off my phone, but I am not carrying a gun.' Silke realised that it was now confirmed that it was Willy, who had broken into her apartment. Who else would know she had a gun?

Willy just smiled and said nothing. He reached forward and grabbed Silke's small bag and pulled it towards himself. Silke resisted.

'What the hell do you think you are doing?' she shouted, pulling at her bag.

'I want to make sure there is no gun in your bag.'

Silke unzipped the bag, 'See, no gun.' She left her bag and mobile phone on the table.

Willy turned to her and smiled.

'I am so sorry about that little altercation, but you do understand that I have to be careful. My father tells me you have some useful information for me. I may also have something for you to pass on to the authorities.'

'You go first,' said Silke,' as I would love to hear your version of the events.'

Willy smiled. This was certainly a gutsy young girl, he thought to himself.

'This all started because Adolf Eicke got involved with the Mayers, Jews bent on revenge against the Germans. My father was a long-time friend of Hermann Heinrich, and obviously he had no grudge against the old man. It was Albert Mayer who suggested that we take him to the island to find a trunk that was buried there. I have to tell you that Heinrich was not murdered, he died of a heart attack. Then it all started to go wrong. I went off to Mallorca and now I have returned. It's as simple as that. I do realise, that thanks to that Jew bastard, I am implicated in a botched kidnapping even if I am innocent.'

'What about the person who was murdered in Mallorca? You were staying at his house.'

Willy nodded, 'I was staying there and then Albert flew in and while I was out he must have murdered the man. Tell me, do I look like a person who could murder someone? I love life. Now, I have heard that Heinrich's son was murdered yesterday. I was in Munich the whole day, but I can bet you that Albert was in Garmisch. Now it is your turn. You told my father that you had important information that could assist me.'

Silke looked directly into his eyes and he stared back at her unflinchingly.

'The police are convinced that Albert Mayer and possibly his father, were behind the kidnappings.

They see you as an accomplice. Mr. Heinrich senior did indeed die of a heart attack. There was no physical evidence that he had been murdered.'

Willy smiled and nodded his head, as this was how he viewed the situation as well.

'I know otherwise,' Silke continued. 'You see, in your background there is a Turkish immigrant who was killed and there is a wife who disappeared.'

'What has this bullshit got to do with the Heinrich kidnappings?' In an instant Willy became aggressive. 'I was never charged with anything.' A smile broke out on his face.

'Willy, it was you who broke into my apartment and injured my friend. I don't believe a word of what you have told me. You are mad, and you must give yourself up.'

Willy's face changed from a smile to a deadpan expression. He stared at Silke and she knew that a line had been crossed. She was now dealing with the evil side of a psychopathic killer.

'You think you are so clever, don't you? Well let me tell you that you have reached the end of the line. Heinrich is dead and now it's your turn. You will soon disappear from our lives.'

Silke put her finger on the number three button on her phone and held it down to engage the speed dial function.

Willy jumped up and grabbed at the phone but missed it, and it went skidding off the table.

At the Munich police station, Bosch heard his phone ringing. He picked it up and caller identification showed him it was Silke.

'Hello, hello,' he said, but there was no reply. He could hear a man calling someone 'a fucking bitch.' Then he heard a woman's voice shouting, 'Oberaudorf; Willy; Oberaudorf; Willy' then the call was disconnected.

Willy had jumped on the phone, causing the screen to shatter and the battery to dislodge. The phone was now useless. He turned around and aimed a punch straight into Silke's face. Blood spurted from her nose, and she fell to the ground clutching her face. In her peripheral vision, she saw the kick coming towards her and she pushed away, riding most of the force but it was still hard enough to wind her. Willy thought he had disabled her and went to the door, where a snow shovel was standing in a corner. He picked it up and came back to finish Silke off. The time for talking was over. He knew he had to act quickly, as he wasn't sure if Silke had managed to get the call connected and to whom.

Silke had reached into the back of her tee-shirt and managed to free the gun. Blood was streaming from her nose, past her mouth and onto the floor. She was shaking from the shock of the attack and when she saw Willy approaching with a shovel in his hands, she shouted, 'Stop or I'll shoot you.'

Willy stopped and looked at her and then at the small gun in her hand.

'That silly toy couldn't harm a mouse,' he said mockingly, as he raised the shovel to shoulder height. He planned to swing the shovel in final coup-de-grace.

Silke remembered what Novak had said about the small firepower of the gun. Only a shot to the head would be effective. But the target seemed so small and she was worried that she would only get in one shot, so she ignored the advice and aimed the gun at Willy's upper right chest area. She pulled the

636

trigger and the sound gave her a fright, but she had made a hit. The force wasn't strong enough to push Willy back. Nevertheless, he winced in pain and Silke could see that he had lowered the shovel.

'Now you will die, bitch.' He tried to raise the shovel, but the bullet had obviously entered a muscle, making movement painful, however, he was not completely incapacitated.

Silke knew she had two shots left. She lowered the gun and fired at his knee. Please let it stop him, she prayed. He swung the shovel and connected with her temple. She fell to the ground, and everything went black. Before Willy could smash her a second time, he heard a police siren coming closer. The bullet had broken his left knee cap. He hobbled out of the house and climbed over the back fence. Blood was pouring out of the wound and a stain appeared on his trousers. He knew of a pathway that would lead him back into town through some fields.

Two policemen entered the cottage. The first thing they saw was the blood on the floor and the prostrate figure of Silke. The first policeman spoke into the phone strapped to his shoulder and called for back-up and an ambulance.

'I think she is dead,' he said, trying to find a pulse on her neck.

A trail of blood led out the back door. They ran outside but by this time, Willy was already deep into the fields. The agonizing pain in his knee, forced him to sit down on the grass. He could hear more sirens in the distance. In a strange way, he was happy.

EPILOGUE

It is one year later.

Willy is incarcerated in a mental institution.

Tracker dogs brought in by the police had found Willy lying under a tree. Loss of blood and the immobility of his knee, had forced him to stop. He was arrested and charged with kidnapping and murder.

A panel of eminent psychiatrists, including Professor Angemeir, were unanimous in declaring Willy Koch legally insane, and he was committed to a state institution in Nuremberg. The bullet in his chest had been removed and despite the prosthetic knee he had received as a result of his injuries, he still walked with a pronounced limp. The staff at the Institution for the Criminally Insane, and this included several psychiatrists, found it hard to accept that he was mad. He was charming and talkative and would spend hours proclaiming his innocence to anyone who would listen.

The body of his wife was never found despite an extensive search in Passau and Oberaudorf.

No visitors ever came to see him, not even his father.

**

Wofgang Koch has died.

Wolfgang Koch had finally been forced to realise that his son was responsible for several murders. He was devastated and refused to visit Willy either in jail or later in the mental institution. He virtually stopped eating, except for a bowl of soup each evening. He realised that he had deliberately blocked any suggestion that his son was a violent person and a potential psychopath. He was a sad and lonely figure. He died six months after Willy's capture.

**

Otto Mayer remains in his house in Antwerp

Otto Mayer was charged with conspiracy to commit a kidnapping by the Belgian authorities but due to his advanced years and the subsequent discovery of his son's body in Switzerland, the charges were dropped. He sold his business and every now and then, letters he had written would appear in the press, notable for their strong anti-German sentiments.

**

The Swiss authorities initially issued an extradition request for Willy Koch to face trial for the murder of Albert Mayer. The request was withdrawn after Willy was declared insane and the case was closed.

**

 In Mallorca, the police were unable to positively link Willy to the murder of Andrew Egan and the case remains unsolved.

**

Sabine Heinrich refused to return to Adlerhost. She stayed with her parents in Hannover before buying a property in one of the smartest areas within the city. Lawyers and accountants are still involved in sorting out the estates of both Hermann and Reinhard. Eva continued to have therapy over several months, before it was decided that while latent problems could present themselves when she got older, she was in a position to enjoy the normal life of a young child.

**

Blondi who had been found huddled on the steps of Hermann's house, was eventually reunited with

Eva. They have become inseparable and she sleeps at the bottom of Eva's bed every night.

**

Silke is recovering from her massive injuries.

When the paramedics arrived at the Koch's cottage, they took one look at the lifeless body of Silke and called for a mortuary van. Then the younger of the two paramedics thought he noticed an eye movement. He bent down and placed his stethoscope against her chest and detected a faint heartbeat. The sphygmomanometer showed a dangerously low reading. A drip was attached to her, and a helicopter was requested, which evacuated her to the central hospital in Munich. An emergency trephining of the skull was carried out, to reduce cranial pressure and control haemorrhaging.

Silke remained in a coma for three days and was forced to stay in the hospital for four weeks, before she was well enough to manage on her own. She was told that some of the fractures to her skull would eventually require plastic surgery. She returned to Vienna but was only declared fit to return to her work six months later. The pre-traumatic and posttraumatic amnesia she initially suffered, caused her much anxiety but gradually her memory of the events returned and she was able to send Bosch a full description of what had occurred. Bosch still maintains e-mail contact with Silke and Sabine has allowed her to phone Eva from time to time. Silke finally enrolled at the University of Vienna, where she is studying for a law degree.

THE END

The Crooked Star

The Crooked Star

The Crooked Star

The Crooked Star

The Crooked Star

The Crooked Star

18423619R00385

Printed in Poland
by Amazon Fulfillment
Poland Sp. z o.o., Wrocław